Ghosts of New England: Skullery Bay

Best Selling & Award-Winning Authors
Lisa A. Olech ~ Kathryn Hills
Nancy Fraser

This is a work of fiction. Names, characters, places and incidents are either the product of the author's imagination or are used fictitiously, and any resemblance to actual persons living or dead, business establishments, events, or locales, is entirely coincidental.

GHOSTS OF NEW ENGLAND: SKULLERY BAY
Ghosts of New England

COPYRIGHT © 2021 by Books From a Romantic's Heart Publishing, and
Nancy Fraser, Kathy Hills, Lisa A. Olech

ISBN: 9798451528129
All rights reserved. No part of this book may be used or reproduced in any manner whatsoever without written permission of the author except in the case of brief quotations embodied in critical articles or reviews.

Contact Information: romwriter96(at)gmail(dot)com

Anthology Cover & Individual Covers by Notes From a Romantic's Heart Author Services © 2021
Cover photos: 123rf, Pixabay, Deposit Photo

Ghosts of New England: Skullery Bay

An anthology unlike any other...
4 Different Centuries
4 To-Die-For Romances
The Same 2 Ghosts!

Widow's Walk (1737)
RITA nominee & Best Selling Author, Lisa A. Olech
He's the infamous pirate, Captain John Jacob Wilder.
She's the daughter of his fiercest enemy.
Their love is the beginning of the legend.

Cast to the Wind and Waves (1837)
Best Selling & Award-Winning Author, Kathryn Hills
She's the heiress determined to restore Fairwinds to its former glory.
He's the solicitor working as a caretaker because of the deadly curse.
Their love will rebuild the legend.

The Bootlegger's Daughter (1924)
Best Selling & Award-Winning Author, Nancy Fraser
She's the daughter of one of the FBI's most wanted criminals.
He's her bodyguard, and not at all what he seems.
Their love will return dignity to the legend.

Jilly's Dilemma (Present Day)
Best Selling & Award-Winning Author, Nancy Fraser

She's the new owner of Fairwinds, a flaky artist who talks to ghosts. Repeatedly.

He's the staid, young professor there to document Fairwinds' history.

Their love will make you believe in the legend.

Widow's Walk
(1737)

RITA Nominee & Best Selling Author
Lisa A. Olech

Widow's Walk

Captain John Jacob (Jake) Wilder wanted the estate known as Fairwinds at any price. Like any pirate worth his share, maybe he'd just steal it. He had grand plans to build his private pirate domain and hide his wealth and mysteries beneath the sprawling grounds of Fairwinds. But soon the magic of the grand house and a kiss of a beautiful woman had him planning a life, a home, and a passion-filled future with a treasure he never dreamed of having—a wife!

Lillian Grace Langdon lived in the shadowed edges of her family, surrounded by memories of a charmed life that had tarnished and faded in the sea air after her mother died. Meeting the dashing Captain Wilder had been like stepping back into the sunshine. The fact that he was a rogue and a pirate despised by her father only added a rebellious heat to that light. Together they grew to deeply love one another as well as the treasured estate, and soon returned Fairwinds back into the magical place it once was. Full of love, happiness, and a brilliant future.

But the winds of fate shifted like the tide, and one stormy night Jake and Lily were cast apart and blown from each other's arms forever. Anguish and sadness filled the halls of Fairwinds and threatened to return the estate to an empty shell. But Lily and Jake proved their love was stronger than death, their souls immortal, and their story became the breath and heartbeat of the grand estate. They became the legend of Fairwinds. It was their haven. Their heaven. Their port in every storm. A fierce blow might have ultimately taken their lives, but it took those same wild winds to unlock the secrets and open the door to their impassioned reunions for eternity.

Dedication

To Macey

Chapter 1

Skullery Bay, Mystic Point, 1737

"Jake, all is secured."

"Good work." Captain John Jacob Wilder clapped his brother on the shoulder. The raid had taken more effort than expected, but the spoils were twice as rich. The five chests of silver alone would more than cover the slight damage to *The Phantom's* mainsail and the surgeon's fee to stitch the few minor wounds of the crew—and the sail. A goodly store of gun powder and shot, chests of spice, hog heads of rum. Aye, the crew was due a chance to crow and had well earned their drink tonight.

Jake tipped his head toward their prisoners. "Finish lashing those bastards to the gunnels, and we can take our leave."

"Aye."

A scrawny lad fought against his captors. "Capt'n! I beg ya. Take me wit ya." He kicked at the two men trying their best to keep hold of him.

"Shut yer hole an' git wit the rest."

"Capt'n," the lad insisted. "I'll fight n' scrape hard fer ya, I will."

Jake turned and appraised the boy. There was nothing to the lad. He was all elbows and knees beneath the rags he wore. "What's yer name?"

"Oliver. Oliver Sharp, Capt'n."

Jake narrowed his eyes at him. "Tell me why I should take on a sorry specimen like you?" His men still held the boy as he shook shaggy hair out of his face and stuck his chin out in defiance. As he did so, Jake noticed the swollen, discolored skin around the boy's eye and along his jaw. His lip had been split. He'd taken quite a beating, and recently.

"I told ya. I'll fight hard. Work harder. Ye won't be sorry."

"Release him," ordered Jake. The men did, and the lad rubbed at his shoulder and shot a sneer at their backs. "Who beat you, boy?"

The lad stuck his thumbs in his pockets and held his ground. "Are ye takin' me wit ya, or not?"

Impertinent whelp. Jake raised his voice. "Answer the question."

"No sense if yer just gonna leave me here with the ruttin' bastard." Oliver glared over his shoulder.

"Who?"

"Rasher," the boy spit out the name.

"Captain Rasher?"

"Ye ken another Rasher?"

"What'd he beat ye for?" Jake asked.

The lad folded spindly arms across his narrow chest. "What ya think?"

Jake had heard rumors of James Rasher's penchant for young boys. "I take it you didn't share his...interests?"

"I did *not*." Young Oliver notched his chin.

Jake pointed at the boy's face. "He give you that eye?"

"He did."

"Go." Jake jerked his head in the direction of the mast where Captain Rasher was currently lashed. "Give it back to him. Then secure yerself aboard *The Phantom*."

"Aye, aye!" The boy practically danced, before kissing his fist and doing exactly as he'd been ordered.

Aiden, Jake's twin brother and First Mate, came to stand by his side. "What was that about?"

"New member of the crew. See he signs the Articles before we dock." Jake turned and looked into an identical set of eyes to his own. There, however, is where the resemblance to his twin ended. As for the rest—height, build, coloring, temperament—they were as different as two brothers could be.

Aiden was driven to the point of obsession. Always had been. His whole being seemed like the string of a bow pulled taut, ready to fly at the nearest target. The younger of the brothers by just six minutes, Aiden had spent his life trying to outrun those minutes by racing to be the lead to each milestone. The first to walk, first to set off in search of his fortune, first to fuck.

He'd married. A sweet girl he called Rose. Primrose Gimbly—now Primrose Wilder. About as sharp as a sack of wet mice, but beautiful, sweet as treacle, and she loved his brother beyond distraction. And now, they'd just learned she carried Aiden's child in her belly.

Jake was content to concede these minor life's thresholds to Aiden if it made his brother happy. It hadn't caused any strife between them. Jake may be the Captain of *The Phantom*, it was one higher rank Aiden hadn't craved since landing a wife, but he'd been the first in line to join the crew and was always the first fist in a fight or the first pistol cocked. Jake couldn't ask for a better man to battle alongside him than his brother.

Back on his own decks, Jake gave the order for all to be away. The crew of twenty-four, make that twenty-five now, set to their individual tasks with well-trained proficiency in the quiet wee hours of the morning. Sails were set and *The Phantom* slipped near silently through the mist like its name implied.

The polished wood planking moaned and rolled beneath his feet as the ship reached speed. Black gunnels glistened in the sparse light of a single lantern placed mid ship. Jake wrapped a hand around a tarred stretch of rigging and relished the low satisfying hum that passed through his hand, into his arm, straight to his soul.

"The skiffs are away," reported Aiden.

"Shares divided?"

"Of course." Aiden followed Jake to the helm. "They'll be met at first light."

"Good."

"This would be a hell of a lot easier if you weren't so free in boasting your position," argued Aiden. "We wouldn't have to hide evidence and scatter our catch to the winds after each raid."

"I've only ever claimed to be the Captain of *The Phantom*. I have never outright confessed to being a pirate."

"You've never outright denied it either."

Jake led the way to the aft deck, taking the stairs two at a time. "Why would I deny it?"

"To keep yourself—and me—from a hemp cravat."

"They would need proof to hang us, and they'll never have it."

"You tempt fate, Jake."

"I tempt nothing. Each plan we undertake is sound. Our raids are fast and fierce. Get the goods off ship and upriver before any British patrol can touch us. Even if The Watch seized the skiffs, there's no way to trace them back to *The Phantom*. The men know what to do if we're compromised. The operation is solid."

Aiden's jaw pulsed.

Jake continued, "You worry too much. Even your wig is graying."

"I blame you for the need to crop my whitening hair. Of course, I worry. I have more to lose these days than you."

"You are free to go whenever you wish," Jake clipped. "I've told you before. Go home. Be a proper gentleman with your wife and babe. Hell, make me an uncle a dozen times over. No one is holding a pistol on you or lashing you to the mast."

"And what about you?"

"What about me?"

"Isn't it time you thought about finding a wife and leaving all this behind?"

Jake scowled. "I'm just getting started. I've no wish to slow down now. In fact…"

Pulling his glass, Jake turned to spy through the murk of the night as they began their sail into the protection of the bay. The looming darkness of Fairwinds manor could barely be seen against the black of the sky. As had been the case for several years, not a single light burned in the grand estate. Jake lowered his glass and continued, "…I'm planning to convince Everett Langdon to part with Fairwinds and secure possession of that house. Then I could come and go as I pleased without running men and goods up and down the river or playing hide and seek with the damn moon."

"What would you want with that hulking estate?"

Jake handed Aiden the glass. "Look there." He pointed. "Along the shoreline to the right where the land just starts to rise."

"What am I looking at?"

"Twin caves."

Aiden huffed and handed Jake back the glass. "Tidal caves. That damn well floods twice a day. What good are they?"

Jake laid a hand on his shoulder and leaned closer. "They can be deepened, brother. Raised. I can run a tunnel—or hell, a bloody maze of tunnels climbing to concealed points on the grounds. Do you have any idea of the amount of goods we could hide away under that hulking estate?"

"There's only one small problem with your plan, Jake. Langdon will never agree to sell you Fairwinds. He loathes you."

Jake huffed. "The feeling is mutual."

"You take far too much pleasure and risks in raiding his ships."

"I can hardly be blamed for the fact his ships continue to cross our path."

"But you do enjoy raising his ire," added Aiden.

"The man is a pompous ass. Arrogant. He's careless and reckless. He hires cheap, incompetent crews, and his ships are overloaded, slow, and far too easy a target. Don't worry about Langdon. I know just how to persuade him. Fairwinds will be mine, and soon."

"And how are you going to convince him to sell it to you?"

"Who said anything about 'sell?' I said, 'part with.'" Determination setting his jaw, he added, "I plan to get Fairwinds the same way I get most of Langdon's property. I'm going to steal it."

After giving the order to drop the main and begin slowing their speed, Jake looked back at Fairwinds once more. A small dim light on the grounds caught his attention. Raising his spyglass, he focused on a lone figure with a lantern moving toward the shore. A female, he guessed, by the curve of her and the length of dark hair. In the gloom she could very well have been a specter with her light skirts and pale cloak. He made a quick sweep of the grounds but saw no one else.

What was a woman doing out alone in the middle of a night such as this? As his ship passed, the mysterious lady raised her lantern a bit higher. Captured in the lens of his glass, the soft light illuminated the most beautiful face Jake had ever seen before the lamp went dark.

Chapter 2

"Here." Lillian Landon handed two lengths of blue ribbon to her sister, Abigail. "See, they're a perfect match to your gown."

"They are. Thank you, my darling." She handed them off to her maid to wind through her pale hair. "What about you?"

"Father is not interested in finding me a rich suiter." Lily pressed her cheek next to her sister's and admired both their reflections in the mirror. "Besides, you're the image of our sainted mother with her fair coloring and blue eyes. Next to you, I'm a mere shadow."

"Nonsense. Your dark hair is lovely. Go, get into your gown, so the maid can braid it into something grand."

Lily kissed her sister's cheek. "It's no use trying to flatter me. All the attention will be on you at the Somerset Ball tonight, as it should be."

A short time later, Abigail, escorted by their father, stepped into one of the grand homes in Mystic Point and Grantham's glowing ballroom. Lily watched the sway of Abigail's train and took special care not to trod upon her hems.

The smell of a hundred beeswax candles sweetened the air with the smell of honey. The sight was elegant and festive with everyone dressed formally for an evening to celebrate the end of summer, but Lily couldn't help the tender tug at her heart as memories flooded her mind's eye.

As Lily predicted, men of all descriptions began circling

her sister like cats to cream. Left to her own, Lily let her gaze travel through the room and got lost in her remembrances of better times, happier times. When their mother had been alive, she and father had thrown many lavish gatherings just like this one in the glittering ballroom at Fairwinds.

They had been happy then, hadn't they? Lily recalled sneaking downstairs with Abigail to hide and watch the parties, pinching sweets from the long, clothed tables running down each side of the room, loving the music from the small orchestra seated on a raised section of floor at the far end of the hall, and getting dizzy following the dancers as they circled and spun in elegant moves.

If she closed her eyes, Lily could almost conjure the image of their beautiful mother with her golden hair smiling and laughing and being the perfect hostess.

"Excuse me."

Startled, Lily's eyes snapped open. A man stood in front of her. Unwigged, his deep auburn hair was pulled away from a ruggedly handsome face. The strong line of his jaw was accentuated by a day's worth of beard against the tanned column of his neck.

"I couldn't help but be curious as to what has put that most delightful smile upon your face."

Eyes the color of a storm captured her. Lily appraised the breadth of wide shoulders encased in the black brocade of his waistcoat and wide-cuffed jacket. Long legs, also swathed in black, ended in tall, polished boots. Even his shirt and stock were dark. And yet, the air about him didn't carry the darkness of his attire. Still rugged, there was an easy charm about him.

Lily tore her gaze from him. Had she been staring? "I was admiring the room. It reminds me of the house where I was raised and the parties we threw there when I was young."

"So last week?" he teased.

"I assure you, I'm older than I appear," she countered and stepped to one side to move past him. "If you'll please excuse me."

He reached out and caught her elbow to stop her. "I've offended you. I'm sorry. My manners don't get much practice these days."

With a gentle shift, she removed her arm from his grasp and resisted the urge to smooth away the tingle his touch had sparked. "I shouldn't even be speaking to you. We've not been properly introduced."

"You're absolutely right. I am John Jacob Wilder. At your service, mistress." He tipped his head in greeting. His easy smile hit her like an arrow.

Lily was quick to lay a protective hand against the sudden flutter in her chest. "Mister Wilder," she repeated.

"It's Captain Wilder, actually." He smiled again. "And you are?" He prompted when she had failed in her fluster to introduce herself.

"Lily," she blurted. "Forgive me." She gathered her composure and held out her hand. "I am Lillian Langdon. A pleasure to make your acquaintance."

At the mention of her name, the good Captain's eyebrow lifted sharply, but before Lily could question his reaction, he lifted her gloved hand and kissed the backs of her fingers. "No, Mistress Langdon, the pleasure is most definitely mine."

Heat raced to her cheeks. Over Captain Wilder's shoulder, she scanned the room. Where was Abigail? Lily hadn't the slightest idea how to engage in conversation with a man. Certainly not a man whose mere closeness was causing such an odd collection of sensations within her. She pulled her hand from his grasp and looked at her glove as if his lips had somehow singed the fabric while her brain struggled for something witty and intelligent to say. Where the hell was Abigail?

"Fairwinds." Captain Wilder whispered. His dark brows knit together. "Were you remembering your time at Fairwinds?"

"However could you have known that?"

"That estate has stood empty for years. Do you visit there still?" The intensity in his gaze disarmed her.

"You do recall what happened to the cat, Captain Wilder?"

"The cat?"

"Yes, curiosity quite did him in." She smiled. "If you'll excuse me, I need to rejoin my sister."

Reaching Abigail's side, Lily released the breath she'd been holding. She placed the cool satin of her gloved fingers against the flushed heat of her cheeks.

Three gentlemen were asking Abigail for a space on her dance card. Looking over her sister's shoulder, she saw they were out of luck. Abigail's card was already full.

"Excuse me, gentlemen, my sister and I are in desperate need of some refreshment." Lily pulled Abigail away.

"Thank you for coming to my rescue," whispered Abigail. "Mister Gibson is most tiresome, and his breath has an unpleasant smell, but Mister Carlisle, I could become fond of him. His eyes are impossibly blue." She glanced over her shoulder. "And he has a kind face. Don't you think?"

"I couldn't know." Lily tugged Abigail closer and dipped her head. "Don't be obvious about it but look to your left. Toward the back tables. There is a tall man dressed in black.

He's with a shorter man. Wigged. Burgundy waistcoat. The one in black said his name was John something. He flustered me so, I've forgotten his name. Do you know who he is?"

Abigail made an exaggerated pretense of looking at the ceiling before glancing in the direction of Lily's inquiry. Her breath caught. "Do you mean the Wilder brothers?"

"Wilder, yes, that's it. He said he was a Captain."

Abigail pulled Lily to a halt. "Yes. He is a Captain. He's the vicious man father is always roaring about ruining him and stealing his fortune."

Lily grimaced. Her father's exaggerated rants were a continued source of embarrassment and rarely had any semblance of truth. "Father is happy blaming everyone else for his failures. He's done quite a thorough job losing his fortune and ruining us all on his own." She hadn't seen their father since they arrived. "No doubt he's slipped into one of the back rooms, had more than his share of brandy, and is racking up more debt at the gaming tables as we speak."

"Perhaps, but Captain Wilder seems all the more willing to take whatever is left," countered Abigail.

"Why would you say that?" Lily's gaze took in the two men once more. Captain Wilder frowned at something his brother said. His dark countenance was oddly appealing. "They seem quite dashing." A warmth spread through her just before the captain turned his shadowed gaze and caught her watching. His eyes held hers captive. For a minute she forgot how to breathe.

"Because that's what they do, Lily. Attack innocent merchant ships. Raid and plunder." Abigail hissed into Lily's ear. "Captain Wilder and his brother are pirates."

***

Jake caught her staring. He'd watched her walk away in her subdued gown the color of which reminded him of dark rum. Realization capsized him. *It was her*. The woman he'd seen walking the grounds of Fairwinds just before dawn this morning. *The face*. Hers had been the face washed in the gentle light of her lantern. She was even more beautiful in the light of a hundred candles.

He hadn't recognized her with her dark hair swept up and arranged in restrained braids. Jake preferred it loose to her waist, blowing in the night's breeze. *It was her*. As soon as she said her name was Langdon, he knew. But this wasn't the Langdon daughter he was planning on seducing tonight. *Son of a bitch*. There were two.

Aiden approached him. "Langdon is already at the gaming tables and well into his cups. You're right, he's reckless in his business as well as his wagering. No wonder he's in trouble." He followed Jake's gaze. "Who is that?"

My future wife. Jake moved to the serving tables. "A change of course." He needed a drink.

"What? Wait, I thought you were after the fair Mistress Langdon." Aiden jerked his chin toward the small cluster of men currently vying for Abigail Langdon's attention. "She's very attractive, but surely you can out charm tonight's competition."

"They can have her. I'm no longer interested in Abigail Langdon." Jake took a large swallow of his drink and watched Lillian over the rim of his glass.

"What happened to the grand plan to secure Fairwinds?"

Jake emptied his glass and secured another. "Plans change."

"Are you going to enlighten me?"

He slapped Aiden on the shoulder. "Don't worry brother. My plan just got more interesting. I'll still get what I want, and more."

Aiden gave him a hard stare. "I don't like that look in your eye."

"What look is that?" Jake feigned innocence.

"The look that has gotten me into trouble since before I can remember."

"Go dance with your Rose and leave me to set my own gambit in motion."

Jake finished his drink and waited until the elder Langdon daughter was led to the dance floor before approaching Lillian again.

"Would you care to dance?"

Jake didn't give her the opportunity to say no before grasping her hand and joining the other dancers.

After a few steps, during a cross over Lillian Langdon tipped her head and whispered, "I had no idea pirates were such accomplished dancers. How would you have had time to learn with all those boots to free and buckles to swash," she teased.

A smile tugged at the corner of his mouth. "Who told you I was a pirate?"

"Well, aren't you?"

"Perhaps."

Lily's skirts brushed the tops of his boots as she passed again. "Either you are, or you're not."

"Tell me about the grand parties at Fairwinds. That is what you were thinking about earlier, wasn't it?"

She shot him a cautious look. "Why are you so interested in Fairwinds?"

"It's too beautiful an estate to be left sitting empty like it is. I never saw it full of life, but I'll wager it was a sight to see."

"It was, still is. It's just…asleep. Dreaming of better days."

Jake grinned. "Someone should awaken her." They were quiet for a few more steps. "I'd love to see it. You could show me."

"Perhaps."

The music ended and the partners bowed and curtseyed to one another. Jake lifted her hand again and kissed its back. "I'll call for you tomorrow morning at eleven."

"I can't see you," she murmured, but there was the spark of something in her dark eyes. Something in the way she hadn't snatched her hand from his grasp. She leaned closer and lowered her voice. "You are loathed by my father, and a man of unsavory character." Holding his gaze, she continued. "I couldn't possibly have you call on me. Imagine the scandal."

Taking a breath, she made a point to straighten her shoulders and give him a coy glance. "Besides, I am otherwise engaged tomorrow between eleven and noon at Fairwinds. I have private business to attend to at my family's estate. I'll be quite busy for hours with no one about to announce visitors or serve tea. It would be ill advised to open the door to any visitor, but especially a pirate." She slipped her fingers from his grasp, dipped into another curtsey, and graced him with the same beguiling smile that had drawn him across a crowded floor toward her earlier. "But then, I haven't determined if you're indeed a pirate or not."

A rush of pure pleasure flooded Jake as her words hit their mark. His plan might proceed far quicker than he hoped. *Bloody hell.*

Chapter 3

    Jake's carriage passed by a small, abandoned gatehouse, up a long-wooded drive, and pulled into the wide circle of a carriageway in front of Fairwinds. The Georgian house was as impressive from the southern entrance as it was from the bay. Stepping out, he was struck by the silence. Still so close to the water, the expansive estate blocked any sounds of the waves hitting the shore.

    He kicked at a clump of weeds rising from neglect in the gravel. The sweep of lawn grew knee high and browned. What must have been well-manicured plantings now threatened to climb the façade. Lillian Langdon was right. The estate was sleeping and had been for some time.

    Multipaned windows gazed out in darkness and stretched in perfect symmetry toward the low-pitched roof. Three dormers lined up with precision across a third floor. Tall chimneys flanked each side between elegant bays of more windows with crowing iron railed balconies. He could just make out the tops of two more wide brick chimneys along the north side. `

    The curve of the front portico bid him between tall pillars. A huge wrought iron lantern hung overhead. His boots crunched the dead leaves collecting in the entryway.

    Silence. Not even the sea birds could be heard. The once rich green paint of the ten-foot entry doors had started to chalk and haze, and the salt air had begun to pit the dulled brass of the door knocker and ornate doorknobs.

All at once the door opened. A startled Lily stood there with a broom in one hand and a dusting rag in the other. Wide brown eyes blinked up at him.

"You're early." Lily snatched a mob cap from her head and brushed stray hairs away from a flushed cheek before tossing the cap, rag, and broom to one side.

"Patience is not one of my virtues, I'm afraid."

Lily glanced behind her and frowned. "*I'm* afraid the maids have all vanished, run off with the stable boys, I imagine. I'm sorry to say Fairwinds has been left in quite a state."

Jake gave a quick laugh and reached out to wipe at a smudge along her jawline with his thumb. The sudden urge to tip her chin and kiss her didn't surprise him. Since he'd crossed that dance floor last night, he'd thought of little else. "If I promise to look past the dust, will you let me in?"

Lily hesitated. Her knuckles brushed where his thumb had been before nodding and standing aside to bid him entrance. "Welcome to Fairwinds, Captain Wilder."

"I insist you call me Jake."

"Then welcome to Fairwinds, Jake." Lily swept her arm wide.

The chilled stale air of the grand estate greeted him when he entered the impressive foyer. Cold soaked the walls. While the exterior of the building was a study of squared symmetry, the inside, like the silhouette of a Rubenesque woman, was a stunning fluid collection of curve and bow. Twin staircases climbed and curved up each side of the massive foyer to meet on the second floor. A bowed wall between the staircases held a door complete with colored leaded glass and matching Palladian window above. Its colors now too dark and dirty to discern.

"This is the foyer, of course." Shutting the door behind him, she extinguished the brightness of the day and cast the space into shadow. "I do wish there were still candles to light. The formal parlor was there." Lily gestured to the wide arching doorway at the foot of the stairs to their left. "What was the library and study were in here." She led him through a twin archway into the room at their right.

Even without candles, the manor's floor to ceiling windows gave enough light to see the room's height and grandeur. In the study, the walls were lined with carved wood shelving surrounding a massive wood-flanked fireplace with a beautifully carved mantle.

"There were so many books filling these cases. Before I could even read a word, I would come in here and sit by the fire. I can still smell the leather of the chairs and the perfume of those thin pages. Mother loved to read in here. Her book collection was vast. It looks so sad and empty without them." Lily ran a hand over one of the shelves and brushed the dust from her fingertips.

"Where are they now?"

"Father sold them or lost them." Her words clipped. She led them back into the foyer and indicated the shadowed impressions of where paintings had once hung. "Books, paintings, furnishings. He lost it all." Lily set her jaw and frowned as she looked about the foyer. She held up a finger. "But there is a painting he couldn't sell or wager." Lily gave him a small grin and her entire being lit like some heavenly creature. "Would you like to see my favorite room in the entire estate?"

Her enthusiasm made him smile. "Absolutely."

Taking his hand, she tugged him through the stained-glass door into a perfect, albeit small, rotunda. The curved walls swept up into a domed ceiling and the painting she'd referred to turned out to be a muted mural that mimicked a bird's-eye view of the bay. A compass rose, done in intricate mosaic tiles patterned the floor. Four doors, standing at each compass point directed them further into the manor. They had entered through the south. The passageway to the north opened into what appeared to be a windowed galley which spilled out onto a grand patio that graced the back of the house and led down a gentle slope to the rocky cliffs edging the sea.

"The dining room was through this passage." Lily pointed to the west. Her voice was little more than a whisper as if the space were reverent somehow. "And that doorway leads into the ballroom."

Jake squeezed the hand still holding his. "The same ballroom you were remembering last night?"

She nodded.

"Show me." He didn't wait for her to respond, but instead pushed through the arched doorway she'd indicated and rushed them both down a short hallway until they burst into a magnificent room. Lily laughed as they skidded to a stop. Two walls of windows and paned French doors leading again to the grand patio flooded the gilt-trimmed room with the brilliant morning's light from the south and west. Even in its current state, Jake could see the room's former glory.

When he looked to Lily, she was staring up at the ceiling. "He couldn't lose that painting either."

The soft depiction of wispy clouds in a windswept sky in the tray ceiling above made you feel as if the room had no roof.

"This perfectly explains your smile last night." Jake lifted her hand and led her into a spin.

The whirl caught her off guard and she stumbled against him. He caught her and held her tight. The smile faded from her lips as her eyes held his. Their breathing continued to dance.

Without another thought he lowered his mouth to hers.

***

The warmth of the sun pouring through the windows of the ballroom was not the cause of the heat that rushed through her. Lily was lost to the sensation of his lips against hers.

She'd tried to imagine what her first kiss would be like. In fact, at one time she'd imagined it happening right in this very room after some handsome boy had danced with her all night. That was where the imaginings of a naïve girl and the reality of this moment ended, however. Jake was no boy, and she was not as naïve as she once was.

Her mind argued with her body. She should push him away. Slap his face. Berate herself for putting herself in such an unguarded position by meeting a man alone. Man, hell, a pirate! But she couldn't do any of those things. She was lost in his kiss. The play of his mouth on hers was too perfect. Felt too good. Had she the power, she would have stopped the clocks and lived in this shimmering sliver of time forever.

Jake pulled away and took a step back. Frowning, he ran a finger over the curve of his lower lip. "I shouldn't have done that."

Lily held tight to his arm to steady the sudden lack of strength in her knees. "I'm glad you did."

"I swear, I didn't come here to seduce you."

"I believe you." She leaned closer and whispered, "It's not your fault. It's Fairwinds. There's magic in the walls." She took his hand again. "And secrets."

"What kind of secrets?"

Lily led him from the ballroom. "You pulled me in here before I could show you." Back in the rotunda, she stopped. "Can you see it?"

Jake frowned. "What am I looking for?"

"The fifth door."

"There's another door?"

"Of course; what's a keyhole without a door?" Lily didn't give him a chance to look but simply leaned back to press against the hidden panel and release the latch.

"Bloody Hell," Jake breathed. "I never would have found that." Moving forward he closed the door and marveled at the seamless construction in the rounded wall.

"I'm told it's a pressure latch, so there's no need for a doorknob."

Jake pushed on the panel to open it again. "Is there a secret room behind to go with your secret door?"

"No. A staircase." She opened the door as far as she was able, and Jake brushed at spiderwebs and leaned in. "A narrow spiral staircase begins in the basement and travels all the way up to the attic rooms on the third floor."

"What do you suppose it was for?" His voice echoed in the deep twists of the stairs.

"Guests."

Jake turned back and raised his eyebrows in question. "What kind of guests?"

"My grandfather, on my mother's side. He was a highly successful Dutch merchant. He built Fairwinds. From the stories I've heard, he liked to keep company with a certain kind of woman. Lots of certain kinds of women. But he had a reputation to preserve, of course, so he built a tunnel from the carriage house and stables into the basement beneath the butler's pantry, and this staircase was so his 'guests' could come and go without any kind of scandal."

"Is the tunnel still passable?"

"I don't know. The only time I ventured down these steps was on a dare from my sister, Abigail, when I was twelve. Halfway to the basement, she shut the door and left me to panic in the pitch black." She tipped in and looked down. "I never went down there again. I can show you where the tunnel starts in the stable, but I can't imagine the tunnel is still usable."

Jake pulled back and nodded. "I'm falling more in love with Fairwinds by the moment."

"And I haven't even shown you the gardens." Lily closed the secret door.

"Then please, lead on." Jake gave the door's frame another pass of his hand. "Perfect."

Out in the daylight, the sun was lovely and warm, but a cool wind blew off the water. Lily pointed out the outdoor kitchen at the end of the breeze way, along with the low-walled kitchen garden and the slated roof of the groundkeeper's cottage tucked into a line of trees.

"I'll show you the stables, but I need to take you through the arbor first. Fairwinds was famous for its rose arbor. My mother planted every type of rose she could acquire. It stretches a hundred yards. The sea roses are my personal favorite even though they are quite common. Abigail loves the beautiful yellow ones with the long stems, but their scent isn't quite as sweet. They've all but passed this time of year, and after four years, have become quite overgrown, but I can't help but think of my mother when I walk through. She would have hated the state of it now."

Lily stopped and fingered a soft petal. Looking back, the serious look on Jake's face stopped her. "I'm talking far too much. You must be terribly bored."

"Not at all. Fairwinds is so much more than I imagined. Why don't you and your family still reside here?"

"Father. He hated living here. He and Grandfather never got along. And after Mother passed, he didn't waste a moment moving us out."

"If he dislikes it so much, why didn't he sell it along with the paintings and the books?"

"He can't." Lily shook her head. "There's an odd clause in my grandfather's will that states Fairwinds can't be sold. It stipulates that the manor must remain within the family for at least one hundred years, plus one day. I imagine it will pass to Halliburton, my brother, and his heirs after that if it hasn't fallen into complete ruin by then. Or father may not wait that long and simply gift it to Abigail upon her marriage."

"What about you?"

"I'm neither the eldest, nor the son. There's little chance Fairwinds would ever be mine.

"But you'd return if you could?"

Lily pulled in a deep sigh and looked back at the manor. "I would."

"You come here often." He'd asked her a similar question last night at the dance. Although the way he phrased it, it wasn't a question. "I've seen you."

"What?" She shot him a glance.

"Night before last. It was you I saw on the cliff edge, wasn't it? With your hair loose and lifted by the night's breeze?" He reached out and tugged at a stray bit of hair before tucking it behind her ear.

She trembled at the intimacy of his touch. "How?"

"I was on my ship." He pointed toward the water. "In the bay. I saw your lantern."

"You could see me from that far away?"

"I was admiring Fairwinds. Through my spyglass." He used his hands to pantomime using a sailor's telescope. "I have a habit of doing so as I pass."

"I come here to walk the grounds some nights when sleep eludes me." She turned back and pointed to the three dormer windows on the north side of Fairwinds. "I used to sit up there and watch the moon over the water when I couldn't sleep. The view is wonderful. But now, I come here to listen to the waves, smell the roses. Remember happier times. It's restful."

"If I owned this manor, I'd breathe new life back into her. Restore her to the beauty she was. Return her magic." He gave her a coy smile. "Perhaps I'd even sneak you through the tunnel and up that staircase to me."

Lily let out a small gasp. "Are you comparing me to a woman of questionable morals?"

"Absolutely not." Jake raised a hand in surrender. "It would be my way of keeping you all to myself." He pointed to the dormers. "And I would raise that section of roof to include a private suite of rooms. With a roof walk that wrapped around like a giant crow's nest to take in the views of the inlet and the entire bay. You'd be able to see for miles on a clear day like this. It would be like sitting on top of the world."

"That would look amazing up there. With matching railings like the balconies below." Lily pointed. She could envision the walk just as he described it. Almost imagine her up there watching the sun slip out of the water at dawn. Waiting to see the ships come into the bay. Waiting to see *his* ship? She turned to appraise him once more.

"You really do like Fairwinds."

"I told you I did." Jake tipped his head toward her. "And now that I've seen it through your eyes, learned its secrets, I like it even more."

They sat quietly for a time on one of the garden's stone benches in the warmth of the sun with the sea birds floating on the breeze above them against a crisp blue sky.

Jake broke the silence. "May I ask you another question?" His voice almost a whisper.

"Of course." She nodded.

"Why did you agree to meet me today?"

"I didn't." Lily smiled. "I was here tending to private business, and you simply happened by." She lifted a quick shoulder. "It would have been quite rude of me to turn you away."

"That story is for everyone but me." Jake returned her smile before his expression turned more serious. "Your father despises me and how I choose to make my way in this world, and yet, here we sit."

Lily sat taller and brushed at a stray leaf that had tumbled into her lap. "My father's opinion means little to me. He's done nothing of late to earn my respect. If I feared meeting you would cause some scandalous behavior and dishonor my family, he's done quite a fine job of that already. We're the gossip on most tongues these days."

Jake had shifted position and sat with his forearms resting on his knees as he looked at the gardens. The view gave Lily the perfect view of his wide shoulders. Her fingers itched to touch him. Stroke his back. Reach for the leather tie holding his hair and set it free.

"As to how you make your way in this world, Captain Wilder, it is only rumored that you are indeed a pirate." He shot her a glance over his shoulder. Lily drew a breath. "You're nothing like my conceptions of a cutthroat freebooter, but if you are..." She dipped her head and grinned. "I find it rather exciting to imagine you battling on the deck of your ship with cannons blasting and swords swinging." She swung her arm wide.

Lily continued quietly. "As I said, I am neither the eldest, nor the only son. I am the shadowy middle where little light reaches and nothing grows, but I do have my own mind. I choose with whom to spend my time." She gave him a quick smile. "It was a fair bet that no one would see us here together. I loved showing you around. I'm pleased to have someone to talk to who shares my fondness for Fairwinds."

Jake turned and held her gaze. There it was again. That look that set her blood to race. Holding his stare, she tipped a shoulder. "In addition to all that, you're wonderfully handsome. And I've found you kiss nearly as well as you dance," she teased.

His eyebrows pushed to his hairline. "*Nearly* as well?" Stormy eyes flashed with indignance.

She gave him a coy smile and stood. "I should show you that tunnel entrance in the stable now." Lily headed back through the rose arbor.

Jake leapt to his feet, caught her arm, and spun her around. "Nearly as well?" Within the tangled rose branches, he gathered her tight to him, cupped her cheek and kissed her again. This kiss was heated and defiant, until it softened and deepened into something more.

At her sigh of pleasure, Jake slipped his tongue into her mouth and pushed his hand beneath her hair to cradle her head. He slanted his head and made her forget everything else except the firm play of his lips against hers and the wave of delicious heat that washed over her.

Within Jake's arms, Lily was nearly undone by an overwhelming sense of safety. She barely knew this man and yet, it was as if she'd found home somehow. Couple that with the awakening passion stirred by his kisses, it kindled a need to find love and be cherished, and she was swept away like a pebble on the beach. He said he hadn't come there to seduce her, but seduce her, he had.

When the kiss broke, they didn't part. With foreheads touching, they stayed in the circle of each other's arms. Their breathing entwined. Jake's heart thumped against her own. Surrounded by the smell of the ocean and the last of the sea roses, Lily fell in love.

She pulled back enough to look into the changing depth of his storm-gray eyes.

"Nearly as well?" his voice rasped. Jake lowered his gaze to her lips.

Lily smiled while running a hand up to the tails of his neck stock. "I may have seriously misjudged your dancing ability." Giving a tug to the cloth, she pulled his mouth to hers and kissed him back.

Chapter 4

"Point her northeast. Drop the Main. I want every inch of sail set." Jake jerked a chin at the newest member of his crew. "Sharp, get yer arse into the nest. Langdon's ship, *Margaretha,* isn't far ahead, and she's loaded to the gunnels. I'm not about to lose her in the mist. Let me know the minute you spot her mast tip."

"It be dark as a hole soon," argued the lad.

"Then we best find her before that. She's never outrun us yet, and I'll be damned if she starts now."

The Phantom hit open water and caught every breath of wind there was. The ship leapt over the tips of the waves as it picked up speed. The ribs popped and groaned under the strain, but her deep hull cut through the water like a blade.

"You're determined tonight," noted Aiden.

Jake followed the sight of Oliver Sharp climbing into crow's nest before he strode to the aft of the ship. "I'm determined every night."

"I haven't seen you for two days. I'm guessing your plan isn't going as well as you'd hoped." Aiden hurried to keep pace.

"You'd be wrong. Did you arrange things for week's end?" Rumor had it that Langdon was planning on playing cards with some of his closest friends at the Grantham estate. It was a weekly event, and Jake wanted in. He climbed the ladder to the poop deck as the ship came alive beneath him.

"Aye. You've a seat at the table." Aiden took over for the helmsman. "You paid handsomely for it, too."

The wind whipped at Jake's hair. The night's chill nipped at his cheeks. "I don't care about the cost."

"Of course not; you'll fleece the lot for that twice over."

Jake picked up his glass and scanned the darkening horizon. "I'll take more than their coin."

Aiden set the wheel and tied it off. "Are we still talking about Fairwinds, or the daughter?"

"She has a name." Jake clipped. He had sighed that very name into her hair when they parted earlier today. Her eyes warm in the late afternoon sun with her sweet lips kissed pink, the sight of her had claimed him.

"Right, Lillian?"

"Lily," corrected Jake.

"And me with a Rose. Are we adding to the Wilder garden?"

"We're adding to the Wilder dynasty. Fairwinds is perfect for what I envision. More perfect than I'd hoped." Jake picked up his glass and scanned the horizon.

"And the girl?" his brother asked behind him.

Jake lowered the glass. "She's no girl." Far from it. She had surprised and delighted him yesterday as she gave him the tour of Fairwinds. It was clear how much she loved the estate. Her devotion had triggered a protectiveness in him. Not only for Fairwinds, but for her as well.

The kiss in the ballroom had lit the fuse, but it was the kiss under the rose arbor that had capsized him. What started as a teasing, had flared into something he couldn't have predicted. And then she had kissed him back.

Lily was something he hadn't expected. He'd spent the rest of that day and a sleepless night trying to sort it all out in his brain.

They'd met again this morning and spent another full day together. Lily had finally shown him the entrance to the tunnel. As she'd predicted, it was currently impassable, but he'd soon remedy that. It was perfectly located for the maze of tunnels he envisioned. There were several small outbuildings, garden sheds in addition to the ivy-covered, stone Groundskeeper's residence. Any one of them would serve his purposes. But there had been more.

She'd led him upstairs and shown him the views from the gables. Jake could envision how he'd renovate the top floor. He imagined making Fairwinds more than a pirate's lair, more than a hideaway for goods, or a decoy when the authorities tried to catch him with the evidence to arrest him. No, it was as if the place bewitched him almost as much as Lily.

Fairwinds calmed him. Made him think of something beyond sailing after his next conquest. The more he saw Fairwinds through Lily's eyes the more he envisioned creating a home. Starting a family. With her.

Dammit, he was starting to believe in the bloody Fairwinds magic.

As the shadows began to stretch long that afternoon, Lily and he took a walk along the cliff edge and down a rocky path to the wide beach below. He wanted to investigate the tidal caves, but the hour had grown late, and the tide had turned and was on its rise.

Jake walked Lily back up to the manor. "I'll be passing this way again, near dawn, sailing back into the bay. Will I see you with your lantern?"

"Perhaps." She nodded.

He cupped the back of her braids. "Will you let down your hair?" Jake brushed her lips with his own.

"For you? Yes," she whispered. "How will I know it's your ship?"

"I'll have a light lit in the crow's nest as we pass."

"Then I'll be here waiting for you."

The thought filled him with a warmth he'd not known. Other men, his brother included, knew the comfort of having a woman waiting to welcome them home. Jake had always hesitated needing that in his life. Not because he rejected the idea of the comforting warmth of a woman's breast, but because that woman who welcomed her man home was the same woman standing on the docks saying goodbye days, weeks, and months earlier.

Too many times, he'd seen those women left heartbroken and alone when their men didn't return. It was a harsh life choosing the sea. Harsher still if you chose to live your life as a pirate. There were only so many ways a pirate could leave that life. Few of them were on his own two feet. More were by being stitched thirteen times into a shroud of sail cloth with cannonballs tied to your ankles before being slipped over the rails.

Jake hadn't wanted to bring that heartache to someone. Or perhaps there was never anywhere he considered home, or anyone he'd allowed to get close enough to care. In two short days all that had changed. It was exhilarating and bewildering all at the same time.

Glancing at Aiden, Jake wasn't about to try to explain something he didn't understand himself. He headed their conversation in another direction. "Run extra powder and chain shot to the forward guns. I want to be prepared for an enthusiastic greeting."

"Taking his ship for a third time, Langdon will want to

beat you in more than cards."

"All part of the plan."

"Capt'n!" Sharp called down from the crow's nest before pointing due east.

* * *

"Again?" At the sound of her father's roar, Lily rushed past the open door of the drawing room and hid behind a pillar in the foyer. The sun had only begun its rise when she returned from Fairwinds. What was her father doing up at this hour?

His bellowing was going to wake the whole household. "Where were the patrols? The Watch? Why didn't anyone stop them? I pay good money for protection. How many times do these bloody bastards have to attack my ships before something is done?"

"The Watch did stop them, Mister Langdon, but there was nothing on their ship that we could link to the *Margaretha*."

"Impossible!" Father threw something against the wall. Lily flinched. "I want the Wilder brothers arrested. I want them both shot. Then hung. Then shot again!"

"Without evidence—"

"Evidence?" he sputtered. "I'll give you evidence. Captain Shepherd and my men will swear it was *The Phantom* that attacked them last night, toppled the forward mast, killed two of my crew, wounded eight, and cleared out the second deck. They took the lot. Every trunk, every bloody crate. Four chests of silver!"

"It would be their word against Captain Wilder and his brother. There is no physical proof. Not a sliver of silver or a dusting of spice that could prove your claims."

Lily's breath caught. *Captain Wilder*? The man she was in love with? The man who she'd watched for before dawn, who's ship slipped through the dark bay unnoticed, saved a single point of light near the tip of its center mast?

She'd almost missed that tiny spark of light. The new moon cloaked the ship to almost invisible. Had she not been waiting and watching, it would have silently sailed past her. But there it was. There he was.

As she promised, she raised her lantern. The chill of the night peaked the sensitive tips of her nipples through the thinness of her shift as she pushed back the hood of her cloak and let her hair fall to her waist.

Other than the pinpoint of light, she couldn't make out anything in the inky darkness, but she could imagine. Was he watching her now? She ran a hand under her hair and fanned it over one shoulder. Did he have his spy glass on her? Could he see her?

As soon as she could slip unnoticed to the stairs, Lily crept up to her room. Closing the door silently, she drew a deep breath and released the clasp on her thick cloak.

"There you are. Where have you been?" Abigail raised the wick on the lamp on her bed table.

Damn. "It's still early; go back to sleep."

"Like I could sleep with Father screaming at the top of his lungs." Abigail swung her legs off the side of the bed and gathered the thick feather-stuffed topper about her shoulders. "It's freezing."

"I'll get the fire started." Lily crossed the room to stir the embers in the grate.

"You didn't answer my question. Where have you been?"

Lily warmed her hands. "I couldn't sleep. I went for a walk."

"You've been taking quite a few walks these days. I swear

since the night of the ball, I haven't seen you."

The night of the ball. How had so much happened in such a short amount of time? Had it only been three days? Was it possible to fall helplessly in love in just three short days? Lily skipped her fingertips across her mouth and remembered every second of every touch, every kiss. Oh, yes, it was most definitely possible. Lily moved to the dressing table and started to run a brush through her hair. With a healthy pink to her cheeks and her eyes bright, she certainly looked like a woman in love. "Can you keep a secret?"

"Of course." Abigail moved closer to the fire and curled up in the wing chair tucking her bare feet beneath her. She burrowed her nose into her quilt.

Lily secured her hair in a loose braid. She spoke to Abigail's reflection. "I've been meeting someone."

"What do you mean you've been meeting someone?" Abigail gave her an incredulous look. "Who? Surely not a man," she scoffed.

Lily spun from the mirror. "Why not a man?"

"Well, first and foremost, it's scandalous to meet a man unchaperoned."

"Don't worry, we've been very discreet." She finished securing her hair and stood.

"*Lillian.*" Abigail gasped. "Are you mad?"

"No, I'm perfectly sane. And perfectly happy. I'm not going to let you ruin this for me, either. I've never felt this way. I'm in love." She held up a hand to stop Abigail's sudden sputter. "I realize it's only been a few days, but it's been so wonderful. I can't stop thinking about him and longing for the next time we can be together." Lily ran her fingertips over her lips again. "The touch of his hands, the feel of—"

"What on earth have you done?" Abigail scolded, her jaw slack.

Lily immediately realized her mistake in wanting to share her joy with her sister. Abigail would shatter her happiness like spun glass if she allowed it. She pulled fresh clothing from the wardrobe. "I've done nothing."

Abigail was at her side in an instant and pointed an accusing finger at Lily's face. "I can always tell when you're lying."

"We've kissed. That's all." Lily moved to pass her.

Abigail kept close on her heels. "And been keeping company with each other? Alone?"

Lily turned and squared her shoulders. She wouldn't let Abigail turn what was happening between her and Jake into something tawdry and shameful. "Yes."

"You realize your reputation will be in ruins if you're discovered."

"I'm past caring about that." Lily grasped Abigail by the shoulders and smiled into her shocked face. "Didn't you hear me? I'm in love." Setting her sister aside, Lily continued to gather her things.

Abigail was quiet for a time. No doubt speechless. Lily gave her an amused glance. "Are you at least going to tell me who?" She finally asked.

Lily shook her head "I don't know if I should."

"Tell me." Her voice took on that pouty whine Lily hated.

Crossing her arms over her chest, Lily leveled a warning. "You promise you won't lecture me or continue to scold me?"

Abigail laid a hand over her heart and blinked innocent pale eyes at her. "I promise."

Lily narrowed her gaze. "Swear I won't hear any

disparaging remarks, or I'll never confide in you again."

"I swear." Abigail insisted.

Lily took a deep breath. "Jake Wilder." Just saying his name aloud made her smile.

"*Captain* Wilder?" Abigail's eyebrows reached for her hairline.

Lily nodded.

"The same Captain Wilder father has been hollering about this very morning?"

"Yes. The same."

"*Lillian Grace Langdon.*" Abigail's jaw dropped in disbelief.

Anger flooded Lily. "You promised."

"That was before I realized what a fool you are. What are you thinking?" She hissed.

Lily planted her hands on her hips. "I'm thinking I should have kept my feelings and my business to myself." What had she been thinking, indeed? She turned away and began dressing.

Abigail grabbed her arm and spun her around. "You're keeping company with a *pirate*?"

"In a manner of speaking, yes."

"Have you lost your senses?"

Lily pulled out of her grasp and sat on the bed to pull on her stockings. "I'm done discussing this with you. You can't possibly understand."

"Oh, I understand," sneered her sister as she stood over her. "You've said it yourself, you're in my shadow, and now that I'm about to be paired in marriage, you have to go off and ruin everything. You're jealous of the attention I got at the dance, and you just had to go out and behave recklessly to get back at me. Do you have any idea how your mistakes can affect my position? What man would want to take me as his wife knowing there's a possibility of having a pirate in the family?"

Lily had never struck her sister before, but if she didn't get out of this room... "My relationship with Jake has nothing to do with you," she snapped as she abandoned her corsets and stepped into her skirt.

"I never thought you'd be so selfish or uncaring." A sob dramatically caught Abigail's words.

Lily shrugged into her bodice and hastily laced its ties. "Selfish? How am I being selfish?"

"You're only thinking about your happiness. You don't care a whit about the rest of us. Think of poor Father. If he ever found out about this it would kill him." Abigail sniffed.

"Enough." Lily shouted, stopping her sister's ridiculous rant. "I came to you as my sister, and I thought you for one would be happy for me. If you're talking about selfish, perhaps you should come over here and take a gander in the mirror." She pushed her feet back into her shoes. "For the first time since we left Fairwinds, I'm happy. Jake makes me happy. He's sweet and caring. Doesn't treat me as if I'm invisible. He listens to me. Appreciates my opinion on things."

"What does he want?" Ice dripped from Abigail's sanctimonious words.

Lily jerked as if struck. "Want? What are you implying? That there's no possible way he could be attracted to someone as plain as me, he must be out for his own gain?"

Abigail lifted a smug shoulder. "This is the same man who seems quite intent on taking everything father holds dear."

"If that were the case, Captain Wilder would be after *you*."

Abigail rolled her eyes. "Oh stop. *'Father likes you best.'*

Please."

"It's true." Lily grabbed her cloak. "Never mind. Forget I mentioned him at all."

"Lily." Abigail softened her tone as she tried to block Lily from leaving the room.

"It's too late. I'll not discuss this another minute. I should have expected you to dismiss my feelings for your own."

Abigail rubbed at her arms and gave her a pitying look. "I just don't want to see you get hurt."

"I'm not going to get hurt." Lily insisted. "Jake and I have developed deep feelings for each other."

"Oh? Has he said so?"

A cold thread of doubt slithered down Lily's spine. "He doesn't have to say the words. I just know."

"Oh, *darling*..." Abigail sighed and looked at her like she was the stupidest creature to ever live.

Lily snapped and pushed her sister out of the way. "You're wrong."

Chapter 5

Racing back to Fairwinds, Lily's tears fell heedlessly as she berated herself for being so naïve. She knew her sister too well. Her reaction was exactly the reaction Lily could have foretold. Why then did she open herself up to such hurt? How could she be so foolish. Because once, just once, perhaps Abigail would not act like Abigail. Perhaps just once she could be how a sister should be. Loving, accepting, encouraging, instead of the spoiled pampered horror that she was.

A cold mist and fog from last night had continued its descent upon the bay. Fairwinds was blanketed by the fine damp that seeped into her clothing and soaked her hems. She sat on the frigid stone bench and wrapped herself tight in her cloak. A deep sadness settled like the mist. Fairwinds looked frozen in a cloud. Cold, gray, lifeless. Lily dropped her face into her hands and cried for it all.

"Lily?"

She jumped at the sound of his voice. "Jake? What are you doing here?"

"I was looking for you."

"We had no plan to meet." Lily looked away and wiped the wetness from her cheeks.

"No, but I hoped." He knelt before her and took her hands. "Why aren't you inside? It's freezing out here. Your hands are like ice. Are you crying?"

"I can't go inside anymore. It breaks my heart to see it like it is. It's so empty, Jake. I'm tired of filling it with nothing but remembrances. Tired of only living in my memories. It's just too sad."

Jake cupped her face. "Is that what's making you cry?"

Lily looked into his stormy eyes. She needed to know the truth. "Did you attack my father's ship last night?"

"I can't answer that." He didn't look away but held fast to her gaze.

"Why not?"

Jake gave a small shake of his head. "Because I won't lie to you, and because to admit it would place not only me, but my brother, and my entire crew in jeopardy." He rubbed her frozen hands between his own.

Even afraid of the answer he might give, Lily had to ask. "Are you with me simply to hurt my family?"

Jake frowned. "No. What makes you think that?"

"Abigail—"

"Is an empty-headed twit." Holding her hands between his he blew a warm breath over her chilled fingers before he pulled her to her feet. "Come with me. I have to get you warm." Jake put an arm about her shoulders and led her to the ground keeper's cottage.

A steel lock barred them from entering. Wrapping a rock in his cloak, he broke a small pane of glass to gain entrance through one of the side windows. "I promise to repair that. I don't trust the chimneys in the manor after all these years, and it will be far faster to heat this cottage than one of the grand rooms in the house."

Jake settled Lily on a long wooden stool, wrapped his own cloak about her shoulders, and then set to the task of building a fire on the small stone hearth. A decaying cache of firewood remained at the back of the building. He gathered what he could still use for kindling. It took him several attempts with the flint.

"My fingers are so chilled I can't hold the stone." But all at once a spark caught the nest of dead grass and leaves. Soon the fire was producing some delightful warmth. Jake warmed his hands over the flames before he added two more logs and once more knelt at Lily's feet.

"Better?" He tipped his head to peer into her face.

She nodded.

He stroked her cheek again and spoke in a low voice. "I hate to see you upset."

Lily pulled a shuddering breath. "I don't know what to think. Three days ago, I didn't know your name or that you even existed. Now, I can't go ten minutes without thinking about you. It has all happened so fast. Too fast. My head is spinning, and my heart…"

"What about your heart?" In the firelight, his eyes were dark as they held hers.

"I fear I've lost it to a man I barely know. Perhaps *I'm* the empty-headed twit."

"No, not you. Never."

"Then what is this?"

Jake gave her a tender smile. "I think they call it falling in love."

Abigail's bitter words echoed in Lily's mind. She was hesitant to ask the question, but she had to know even if the answer broke her heart. "And do you love me in return?" she whispered.

Jake lifted her hands and kissed their backs. "The first time I saw you on the cliffs, I couldn't believe how beautiful you were. I convinced myself that you weren't real. A figment.

A spirit wandering the grounds. But then I saw you at the ball. I knew I had seen your face before. It took me a moment to realize it was you. But when I did, it was as if my heart kicked in my chest.

"I've spent the last few days thinking about little else but being with you, too. Yes, it has all seemed like a whirlwind. Like that spark catching the kindling and bursting into flame." He reached out and traced the lower edge of her lips. "Then, God help me, I kissed you. I knew right then I was in trouble." Jake sat and scooped Lily into his lap.

She arranged their cloaks about them. The smell of damp wool added to the shared warmth of their private cocoon.

"But it wasn't until this morning when I realized it," Jake continued. "Seeing you on the cliffs again." He slipped the backs of his fingers over her cheek. "Seeing your beautiful face in the lantern light. Knowing that you were real. Knowing that you were there for me. I saw you smile, Lily. The wistful smile that had me crossing a crowded dance floor to learn your name. That smile into the dark this morning was for me. It was mine. *You* are mine." He laid a gentle kiss on her mouth. "And if you've lost your heart to me, I'll take good care of it, if you promise to do the same with mine."

Jake touched his forehead to hers. The warmth of him chased the chill from her bones, and the doubt from her heart. He loved her.

"You were wrong about something else, too," he whispered.

"What was that?"

He cupped her cheek. "You said you were a shadow. The shadow in the middle where nothing grows. You are *nothing* like a shadow. You're smart and have a clever wit. Do you know when you glow? When you light up like a thousand candles? When you talk about Fairwinds." Jake ran the tip of his thumb across her lower lip. "And the way your eyes shine after you kiss me. You're as blinding as the bloody sun."

A sob caught in Lily's throat at the tenderness of him. Her eyes filled with tears.

Jake frowned and wiped at the wetness on her cheek. "Please don't cry. I can't bear it."

"Not even when they are tears of happiness?" She gave him a watery smile.

"Not even then." He kissed her.

Lily laid a hand upon his chest to feel the beating of his heart. Had she ever felt more cherished or safe?

She was feeling something more, too. A different kind of warming. Wrapped together like this, wanting to kiss him, and have him touch her, she couldn't help but think of the prospect of lying with him. Abigail had explained the unpleasantness of the act—in graphic detail. At least the first time, but somehow Lily hoped she'd lied about this as well. Maybe it wouldn't be as bad as either of them imagined.

Lily laid her cheek against the soft linen of his shirt. Jake wrapped her in his arms.

He pulled away. "Dammit, woman, what's happened to your corset?"

Heat rushed to her cheeks. "I left my house in rather a hurry."

Jake glanced down and gave what sounded like a strangled groan. "Your bodice is barely laced." His voice was low.

Lily looked at the unconfined state of her breasts. "I wasn't expecting to meet anyone." The fire was warming the small room. The heat that flushed her cheeks seemed to be spreading. Lily pushed back the hood on her cloak and pulled the thick braid of her hair over her shoulder. "I didn't have time to do my hair up properly either."

Jake's breath left his lungs in a rush.

Lily untied the lacing and unplaited the braid. "But you prefer it down. Isn't that what you said?"

"Aye." His voice had a decided huskiness.

Lily wanted him to wrap his arms about her again and hold her tight. "I imagine there are certain benefits to not having to fight through whale bone." She arranged one of his arms about her waist and lifted his other hand and boldly placed it on her breast.

"Lily..." he sighed against her mouth as he kissed her again and his hand began a caress of her breast. Her nipples, already peaked due to the cold, sent delicious shivers to her thighs when his palm brushed a firm tip. Lily drew a shaky breath and clutched at his sleeve. Her lips trembled beneath his in a mixture of uncertainty and blooming desire.

"No. Stop." Jake pulled his hand from her and set her away from him. He pushed his cloak aside and stood.

"But—"

"This can't go any further." Jake pulled in a deep breath. "What am I doing? You're an innocent." He threw a hand toward her.

"But I'm ready. I consent." His abrupt rejection sent her emotions on another tumble. "I thought you wanted—"

"Oh, I do. I want you so bloody much I can scarcely breathe." He planted his hands on his hips. "But not like this. Not your first time. Not here in the dust and the dirt. When I make love to you, you'll be my wife," he snapped. "And I'll do it properly. In a proper bed."

Air left Lily's lungs as she stood knocking her sodden cloak to the ground. "Your wife?"

"Yes, dammit, my wife. You'll be all mine. And soon." His eyes raked over her as the muscle in his jaw tensed. "The sooner the bloody better."

As her heart soared, a sobering thought caused it to fall and shatter at her feet. "My father will never agree to it."

"You leave your father to me."

Chapter 6

"What the hell are *they* doing here?" Everett Langdon slammed a fist on the table, disrupting everyone's neatly stacked coins.

"Captain Wilder purchased a seat, same as you Everett." The host for this evening's game, Horace Grantham, pulled two decks of cards from an intricately carved ivory box.

"Mister Langdon." Jake inclined his head and greeted the florid-faced man.

Langdon jumped to his feet. "I'll not play with thieves."

Jake pulled a small stack of five-pound notes from his coat pocket. "That is certainly within your right, sir. I, for one, have no objections if you leave." He glanced at Aiden before looking back at Langdon. "The night is young. Perhaps you'll find another game more to your liking somewhere else."

Everett Langdon looked at the hand already in play. "I'm not leaving without my money."

Grantham tugged at his sleeve. "Sit down, man. You're winning for once. You'd be a fool to walk away now."

"You're far more experienced at cards than I, Langdon," Jake goaded. "You should stay. Hell, maybe tonight's your lucky night. You could win my money as well."

Langdon still stood. He jabbed a finger at Jake's face. "You're a cheater, a murderer, and a thief."

Jake held up his hands in surrender. "I'm just here to play a few hands of cards. If it makes you feel better…" Jake stood, took off his coat, and rolled the wide sleeves of his shirt well past his elbows before sitting back down. "I'm unarmed for starters. Surely Mister Grantham will be happy dealing the cards, and I'll swear to keep to my seat and have my hands in full view the entire time. I couldn't possibly cheat you or anyone." He gave Langdon a cool smile. "Someone bring me an ale. And bring Mister Langdon another drink to calm his obvious nerves."

"What about him?" Langdon shot a glare at Aiden.

Aiden sat in a chair behind Jake and placed a hand over his heart. "I'm just an observer. Just here to make sure Jake doesn't lose his head and bet away my inheritance."

Jake smirked, still holding Langdon's furious gaze. "Don't worry, brother, I'll only wager my half."

"Hard sailing half a ship, brother," Aiden quipped.

The other men in the room laughed as the drinks were brought and Langdon reluctantly returned to his seat. He won the hand in play, and a fresh deck of cards was then unbanded and shuffled by Mister Grantham. Cards were dealt and play commenced.

A few hours later, Jake and Aiden, sans all their money, boarded their carriage and left a very smug Everett Langdon counting his newly acquired winnings.

"What the hell was that?" Aiden snapped as soon as their carriage was underway.

Jake brushed at his breeches. "We lost."

"No." Aiden shook his head and pointed behind them. "We didn't lose. You purposely let that bastard Langdon win. I saw your last hand. You had him. And it wasn't the first time either. You threw away a dozen winning hands."

"Just laying the trap." Jake assured his brother. "Now I know exactly how the man plays, and I've bolstered his confidence at my incredible lack of skills. It was worth losing a little tonight to make him cocky for the next time. Speaking of which, make sure I've a seat at the next game."

"How long are you planning to lose?"

"Cease your worrying. I've got everything well in hand."

Well in hand. The image of Lily in the groundkeeper's cottage, looking every bit a woman seduced continued to haunt him with her hair falling to her waist, and the tips of her chilled nipples peaking the linen of her shift, the beautiful roundness of her breasts, unrestrained and begging to be fondled, caressed, tasted. *Dammit.* It had taken everything in him to take his hands off her and stop things.

He shifted in his seat as his brother fumed next to him and the carriage moved along the dark street. The state of his cock was causing him no end of discomfort. He'd already doused himself in icy water once today. If he didn't take Lily to his bed soon, he'd end up freezing to death.

"Have patience," Jake's words came out clipped as he shifted the position of his erection. Was he talking to Aiden, himself, or to his ready arousal?

* * *

Lily slipped into the house through the servant's entrance. She'd been out on the cliffs again, welcoming Jake back into the bay. The clear shine of the night's moon had given her a beautiful view of *The Phantom* as it carved silently through the calm seas leading into the bay. Still a lamp lit in the crow's nest for her. Could one perish from feeling too much love in their hearts?

"Finally."

Lily came up short as she entered the foyer and found her sister waiting. "Abigail, you scared me half—"

"You ought to be scared." Her father emerged from the darkened drawing room. "Your sister tells me you've been keeping company with that bastard Wilder."

Lily gasped and shot a horrified look at Abigail. "How dare you betray a confidence."

Abigail laid a dramatic hand to her chest. "I had to tell him. You're out of control, Lillian. I did it for your own good."

"Am I to understand you've been meeting him regularly since the ball?" her father barked.

Lily notched her chin. Abigail had obviously told him everything. No use denying it. "Yes. I have."

"For nigh two weeks, you've been wantonly bringing disgrace to this family?" He raised his hand and before Lily could react, her father issued a vicious slap across her face.

Lily gasped and held a hand to her abused cheek. Tears burned as her face stung beneath her palm, but she refused to cower. "The only one bringing disgrace to this family, Father, is you."

"Insolent chit!" He raised his hand again.

Abigail was quick to step between them. "No, Father!"

He shouted at Lily over Abigail's shoulder. "You'll not see him again. I forbid it."

Lily met his furious glare. "You can't stop me."

"We'll see about that. If I have to, I'll lock you in your rooms. You will not defy me!" Father's face was florid. Spittle gathered in the corners of his mouth. "I can't even look at you. Be gone from my sight."

"Happily." Lily lifted her skirts and fled up the stairs with Abigail on her heels. But before she could follow her into their rooms, Lily was quick to slam the door and do the locking herself.

"Lily, open the door." Abigail pleaded through the wood. "Please."

"Go away." Lily lifted a hand to the sting of her cheek. Fury burned through her. She should have known Abigail would betray her. Pacing the room, her anger flared as she struggled with what to do next.

"I'm so afraid for you. I only wanted to help." Abigail's voice was muffled through the door.

"You've done enough. Leave me *the bloody hell* alone." Lily kicked over a chair.

Beyond the door, she heard Abigail gasp. "See, I knew getting involved with that man would ruin you. You're already talking like a filthy sailor."

Lily picked up a book off her bedside table and hurled it at the door. Abigail gave a small shriek and escaped down the hall.

Rage and indignation stormed within her. She'd be with Jake whether they liked it or not. If only she could send word to him somehow. They had plans to meet next morning. Jake assured her that after tonight they could finally be together. That somehow, he'd convince her father to let them wed. He'd cupped her cheek, kissed her lips, and told her not to fret. *"All will be well, my darling."* After what just happened downstairs, that would take some sort of miracle.

Lily dropped onto the stool before the vanity and gave herself a hard stare. Her cheek flared red. She didn't care what Father or Abigail said. She and Jake didn't need their blessing. To hell with them. She wouldn't wait until morning. Father would leave as he did every night for the gaming tables after dinner, and all Lily would need do is wait for Abigail to fall asleep, and then she could leave once and for all.

She'd pack what she could carry and find Jake. Head toward the piers. Perhaps seek him out aboard *The Phantom*. She'd tell him it was hopeless. Her family would never see him as anything other than a pirate, and if he truly wanted to have her as his wife, they would need to sail off and get married somewhere else. Make a life in a new place, a new town. Perhaps along the southern coast. The weather was warmer there. They could build their own Fairwinds. She would plant her own rose arbor.

They'd be happy. Fill their home with children. Jake's brother Aiden's wife was due to have a baby in the new year. With any luck, she and Jake would have their own come summer.

Lily ran a hand over the flat of her stomach and tried to imagine it round with a babe. Jake's son. It would be a boy first. She was sure of it. Would he be John Jacob, Junior with his father's changeable eyes?

One thing was certain. Lily met her gaze in the mirror once more and ran her fingers over her injured cheek. Their child would never know a day where he questioned being loved. He would never doubt his place in his parent's hearts or know the sting of their hand. The home she built with Jake would know nothing but love and happiness. On that she would wager her life.

As the morning melded into the afternoon and the shadows grew long into the day, Lily's mind settled into her visions of a beautiful future for her and Jake. She need only bide her time. A few more hours and she could be gone from this house and back in the safety of Jake's arms. Lily curled up on her bed and forced herself to be patient.

"Lily!" Abigail was back and pounding at her door as the

sun finally made its slow descent into the west.

"I'm still not speaking to you. Go away." Lily called out.

"Forget all that. Father has been shot!"

Chapter 7

Lily jumped to her feet. "What?" Fumbling with the key, she wrenched open the door.

Abigail was crying and wringing her hands. "Down at the pier. I don't know what happened. All I know is after his row with you, he left in a horrible temper. Said he'd deal with Captain Wilder himself. A messenger just brought word that he is gravely wounded." She held a crumbled note in her fist and sobbed. "He's on the *Margaretha*. Oh, Lily, he could be dying. We must go to him. Now."

Panic raced through Lily as she grabbed her cloak and chased after her sister. "You don't think Jake had anything to do with this, do you?"

"I don't know what to think." Abigail wept into the note. "We've already lost Mother; we can't lose Father, too. What would become of us?"

Hurrying, they climbed into the carriage waiting out front. The horses leapt as the driver's whip snapped. Lily wrapped an arm about the shoulders of her distraught sister and tried to quiet her as they raced toward the docks.

Could Jake have shot her father? No. That's ridiculous. He wouldn't. He couldn't.
But he's a pirate, her thoughts warred with one another. If tempers flared...

"Leave your father to me." Jake's words echoed in her mind.

In no time they were at the pier. The carriage brought them as close to the *Margaretha* as it could. Abigail was out before the wheels had stopped moving. Lily lifted her skirts and raced after her. Their heels echoing on the wooden dock and up the wide planking before they dropped onto the decks of her father's ship.

Abigail barely slowed. Men aboard watched as she sped past. Down the ladderway, to the space below decks. Lily blinked to get her eyes to adjust to the sudden blackness.

"Abigail, slow down, I can't see where I'm going." Lily reached the bottom of the ladder by feel alone.

"Take my hand." In the dark, Abigail's hand found hers and gave her a sharp tug. "He's likely in Captain Shepherd's quarters."

"How can you see down here?"

"I don't need the light. We've been on this ship countless times. Don't you know your way?"

"Not when I'm in a panic." Lily braced herself for what she might see. Steeled herself for what she might learn. If it was true, and Jake shot her father… No, she wouldn't allow herself to think such a horrific thought.

Reaching the aft of the ship, Abigail didn't bother knocking before rushing in. Light flooded the tight corridor as Abigail pulled Lily into the cabin behind her. Half a dozen lanterns lit the space. Lily shielded her eyes at the onslaught of light after the utter darkness of the passageway.

Abigail was quick to release her hand and shut the door. Lily's gaze flew to the narrow cot set into the side of the ship. It was empty. "Where?" She spun to her left. The room was empty. "Where is he?"

Lily heard the key scrape in the lock. Turning back, she

found Abigail against the door. Her color was high as she bent to catch her breath. When she straightened, the cold determination in her eyes made Lily gasp.

"Where is Father?"

Her sister pressed the backs of her hands against her cheeks. "By this time of the evening, I imagine he's several drinks into his cups and probably losing my dowery at the tables." Abigail tugged on the hems of her bodice and brushed at her skirts.

"He—he wasn't shot?"

"No. He's quite healthy for a man despite his age and habits."

Lily's brain spun. She gave Abigail an incredulous look as she tried to make sense of what was happening. "What the hell is going on? Get out of my way." Lily pushed at Abigail, but she stood firm. "Move aside, I'm leaving."

"The door is locked and there's a guard on the other side, Lily." She gave her a pitying look. "You're not going anywhere...well, that isn't entirely true." Abigail smirked.

Lily clapped a hand to her forehead. "What are you talking about?" Around her the ship began to creak and moan. Overhead she could hear the crew's boots as they moved hurriedly about the deck. "Good God, are we moving?"

"Yes."

"Where? What? Dammit, Abigail, if you don't tell me what the hell is going on, I swear I'll snatch all the hair from your head."

Abigail's hand swept over a small collection of trunks lining the walls of the cabin. "We're going on a trip, you and I. Father thought it best if I took you on an adventure."

A cold wave of realization crashed over Lily. "I'm not going anywhere with you." She tried the door before pounding on the boards. "Open this door, at once."

"The guard has direct orders not to open that door until we are well out to sea."

"Out to sea?" Lily spun around. "Are you kidnapping me?"

"Of course not. We're saving you. It was the only way we could get you away from that...that pirate."

"Get me off this damn ship," Lily growled.

"It's too late. The next time we set foot on dry land, we'll be back in England. Father's shipping us to Aunt Prudence."

"Like hell he is." Rushing to the back row of windows lining the fantail of the ship, Lily watched as they pulled further away from the pier. She wrenched open one of the diamond-paned windows and tried to judge the distance to the water below. She'd swim back. In the growing darkness of night, the water looked black and bottomless. If she jumped and survived the drop, the weight of her skirts would surely drag her to the bottom of the bay. Hell, she'd just have to take that chance.

Abigail grabbed at her sleeve and wrenched her away. "Are you insane? Get away from there."

"No," Lily snapped, "you're the one who's insane, if you believe I'm staying on this ship for one more minute."

"Listen to me, Lillian Grace Langdon, he lied to you. Whatever you believe you have with Captain Wilder is part of his plan to ruin our family forever. Father's men heard him talking to his brother. Boasting how he'd convinced that dim-witted Langdon girl into believing his lies, falling into his arms with the least provocation, swooning at a few chaste kisses. He set out to deceive you from the beginning. He's been lying to you this entire time."

Lily clapped her hands over her ears. "I won't listen to you.

Abigail pulled sharply at Lily's hands. "When are you going to get it through your mule-stubborn head? Jake Wilder is a thief and a murderer. Do you actually believe he has feelings for you?"

"You're wrong. He does love me. He said I hold his heart. He's been kind and tender. Something you know nothing about." Lily pushed past her sister and pounded on the door again. "Let me out!"

"Did he lay with you?" Behind her Abigail's voice lowered.

Lily spun back. "No. He's been a proper gentleman. He said he wanted to wait until we were wed to claim me. To do it properly, in a lovely bed."

"Oh, Lillian, don't you see how ridiculous that sounds? He's a rouge. A pirate. He tosses women's skirts for sheer enjoyment. The only reason he wouldn't toss yours is he didn't want the possibility of a bastard growing in your belly."

"He wants to marry me."

"And you fell right into his trap. Marry you? He lives on a ship, Lily. I can just picture you out on the high seas. Eating roasted rat and swilling rum. Or no, more likely he'll leave you behind in some hovel with his horrid children latched to your breast. Abandoning you and his filthy spawn somewhere to wait for him while he's out raiding ships and killing their crews."

"He wants to live at Fairwinds." Lily snapped, but as soon as the words left her mouth, a feeling of dread spread through her limbs. *Fairwinds*. Could all of this—his courting her, wooing her—was it all to get Fairwinds?

"Ha! I knew it." Abigail crowed. "Of course he wants to marry you. That's the only way he can get Fairwinds. Now it all makes sense. Father can't sell. It must come through one of us. He knew *I* wouldn't give him the time of day, but *you*... You'd fall for any man who crooked his little finger in your direction. Of course he'd pick you. The only reason he spent time with you was to secure the estate for his own. Did you actually believe a man like that would be interested in someone like you?"

"Shut your mouth." Abigail's words had turned to swords. Each one cut ever deeper into Lily's heart.

Abigail kept stabbing. "Even if he did get you to marry him, I guarantee there would be no wedding night. Proper bed or not. Think about it. He couldn't have risked it. If he made you with child, he'd have to stay wed to you. It was his plan all along to get Fairwinds. Once the papers are signed, if he claimed the marriage wasn't consummated, he'd be free to cast you aside."

"Please. Stop." Lily dropped to the side of the cot and covered her ears again. Her mind flittered through each tender moment with Jake. Abigail had to be wrong. But what she was saying would explain Jake's fierce interest in Fairwinds. They had talked about little else in all the time they'd spent together. Could all his tenderness have been a lie? A cruel means to an end? "I don't know what to believe anymore."

"Oh, my dear naïve sister. Jake Wilder used you. Played you for a fool. Thank goodness you've escaped him and his hideous lies before it was too late." She sat beside Lily and wrapped an arm around her shoulders. "You'll come to thank me and Father for saving you from the heartbreak and humiliation of having him say these same words to you when he tosses you out."

Abigail tipped Lily's face to look at her. She brushed tears from Lily's cheeks and spoke more gently. "Do you honestly believe I would set aside my hopes for a husband and make this journey with you if I didn't believe I was protecting you from a horrible fate? Aunt Prudence is an odious woman, true, but Father assures me she is associated with some of the finest families in London. Perhaps she'll arrange a meeting for me with a tall, handsome Duke? Won't Mister Carlisle lovely eyes pale by comparison to that? Then it will be your turn. You'll see, you'll soon forget all about this. You'll forget all about Captain Wilder."

Lily closed her eyes and leaned into her sister's embrace. Visions of Jake's face filled her mind. The pain in her chest at his betrayal stole her breath. Abigail patted her arm and stroked her sleeve.

Around them the *Margaretha* groaned as she gained speed. Opening her eyes, Lily looked toward the back windows to watch the harbor lights flicker and fade into the evening's mist as the ship made its way out of Skullery Bay.

Had she been a fool? Were Jake's kisses lies too? Had her heart made her blind to what was really happening? It was one thing to lose trust in another person, but quite another thing to lose trust in one's own heart. She made a silent promise to herself that she'd never make that mistake again. If her heart ever healed, she was sure to carry the scar of this for the rest of her days.

In this one thing, she knew Abigail was wrong. Lily would never forget any of this.

Chapter 8

Jake sipped his brandy as he appraised Everett Langdon over the rim of his glass. His arrogance tonight was even more pronounced now that Jake had given him a false sense of confidence. He pulled a small stack of notes from his pocket.

"I'm surprised to see you back here, Captain Wilder, after the beating you took at this table just last week." Smugness oozed from Langdon like a fetid fog.

"I have a feeling my luck is about to change."

"Luck is a fool's bet." Langdon laughed, as did the other men at the table. He drained his glass and bid another. "Grantham, we need a fresh deck."

The room was thick with the smoke of Grantham's cigars, and the mood was far more cordial than it had been, but still Aiden sat a fair distance behind him, and Jake removed his waistcoat and rolled up his wide sleeves to appease Langdon's accusations of cheating.

When this night was over, Jake wanted no question as to the validity of his winnings. Tonight, he would walk away from this table with everything his heart desired.

The first hand, Jake threw away three perfectly winning aces to Langdon's trio of sixes. It would be the last hand he'd give willingly to Langdon.

For the next hour Jake won nearly every hand. Langdon lost them all. He bellowed at the servants for more drink. Sweat broke out on his oily brow.

Soon several of the men left the game. Their money now neatly stacked in front of Jake.

"Dammit, Wilder." Grantham threw in his cards and pushed away from the table himself. "You win again. I need a break."

"Grantham, don't you dare move. You're still dealing," snapped Langdon.

Jake gave the man a small shrug as he pulled his winnings toward him. "Perhaps we should give the man a rest."

"Nonsense," Langdon ordered. "Deal."

Grantham narrowed his eyes as he passed out the cards for the next hand. "You know Langdon, I'm almost going to enjoy watching you lose your shirt tonight."

Jake smirked. "Good thing for Mister Langdon, I'm not interested in winning his shirt." He watched the cards as they fell in front of him. Jake let them lay.

Langdon scooped up his cards at once. "We'll just see whose luck is about to change."

Grantham looked at his cards, grunted some obscenity, and threw them into the center of the table. "I'm out."

"Looks as if it is just us two." Jake met Langdon's glare.

"Just play your cards, Wilder." Langdon's speech held a hit of alcohol slur.

"I have a better idea, Mister Landon. Why don't we wager for something bigger than a few coins?"

Langdon narrowed his eyes.

Jake continued, "One hand."

"You haven't even looked at your cards," scoffed Langdon. He turned to the others watching. "Fool."

"Then the odds would be in your favor, yes?" Jake took a sip of his drink.

"What's the wager?"

Jake pushed the stack of bills and coins in front of him across the table. "I'll wager all of this." He pulled another stack of ten-pound notes from a front pocket of his breeches and tossed it into the pile of money. "Plus, another hundred pounds."

Langdon's gaze dropped to the pile of money and back to Jake. "I can't match that, and you know it."

"Ah, but I think you can. I want Fairwinds."

"Ha," Langdon scoffed. "I can't gamble away Fairwinds. It's locked in the provisions of my late wife's estate. Had I that option, the bloody hell hole would have been gone years ago. The place is nothing but a constant reminder of her overbearing arse of a father, and a constant drain on my pockets. I'd give the damn place away if I could."

"But I understand you can give it away." Jake waved away a servant who came to refill his glass. "I'm aware of the situation with the estate, but I'm also aware that you can gift Fairwinds to your daughter upon her marriage."

Langdon didn't blink. "Are you proposing that I wager the hand of my daughter?"

Jake cocked an eyebrow. "That would be the bet."

"Now see here." erupted Grantham. Several of the other men voiced their objections stating the crassness and unsavoriness of such a thing. "You can't wager for a woman."

Jake's gaze never left Langdon's. Had it, he would never have noticed the small smile that tipped the corner of the man's mouth. Not the reaction he anticipated. Langdon was lousy at bluffing. Either he had an exceptional hand, or he was up to something. "Well, what say you?"

"Which daughter?"

"Langdon, for God's sake man, you can't be considering—" Grantham sputtered.

"Not my Abigail." Langdon shook his head. "Over my dead body."

"No, I want Lily."

Langdon leaned back in his chair. "So, let me make sure I have this correct. You are putting in all your winnings, plus one hundred pounds, for the hand of my disagreeable daughter, Lillian, and an empty hulk of a house."

The man's obvious disdain for Lily dripped from his words. Jake's hands curled into fists.

"That's right. I want Lily and Fairwinds. Nothing more."

Langdon stroked his chin. "And I want *The Phantom*."

Jake lifted a shoulder. "If I lose, it's yours."

Aiden was out of his chair. "Jake, what the hell are you doing?"

Langdon flashed a smug smile towards Aiden. "Your brother has just stolen your half of the ship. Perhaps now you won't be so quick to do his bidding."

The muscle in Jake's jaw twitched. He could feel the heated glare of his brother fanning his back. He'd deal with his anger later. "Well, Langdon?"

The small smile returned to tip the corner of Langdon's mouth. "I'll take your wager, with two small conditions."

"What's that?"

"If you win, you first agree never to set foot on another one of my ships again, and second, you have to marry my daughter immediately." His wicked smile widened to spread across his face. "Before sunrise tomorrow, or you lose and the whole deal is off. I win the pot and your ship, and you end up with nothing."

Jake didn't hesitate. "Agreed."

"I can't believe what I'm witnessing," fussed Grantham. "The two of you are beyond reprehensible."

"Aye, perhaps, but you are a witness to this Mister Grantham, make no mistake about that." Jake turned and retrieved a roll of parchment from his coat. "And you'll sign as to just that." He handed the letters to Langdon. "Should I win, of course."

"Just pick up your damn cards, Wilder, and let's get on with this."

"Very well." Jake gathered the cards before him and fanned them in his hand. He'd been counting face cards and he knew what his chances were.

Langdon frowned at his cards, pulled several, and dropped them to the table. "Give me three." Grantham did just that and turned poised to make Jake's play.

Jake slid a single card toward the man and took his draw card.

"Well, Langdon?" Jake jerked his chin toward his opponent's cards. "What do you have?"

"Seems tonight won't end so horribly after all." Langdon grinned and set his cards down face up. "A full hand, three queens and a pair of tens." Around them the others murmured their relief. As he began to gather up the coins, he added, "Have your men off *The Phantom* by eight bells tomorrow, and the next time I see my daughter, I'll be sure to let her know how she escaped a disastrous future with a conniving pirate tonight."

Jake stood and tossed his cards on top of the winnings. "I'll tell her myself. Four kings." Chaos erupted. Grantham was on his feet. Jake pushed the letters at him. "Now be a good witness and sign these. Seems I have a wedding to attend."

"I'll do no such thing. I'll not be a part of this...this disgraceful display—"

Jake pulled a small pistol from inside his boot and pointed it at the man. "I think you will."

Aiden was at his side and pulled a similar weapon.

"By all means, fetch the ink. Sign them," Langdon agreed over the commotion. "Give them here, they'll need my signature as well." He gestured to the room. "Hell, we'll all sign them." He emptied his glass and waved it at the parchment. "Where's my quill?" Grabbing the sleeve of a servant, he relieved him of the cut-glass decanter he carried and ordered him to bring ink, at once. He filled his glass to the rim and raised it in salute.

A wave of unease crashed over Jake at Langdon's reaction. He'd seen him upend the table over losing a few hundred pounds, and here he was casually drinking after he'd lost his daughter and an entire estate. Could he loath both so much?

When the servant returned, Langdon was quick to snatch the ink pot and quill from the man and scribble his signature at the bottom of Jake's legal letters. He blew on the ink to dry before tossing them at Grantham to do the same. Still, he was quiet.

Jake rolled down his sleeves and donned his waistcoat before pushing the parchment into his breast pocket. His gaze still locked with Langdon's. "Aiden, please gather my winnings, and roust the minister from his bed. I'm off to claim my bride."

Langdon lifted his glass once more and began to laugh. "Good luck with that."

"Keep drinking, Langdon. Come morning, I fear your sore

head won't be your only regret." Jake pushed the pistol back into his boot and moved to leave.

"Not I. Come morning I'll crow like a bloody rooster after I finish blowing your precious ship into splinters. Perhaps I'll shout for joy from the roof of Fairwinds. That might be a lovely touch, aye?"

Jake turned back. "Come morning, Fairwinds will be mine, and you'll do well to stay off my roof or I'll have you shot for trespassing."

Langdon slammed down his glass and stood. "You lost. You bloody bastard, you lost. Don't you see? When the sun rises tomorrow, I will have finally beaten you! I'll have *The Phantom* and your days of getting rich off other men's backs will be over. Fairwinds will never be yours, and neither will my darling Lillian." He straightened. "Do you think for one minute I didn't know about your interest in Fairwinds or your disgusting relationship with my daughter? Stupid, stupid girl. She actually believes she's in love with you." He tsked and dropped back into his chair before refilling his drink. "I'm sure her time away will do her good, however. A few months abroad and she'll forget all about you."

"What are you babbling on about? Lily isn't going anywhere. Not without me."

Langdon swirled the liquor in his glass and sneered at Jake. "I wouldn't bet on that. Lillian is at this very moment on the *Margaretha* headed toward England. She set sail on the tide." He gave Jake a pitying look. "Sorry, Captain, you lose."

Chapter 9

"I want every bloody inch of sail we've got." Jake yelled at the crew.

"Do you honestly believe we can catch the *Margaretha*?" Aiden called after Jake as he ran the length of the ship, pushing the crew, securing lines, vowing silently, "*I'm coming, Lily.*"

At least one bit of luck was with them. Jake peered up at the pale light of the moon in the crystalline sky.

"Sharp," Jake grabbed the boy's arm and dragged him mid ship.

"I know, I know, crow's nest, the first tip of a mast. I remember."

"Good man." Jake clapped him on the shoulder and nearly pushed him up the rigging.

"Brother, there's no way of knowing how far ahead they are. They could be hours away. We'll never reach them before dawn. And even if we did, what then? You can't even board the ship."

"I cannot board the ship, true, but I made no such provision for you or another member of the crew."

"And do you suppose the crew of the *Margaretha* will simply let us stroll aboard? If we get that close without any fire power to clear the way, they'll blow us out of the blasted water," Aiden argued.

Jake tossed several crates overboard trying to lighten their load. "They won't engage us with a woman aboard."

"How do you even know she's there? Langdon could be lying to you. He said it himself, he wants to see *The Phantom* blown to driftwood. What if he's sent you on fool's errand to get us all killed?"

Jake spun on him and grasped him by the shoulders. "I have to take that chance. Don't you see?"

"You could end up losing everything if you're wrong."

"If I lose Lily, I've already lost everything." Jake planted his hands on his hips and studied the toes of his boots. "Take the skiff and four men. Go home to Rose. There's enough gold hidden to compensate you for your half of *The Phantom*. Take it. Live your life as a gentleman. Build your home. Raise your growing family."

"And leave you? We came into this world together, and with any luck, that's how we'll go out." Aiden shook his head and laid a hand on Jake's shoulder. "You and I have sailed together into countless storms and battles we never thought to survive. I'm not going anywhere. Rose is surrounded by six sisters, four brothers and parents who adore her. If I'm not there, she'll barely notice."

Jake looked into eyes identical to his own. It was true, the wild Wilder brothers had been through a life of scratching and scraping for food and a roof over their heads at times, storms and battles that tested their strength and their bond, but they always fought back-to-back and side-by-side through the worst of it.

"We're not going out this night or any time soon, brother. I promise. Have the crew make ready the cannons. Twice the powder with none of the shot. When we find the *Margaretha*, we'll make all the noise of an attack without ruffling a single edge of sail."

"And then?"

"Then I'll ask you to go fetch my bride, and the captain to marry us."

* * *

Finally able to leave the Captain Shepherd's quarters, Lily went topside to get away from her sister. Abigail had done nothing since they left Mystic Point but chide her on her foolishness.

Lily needed air, space, time to think, and time to try and forget. Had she been blinded by a few kind words and tender kisses? Was she truly that naïve? The fullness of the rising moon cast a pale path upon the water as if you could step off the ship and walk across the sea to its honey-colored face. Its brightness dimmed the stars, but the sky still enveloped her and made her feel oh so small and terribly alone.

She closed her eyes to the sting of fresh tears only to see Jake's handsome face behind her closed lids. The image of his smile, seeing the love for her in his eyes. Had all of it been a ploy to get Fairwinds? *Ridiculous.* But the rebellious part of her mind argued the validity of such a thought. She'd believed it quaint and lovely to only meet at Fairwinds. Walking the grounds together. Showing him the secrets and beauty of the house. Kissing in front of the fire in the groundkeeper's cottage. He'd been so attentive. Lily had thought it wonderful that he shared her appreciation of the once grand estate. Little had she known it was the estate and only the estate that he was interested in. She was just a means to an end.

Lily smoothed her hands over the wide polished gunnels of the *Margaretha*. The ship Father had named after her sainted mother. "I could really use some of your gentle advice,

Mother." As the years passed, Lily's memories of her beautiful mother had begun to fade around the edges. Try as she might, Lily couldn't quite remember the sound of her mother's voice anymore. "Perhaps if you simply could give me some sort of sign that you can hear me, let me know if I've truly made a mistake in giving my heart to a pirate."

The loud clang of a warning bell split the silence of the night. Over head the lookout shouted, "Ship! Starboard aft! Coming straight for us at full sail!"

No sooner had the words left his mouth than the report of cannon fire blasted behind them. Around her, men took cover and awaited the hit of the shot, but no thunderous blow came. Had the other ship overshot?

Abigail came screaming from below. She found Lily crouched behind a stout barrel and began dragging her to the ladderway. Chaos erupted on deck as men flew in a dozen directions at once.

Captain Shepherd shouted to come about and prepare to return fire. The quartermaster cursed as he lowered his spyglass. "It's those bastards on *The Phantom*."

The Phantom? Jake? Lily wrenched her arm from Abigail's grasp as another blast exploded from behind. No shot hit. She flew at the captain. "You can't fire on him."

He shook her off. "Like hell I can't. Get below."

"You're not about to risk the life of my sister and myself, are you? Our father would kill you with his bare hands should anything happen to us. Plus, can't you see Captain Wilder isn't shooting at you?" Lily pointed toward *The Phantom*. "There's nothing in their guns except noise."

"We've been attacked by Captain Wilder and his crew three times in the last six months. Spent the last week and a thousand pounds replacing the mast and rigging they brought down the last time. Your father would kill me with his bare hands should I let that happen again," Captain Shepherd countered.

"You just confirmed what I'm saying. The last time, they brought down your mast. If Captain Wilder indeed wished to raid the *Margaretha* again, do you believe he would not bother to use cannonballs?"

"Get below, Mistress Langdon, and let me do my job."

Lily clutched at his sleeve. "But you must listen."

"Lily, stop this nonsense and come along." Abigail made a brutal grab for her arm and nearly dragged her below.

"I don't know how, but he knows I'm aboard, Abigail. You were wrong. Jake loves me, and he has come for me."

"God Lord, Lily, we're under attack by pirates, and you're still convinced you're a lovestruck heroine in some romantic drama. Our very lives are in danger!"

Once more Lily found herself locked away in the captain's quarters. She rushed to the back windows and watched as *The Phantom* grew larger and more menacing the closer it came.

"Come away from there." Abigail looked through the drawers in Captain Shepherd's desk. "There has to be something in here we can defend ourselves with. Help me look."

The closer the other ship sailed, the more convinced Lily became. A glimmer of hope flickered in her chest. "We're not going to have to defend ourselves."

Behind her Abigail brightened. "Here's a pistol."

"Have you ever fired a pistol?" Lily knew the answer.

"It couldn't be difficult. Point at something and pull this part here." Abigail tapped the side of the trigger with a timid finger. She turned the weapon this way and that in her hands. "Do you suppose it's loaded? I've watched father load his weapon a few times. I think it's powder, wadding, ball, tamp, more powder, or is it ball, powder, tamp, powder wadding?" She pulled the tamping rod from the end of the gun and looked at it as if it could speak. "Then I remember something about a pan, and a half cock of the flinty part."

"You'll end up blowing your fingers off."

Abigail laid the weapon down gingerly. "Perhaps you're right." She made another slow scan of the room. "Oh, swords." She dragged a chair over and climbed to take down a pair of crossed swords mounted behind a shield upon the wall.

"I think those are decorative."

"They look weapon-ly enough for me," Abigail countered.

Commotion over their heads caught Lily's attention. Pistols fired. Men shouted. It sounded as if hell itself had arrived. For the first time fear entered the churning of emotions in her brain. Perhaps Abigail had been right all along? What if Jake wasn't coming to rescue her like some castled damsel? The battle ragging overhead sounded real enough. Confusion muddled her thoughts. The small flicker of hope she's felt moments before snuffed out like a pitiful candle.

If Jake didn't know she was aboard, the firing of his cannons without shot could simply mean he didn't want to damage the ship. Perhaps this time he was determined to take everything—the storerooms and the *Margaretha* as well. Lily laid a hand against her forehead. She didn't know what to think anymore. What to feel. Who she should believe.

Behind her, Abigail had managed to pull the display of swords, shield and all, off the wall. Abigail gave a small screech as it crashed to the floor. Leaping off her chair, she began tugging on one of the hilts. "Lily, help me free this damn sword."

More gunfire and shouting could be heard overhead. A quick look out the stern windows confirmed that *The Phantom* was upon them. The battle above swelled. Blades met. Pistols fired. Men cried out in pain. The smell of sulfur filtered down through the boards.

Abigail looked toward the ceiling with pure terror in her eyes. Panic overtook her. "They're aboard. Good God, Lily, we're being captured!" With a mighty yank, she freed one of the blades.

Before either of them could prepare themselves, the door swung violently on its hinges hitting the wall with the force. Two men in filthy clothing, one stained with fresh blood, burst into the room with pistols drawn.

Next to Lily, Abigail gave a small pitiful squeak before fainting into a heap of skirts. Her newly found sword clattered to the floor. Lily was quick to pick it up and hold it out toward the fearsome looking men.

But once inside, the men lowered their weapons and stood to one side allowing another man to enter. Lily recognized him immediately. Smartly uniformed, wigged. Aiden Wilder pushed his pistol into a wide leather baldrick as he came forward.

"Mistress Langdon." He dipped his head in a small bow. "We've not been formally introduced, but I've been sent here by my brother on an errand of great importance."

"Where's Jake?" The trembling in Lily's arms made the sword in her hands shake.

"He's aboard *The Phantom*. I'm to bring you to him."

Lily narrowed her gaze and pushed the sword at him. "If I'm of such *'great importance'* to your brother, why isn't he here himself?"

He held his hands out from his sides. "I assure you all will be made clear, if you'll just set aside your weapon and come with me."

At her feet, Abigail moaned and began regaining consciousness. "I'm not leaving my sister."

"I give you my word, no harm will come to her, or to you, Mistress, but it is imperative that we leave this ship now."

"And I'm supposed to believe pirates?"

"Leave her the sword for protection. I swear to you my men will vacate the *Margaretha* with me and leave the ship and your precious sister unscathed."

Lily pointed to one of the men. "And the blood on his shirt? I doubt he earned that shaving."

Aiden sighed and placed his hands on his hips. "Yes, there was a short, intense difference of opinion topside, but we did not draw first blood, nor take vengeance on those who did." He pulled his pistol once more and held it out to her. "If it will make you feel better, take my weapon. It's loaded and primed. Hold it to my back if you wish. I can think of nothing else to convince you that you are safe. But time is wasting, and if I don't bring you to my brother posthaste, you won't have to worry about shooting me. He will."

When he smiled, Lily could see the strong resemblance between the two brothers. He shared Jake's eyes as well. The realization tugged at her confused heart.

"I want to believe you."

He pushed his pistol toward her with the barrel pointed toward his chest.

"And no harm will befall her?" She tipped her chin toward Abigail.

"None, I swear to you." Aiden placed his free hand over his heart.

"Lily?" Abigail was waking. Pale, but otherwise she appeared to be well.

"You dropped your sword." Lily placed it beside her sister and cupped her chilled cheek. "I'll be back. All is well. You're safe."

"What? You're leaving me?" Abigail scrambled to sit.

"You're fine. I need to talk to Jake." Lily looked toward Aiden.

Abigail's color returned. Pink flushed her cheeks. "So he can twist your thinking with more lies?" she snapped.

"No, so I can know once and for all what is the truth." Lily stood and took the gun from Aiden's hand. "After you, gentlemen."

Chapter 10

Jake paced the deck of *The Phantom*. Where the hell was Aiden? How long did it take to collect one woman? Time was wasting.

Across the boarding ladders to the other ship, he could see his crew holding the decks of the *Margaretha*. He'd warned every man to check their weapons and make the capture of the ship and its captain as quick and painless as possible. *"If you raise one splinter of wood on that ship, I'll kill the lot of you myself."* But the *Margaretha's* crew had understandably not heeded that warning themselves. Several men lay injured. His own crew included, but from where he stood, nothing looked life threatening. A low fog of smoke settled upon the scene.

Captain Shepherd had been forcibly encouraged to cross over to *The Phantom* and was escorted below. Jake checked the sky. The moon was near the completion of its rise. They needed to make haste. He began pacing like a nervous groom.

He saw Aiden then, with two more of his men walking with their hands raised in surrender. "What the hell? Where's Lily?"

It wasn't until they reached the boarding ladders that he saw her. She was holding his brother at gunpoint? With his own gun, by the look. *Bloody hell.* The other two men crossed over.

"She's a feisty one, Capt'n." One of the men jerked his chin back toward Lily.

Across the span between the ships, it appeared Aiden was

in deep discussion regarding their route. Lily peered over the railing at the dark abyss to the water below and refused to cross.

Clouds had begun to reach thin fingers across the sky to dull the light of the moon, and the seas were starting to rise. Tossing his waistcoat to one side, Jake headed across the ladder to get her. Hanging tight to a line, he stopped a few yards from the rails of the *Margaretha* and stretched out his arm.

"Lily, take my hand; I'll bring you across."

"Jake. I don't know what's happening. He won't tell me anything." She waved the pistol at Aiden. "And I'm not coming across until I know what's going on."

The ladder jostled beneath him as the two ships moved independently. "Can you please give my brother back his weapon, and could we have this conversation in a less precarious place?"

Lily gave a quick shake of her head. "I'm not leaving this ship until I know the truth."

Jake took a steading breath and reined in his impatience. "What truths do you wish to hear?"

She peeked over the railing again. "I'd rather not have to shout; come over here."

"I can't. I swore to your father I'd never set foot on his ships again."

Her eyes widened. "Why?"

Lily gasped as the ladder bucked and knocked Jake to his knees. "Because he misled me. Made me swear to certain circumstances knowing you were already aboard. He knew I'd come for you but plotted against me being able to reach you in time."

"In time? In time for what?"

Jake's knuckles whitened as he held fast to his perilous perch. "To bloody well marry you!"

Aiden was quick to catch his pistol before it hit the deck boards. Lily's jaw went slack. "You…You're here to marry me?"

"Yes, and if you don't take my hand and get over here, it will be too late."

"Father agreed to this?"

"In a manner of speaking, yes."

Lily was quiet for a moment, her gaze locked with his. "Are you marrying me to get Fairwinds?"

"Yes." He wouldn't lie, not to her. He'd already made her that promise. "But that was before I knew you. Before we'd ever spoken. All that changed. Now, I'm marrying you because I'm in love with you. I wanted Fairwinds for myself, but now I want it for you. For us. Like we talked about. All our plans, I want to make them happen with you. Make it ours. Make it our home."

Another swell unsettled the ladder, nearly knocking Jake into the churning sea below. Lily let out a scream as he clung to the rungs and rode the crest. "Dammit, Lily, give me your hand."

Hoisting her skirts, she rushed toward him. Jake grasped her hand then her waist as she nearly knocked them both into the sea. He backed them both off the ladder and onto the deck of *The Phantom* before he took her face in both his hands and kissed her soundly. "Welcome to my ship," he murmured against her lips.

Their kiss broke at the sound of Aiden's boots hitting the deck boards behind them.

"Come with me." Jake still held tight to her hand. He

turned to his brother. "You as well."

Jake was quick to lead them across the wide rolling deck, down the tight ladderway and aft to unlock the door to his quarters. The cabin was lit by several lanterns that swung lazily in their holders.

"Captain Shepherd?" Lily turned to Jake in question.

The man sported a fresh black eye, and had his wrists lashed to the post of Jake's cot. "The good captain doesn't know it yet, but he's going to have the honor of marrying us."

Lily looked at him with wide eyes. "Now?"

"I'll do nothing of the sort," blurted Shepherd.

"Yes, now," he answered Lily. "Oh, and you will," he insisted of the other captain.

As if on cue, Aiden lifted his pistol and pointed it at Shepherd.

The man didn't flinch. "You're crazy if you think I'll marry Langdon's own daughter to the likes of you. He'd have my bloody head on a platter."

"But if you don't, I'll have to shoot you." Aiden shrugged before cocking his weapon. "Seems you have a choice, Captain Shepherd. Die now or die later."

"Fine, shoot me. It would be quicker and far less painful than what that bastard Langdon would do to me when he finds out."

"But you have orders to sail to England." Jake reminded him. "That alone means it will be months before Langdon's punishing hand can reach you, even if you foolishly decided to make the long journey back. Or you could crawl out from under his heavy thumb and be your own man for once." Jake crossed to his desk and pulled a leathered sack of coins and threw it to land at the man's feet. "And, of course, I would heartily pay you for your services."

"Untie me. What do I care if you wed his offspring? You deal with his wrath. Just let me get back to my ship."

"I give you my word. You'll return to the *Margaretha* and be on your way just as soon as you say the words."

"Fine," Shepherd snapped. He glared at Jake and turned to Lily. "What's your full name?" Aiden cut the man's ropes.

Lily looked back and forth between the men. Jake captured her gaze and held it. "Tell him your name," he whispered as he gave her hand a gentle squeeze.

"L-Lillian Grace Langdon."

"Do you, Lillian Grace Langdon, take…" Shepherd rubbed at his wrists and gave Jake a pointed stare.

"John Jacob Wilder."

"Do you take John Jacob Wilder to be your lawfully wedded husband?"

Lily nodded.

"You have to say either 'yes,' or 'I do.'" Shepherd grumbled at her.

With a quick look of surprise, Lily answered, "I do."

"And do you take her," Shepherd flipped his hand between Jake and Lily, "to be your lawfully wedded wife?"

Jake held her gaze and smiled. "I most certainly do."

Shepherd tugged at his cuffs "Where's the ring?"

"Damn." Jake shot a glance at Aiden. "I forgot the bloody ring."

Shepherd huffed a sigh and made a quick scan of the room. "Give me your knife." He held his hand out to Aiden for the knife that had just cut him loose and snapped his fingers impatiently before snatching it from Aiden's hand. With it, he split the hemp of the rope and sliced off a short length of twine, which he passed to Jake. "Tie it on her finger and repeat after me. "With this piss poor excuse for a ring, I wed thee."

Jake glared once more at the man before tying the twine around Lily's slender finger. "With this piss poor excuse for a ring that I will soon replace with gold, I wed thee.

"Good. Then By the authority of my station as Captain of the ship known to all as the *Margaretha* and the power granted me by King George the Second of England, I pronounce you man and wife. Go ahead and kiss her." Shepherd didn't wait a beat before stooping and gathered the bag of coins at his feet. "Now, if you'll excuse me."

"Aiden, if you'll please escort Captain Shepherd back to his ship, we'd both be most grateful. And gather my new sister-in-law, Abigail. I doubt there's any reason now for her to make the trip alone. We'll return her at once to the safe harbor of her father. She can surprise him with the good news of our nuptials. Give the order to turn about. Full sail back to Mystic Point."

A smile tipped Aiden's mouth. "Aye, Captain, at once. And congratulations. Best wishes to you, as well, Missus Wilder."

As the door closed behind them, Jake turned back to Lily. She was looking at the bit of string tied to her finger. "Missus Wilder."

Jake took her hand and ran his thumb over the knotted twine. He touched his forehead to hers. "That was a poor excuse for a wedding, I know, but before this night is over, I'll make it all up to you. You have my promise."

"You forgot to kiss me," Lily whispered.

"Oh, aye, so I did. I can remedy that immediately." Tipping up her chin, Jake wrapped his arms around her and lowered his mouth to hers in a searing kiss. She was his. While he regretted the way in which it all happened, the fact remained, here in his arms was everything he hadn't realized he needed. For the first time in his memory, it wasn't about him or what he wanted. It was about her. Making her happy. Keeping her safe. Laying the world at her feet. She was his wife.

"Lily," he murmured against her lips. "My Lily."

Chapter 11

Jake held Lily tight in his arms. Her mind continued to try and make sense of it all. "I'm still confused as to how we got here. How did you manage to catch the *Margaretha*? How did you know where to find me?"

"Your father told me exactly where you were, and my ship is faster." Jake proceeded to tell her everything that transpired between him and her father earlier.

The shock of his words made her head spin. Lily pushed out of his embrace. She needed air. She couldn't look at him and turned away. Disbelief caused her heart to pound. Jake and her father had wagered her future? Bid on her like livestock at an auction? Used her and her feelings as nothing more than a bargaining chip?

"But, I won," Jake concluded behind her. "I found you, beat your father's contrived conditions, and now your mine. Fairwinds is mine and—"

Lily spun on him. "So I was just a playing piece? A pawn in both your games?"

"No." Jake stood in front of her and held her upper arms. "It was the only way I could think of to get your father to agree to our marriage."

She closed her eyes to block out the sight of him. "All so you could own Fairwinds." Lily stated woodenly.

"I told you in the beginning that was my original plan. I admit it." When she started to pull away, Jake tightened his grasp. "But damnit, Lily, that was before."

He tipped her chin so she had no choice but to look into his stormy eyes. "That was before I'd met you, spent time with you. Then all I wanted was you. Tonight, I put everything I had on that table including this ship. I risked everything for you. And even when I won, your father tried to see to it that I still wouldn't have you. I'd still lose everything if I didn't reach you and marry you by sunrise."

"And what if you'd lost?"

Jake gave a small shake of his head. "Then I would have thought of another way. I wouldn't have stopped until I found you."

"And Fairwinds?"

"To hell with Fairwinds. It stopped being about that old estate the moment I spoke to you at the ball. Am I happy to have it now? Yes, because you love it there, and it makes you happy and light up like the sun. I plan on doing everything in my power to keep you happy, but if you want to live somewhere else, Fairwinds can bloody well crumble into the sea."

Lily frowned trying to believe him. "Then why did you even want it to begin with?"

"The caves."

"The ones on the beach?"

"Yes. I had grand plans to construct tunnels and storerooms beneath the grounds to hide our cache without detection."

Lily couldn't have heard him correctly. "You-you wanted to turn Fairwinds into a pirate hideout?" A shaking began in her body.

Jake nodded. "That was my plan." He ran his hands up

and down her arms. "But don't you see none of that matters now."

"I don't know what to think anymore. I-I..."

"Lily, say the word and I'll turn this ship in any direction you choose, and we can start our life wherever you wish. I love you. You're my wife, but if knowing the truth has changed your feelings—"

"And what if I no longer want to be wed?" She blurted and pushed away from him. "I still feel like I'm nothing but a pawn in your game. This is all too much." Lily wrapped her arms about herself and tried to still the trembling.

A knock sounded at the door. Before either of them could respond, Aiden opened the door a crack. "The skiff is ready to take you and Lily to Fairwinds."

"Thank you." Jake looked back at her and held her gaze for a long moment. "I'm not sure it's needed anymore."

Aiden opened the door fully. "What? I thought—"

"Seems the lady is having some misgivings."

Lily's gaze shifted back and forth between twin sets of identical gray eyes. Waiting for her to...to what? The pull and tug of her emotions only added to the nausea she was experiencing aboard *The Phantom* as it rose and fell in the rising seas.

She turned her back on the two of them and took several deep breaths. Being in Jake's quarters, however, tidal waved her senses with everything...him. She could smell the spiced scent that lingered on his skin. Saw his coat and baldrick hanging on pegs along with various weapons. How many lives had been ended with those weapons? Chests of goods lined the walls at her feet. Stolen goods?

All around her were the organized tools of his trade—

charts, spinnaker, ship's log. This was truly who he was. Captain, seaman, *pirate*. She'd foolishly romanticized all of it while she was losing her heart to a man she knew nothing about. A man she'd married with a twine ring. Lily pressed her hand against her corsets as she fought to take a decent breath.

Jake came to stand behind her. He stroked her shoulders. "I realize it's all a great deal to accept right now, but I'm asking you to trust me, and come along," he urged. "If we wait to much longer, the seas will become too rough, and we'll not reach Fairwinds before sunrise."

Lily finally snapped and spun on him again. "Sunrise? Sunrise! Ah, yes, your blasted bet and the dreaded curse of sunrise! By all means, put me in your skiff, tie me to an oar for all I care. Then you'll win your bloody wager and keep your precious ship and capture your prize of Fairwinds." Her voice raised a full octave. "But once the light of that damnable sunrise hits my face, my part of your plan will be over." She held her forehead. "What could I have been thinking? Why did I ever believe the word of a pirate? Fear not, my *husband*, you'll not need to pretend to love me after this night. You'll be unfettered. You can be rid of—what did your men call me—the dim-witted Langdon daughter. Our marriage will be annulled, and you'll be free to paint Fairwinds purple and dig tunnels straight to hell if you wish." She drew a shaky breath and glared at him.

Her anger filled the room. Silent tension pulsed in the air around them.

Jake's stormy eyes darkened before narrowing. His anger joined hers. "Very well," Jake ground out between his teeth. The muscle in his jaw flexed. The tense air fairly sparked between them.

A new shiver ran through Lily. She'd never seen Jake angry. It was a sight she immediately regretted provoking. It was as if part of him turned cold and dark. He looked every bit the fearsome pirate he was rumored to be.

He grabbed her firmly by the arm and pulled her toward the door. "We're leaving," he growled at Aiden as he grabbed a cloak from a peg near the door. Pushing out into the dark narrow corridor, he didn't speak, nor slow his steps. He pulled her up the stairs and onto the lanterned deck.

Jake never stopped or slowed. Lily had to run to keep up with his long, determined strides. Passing an ashen Abigail, Lily held up her left hand and showed her sister her twine ring.

Lily shouted back to her, "Tell Father he lost far more tonight than his bloody wager."

In response to her words, Jake tightened his hold and quickened his steps.

A small boat clung to the left side of *The Phantom* and hung precariously on a series of pulleys and ropes. She started to object to boarding, but the look on Jake's face silenced her. He deposited her without ceremony on a low bench in the back, wrapped her in his cloak and left her to join the four other men who were positioned toward the bow, facing her.

"Away," Jake barked.

Men on *The Phantom* began lowering them on the ropes toward the dark waves below. Lily hung on to the sides of the small ship and prayed they wouldn't drop them. All the while, her gaze never left Jake. He wouldn't meet her eye. The pulsing muscles in his jaw continued to chisel the lines of his face.

Before long, they were safely in the water. A single lantern at the bow lit the scene as the men used their oars to push them away from the other ship. The small skiff tossed on the waves as Jake and the others secured their oars in their locks and worked in unison to pull them through the water and away from *The Phantom*.

Looking off to her right, Lily could barely see the lights of Mystic Point through the mist that had begun to settle over them. Ahead, she could just make out the dark edge of the cliffs at Fairwinds against a lightening sky. A lantern burned on the beach.

Lily tucked into the warmth of Jake's cloak. Tears threatened, but she refused to let them fall. She'd been a fool, just as Abigail had warned. To think a man like Jake Wilder would fall in love with her, and she'd believed him. Believed his kisses. His tender words. How could she have been so impetuous?

Because those kisses and tender words had reached a neglected part of her heart and ignited a need so deep, the thought that it had all been fake capsized her. Lily closed her eyes to the shaft of pain that stabbed through her chest.

With each stroke of the oars, Lily's body jerked forward as they pulled closer to the shore. Before she knew it, the sound of gravel rasping the bottom of the skiff announced their arrival. The four men leapt from the skiff into the shallow water and hauled the heavy boat up onto the beach. A welcoming lantern burned at the foot of the cliffs where the narrow set of stone stairs led up to Fairwinds.

Jake got out and looked toward the eastern sky before holding out his hand to her. His anger radiated off him like the coming sun. He wasn't the only one. Her own anger and heartache had her straightening her spine and refusing his help to disembark as she negotiated the tipping skiff at the edge of the waves. She leapt from the skiff and nearly ended up taking a dive into the sand.

Storming toward the sea stairs her mood continued to darken. Angry, indeed. If anyone had a reason to be furious, it was her. At Jake, at her blasted father, at Abigail, but mostly at herself for letting her feelings blind her to the reality of what was truly happening. Lily berated herself as she climbed the narrow stone steps. In future, she would not be so easily swayed by a set of wide shoulders and a rakish smile—

Lily reached the top of the stairs. The sight she beheld stole her breath away. Gasping, she looked back at Jake. For the first time since leaving *The Phantom*, his dark gaze held hers. "What have you done?" she whispered.

Turning back, she followed the line of small lanterns that edged the path leading from the cliffs through the grounds of Fairwinds. Torches burned bright at the entrance to the arbor where a man stood waiting. Was that the minister?

Walking along the lighted pathway, she reached the spot. Where the roses on the arbor had all but faded, fresh roses and greenery was tied on with wide white ribbons. Their ends danced in the gentle breeze. Pink and yellow rose petals were scattered on the ground in front of the officiant.

Beyond, several lights burned within Fairwinds. Two servants stood waiting on the patio. From here she could see the ballroom softly glowed, as if dozens of candles had been lit within.

Lily spun back to Jake and repeated "What have you done?"

"Better that I tell you what I *haven't* done." His voice still carried a grated edge. "I didn't lie to you about my feelings or my desires. I never *pretended* to love you."

Hearing her own words tossed back at her made her gasp.

Jake pulled in a deep breath and continued, "I wanted to marry you, here. Properly." His words softened and he took a step toward her. "Captain Shepherd was merely assurance should we not make it back in time, but that was hardly the wedding I wanted for us. Hardly the wedding you deserve. You're wearing a bloody bit of rope for a ring." He shook his head. "So, before I headed off to find you, I set some things in motion here." His hand swept the scene.

Looking around Lily stammered, "I—I don't know what to say."

"Dammit, Lily, say you believe me. Tell me you love me. Say you still want to be my wife. Marry me again. Now. And promise me that when the sun does rise, you won't leave me."

His words caressed the bruises of her heart. Lily flew into his arms and kissed him. Between kisses she rushed to assure him. "I do love you. I never should have doubted you. I believe you. I'm sorry I said those ugly things. I was upset and in shock. I love you so much. Please tell me you forgive me."

Jake's arms crushed her to him as he deepened the kiss and ended the need for any more words.

Behind them the minister cleared his throat. "The sky lightens, Captain."

Jake loosened his hold. "Ah, yes."

Lily turned and ran a smoothing hand over her hair and skirts and smiled at Jake. "We're ready, Father."

Jake gave a small shake to his head. "No, we are not. Another few minutes, Father, please?" He raised his hand and summoned the servants from the patio. To a young woman, he said, "Primrose, please show the bride where she can change."

"Change? But I—"

Jake cupped Lily's cheek and dropped a tender kiss upon her lips. "Just go with Rose, and hurry."

Lily was quick to follow Aiden's wife Rose. The slight woman with bright auburn hair and striking green eyes was bursting with excitement, and her enthusiasm was contagious. She gathered Lily's hand and rushed her inside. All the while chattering about how romantic it all was, how happy she was to soon have another sister. They were destined to be the best of friends. Aiden had told her how smitten Jake had been behaving these last few weeks. They thought he'd never find a wife, but here she was.

In what had once been the dining room, Lily was set upon by a small crew of lady's maids that helped her change into a beautiful satin gown the rich pink color of sea roses. At the same time, Rose pinched at her cheeks to bring up her color while still another fussed with the arrangement of her hair and pinned it up loosely with tiny rosebuds and ribbons. Jake had thought of everything. The final touches were a pair of gold wrapped rubies secured to her ear lobes. "A gift from the groom, my lady."

In no time she was back at Jake's side, standing before the officiant with an armful of ribboned roses and lilies. A sudden flutter of nerves twittered in her belly.

"You look beautiful." Jake's smile calmed her. He loved her. How could she have questioned that? She made a silent promise she'd never make that mistake again.

"And you are the most handsome man I've ever seen." The dark black of his formal waistcoat lay in sharp contrast to the brilliant white of his stock. The embroidered pattern on his satin vest, black on black, gave him the look of a sophisticated gentleman.

He didn't take his eyes from her. "Now, Father. Make haste."

"Of course." The minister cleared his throat again. "Captain John Jacob Wilder, do you take this woman, Lillian Grace Langdon, to be your wedded wife, to have and to hold from this day forward until you are parted by death?"

"I do."

Lillian Grace Langdon, do you take this man, John Jacob Wilder, to be your wedded husband, to have and to hold from this day forward until you are parted by death?

"With all of my heart, I do." She smiled at the sudden catch in Jake's breath.

"Do we have a ring?"

"Yes." Holding her hand, Jake tugged the short piece of twine off her finger and tucked it into his pocket before pulling out a wide circle of gold set with a large center ruby hugged by two triangular diamonds. He slipped it onto her finger and cursed softly. "It's too large."

"Nonsense, it's perfect," Lily insisted, squeezing his fingers. "Go on, Father."

Pinks and lavenders threaded the sky behind the low buttery moon when Jake repeated the minister's words, "With this ring, I thee wed and with it I bestow all of the treasures of my mind, heart, and body."

"By the power given unto me by God himself, I pronounce you are man and wife. You're free to kiss your bride, Captain Wilder."

Jake didn't wait for the man to finish the sentence. He pulled her into his arms and crushed his mouth to hers after the words, "You're free to kiss—"

Lily's heart soared in her chest as he enveloped her. "We

made it," she gasped between kisses.

"You're officially, legally, blessedly, and completely mine. Now there can be no question."

"Not when you've married me on land and at sea," Lily teased. "Be warned, Father, he may wish us to climb into the trees next and have the birds of the air witness our union for a third time."

"Best wishes, Missus Wilder." The minister shook both their hands. "Congratulations, Captain."

Jake thanked the man and paid him handsomely for his service before taking Lily's hand and raising it to kiss the backs of her fingers. "Come."

With the sky ripening to gold around them, Jake led her across the patio and through the open French doors into a glowing ballroom. Tall branches of candles burned. A small table, set for two, sat in the middle of the wide space. Its long white tablecloth pooled onto the floor. A servant stood at the ready with a bottle of wine. Jake held her chair as a quartet of musicians began to play a soft tune.

"This is all too much—" Lily gave the quartet a closer look. "Are those? They are. Those are your men. The ones who rowed us ashore."

"Aye, they are the musicians from *The Phantom*."

The four looked freshly scrubbed and wore shirts the color of rich wine. One played what looked like a lute. Another bowed a fiddle. There was one softly playing a whistle pipe and a man drumming a bodhrán. For all their rough appearance, the music they played seemed like something from a dream.

Looking back at Jake, she caught him staring and gave him a smile. "It's lovely. It's all lovely. I shall not forget this night or this day for the rest of my life." The first rays of the rising sun had finally reached Fairwinds.

"You are what I shall never forget. Just when I imagine you cannot get more beautiful." He gave her fingers a squeeze. "Dance with me."

Lily took his hand and followed him a few steps away from where they sat. Jake gave her a small spin, like the first time she had shown him the ballroom, before he drew her into his arms. He held her tight and began to sway gently to the music.

"I don't know the steps to this particular dance."

"There are no steps," he whispered into her hair as he slipped an arm about her waist and pressed the length of her against him. "'Tis simply a way to hold your body close to mine."

"That is beyond scandalous, Captain. There will be talk." Heat flooded Lily's limbs at the feel of him pressed tight to her. His now familiar scent filled her senses. "If you continue this behavior, you'll have to marry me to restore my honor."

"I've already done that," he murmured into her ear. "Twice."

"Ah, yes, so you have. Then by all means, compromise me." Lily grinned into his shoulder. "But not in front of the men."

"Very well." Jake raised his head. "Turn about," he ordered the orchestra, and to Lily's delight the four men did so and presented their backs without missing a single beat.

Lily laughed as they turned. "You as well," Jake ordered their servant. The man couldn't quite stifle his grin before he too turned away from them.

"It seems you are very skilled at removing any and all obstacles, Captain Wilder."

"When I desire something...someone, as much as I desire

you, I don't know the meaning of the word." He tightened his hold, tipped her back, and kissed her. Deeply, passionately.

Lily clung to him, welcoming the sweep of his tongue into her mouth. Her body trembled with awakening want mixed with an innocent's nervousness.

Straightening, Jake continued to capture her mouth with his. Their breathing raced. One hand pushed into her hair to hold her head while the other traced the curve of her ear and down her throat. The heat of his touch near singed her skin.

When a single finger dipped into the tight pressed valley between her corseted breasts, she let out a gasp. Not one of shock, but one of pure delight.

"Jake," she breathed as his mouth followed the trail of his fingertip.

"Are you hungry?" he murmured against her skin.

Her brain couldn't think past the feel of his lips on the apex of her cleavage. "Hungry?"

Jake finished raining kisses over the swell of her breast before pulling back and resting his forehead against hers. "I don't think I can wait through a five-course meal to be with you."

"But there's cake." Lily's breath stuttered.

"I'll feed it to you in bed," he growled.

"Please tell me it's a proper bed?"

A slow grin tipped the corners of his mouth before he captured her lips again. "Not for long."

Chapter 12

Through the alcove with the hidden door and out into the foyer still stark and bare, Jake ushered Lily to the second floor. Leading her to the northeast corner of the house, he opened the door to the room he'd requested.

The sound of Lily's surprised breath was better than any music still filtering up from the ballroom.

"It isn't grand, or large, but 'tis a start." Jake admired the work his small crew of hired house servants had accomplished in short order.

The room gleamed in the early morning light. Every surface had been scrubbed and polished. The windows on two sides of the room fairly sparkled. A wide bed stood against the west wall and was plump with a fresh goose feather mattress, linens, and a quilted spread covered with pieced, intertwining rings of yellow and blue.

"How on earth did you do all of this in one night?" Lily sighed. She fingered a vase of the same roses and lilies as she carried earlier.

"I hired help. In truth, I stole them from my brother's household for the night. Primrose would have my head if I were to take them on permanently, however. Although after seeing what they accomplished, I'm tempted to make them an offer."

A small fire had been lit in a narrow fireplace taking the chill from the room. Two matching wing chairs covered in a rich blue velvet flanked the fire with a small table between holding a decanter of what looked to be brandy with two short-stemmed glasses waiting to be filled. Jake filled them both and handed one to Lily. She took a large swallow and seemed to regret it, placing a hand to her throat with a gasp.

He took the glass from her and set his aside also before moving closer to her. "Perhaps we should leave the brandy for later as well."

"We could have it with our cake," Lily teased, stepping aside. She wrung her hands and gave him a forced smile before glancing at the bed. "My, what a proper bed that is. Just as you said."

Jake tried to sooth her obvious apprehensions. He caught her arm as she skirted him once more. "Indeed, quite proper. I'm not going to force you into it either." He cupped her cheek.

"It's not that I've changed my mind, or that I don't want to do my duties as your wife. I just…I'm a bit nervous."

"Then we'll take things nice and slow." Good advice for both of them. Given the wooden state of his cock, if he didn't cool his ardor, their joining would be over before it began, and he'd end up hurting her in the rush. "Perhaps I will have my brandy now."

Stripping off his coat, he tossed it over the back of one of the chairs and tugged at the ties to his stock. Had the room become a good deal warmer?

"Here, let me help you with that." Lily stood before him and unwound the silk from his neck. He drowned in the darkness of her eyes. "I haven't thanked you for my beautiful ring. And this gown. I suppose Primrose had something to do with this, as well?"

"Everything but the color," he corrected.

Lily looked down and plucked at her skirts. "You picked pink?"

Jake followed the path of her fingers as she traced the edge of her neckline. "It suits you." His voice broke. *Dammit.* Reaching out he tugged at the ties of her lacings and released the bow.

Lily's breath hitched and he stopped. He broke away and refilled his glass. "Of course, all of this would have been quite in vain had you refused me." Jake swept the room with his hand.

"No wonder you were so angry."

"I wasn't angry about that, Lily. I was angry that somehow you believed I wanted this house more than I wanted you." He sat before the fire and removed his boots. "Every time I sailed past Fairwinds, I would look at those caves and imagine the storehouse I could build beneath these grounds. I drew a maze of tunnels and rooms I'd build. Secret passageways to hide my bounty so my crew and I could slip away without capture." Jake unbuttoned his vest and loosened the neck of his shirt. "Then I met you at the ball. The next day we were here, and I began to see Fairwinds as something else." He leaned forward and poked at the fire with the iron hanging alongside the hearth. Lily came and sat in the adjoining chair. She picked up her glass and sipped at her brandy.

"When Aiden and I were boys, we were poor. The poorest of the poor. Our father was a seaman on a merchant ship. We wouldn't see him for months at a time. Mother did everything short of selling one of us to get food to eat and clothes to cover our scrawny behinds. That's why Aiden dresses like he does." Jake shot her a glance before returning his attention to the dancing flames. "Only the finest cloth. Hand tailored. The most expensive wigs. I never shared that desire. Yes, I wanted better for myself, but better so I wouldn't have to scrape every damn day. I don't need custom-made boots." Jake lifted his boots by their tops and set them next to his chair.

"It wasn't until that day. Seeing Fairwinds through your eyes. Hearing how it had been your home." He gave a slow shake of his head. "I never knew what that meant before then. It struck me with how much I wanted it. This home. Your home. I wanted to give that to you again. Make it ours."

Neither spoke for a moment. The only sound in the room was the crack and pop of the wood in the fire.

"Your father is the one who enlightened me most," Jake admitted finally.

Lily almost choked on her brandy. "How did he manage to do that?"

Jake looked over at her. "He kept talking about this empty building and crumbling estate. He was right. It's not the walls and floors or even the painted ceilings that make this anything other than a hollowed-out shell. It's you, Lily. You're the one that makes Fairwinds a home. It all became clear to me as I raised the sails of *The Phantom* to come after you last night. *You* are my home. Whether I'm with you here or whether we travel to the ends of the earth together, as long as you're with me, I'm home."

Tears welled in her eyes. Jake reached across and took her hand, giving it a squeeze. "I'll find another place to dig my tunnels and hide my stores. I just want to know I can always come home to you."

Lily rose and came to sit in his lap and wrap her arms about his neck. "Yes, my love, you can always come home to me." She laid a gentle kiss on his lips. "In fact, I insist upon it."

Jake settled her weight against him and relished the simple feel of her in his arms.

"Jake?"

"Yes?"

"I realized something last night, too."

He pulled back enough to look into her face. "What was that?"

"I've fallen in love with a pirate."

"You've only come to that realization now?"

"Being on *The Phantom*, standing in the captain's quarters, your quarters, I saw that side of you for the first time. Understood the truth of what it all means. Surrounded by your weapons, I saw the ferocity in your anger. Felt the strength of you. Your power. You were terrifying."

"My temper gets the better of me sometimes, but you have to know I'd never raise a hand to you. Ever."

"I believe you. It was just…It was frightening to witness such intensity, but it was also a thrilling sight to behold." She gave him a coy smile. "It captured even more of my heart."

Jake frowned. "What are you saying?"

"I'm wed to a handsome, fierce pirate, and I'm excited to hear all your tales of dangerous adventures and conquests. I want you to have your tunnels. I want you to make Fairwinds your pirate lair. Hide your treasure. Store your goods unnoticed. Come and go under their very noses. I'll claim I know nothing. Let Fairwinds be your safe harbor, a secret hideaway, as well as our home."

Jake's heart soared. Had he not already been completely and hopelessly in love with her, he'd have fallen for her in that moment. He kissed her then, tasting the sweetness of brandy on her lips.

They stayed just that way long after the logs on the fire had burned down to nothing but embers and the sun rose higher in the sky. Their kisses went from sweet and chaste to white hot and back again. They finished the brandy, talked about his secret tunnels, Aiden and the sweetness of his Rose, and about expanding the third floor to create a little piece of heaven, a private place just for them, to make Fairwinds their own.

"And perhaps a nursery?" Lily teased the open neck of his shirt.

While they'd been wrapped in each other's arms, between teasing, stirring kisses, Jake had worked at undoing the lacings of her bodice. With and without her notice. One eyelet at a time. He slipped a searching hand past the neckline of her gaping shift to caress the buttery soft fullness of her breast. She arched with pleasure as he trailed his lips along the column of her throat.

"You do want to have a child, don't y—oh, Jake, that feels…"

"We'll build a fine nursery," he murmured against her skin, "and fill it with a dozen babes."

"A dozen?" She gasped as he tweaked at the tightened tip of her nipple.

"One at a time, of course. Or maybe two. I'm a twin after all." Jake moved his kisses up to trace the shell of her ear.

Lily squirmed in his arms. "Are you suggesting we never leave our bed?"

"We would have to get in our bed before we can leave it," he teased.

"I suppose it is time. You've been up all night."

Her naïve statement had him rolling his hips to ease the

increasing ache in his pants. He released a small groan. "Aye, it feels like I've been *up* for days."

Lily stood and finished what he'd started by first removing her bodice and then releasing the ties of her skirts to let them puddle at her feet. The soft linen of her shift caught seductively upon the peaks of her breasts as she reached up to pull the pins and ribbons from her hair.

Tiny rose buds tumbled into the pile of skirt. "I'm ready. Take me to your proper bed, Captain Wilder.

In a single motion, Jake stood and swept her into his arms. "Very well, Missus Wilder."

Chapter 13

Jake pulled the shirt over his head and began to unbutton his breeches. Behind him Lily was quiet. Too quiet. Turning, he frowned. She was laid out on the bed, arrow straight, eyes screwed tight. Her dark hair fanned the pillow.

"What's the matter with you?" When he touched her shoulder, she flinched. "Damn, I forgot you're not used to the strength of the brandy. Are you ill?"

"No, I'm not ill, or drunk. I'm ready."

"Ready?"

"For you to take your husband's privileges." She looked at him with urging eyes. "You know, claim me. Take my innocence. Pillage me."

"Pillage you?" he grinned.

She nodded. "I'm nervous. I've been told…things…"

"Like what things?"

"That there is pain and blood, but I should just hang on and it will be over 'fore I know it. Abigail always says, if there is any grace in God, she'll conceive a son on the spot, give her husband an heir, and never have to lie with him again."

"Abigail is the dim-witted Langdon daughter." Jake removed her fingers from the death grip she had upon the bedding. He kissed their backs. "I'm not about to rut you like some rabid beast."

Her eyes widened. "You're not?"

"Of course not."

"But you're a pirate. Pirates are experienced...pillagers."

"True." Jake stifled a laugh and kissed her chilled fingers again.

"And you've been with many women?"

Opening her hand, he laid a warm kiss into her palm. "A few. But none were you." Jake pulled her to seating. "Yes, the first time can be painful, but only for a short time and there are ways to ease some of the pain. Pleasures as well." He gave her a tender kiss. "Like when I touch you." Jake murmured against her lips as he loosened the neck of her shift and pulled it off one shoulder.

"I do like that."

"I want to learn everything you like. To pleasure you." His voice sounded like gravel to his ear. "Tell me what you like, Lily."

"Oh." She gave a little sigh. "I like it when you kiss me. I like that very much."

Jake tipped his head and covered her lips gently with his own. At another sigh, he slipped his tongue between her lips and kissed her until he felt her begin to relax beneath his hands. "Kiss me back." He whispered then smiled at the tentative tip of her tongue.

Moving his kisses to her jaw, Jake teased the space below her ear and down the side of her neck. "What if I kiss you here? Do you like this as well?"

"Oh, my, yes."

"What if I kissed every inch of you?"

Lily squirmed in response. "Every inch?"

He finished opening her shift to her waist and slipped a slow hand inside to caress the softness of her breast. He brushed his thumb over the tip, making Lily breathe a soft gasp. "I could kiss you here. Do you like it when I touch you? Tease you?"

"Jake…"

He laid her hand on the plane of his chest. "You can touch me as well."

"A-and, you'd like that?"

"Mmm, hmm," he whispered as he trailed his lips over the rapid pulse at the base of her throat, before dipping his head and pulling her pebbled nipple into his mouth and sucked."

"Oh, Jake." She clutched at this shoulder and writhed in his arms. "Oh…"

He raised his head. "That feels good to you?"

Lily's breath came quickly as she nodded.

Jake smiled and lowered the thin linen of her shift to pool at her hips and drank in the sight of her. Beautiful. Lily. His wife.

"You take my breath," he huffed, cupping each tender breast and kissing her there. "You're perfect."

"I'm not." she blurted and tensed once more. "I'm far from perfect. I have an ugly birthmark."

Jake's gaze roamed over her. "I don't see any birthmark."

Lily clutched the fabric at her side. "It's on my hip. Mother once told me I must have struggled in the stork's beak, and he had to carry me to her by the corner of my britches. I'm embarrassed for you to see it."

Jake lifted his arm and showed her the white line of a scar he'd earned along with two cracked ribs capturing *The Phantom* from her previous host. And yet another scar across the top of his right arm. "I'm not perfect either."

Once more, Jake plucked tight fingers away from their white-knuckled grip and kissed their backs. "You mustn't ever be embarrassed to show me your body."

Grimacing, Lily hesitated before pushing the fabric lower and turned. Sure enough, on the gentle flair of her hip was a small mark the color of claret against the alabaster of her skin. "It's hideous." She covered it with her hand.

Jake brushed her fingers aside. "It's a heart."

"No, it isn't." She peered back over one shoulder.

"Aye, it is." He traced it with a fingertip. "The edge is ragged, but it is most definitely a heart." Jake bent to lay a kiss upon it and used the advantage of his position to slip a hand lower over the full roundness of her behind.

"Jake," she whimpered.

"Still perfect," he breathed against her skin. In one skillful move, he had her free of shift and laid her back against the pillows. Jake continued to stroke and kiss her.

"Everywhere you touch me…" Lily moved beneath his caresses and arched into his touches. "It's like I'm on fire."

"Am I hurting you? Burning you?" His tongue teased her navel.

"No, oh Jake, it feels…so good."

Jake moved higher and captured her mouth again. She kissed him hungrily as he reached to thread his fingers through the soft curls covering her sex. Lily gasped and stilled. Jake felt her heart pounding under his own. His gaze held hers as he nipped at her lips.

"This will feel good as well, I promise." He moved his hand up one of her thighs and urged her to spread her legs for him. Her heat fanned his fingers. The pulse of his trapped cock nearly strangled him. Sweat prickled across his chest at the effort it took to harness his control.

Slipping a finger along the satiny clef of her, he moaned at the wetness he found there. It bathed his fingers as he stroked and teased her swollen flesh.

"I'm...I'm wet there, I'm sorry. I don't know why."

Kill me. "It's perfectly normal. Your body is making you ready for me."

"Oh. Oh!" Her breath caught as he slipped a finger into her opening. The walls of her quivered. She opened her knees wider and rolled her hips.

Jake's thumb swirled over the slick bud of her clitoris while slowly and gently sliding his fingers in and out of her sheath, preparing her, teaching her the rhythm he would soon find with his cock. Bracing on one elbow he looked down into her face, watching her discover her body's passion. Watching her learn her pleasure.

Lily opened her eyes and gazed up at him. Her lips parted as her breathing raced. Her hair clung to the dampness of her heated cheeks. "I feel...oh, Jake... It feels like I'm rushing toward...oh, God...I don't know what."

"Do you want me to stop?" he teased.

"No."

Jake smiled. "Good. Let your body take you there."

"Take me where?" She clutched at his arm with one hand and reached for the headboard with the other. Closing her eyes, she arched once more, spread her legs wider. "Oh, God." Her hips instinctively moved in opposition to his fingers.

Somewhere along the way, the front flap of Jake's breeches had lowered. His cock stood proud against his belly. He was fit to burst, but he needed her to find her release first. Jake increased the pressure and quickened his strokes. Lily cried out again.

He kissed her throat, tasting the salty glow of her skin.

"Feel it, my love. Feel me loving you. Every stroke, every kiss," he nipped at her collar bone, "every—"

"Ah! Jake!" Lily's body jerked beneath him. She pushed her hips higher. Her nails bit into his arm. He pushed his fingers deeper, faster. A rush of hot cum ran over his knuckles.

Dear God, she was glorious. Her orgasm continued to roll through her until she whimpered and pushed weakly at his hand.

Jake gathered her into his arms and pulled her into his lap. His hard cock lay trapped between his belly and a beautiful, ragged-edged claret heart.

Lily wrapped her arms about his neck. Her body still trembled. She kissed him and pressed her chest to his. "I was wrong. I... that... What you did to me. It felt as if...I had no idea."

"We're not done yet." He stroked her back. The muscle in his jaw pulsed as he held on to the last shreds of his control. Warm and soft, she felt like heaven in his arms. The musky scent of her skin aroused him even more. "I wanted your first time to make you want a second. I want you to come willingly to my bed. Eager for what we do here. You're my wife. My lover. We can fill our nights with pleasuring each other in all kinds of ways." Images of those ways fill his thoughts. Running a finger over his lip, he tasted her on his tongue. He wanted more. What would she do when he put his mouth to her sex?

"And what about your pleasure?"

"Right now, this is about you."

"Well unless you've forgotten to remove your pistol along with your breeches, I have a very firm cock pressed into my hip that might suggest otherwise." She gave a small wriggle to accentuate her point.

He groaned. "I'm doing my best not to toss you on your back and brutishly plunge into you. I don't want to hurt you, but good Lord, I can't think past my wanting to be inside you." His voice dropped low once more.

She pulled away enough to look down at the cock in question. "I don't see how you can possibly fit."

Jake groaned again and closed his eyes. His cock pulsed with impatience. "You'd be surprised."

"It might be a tight squeeze." Lily gave him that smile. The one that had made him cross a crowded room and fall in love with her the night of the ball. The one that said she was no timid maid. That regardless of her innocence, she possessed an independent, confident spirit he found intoxicating and utterly arousing. She ran a hand over his chest before laying a kiss at the base of his throat.

Slipping off his lap and laying down she trailed her fingers down his arm. "I've always heard that one should finish what one starts, Captain Wilder." Lily raised his hand and placed it upon her breast and arched into his touch. "Don't you have some more pillaging to do?"

Chapter 14

The next several months were an endless flotilla of workmen both above ground and, to her husband's delight, below. Servants were hired, and the Captain and Missus. Wilder were blissfully happy making Fairwinds everything they hoped it would be.

Fall crept into winter with long nights of discovering each other's pleasures. There was much pillaging. On the sea and most assuredly in their bed.

Spring returned beauty to the sleeping grounds of Fairwinds with newly tended gardens and flowering trees. Lily filled each room with the scent of roses. Spring also brought mud as it does in New England. If not to the formal pathways and gardens, at least to the tunnels being constructed below her feet. Jake's boots reminded her of this sodden condition daily.

Lily had spent the morning in the groundskeeper's cottage giving the building a much-needed tidying. Shooing away the other servants, she appreciated the chance to work and relished the quiet solitude away from the constant noise of construction.

The last few weeks had been a strain. With the warmer weather all activity around the estate had bloomed into organized chaos, but Jake captained it all with relative ease. Including the hiring of the new groundskeeper and stablemaster, as well as most of the staff. The secrets of

Fairwinds continued to grow, and Jake trusted only his own men to keep those secrets.

Turning from her task of cleaning the ashes from the hearth, Lily jumped in surprise. "Jake! You frightened me to death. Where did you come from?"

He pulled her into his arms. "That would be my little mystery." He smiled against her lips.

She pushed at his chest playfully and put a finger under her nose. "No mystery. You and your horrid boots have come straight from the tunnels."

Jake tightened his hold, refusing to release her and kissed her before looking at the mess he made on the freshly scrubbed slate tiles. "How are you so sure? This muck could have easily come from inspecting the new tilling of the kitchen garden."

Lily gave her head a quick shake and wrinkled her nose. "You smell like the inside of a dank barnacle."

"Do I? And how would you know what a dank barnacle smells like?" he teased, brushing the end of her nose with his own.

"I've witnessed a ship or two careened in my lifetime. The scent is familiar as well as unpleasant." Lily pointed to the open door. "Out."

Jake obliged in removing his offensive boots to outside. "But you should see what my men have done below. It's made so one can come and go without detection from the house, the stable, even this cottage."

Lily cleaned away his footprints and gave him a pointed look. "I have no interest in your muddy maze. You know, you missed our portrait session this morning," she scolded. "Again."

Jake growled, "The man could have painted the entire house by now. How long does one portrait take?"

"It takes far longer when the groom doesn't keep his promise to pose for his own wedding portrait."

Jake lifted her to her feet and set her wash pail aside. He cupped her face and swept a thumb over her cheek. "None will care if my image is there or not as long as your beautiful face is captured for prosperity," he cajoled.

She would not be swayed by his charms. Not this time. "Jake, you promised."

"Aye, I did."

"And dressing one of your men in your wedding suit to stand in your place was not appreciated by Monsieur Fortier."

"Monsieur Fortier knows no sense of time. I'm a busy man. When he finally gets around to painting my face, I'll be there. I swear to you."

"And you'll smile and not look like a man heading to his execution?" Lily traced the lower edge of his lips.

"You ask much, woman." Jake ran a fingertip along the front of her throat and down into the shadow of her cleavage before tugging on her lacings. "There could be a high cost for that smile. I'm wondering, what are you willing to give in exchange?" His voice took on the low rasp that sent tremors to her thighs.

"I thought you were a busy man?"

"Aye, and I'm busy seducing my wife right now." His lips followed the path his fingers had singed moments before. "I believe the last time we found ourselves on this very spot, we may have left a few things undone." Jake kissed the top of her breast while his hands clutched and raised the fullness of her skirts.

"I remember," she breathed as cool air tickled the backs of her legs. "If I recall, you didn't want to take me in the dirt and the dust."

"I see no dust now." His kisses were making her knees weaken.

Jake's quick fingers finished unlacing her bodice. Between kisses, her skirts dropped to her shoes. Lily tugged at his shirt and let one hand lower to stroke the length of his arousal through the wool of his breeches. "You had other objections if memory serves. Something about a bed?"

"The cot will suffice." He pulled her backwards toward the narrow sleeping pallet.

"We *are* alone." Lily fumbled with the buttons holding the front flap of his trousers.

"Then I say we take full advantage of the situation." Jake's breath caught as she released his erection from its confines and gave it a gentle caress. He groaned into her mouth as he crushed his lips to hers.

Lily tugged up on his shirt as he tugged down on her shift. The combined result was them both bare from the waist up when they hit the edge of the cot. Lily's shift circled her middle as she rushed to lift it enough for her to straddle his lap.

Passion flared, and their movements became frantic and rushed as the heat between them flashed like a flame to powder. In one motion, Lily impaled herself on the upward thrust of Jake's cock, fusing herself to him. Taking him deep and full within her.

Jake grabbed at her hips and rained kisses across her chest as she took control from him. Rocking and riding over him faster. Lily closed her eyes to the swift building of her own orgasm. One hand clutched his shoulder while the other braced against the rough stone of the wall.

"Slow, Lily, I'll finish too soon."

"No," she huffed. Sweat made their skin slick. "Come with me." She increased the pressure and tempo of her hips.

"Bloody… Hell…." he ground out as he arched his back. Jake bit at his own lip. His darkened gaze locked with hers. Moving his hand from her breast he reached lower, adding the pressure and swirl of his thumb to her sensitive flesh to send Lily into a freefall of crashing climax.

Jake tightened his hold on her thrashing body and drove hard and deep, meeting her powerful release with a fiery surge of his own.

"Dear God, I'm wed to an insatiable wench," Jake gasped. "What have I created?"

Ridding themselves of their damp tangle of clothes, they laid naked on the narrow cot. Lily stroked the damp hair on his chest. "I pray you've created a babe."

Jake gave her a small nod and tightened his hold. "I pray that as well."

It was just before winter had set in in earnest when Lily had been late with her courses. For more than a week, they had been the most excited couple on earth at the prospect of bringing a child, their child, into the world.

Lily had been devastated when they'd been wrong. It broke her heart still to remember.

Jake had been at sea for several days. Lily feared his return. She didn't know how to tell him she wasn't pregnant after all. Aiden's wife Rose was round and ripe with their babe, and all Jake could talk about was how the two cousins would be the best of friends.

He'd come home with a gift and rushed to show her. Jake

found her in their room curled up before the fire.

"There is my beautiful wife." Jake set aside a large parcel wrapped in a heavy cloth and tied with string. He knelt before her and kissed her hands and then her lips. "I've brought you something. I know it's a bit hasty, but I couldn't help myself." He pulled the package in front of her. "Did you know, my man, Oliver Sharp, fancies himself a bit of a carpenter? Seems he knows his way around a saw and hammer. Saw a bow-top chest he'd built for himself, and I asked if he could build something for us." He pulled at the twine. "Four days, Lily. He built this in only four days."

Pulling away the cloth, he revealed a beautiful white pine cradle. It looked like a tiny skiff with lapstreak side boarding and wide rockers fore and aft. The workmanship was stunning with polished rails and brass trimmings.

"I've got him working on a wee set of oars as well." Jake joked as he ran a hand the length of the piece. "We'll need a mattress of course, but I spoke to our sail mend—"

Lily began to cry and crumpled into his arms. At the tightening of his embrace, she hadn't needed to find the words after all. He knew.

Jake had simply held her, stroked her back and shushed her like a child waking from a bad dream. They stayed that way for a long time until he kissed her hair. "The cradle will wait. You'll see, my love, we'll need an entire fleet of cradles before we're done. There'll be so many children, they'll hang like monkeys from the chandeliers."

A few days later, Rose gave Aiden a beautiful daughter. They named her Pearl. She was the most perfect child Lily had ever seen. And though it sometimes hurt Lily's heart to look at her, Lily loved her. She and Jake had agreed to be her

Godparents, and they vowed to guard over her should anything happen to Aiden and Rose.

The responsibility of family bonds was strong with Jake and his brother, and it was during this time, Lily tried to bridge the chasm that had formed between her and Abigail.

As predicted, Mister Carlisle with the impossibly blue eyes had turned his gaze toward another and Abigail had opted for wealth and prestige over love and was soon betrothed to Mister Gibson. His breath was worse than Jake's mucky boots.

Her father was another chasm completely. Try as she might, Lily couldn't forget or forgive his actions where she was concerned. His careless disregard for her and her happiness couldn't be ignored. Indeed, he was more furious at his loss of face when Jake had beaten him at his contrived plot the night she and Jake married, than at the idea of his youngest daughter's marriage to a rogue pirate.

Of course, he continued to wager on the fact that Lily was indeed some naive creature and tried to work his wiles with her to catch Jake so he could see him arrested and hanged. But he was transparent as window glass and Lily's intelligence and devotion to Jake surpassed all. Everett Langdon never stood a chance. But that didn't stop him from trying.

Jake kept his word, however, and never stepped foot on any of her Father's ships again, but that hadn't slowed down his prowess as a pirate. With the increase in trade along the east coast, there was no end to conquests. And with the addition of the labyrinth of tunnels beneath Fairwinds, The Watch was no match for Captain Jake Wilder and the crew of *The Phantom*. Jake could greet dinner guests, beg their forgiveness as he was called away for an "issue" with something on the estate, escape through the tunnels, lead his crew to make a raid, unload the goods, and still make it back to the dinner table before the wine was poured. With nary a hair out of place and none the wiser just as long as he left his smelly, dank, barnacled boots elsewhere.

Chapter 15

It was late August when Fairwinds was quiet once more. Construction was completed. The third floor had been transformed into Lily and Jake's personal oasis. Their private quarters were just that. Private. The servants had strict orders not to disturb them unless Fairwinds was on fire or under attack.

Like the ballroom, most of the walls of their quarters were comprised of French doors and floor to ceiling windows which gave them a view of Skullery Bay and the harbor that was spectacular. On sun-drenched days you could see for miles out to sea where the horizon and sky faded into one. Drapes kept out the drafts on bitter nights, but Lily preferred to keep them open because on crystal clear nights it was as if you could get lost among the stars.

Their proper bed was wide and beautifully hand carved with vines and ivy. Thick, rich bedding made it feel as if you were truly in the clouds. A matching secretary sat tucked in a corner, and a thick padded love seat was placed cozily before the fireplace. Sumptuous hand-woven rugs covered the original wide pine flooring. They warmed the space but failed to deaden the persistent squeaks that still prevailed with some of the old floorboards.

As they'd talked about that very first day, an impressive roof walk had been constructed beyond the French doors to decoratively wrap around the very top of Fairwinds like a wrought-iron crown. Built to give access to the four large chimneys, it was also the perfect place to feel like a bird.

While loving the walk, it made Lily uneasy to venture out there.

"You're perfectly safe." Jake shoved at the elegant railings to show Lily how sturdy they were.

"Please don't do that." Lily's stomach lurched. "We're so high."

"Keep your gaze on me. Come now, take my hand. I've had six men up here working at once. I assure you it's solid and secure."

She moved to him slowly and cautiously. Soon Jake's comforting arms wrapped around her and chased much of her anxiety away. She shivered. "It's so windy up here."

"Aye. Like sitting on top of a mast, but at least Fairwinds isn't pitching and rolling and riding the waves beneath us."

"Thank goodness." Lily clutched at his arm while he pointed out the farthest most points at the mouth of the harbor where a small light house stood on a rocky knoll.

"From that point, there is nothing but open ocean clear to England. See how the water gets dark? It turns a deep blue. Soon you lose sight of land, and all that surrounds you is miles upon miles of water. That's where we set every inch of our sails and catch the power of this wind. *The Phantom* races over the tips of the waves. With all her sails filled and the rigging taut, she hums." Jake turned her in his arms. "Hums like a well-pleasured woman." He kissed her and let his hands roam over her, seeking to move past the fullness of her skirts and the cage of her corsets to caress her.

"Are you comparing me to your ship?" Lily pushed his hands away and feigned offense.

"You do have sleek curves and beautiful lines." His insistent hands lifted her hems while sweeping his touch up her thighs. "And you roll and moan beneath me when the waves get high." He growled against her neck.

"Jake." Lily gasped as his fingers teased her. She shifted her stance and moved against his touch. Her breathing began to race as she tugged at the waistband of his breeches. "Your ship and I are both strong and demanding, however. We do require frequent attention."

"Aye, that, too." Jake murmured between kisses as he pulled her back through the open doorway and onto their bed. "Hard work for a captain." He ran her hand down the firm length of his erection. "Good thing I'm up to the task."

She stroked him. "Shall I order 'all hands on deck?'"

Jake quickly pinned her beneath him and trapped her wrists over her head. "Not all hands."

* * *

"Mistress, you have a visitor."

Lily looked up from her book. "Am I expecting someone and have forgotten?" She slipped her teacup into its saucer.

"No, ma'am. The woman says she is your sister."

"Abigail?" Lily untucked her feet and smoothed her skirts as she rose. "Please see her in and perhaps have Cook send in some fresh tea?"

While things were cordial if not strained with her sister after the events of the last year, Lily couldn't help the initial flare of unease and tension she still experienced at the mention of Abigail's name.

"Lily!" Abigail rushed into the library and pressed her cheek against Lily's. "It's been too, too long, my darling." She pulled back. "You're looking quite well."

Since Abigail's recent, yet unfortunate marriage to Mister Gibson, she'd found a fondness for sweets. Her corsets looked impossibly tight with a generous display of pale décolleté pushed near her chin. Her cheeks were bright and shiny.

"As do you, sister. Please have a seat. I've asked for tea to be brought."

"Lovely. Yes." Abigail perched on the edge of one of the leather chairs. "Goodness, Lily, this room is just as I remember it." She looked back over her shoulder. "I swear if I turn in time. I might see the ghost of our sainted mother reading in a corner." Abigail shook her head. The stiffened curls at her ears didn't move. "Why she found all these dusty books so interesting was always a mystery to me."

A servant entered with a tray. Lily held up her hand. "We could take our tea on the patio, if you'd rather."

Abigail licked her lips and brushed at her skirts. "No, no. This is fine."

Lily went through the motions of pouring, while Abigail helped herself to the plate of biscuits and petit fours. Silence stretched between them. Lily took a sip of her tea and sat back. "So, what is it you want?"

Abigail's eyebrows rose as she dabbed at her mouth with her napkin. "Can't I simply wish to see my only sister? I've missed you."

"I haven't been abroad, Abigail. You've known where to find me." Lily set her cup aside.

"But you've been busy, and I've been busy." Abigail flipped a hand between them. "Both of us married women now. Running large households."

"How is Mister Gibson?"

Her sister lifted a shoulder. "He's the perfect husband.

Wealthy. Distant. Inattentive. Unobtrusive. What more could I ask for?"

"Does he still, you know?" Lily ran a discreet finger under her nose.

Abigail held up a hand. "It's better. I make him carry a tin of fresh mint leaves and parsley to chew. I hardly notice anymore, but then we're not together much. He's…busy."

"It seems an epidemic, all this business."

"He and father have become quite close since our dear brother left for school abroad. Mister Gibson is helping to shore up some of Father's failing enterprises. Something having to do with father's ships meeting Mister Gibson's ships. They're bemoaning all the new tariffs. I have no idea really, but Father is most anxious about gold weights and tide charts lately." Abigail rolled her eyes. "When they start talking profits and the like, I tend to stop listening. But they both seem in good spirits about it all."

"Good." Lily lifted her cup and spoke into her tea before taking a sip. "Perhaps *your* husband can distract Father from his relentless pursuit of *my* husband."

"I know nothing about any of that, Lily. Although, you know how Father can be. He hates being bested above all." She again flipped a dismissive hand. "And what of your Captain? I suppose he is forever at sea leaving you in this horrid mausoleum all alone."

"Not at all. Jake and I are together…frequently." A shimmering rush accompanied the turn of her thoughts. This morning their lovemaking had left her limbs trembling for close to an hour. She grew damp at the very thought of what he'd done to her with his tongue.

"How sad for you." Abigail patted her sleeve and gave her

a sympathetic look.

Another image filtered through Lily's mind. Jake was due home day after tomorrow. He loved it when she met him out on the cliffs, welcoming him home. Their reunions were becoming even more heated than their farewells.

Once they had gotten so carried away with one another, they barely reached the third floor. They hadn't made it to the bed. Even the cold polished floor didn't cool their overheated passions. It *was* the day she'd ordered the carpets, however.

Lily cleared her throat and set her cup aside. A flush warmed her cheeks. "We've just finished renovating the third floor. Would you care to see?"

Abigail spoke around a mouthful of cake. "The third floor? Where Grandfather entertained his whores?"

"Yes, but don't worry. We've remodeled. I'm the only whore entertaining there now." Lily rose and smoothed her skirts.

Abigail followed her lead and stood. "Oh, Lily. You shouldn't say such crude things. What will the servants think?" She snatched another bit of cake before leaving and popped it in her mouth.

Lily opened the door to her and Jake's new quarters and waited for Abigail to catch her breath after the climb.

"Oh, you've built a widow's walk." Abigail pressed a hand to her corsets and continue to huff for a decent breath.

"Don't call it *that*," scolded Lily. "It's a roof walk. We built it to help with the upkeep of the chimneys."

"It's also called a widow's walk."

"Only by widows." A cold shiver raised gooseflesh on Lily's arms. "Don't curse me like that Abigail."

"I wouldn't call that a curse." Abigail dabbed at the sweat

on her upper lip with the napkin she still carried from downstairs. "I've come to think being a rich widow isn't the worst fate a woman can meet." She opened the French doors only enough to stick her head out. "It's terrifying out here." She shut the door and shuddered. Scanning the room, she asked, "So where do you sleep?"

"I sleep here."

"Oh, the décor is so masculine, I assumed. Is that your husband's room at the other end of the hall?"

Lily smoothed the bed's coverlet of deep reds and warm browns. "No, Jake sleeps here with me."

"Whatever for?" Abigail's eyebrows reached for her hairline. "Mister Gibson and I have separate wings, for heaven's sake. Didn't I tell you what horrible business all of that…that," Abigail wiggled her fingers toward the bed, "vile act requires?" She winced and curled her lip. "Mister Gibson is allotted one brief encounter once a month to get me with child. Fortunately for me, his appetites are much like Grandfather's in that regard, and I'm happy to have other women see to those particular vulgar needs." Abigail grimaced again and pressed her napkin to a damp temple. "So, what's the room down the hall then?"

Lily led her to the small bright room done in a soft buttery yellow. Sheer curtains puffed at the window. The cradle Oliver Sharp built stood ready for a child not yet conceived. Layettes sat neatly folded. Waiting. A matching pine rocking chair sat before an embroidery hoop. Lily had started to stitch playful fish along the edge of a kitten-soft blanket the color of the sky. With each stitch, she prayed that by the time it was finished she would have Jake's son growing strong in her womb.

"The nursery." Lily whispered the words.

Abigail spun on her and dropped her stunned gaze to Lily's stomach. "Are you with child then?"

Lily laid a hand low on her belly. "No. Not yet."

"You've been wed almost a full year, and you sleep in the same bed." Abigail frowned. "I would have thought you'd be with child long before now."

"I'm told it takes time."

"I've told Mister Gibson he has six months," Abigail quipped before sweeping out of the room and moving back down the hall to the stairs.

Lily gave her a quick tour of the downstairs before leading Abigail out onto the patio. A light breeze from the sea cooled the air.

"You really have done a lovely job here, Lily. Everything, the house, the grounds. So like when Mother was alive, but fresh and new and completely you. Fairwinds has never looked so welcoming." Abigail took as deep a breath as she was able. "I have missed you. I find myself terribly lonely these days, I'd like very much for us to be close again. Perhaps be welcomed here more often? I know Mister Gibson is most anxious to meet your captain." Abigail made a tiny gasp and clutched Lily's arm. "Oh, I have a wonderful idea. You should throw a ball. Just like the ones Mother used to host. In celebration of your upcoming anniversary." Her cheeks flushed pink with excitement.

"I don't know." Lily shook her head. "Jake and I have finally gotten the estate back to ourselves after months of workmen tramping about. The thought of all that planning, the extra staff, accommodating guests."

"But you must celebrate, and Fairwinds looks lovely. Don't you remember Mother's dances? I could buy a new gown. And

I could help you with the preparations. See to the food and the flowers. You could borrow some of my staff." Abigail gave her a pout. "Please? It would be a way to spend more time together again. As we were. Before you were stolen from me."

"I wasn't stolen. I fell in love."

Abigail huffed. "I don't believe in love."

They walked in silence out to the cliffs. Lily wasn't sure how to respond. How could she convince her sister that love was real? Amazingly, earth-shakingly real. As real as flesh and bone and the ground beneath her feet.

It wasn't just her and Jake, and their nights of bringing each other pleasure. It was more. It was standing on these cliffs feeling his love coming over the waves toward her. Waiting with heart aching anticipation for his return. It was in the air she breathed into her lungs. The sun caressing her face.

Turning back, she looked at the beauty that was Fairwinds. Love was why she was here. Her mother had loved this place. It was in the stones. She'd planted it with each rose in the arbor. Love hung in the leaves on the trees in the surrounding woods. Now, it was Lily's turn to refill the estate with all the love she could manage.

Lily turned and saw her sister with different eyes. Pushing past their strained relationship, and their history, she was still her sister. Pity for her tugged at Lily's heart.

"Fine. We'll throw a ball."

Chapter 16

Between kisses, Lily danced with excitement at Jake's return. "I have a surprise for you." She pulled him toward the house. "Actually, I have three surprises for you."

Jake growled and pulled her back into his embrace. He'd only been gone a few days, but he missed the feel of her body pressed against his. Missed her sweet smell, the taste of her mouth. "Am I going to like any of these surprises?"

"One possibly, one hopefully, and one definitely," she teased while trying to escape his determined hold.

"Are any of them in our bedroom?"

"One is close by."

He tugged at her ties, his voice lowered as he nuzzled her neck. "Good, let's start with that one."

Lily gave him a smile that rivaled the sun and raced him into the house and up the stairs to their rooms.

Panting, she moved toward the door leading to the roof walk. "It's out here."

"You hate it out there."

"I'm coming to like it better. You'll be proud of me, I'm getting used to the heights." She pulled him onto the walk. "And now I have this to see while I'm watching and waiting to see you sail home." She waved her hand toward the very peak of the roof.

"Lily..." He breathed her name. "It's *The Phantom*."

"Yes." She beamed. "Do you like it?"

Jake moved as close as he was able. Sitting on a tall post secured with iron plates to the pitch of the roof sat a perfectly scaled replica of his ship done in wrought iron, brass, and copper. A wide blade fanned from the back, like the ship's wake, and steered the ship in the direction of the wind. Below sat the directional with points north, south, east, and west indicated by elegant initials in brass. Below that, an ornate sphere in brass and copper resembled the globe. The rich metals sparkled in the sun. Mixed with the darkness of the iron, the piece was magnificent.

Lily slipped her arm through his and pressed close to his side. "I was going to save it for your anniversary gift, but when I saw it, I simply couldn't wait. Isn't it grand?"

"It's…" He didn't have the words. The weathervane was the final jewel in Fairwinds' crown. His ship, riding the wind atop his home. *His home.* After the months of work and toil, here he stood. Jake had dreamed of making Fairwinds his, but never did he imagine he'd feel such pride. Never did he dream he'd share it with the most wonderful woman by his side or experience the fierce rush of protectiveness or belonging he felt here.

Jake shielded his eyes as he looked up at the stunning weathervane. He couldn't have imagined a more thoughtful, meaning-full gift. Emotions tied his tongue.

"You don't like it. It's too large, too ostentatious." Lily shook her head beside him and seemed to deflate. "I'm sorry. What was I thinking? I'll have them take it down—"

"Don't you dare. It's bloody perfect." Jake crushed his mouth to hers. "You're bloody perfect."

"Remember that when I tell you about your last surprise," she warned.

Jake pulled back and gave her a hard look. "And the second surprise?"

"Monsieur Fortier has finished our wedding portrait."

"It's about damn time. Where is the masterpiece?"

"Downstairs. In the ballroom." Lily rained tiny gentle kisses over his mouth and along his jaw.

"I thought we were hanging it in the library?" Lily's lips trailed to his neck. He knew this trick. She was trying to distract him. It was working. The tightening of his britches was most distracting. He slipped his arms around her waist.

"Because of the unveiling." She ran the tip of her tongue to the base of his ear while her fingers slipped the buttons of his vest from their holes and loosened the sash at his waist. "At the ball." Her lips continued to kiss along his jawline. "To celebrate our anniversary." When she moved to capture his mouth again, he stopped her by placing two fingers against her lips.

"A ball?"

"Yes. Surprise, we're having a ball. Two weeks from tomorrow."

When he groaned, Lily rushed to convince him how wonderful it could be. They could show off Fairwinds, fill the ballroom with good food and music.

"We could invite Aiden and Primrose and my family as well," Lily continued.

"Your family?" Jake frowned. "Does that include your bastard father?"

"We really can't invite people to a ball at Fairwinds without including him. I'm not thrilled about the prospect either, but Abigail assures me all will be fine. Father is on to new obsessions other than you." Lily rushed to say, "It seems he and Mister Gibson are embroiled in some business dealings with one another, so he's far too busy to give you or *The Phantom* a second's notice."

Jake had trouble believing Langdon would ever cease his revenge on him and *The Phantom*. "What kind of business dealings?"

"I don't exactly know, but Abigail said something about ships meeting and moving goods. It has something to do with tariffs and gold weights." She lifted a shoulder.

"Gold weights?"

Lily pressed another kiss against his tightening jaw. "What does it matter? The important thing is you are no longer his focus."

Jake held her away from him. Her dark eyes pleaded. Battling a ship full of cutthroat thieves was easier than saying no to Lily. "What are the chances I can talk you out of filling our home with strangers and people I never liked?"

Lily blinked and gave him a small smile. "Practically none."

"I feared that. Fine, have your ball." Lily bounced in his arms. "Are we done with all the surprises now?"

She wrapped her arms about his neck. "I believe we are."

"Good. May I take my wife to bed now?"

"I believe you may."

* * *

"Brother? Jake, dammit, are you deaf?"

Jake studied a chart spread over a makeshift table outside the main storeroom within the labyrinth of tunnels constructed beneath Fairwinds. "Aiden, I didn't hear you."

Aiden added his lantern to Jake's "I gathered as much. I've been hollering at you for the last five minutes." He set a map before Jake. "The gates are finished at the cave ends."

"And fifty feet in?"

"Aye." Aiden pointed out the location of six iron gates strategically placed throughout the maze of tunnels they'd created. "The tunnel leading away from the stables is cleared. You can slip past the rain of horse droppings and head straight into the house, here."

"Good." Jake studied the webbed plans before him. Now he could access the entrance under the butler's pantry and have access to the spiral staircase straight to the third floor. "And the off-load storeroom?"

"We hit a fair bit of stone out there and had to set it higher than we thought. The men will grumble at the climb, I'm sure, but it's level to the point where it exits into the stone cottage."

"I've hidden the entrance in the floor. You'd never know it was there. As long as the groundskeeper can be trusted, and I can keep Lily from setting some bit of furniture atop, we could run the crew out through there and hide them in the east woods if we need to."

"Do you want another gate there?" asked Aiden.

Jake nodded and pointed to the plans. "Aye. Here."

"Consider it done." Aiden rolled up the tunnel map and tucked it under his arm.

Looking back at the sea charts, Jake scrubbed at his jaw. "What do we know of a man named Gibson?"

"The same Gibson who's your brother-in-law?"

"The same."

Aiden lifted a shoulder. "Successful merchant. Four large schooners to his name. Fast ships. Full, regular crossings. Usually travels in pairs. We engaged one once. More than a year ago now. Don't you recall? They were near empty."

Jake straightened. "Right, I remember. We thought it odd how light our haul."

"We joked that someone had raided them before we arrived." Aiden nodded.

"Not raided." Jake crossed his arms over his chest. It was all starting to make sense. The pieces to the puzzle were falling into place. Lily was right. Langdon had a far more lucrative quarry than chasing *The Phantom* about, hoping to catch them with the evidence he needed to hang the lot of them. No, he was after bigger, fatter fish.

"What are you talking about?"

Jake shot a glance at Aiden. "The tariffs at the harbor have gotten steep of late."

"Not news, brother. They've been rising steadily."

"And they target those coming across the Atlantic with full stores, am I right?"

Aiden nodded. "Of course, they're the ones with the most goods to tax."

Jake tapped a finger on the charts before him. "And those slow ships running up and down the coast? Like the *Margaretha*?"

"The tax has already been paid on most of their stores and it's been sold off for profit."

"What if a ship like the *Margaretha* was to rendezvous with one of Gibson's schooners and bring those goods into Mystic Point themselves?"

Aiden lifted an eyebrow. "They'd avoid the tariffs, for one thing."

"And if the owner of the *Margaretha* had enough influential friends, he could get The Watch to look elsewhere while he unloaded his ship at the docks."

"It would cost him plenty."

"More than the taxes?"

Aiden huffed. "Not even half."

Jake nodded. "Aye. We still have a man in The Company, correct?"

"Correct."

"I want shipping logs on Gibson's ships."

"Are we planning on giving chase to the *Margaretha* again?"

Jake gave a low chuckle and began rolling up the parchments before him. "No, I'm thinking of being in front of the *Margaretha* for once."

"Gibson's schooners are fast, Jake. With enough sail they can easily outrun us."

He slapped Aiden on the shoulder. "Not when they're loaded to the gills with gold."

* * *

"Do you have to go?" Lily dropped the neckline of her shift, bared one breast, and gave him a seductive smile. "Will nothing change your mind?"

"You're wicked, Missus Wilder." Jake stopped dressing and pulled her against him. She was still warm from their bed.

"I've been taught well." She wrapped her arms about his neck.

Jake brushed her lips with his. "What have I created?"

"A siren." Lily breathed between kisses.

"Sirens lure lovestruck sailors to the bottom of the sea."

"Can they also lure them back to their beds?" She moved his hand to cup her breast.

Jake growled against her shoulder. He nipped her skin there making her gasp. "Woman, you're insatiable." He shifted the position of his arousal and buttoned the flap of his breeches. The musky scent of their sex surrounded him. "I have to go. I told Aiden I would meet him."

"But Aiden has already done his husbandly duty and planted yet another babe in his lovely wife's belly. Baby Pearl and now his second, and we've not even had one."

Jake captured Lily's chin. "I swear to you. This is the last time. The bounty is too great to let this raid pass. After this capture, I'll never have to pirate again. We'll have gold enough for our children's children's children to live in a home as grand as ours for the rest of their lives." Jake swept his hands down Lily's back and over the roundness of her bottom. He hauled her against his growing erection. "I promise you, when I return, I will take you to bed and will not cease in my husbandly efforts until you, too, grow round and ripe with my babe." He splayed a hand over the flat of her belly.

"You'll ravish me?" Lily sighed against his lips.

"Daily."

"Pillage?"

Jake tested the firmness of her behind. "Aye. I'll pillage like I've ne'er pillaged before."

Lily squirmed in his arms. "And do that special thing you do with your tongue?"

"Are you trying to kill me?" Jake moaned.

"No, I'm trying to get you to stay here with me tonight."

"I told you…"

"Yes, I heard you." Lily pushed away. "But we don't need gold for our children's children's children. Let them get gold for themselves. I don't want to foster spoiled, lazy grandchildren. We have more than enough to give them a brilliant beginning. I have everything I'll ever need right here."

Lily tugged at his shirt sleeve and pressed her body against his again before she kissed him.

"I'll only be gone two days."

"And two nights," she pouted.

"Aye, and two nights, and then I will be right back here." He kissed her. "In this very spot." He slipped his tongue between her lips in a quick, teasing sweep. "Wanting to love you and touch you." Jake ran his hands over her curves again. "And loving you forever."

"And you'll be back in time to escort me into the ballroom?"

"If not, I'll have one of my men dress in my wedding suit to escort you," he joked as he released her and gathered his coat and baldrick.

Lily retied the neckline of her shift. "Do not tease me, Captain Wilder. I've worked too hard on this silly ball."

He laid a hand over his heart. "I give you my word, I'll be back in plenty of time for the ball."

"And you'll never leave me again?"

"Never. You have my promise." Jake tipped her chin and kissed her once more before leaving.

*　*　*

The seas were angry and getting angrier as a fierce storm lowered its fist on Jake and the crew of *The Phantom*. Waves crashed over the bow sweeping anything not lashed down to crash against the ship's sides as a wild hurricane engulfed the ship from every direction.

"We're riding too high, Captain," yelled his boatswain.

In anticipation of loading the heavy gold from Gibson's ship, Jake had the ship stripped of everything not essential. He'd made a crucial mistake. Now they hadn't the weight needed to hold fast in the rising seas.

Jake strained to hold the wheel and keep *The Phantom* hitting the towering waves head on. He yelled over the rising winds. "Get everyone below."

With all the sails secured, Jake cleared the upper deck. Night closed in fast and with a howling fury. If they could just ride her out until dawn.

Jake screamed obscenities into the growing darkness as another surge hit the port side of the ship, nearly ripping the arms from his shoulders. He gripped the slick pegs of the wheel and leaned all his body weight against the watery blow as the ship veered sharply to starboard.

"Ahhh! Dammit! Straighten out, you bloody bitch!"

Aiden fought his way through the tempest to help Jake hold the wheel. Together the two of them struggled to straighten her out and keep *The Phantom* from keeling over.

"Get below," shouted Jake. Rain and seawater lashed at his face and stung his eyes. His clothing plastered against his body. Icy water filled his boots. "I can hold her. Go. Now! That's an order!"

"After you," Aiden shouted back.

"Stubborn bastard!"

"Like my brother!"

The storm surged. Lightening clawed its fingers through the black chaos surrounding them. The scream of the wind and the roar of the ocean shrieked their chilling arrival into hell.

Jake pulled at the last shreds of his strength. He wouldn't give up. He couldn't. He gave Lily his promise to return to her. The soft image of her seducing him to stay with her beckoned to him through the night.

Hang on. Dammit just hang on. He and Aiden fought the wheel together.

Cold fear gripped Jake as a flash of lightning lit the violent tempest around them and illuminated a horrified look on his brother's face.

They were lost.

Jake never saw the wall of water that hit them. The force of the wave slammed the air from his lungs and hurled him into a black watery abyss.

"*Lily!*" He cried out her name from the depths of his soul.

Chapter 17

"Where is he? He promised he'd be home in time." Lily spoke to her reflection in the mirror as she secured her ruby earrings and smoothed a stray curl. "He better not rush through those damn tunnels at the last minute and drag mud and stink into the ballroom." She'd had the staff working for days to shine the floor tiles to sparkling. They'd all worked hard over the last two days.

The chandeliers were polished, the candles lit. The ballroom sparkled. Everything was ready. The kitchens were alive with preparing delicious food. The musicians were tuning up. Tonight was going to be as magical as she remembered her mother's dances to be.

Lily smoothed the skirts of her rose-pink gown. The suit Jake wore when they wed had been pressed and waited for him on the bed.

For the fourth time in the last hour, she made her way out onto the roof walk to look for him. Dark clouds had begun to build, and night was falling fast. A chilled wind raised gooseflesh on her arms and had her looking toward the beautiful weathervane she'd given Jake. With a slow creak, the vane turned to indicate a shift in the wind from the northeast. It brought with it the crisp smell of the sea as well as the promise of foul weather.

Lily fiddled with her wedding ring, spinning it on her finger, and prayed Jake brought *The Phantom* in well ahead of the storm. A cold shiver had her teeth chattering.

Opening the door to go back inside, the building wind gusted behind her and nearly ripped the doorknob from her grasp. The first drops of rain dotted the floorboards.

"Lillian? There you are. Are you coming?" Abigail fanned at her flushed cheeks.

Lily shook her head. "Jake's not here."

Abigail flipped a hand at Jake's clothing. "I can well see that."

"I should wait for him." Lily pressed a hand at the worry fluttering in her belly.

"Mister Gibson says the seas are up. Jake could be hours yet, and your guests are arriving. I'm sure he's on his way."

"The winds have turned." Lily paced and wrung her hands.

Abigail stopped her and took hold of her hands. "Cease worrying. He'll be here." She lifted Lily's hand to run a thumb over the ruby in her ring. "I saw you two kissing quite passionately in the gardens the other day. Even I cannot deny what is so obvious. I could be quite jealous at your closeness. Anyone with eyes can see the love between you. He won't miss your anniversary, Lily. He'll not let a little rain keep him from you. He adores you." Abigail plucked at the sleeves of Lily's gown. "Come now, you're looking beautiful. The color is lovely on you. Everything downstairs is perfect and waiting for the lady of the house."

Lily gave her a quick nod before glancing once more out past the walk to the darkened skies beyond. Her gaze shifted back to Jake's wedding suit.

Hurry, Jake. I'm waiting for you.

Hours later, the storm was upon them in earnest. Most of

the guests battled the drenching rains and buffeting winds to leave early.

Worry no longer fluttered. It gnawed at Lily's stomach. Among the few to remain, Lily spotted her father and Abigail's husband looking nearly as concerned about the storm as she. She overheard their conversation.

"I can't afford to lose the *Margaretha* in a bloody nor'easter. She's all I have left."

"I can't predict the weather, Langdon. You and I both know I've far more to lose out there than anyone."

No, thought Lily, *I've far more to lose "out there" than both of you combined.*

She stood before Monsieur Fortier's portrait sitting prominently on a strong easel for tonight's unveiling. She ran her fingertips over the image of Jake. A smile tugged at her lips as she remembered when she had shown Jake this particular surprise.

"You're beautiful, of course, but this looks nothing like me." Jake motioned toward the painting.

Lily slipped an arm through his. "Of course it does. It's a fine likeness."

"If I was six inches shorter."

She lifted a shoulder. "You should have had a taller man stand in your place."

Jake leaned closer to inspect Fortier's work. "What has he done to my ear?"

"He's given you an earring. Like a proper pirate."

"To punish me, I suppose." Jake shook his head. "I'm lucky the bastard hasn't set me on a bloody cannon with a knife between rotting teeth."

"I like it. I think you look terribly dashing." She reached

out and teased his earlobe. Leaning in, she kissed the side of his neck. "Rakish. Dangerous." She gave a light bite to said earlobe.

Tightening his hold, he turned to capture her teasing mouth. "Then perhaps I'll have to oblige my pirate wife and hang some gold from my ear. Tell Monsieur Fortier I'll take the cost out of his pay."

Turning from the portrait, Lily saw the one person sharing the depths of her fears tonight. Primrose.

Standing before the French doors, Rose hadn't moved in more than an hour. Lily went to her and grasped her chilled hand. Rose turned a tear-stained face to hers.

"What if we lose them, Lily?"

"Don't say that. Never say that." Lily rubbed at her fingers.

"What will I tell Pearl?"

"You'll tell her that her father loves her."

"But…" Rose laid a hand over the slight curve of her belly. "What if he never meets his son?"

"Stop talking like that. We can't give up hope. Jake and Aiden are on their way home to us."

"I have a bad feeling, Lily. I felt it earlier. Like—"

"Stop." Lily's panic welled in her chest. "I beg you, stop. I'm going to have my sister's husband take you home in their carriage. Aiden could already be waiting for you there. Cold and wet and hungry. What a story they'll have to tell us upon their return. I'm sure by this time next week, we'll all be gathered around the dinner table scolding them both for worrying us so."

Rose sniffed and wiped at her eyes. "You sound so sure."

"I am." Lily gave Rose a quick hug. "Go home, give Pearl an extra hug from me and her favorite uncle tonight. You'll see. Come morning, the storm will have passed, and this will all have been a bad dream."

Lily paced the third floor long into the night. As every gale-filled minute blew by, her worry increased. Foolishly she continued to venture out onto the walk, even though the rain and the wind blinded her and made the high walk treacherous. Each time she struggled to close the door against the buffeting gusts. Lily clung to the railing and peered into the turbulent night, hoping and praying to see some tiny flicker of light. One single lantern burning at the tip of a mast. *Just one.*

But as the storm continued to rage, Lily's imagination conjured every horrific possibility to face Jake and the crew of *The Phantom*. In the wee hours of the morning, she dropped to her knees by the side of the bed and prayed.

"Please, please, let them be safe. Let them have found a protected harbor to ride out the storm. Bring him home to me. Please."

Climbing into their bed, she placed the arms of Jake's waistcoat around her and clutched the silk of his neck stock. It still carried his scent. Lily curled into a ball, she fought to push away her fears. Pressing the silk to her face, she breathed in the smell of him and started to cry.

Three days. It had been three days since the night of the storm with no sign of Jake, Aiden, the crew, or *The Phantom*. All those around her tried to brace Lily for the truth.

According to Abigail, the *Margaretha* had been lost. Their father's holdings were gone, and he was now penniless. Ruined. Mister Gibson also suffered extensive losses, but much of his fleet had been in port and was spared. No ship on the open sea that night survived the storm. Mystic Point began to mourn their dead.

Stubborn denial had Lily refusing to believe *The Phantom* was lost. For three days she had paced the roof walk for hours, hoping that she would blink and there they would be, sailing home out of the rising sun, flying into Skullery Bay with their sails bowed, dancing over the tips of the waves back to Fairwinds.

After dark she walked the cliffs with her lantern, calling out for Jake into the cold mist. Lily wandered back and forth for hours through the night, afraid if she slept, closed her eyes for even a minute, she would miss seeing them, miss being there to welcome Jake home, miss racing into his arms and having him crush her in his strong embrace. She swore once she was back in his arms, she'd never let him go.

* * *

Jake walked in darkness. For how far and how long, he didn't know. Everything was silent. The ground beneath his feet neither rose nor fell. His steps made no sound.

Where the hell am I? The last thing he remembered was being slammed by a stone wall of seawater. Starboard became port. Up became down. *The Phantom* rolled and tumbled like a child's toy in the churning seas.

Then he was walking.

A light moved in front of him, simply crossed his field of vision a far distance away. His steps increased until he was running. As he drew closer, recognition dawned.

He was home on the cliffs. The sea grass crunched beneath his boots.

"Lily?" Oh, thank you, God, it was her.

"Wait, brother." A voice stopped him.

Jake turned. Aiden stood behind him. Where had he come

from? Fairwinds seemed to appear in the background, but the image was distorted somehow, as if he viewed it through a water glass.

"Aiden, what the blazes is going on?"

"You're going the wrong way. You need to come with me." He tugged at Jake's sleeve.

"No. Lily." He pointed back to her. "I need to see her. I made a promise."

"It's too late for promises." Aiden pulled at him again.

"No. Stop." Jake wrenched his arm from Aiden's grasp. "I'm not going anywhere but home." He turned back toward his wife. "I need to see Lily. Take her in my arms. Hold her. Kiss her. Do you know her hair smells sweeter than any flower I've ever smelled? And her lips…they are so soft." He ran a finger over his lip. "I need to feel her lips on mine again, Aiden. I love her. I'm sorry." When Jake glanced back at Aiden, he was gone.

Jake rubbed at his eyes. The sky had begun to lighten with the dawn. His vision continued to waiver as he took in his surroundings, until he looked back at Lily. She was perfectly clear in his sight, perfectly beautiful with her dark hair long and free, the wind blowing back her cloak and pinning her shift to her body. The chilled air peaked her nipples and pinked her cheeks. Had he ever seen her look so lovely? He needed to sweep her into his arms and carry her to their bed.

"Lily?" He called out to her, but she didn't respond. "Lily."

She raised her lantern and moved to face the bay. Was she angry with him? "I'm late, I know. Can you forgive—"

Lily turned. The light from her lantern caught the wetness on her cheeks. She was crying. It tore at his heart. "I'm so sorry." He reached out to pull her into his arms and soothe her, but his hands somehow missed. Lily lifted the hem of her skirts and seemed to pass through him as if he were nothing more than air.

"Lily?" He spun around to watch her walk away.

What the hell is happening? He looked down, patted his arms, his chest his abdomen. He was solid, but she had…

He moved to catch up with her and reached out to grasp her arm to stop her, but his hand caught nothing. Lily never slowed. She hadn't heard him. Hadn't felt him. She continued to walk with slow steps back to Fairwinds.

As the sea wind lifted her cloak again, Jake noticed something else. The wind never touched him. It didn't lift a single hair on his head or ruffle a cuff. Nor did he feel its cool brush against his cheek.

A cold realization made him choke. "Dear God, I think I'm dead."

Jake continued to wander Fairwinds. For some reason, he couldn't walk the grounds or even visit the cliffs again, but he continued to move through the halls and the tunnels beneath just as far as the caves.

None acknowledged him. None heard him. Servants passed through him with a shiver. He tried every door leading to the outside. All were locked to him. It was maddening. No matter which direction he headed, however, he always ended back on the third floor. In the very spot he promised to return to, even though doing so tore the heart from him. If not for seeing Lily, he'd have believed he was truly in hell.

Lily never rested. She stopped using their bed as if to lie there without him was too painful. Instead, she would curl into herself on the loveseat before the fire and cry herself in a fitful sleep for an hour or two. She'd wake and call out for him and then seem to remember and begin to cry anew.

Jake knelt before her, unable to touch her, unable to feel her. "I'm here, Lily. I wish you could hear me. I'm right here. I love you." *Perhaps this is purgatory after all. Judgement for all my crimes. Punishment for the life I led.*

Soon, Lily refused meals, choosing to spend hours walking the roof walk and out along the cliffs. She grew thin and pale. Dark smudges deepened beneath her eyes as each day passed into the next.

Their wedding portrait now hung over the fireplace in their room, but seeing it only seemed to cause her more heartache and drove her out onto the roof walk once more.

Hard as it was to watch Lily grieve for him and witness her health fading like the last roses of the summer, Jake stayed. He was with her, and that was all that mattered.

Out in the cold, day and night, had taken its toll on Lily. A fever began to burn within her and brought a sickness to her lungs. Her fits of hysterics and temper along with her erratic actions had frightened much of the staff and many had left. Still, she roamed the walk and clung to the ornate railings, calling out to him in the mist.

Anger and frustration built in Jake as he watched her wither away. There had to be some way to reach her. He was a man of action. He was a bloody pirate, and she was his wife. Lily was stronger than this, and yet grief was winning the battle. She needed to fight.

"Dammit, Lily, I'm here," He screamed to her through the panes of glass. "Come in from there. Warm yourself. Dammit, woman!"

Lily turned. Jake gasped in surprise. *Bloody hell.* Had she heard him? "Lily?"

"Jake?" Her cheeks were bright with fever.

Can you see me? He raised his hand. "I'm right here, my love. Standing right here."

Lily clutched at her heart. "Jake…"

Chapter 18

Dragging the heavy cradle to the back wall, Lily pushed and shoved it deeper into the nursery. The unfinished blanket still stood in her embroidery hoop. Layettes neatly folded. Lily threw it all into a corner. All of it. Her energy sapped as she moved the rocker and knocked it over.

Tears blinded her as she fell to her knees and began clawing at the rough mixture of gravel and sand. Scooping great handfuls, she plastered it in a haphazard frenzy, pressing bricks across the threshold, cementing another brick on top of the others.

Abigail gasped behind her and rushed to tug at her shoulder. "Lily, darling, stop. What the hell are you doing?" Primrose along with a frightened maid stood wide-eyed behind her.

"I brought Pearl by for a visit. I thought it would cheer her." Rose cried into a black-trimmed handkerchief. "This is my fault. I was only trying to bring us both some comfort. Pearl loves it here. But…Lily was so…upset. When she saw us… I didn't know what to do, so I sent for you." She clutched at Abigail's sleeve. "I'm so sorry. Lily, I'm so sorry." Rose laid a soothing hand on Lily's back.

"Leave me." Lily pushed her away with her elbow. "All of you. Leave me."

"You're distraught. Please," Abigail pleaded. "You're not thinking sanely. Please. Come away from there."

The rough sand of the mortar bit into Lily's fingertips as she continued to scratch at the mixture. "I can't. I have to finish."

"You haven't slept, my love. Maid says you've not eaten in days. You can't continue like this. We're worried for you."

"I can't..." Lily threw more mortar at the mess she was constructing. Tears blinded her. "I can't!"

Abigail dropped to the floor in front of her and tried to gather her into her arms. Part of Lily wanted to dissolve into her sister's arms and cry until she was nothing but dust to blow away on the wind. But she wouldn't find any comfort in her arms. Abigail couldn't understand. Even Rose in mourning for her own husband couldn't comprehend this. She couldn't possibly know the depth of her pain each time she stood in this doorway.

"I can't see this room again. These things. I never want to see them..." Lily shoved at her sister's embrace to keep bricking up the doorway. "...again!" A sob wrenched from her throat. "Leave me!"

Abigail wouldn't lessen her hold, no matter how hard Lily fought.

"All right, all right." Abigail grabbed her roughly by the shoulders. "If you promise to come with me now, let us clean you, feed you, and settle you into your bed, I'll have a team of men up here within the hour to do this work. They'll fill the door. You'll never have to lay eyes on any of this ever again. I swear. Please, Lily, please come away from here now."

Lily struggled to pull in a full breath without being wracked with her worsening cough. "The window, too."

"Yes, love, the window, too."

"Like this room never existed." She gripped at Abigail's

arms. "Like our dream was never dreamed. Erase it from my mind." Lily clutched at her chest and coughed. "Wall it away in my heart. Please, Abigail, I can't breathe through this sadness."

"I know, love, I know." Abigail tried to pull her closer.

Lily pushed away and shook her head wildly. "No, you can't possibly know. No one understands. I love him. I still love him. I love the children we were to have. I still picture them in my head. It won't stop. I tried to make it stop. I think I'm losing my mind." Lily grabbed at Abigail's arms. "I swear I hear his footsteps on the stairs. Smell his awful boots. Then, I saw him. Last night." Lily pointed a shaking finger down the hall. "Standing in our rooms. He was calling my name. I heard him clearly. I did. But when I opened the door," she sobbed, "he vanished. Like he was never there."

Abigail shot a frightened look at Primrose and shook her head. Rose gave a pitying sob and rushed to leave.

"You're exhausted. When was the last time you slept?" Abigail tugged at her again.

Lily struggled to her feet and coughed. "I..." Unable to stop herself, her gaze swept the nursery one last time. A razored shaft of grief nearly sliced her in two. She closed her eyes and turned away. She'd forgotten to add one more thing. One more thing to bury in this room along with her heart. Lily wiped her hands on her ruined skirts and stumbled back toward their bedroom.

Abigail was quick to follow. "Lily?"

"Help me." She dragged a chair to the fireplace and started to climb.

Her sister pulled her back from the edge of the fire. "You'll catch your skirts! Stop! What are you doing?"

Lily sobbed and pointed to their wedding portrait hanging over the mantle. "Put that in the nursery as well."

"Fine. Whatever you want. Please."

"I can't look at it anymore."

"Of course, I'll see to it."

"And this, too." Lily slipped the ring from her finger and handed it to Abigail.

"No, Lily, you're grieving now, but one day you'll regret all of this, and you'll want to wear your ring."

"No! I can't bear it." She forced it into her sister's hands.

Abigail slipped the ring into a pocket and wrapped her arm around Lily's shoulders. "Darling, shhhh, please. I have a wonderful idea, why don't I have your maid pack a few of your things and you can come home with me. It will be like old times. You won't be haunted by your memories. You can rest and get well. I'll instruct the remaining staff here to close up Fairwinds and you can come live with me."

"No." Lily pulled out of her embrace. "I'm *never* leaving Fairwinds. He's here, I tell you. Jake's here. I saw him. I know he disappeared, but he'll come back. I need to be here when he does."

"He's not here, Lily. It's all in your mind. The fever has you seeing things that aren't real." She placed a hand on Lily's forehead. "God, you're burning up."

Lily pushed her hand away. "You're wrong. He'll return, and I'll be here waiting."

"Jake isn't coming back."

Lily put her hands over her ears. "I'm not leaving." She turned and clutched at Abigail's sleeve. "Ever. I won't go. Bury my bones on the cliffs if you must, but I'm staying here."

"Fine, fine…" Abigail placated as she moved Lily toward

the bed. "If you promise me to stay in this bed until I can return with the doctor, you can remain." She turned and gave the maid a shove. "Build up the fire then fetch her a strong broth."

The maid stumbled with a frightened look over her shoulder. "But Cook isn't—"

"I didn't ask you for excuses," Abigail snapped. "Bring my sister some broth at once."

"Yes, ma'am."

As the maid raced out of the room, Abigail yelled at her back, "The fire. Dammit."

Lily laid in the bed. As Abigail continued to fuss and sputter over the incompetency of her staff, Lily was wracked with a deep and sudden weariness. Perhaps if she just closed her eyes for a minute. Abigail's voice faded into the distance. *Please, God, give me a moment's peace, to rest.* Her head pounded. Her lungs burned. "Jake…"

"I'm here, my love. Can you hear me?"

"Yes…" Lily opened her eyes and scanned the empty room. "Where are you? I miss you so much."

"I'm right here."

Lily caught a whiff of a familiar smell and smiled. "You've been in the tunnels…. I even miss your mucky boots."

In her mind, she heard him laugh. Struggling to sit she scanned the room once more. "I want to see you." Silence was her answer. "Jake?" Lily pushed back the covers and swung her feet to the floor. A fit of coughing seized her as she struggled to her feet.

Opening the French doors, she once more braved the cold of the roof walk. She had seen him from out there before and prayed for one more glimpse even if it were just for a second.

Even as her rational mind told her it wasn't real. He had been real to her. Until she foolishly opened the door and made him disappear. She wouldn't make that mistake again. Lily closed the door tight behind her.

"Jake?"

Another coughing fit had her clinging to the icy railing. It was so cold. One sighting and she would get herself back to bed. Just to see him once more and she could rest. Her legs failed her, and she slid down to sit with her back against the iron balustrade. Breathing became a struggle. She closed her eyes to the effort.

"Lily?"

When she opened her eyes, Jake was there. She could see him clearly through the glass. Hear him. It wasn't cold anymore, and her lungs had ceased their battle. Lily pulled a deep breath and got to her feet. She pushed the hair away from her face. Her head no longer pounded.

"Jake, I see you, my darling. I do."

"Aye."

Beyond Jake, the maid came into the room with a tray and let out a high-pitched scream, dropping it all to the floor in a horrible crash before rushing out.

"I guess she doesn't find you near as handsome as I, Captain Wilder." Lily smiled at him.

"I doubt she can see me. I think it's you that made her scream."

"Why on earth would I make her scream?" Lily followed Jake's line of sight. There she was…or more to the point, there was her body, curled against the side of the railings, her face white as chalk. "Oh…yes, that would be more likely." She looked back at Jake. "I didn't imagine dying would be so quiet;

did you?"

Jake shook his head. "I died in the middle of a storm. It wasn't quiet."

"But you know what I mean, you're alive one second and then you're not. Why did I think it would be more dramatic?"

Jake smiled at her and lifted a shoulder. "Again, I died in a storm at sea. It was rather dramatic."

"I suppose." Lily was struck with a thought. "Oh, Jake, if you're dead and I'm dead…does that mean you won't vanish again?" She didn't wait for him to answer. Lily raced to the door, but when she moved to turn the knob, her hand passed straight through. "No. This can't be. Oh, Jake…" She tried once more to open the door. "Is it worse that you vanish or that I can't ever touch you?"

"We're here together. Trust me when I say that's more than I'd begun to hope for."

"But I want to hold you, and have you hold me. Kiss me. Love me. If my hand can pass through the knob, why can't I pass through the door? Or the window?"

"Even if you could, there's no guarantee I would still be visible to you. I'm afraid I don't know the rules in all of this, Lily. I'm just happy to see a smile on your beautiful face. To tell you how much I love you again and have you hear my words."

"Oh, Jake…"

"We'll figure out a way, Lily. Whatever that may be. Even death can't conquer our love, don't you see? We're still at Fairwinds. Together again."

"Not quite together, Jake, but close. Closer than we were yesterday. Perhaps now I can bear to face tomorrow."

Chapter 19

As the last of the summer roses withered on the vines, time and space ceased to be important. Yesterdays and tomorrows melted into one another. Senses like smell and touch lost their meaning. Cold or warmth no longer existed, as if that part of living had been taken away. Or perhaps it was what made one alive, feeling the sea air, the warmth of the sun, smelling the crisp fall leaves. It was as if the world lost a wee bit of her color.

Lily and Jake soon discovered the breadth of their separate worlds. While Lily could still walk the grounds and along the cliffs, Jake was bound to the inside. He could venture out to walk the tunnels and as far as the entrance of the caves, as long as he came and went via the spiral staircase beneath the butler's pantry.

Lily continued to pace the walk. However, she could only peer in at the third floor from outside. She'd tried every door on the estate to get back inside without success. Was she to spend eternity peering into Fairwinds like a beggar with their nose pressed to the glass?

Was the universe playing a cruel joke on them by allowing them to remain together, yet keeping them apart?

"You know, you don't have to stay here," Jake spoke to her one night from what had become their favorite place, through the French doors. Earlier they had both watched from their separate vantage points on the third floor as a small group of mourners lowered the remains of Lillian Grace Langdon Wilder into a small, marked grave placed out on the cliffs.

"And where would I go?" Lily leaned her head against the glass.

"I don't rightly know."

"I'm not going anywhere. Not without you."

Jake huffed. "There's little chance, if there is such a thing as heaven and hell, that you and I would end up in the same place."

"Perhaps we did. Perhaps Fairwinds is just that. Both our heaven and our hell."

One by one the remaining servants left Fairwinds amid rumors that strange sights and sounds could be heard around the estate. Abigail returned only once more to order the house be closed. Before long, Fairwinds slept once again…or so it would seem.

Lily watched as a gray day faded into a dark night. The tops of the trees danced with a building wind. The ornate weathervane still stood, bright and new in its place atop the house. It creaked its announcement of the wind's shift from the northeast.

Rain began to fall around her. She tipped her face up, missing its cool feel upon her face as she recalled the last time a storm brewed like this. Looking through the windows, she saw that Jake had returned from his evening's wanderings. The last time a nor'easter blew, was the night she feared she'd lost Jake forever. It was a night that changed her life forever.

Looking down, Lily realized to her surprise she wore her pink gown. Around her the world swirled and became turbulent as the storm grew stronger with each passing moment. With a mighty burst of wind, the French doors behind her crashed open.

Lily spun to find Jake standing in the very spot she first saw him. He stood in the very place where they had last kissed. Where he promised her he'd return.

"Lily?" He wore his wedding suit. "The bloody door…"

Rain soaked the flooring past the doorway. Lily's breathing began to race. Everything in her wanted to rush into his arms.

"I'm afraid, Jake. What if I take a step over this threshold and you vanish again? I could lose you forever."

"The time before, I only vanished from your sight, Lily. I never left." He held out a hand to her. "I'll never leave."

Longing flooded her.

"Come here, Lily," he urged. His voice a gentle plea.

Holding her breath, she stepped over the threshold and grasped at his hand. All at once the room around them came alive. A fire flared in the cold fireplace. Lily felt the warmth of the flames fill the room. Candles flickered in once empty sconces. Dust covers disappeared. Their grand furnishings shone in the soft light.

He still held tight to her hand.

"Jake…"

He pulled her into his arms and nearly crushed her against him in a tight embrace. "Thank you, God!"

Lily cupped his face relishing the warmth of his skin, the prick of his unshaven face. "Jake!"

Laughing and crying, they ran their hands over one another. Touching, testing, proving to themselves that what they were seeing, and feeling was indeed happening, was real. And then he lowered his mouth to hers and kissed her, and the world was all at once whole and right again.

When Lily's knees betrayed her, he scooped her into his arms and carried her to their bed and laid her on the coverlet of rich reds and browns and covered her with his body. His scent filled her senses. She clung to him.

Their kisses went from desperate to a depth of wild passion Lily had never known. They tore the clothes from one another as the winds of the storm began to howl and moan around them. The rough feel of his hands on her skin made her gasp. She clawed at his back as he ripped the last of her clothes away and pushed open her knees.

In one thrust, Jake buried himself deep within her. They both cried out each other's name as they bucked and rocked against one another in a frenzied dance. Jake drove into her over and over. His pace soon raced past her own as the first tidal wave of orgasm crashed over her.

Clutching to the headboard her body jerked and clenched beneath his. The power of him stole her breath. She arched into yet another climax, crying out. He fused into her and reached a grinding release of his own until he collapsed at her side. Their skin slick and glowing with sweat. They both fought to breathe.

The storm continued to rage inside and out. Later they made love on the floor in front of the fire. Golden light from the fire bathed their heated skin. After Jake pulled her close. Lily draped her leg across his body and trailed lazy fingers over the rise and fall of his chest.

"Could we stay just this way forever?"

"That would be heaven, indeed." He tightened his hold.

The logs in the fire popped and settled. The winds outside still blew a gale. Rain still lashed against the house. Lily kissed

Jake's shoulder. "I'm sorry."

"Whatever do you have to be sorry for, my love."

"I didn't believe you." Lily rested her head on his chest and heard the beating of his heart. "I didn't trust your word. You promised me you'd return, and I let my grief take over my heart. I gave up on your love. I lost my faith and my hope."

"Neither of us could have predicted this fate. I'd always believed death was the end. Who could have imagined?" Jake stroked her back and along her hip before tracing a finger around the claret heart that marked her there. "I know now why your birthmark has a ragged edge," he murmured into her hair. "Your heart was broken, and I couldn't perfectly piece it back together." His hold tightened. "I'm sorry I put you through such heartache."

"I went quite mad with it, truly. *I'm* sorry I buried our portrait and your beautiful ring behind a wall of brick." Lily lifted her empty hand and shook her head. "Abigail was right. She said I would come to regret it one day. Now it's gone."

"It's not gone. Abigail put it into her pocket. I saw her slip it on her finger before she left the house."

Jake stretched out an arm and grasped at the tails of his coat that had landed over one end of the loveseat in their rush to rid themselves of each other's clothing. He pulled it toward him.

"What are you after?"

"Do I still have it?" He fished through one of the pockets and pulled out a crumpled bit of twine and tied it to Lily's finger as he'd done on the night they'd married. "I can't promise to replace it with gold and rubies this time." He kissed the backs of her fingers.

"You need not replace it. I love my twine ring." Lily held

up her hand once more and admired it in the firelight. "It makes me feel a wee bit better knowing that my other ring is safe in Abigail's keeping now. I may even forgive her for not putting my full name on my gravestone. Do you know it just says, *Lillian Grace, Wife of a Pirate*? As if adding *Wilder* would have disgraced me."

"Adding *Langdon* would have been worse."

"I suppose," mused Lily. "I do like forever being known as *Wife of a Pirate*." She kissed his chest. "But without Monsieur Fortier's painting, no one will see my beautiful gown."

"That damn portrait…" Jake pulled Lily atop him. "I'm happy you buried that."

"I liked it." Lily kissed her way up Jake's neck and nipped at his ear. "You never did get that earring for me."

Jake grasped her hips and ran his hands down the back of her thighs. "I was busy dying in a storm, remember?"

"Ah, yes, in a very dramatic fashion, I understand." Lily straddled him and rose. The firm length of his erection lay long and split her heat.

"Are you mocking me, woman?" Jake rolled his hips and ran his hands up to caress her breasts.

"No, I'm loving you." Lily lowered herself upon him. "Forever."

Rain beat against the windows and into the open door to soak the boards of the floor as their lovemaking matched the drama and intensity of the storm beyond the walls, beyond the walk, beyond time until they fell into an exhausted sleep within the shelter of each other's arms.

When Lily opened her eyes, the clouds had swirled themselves out to sea. The weathervane showed a steady westerly breeze and the sun blazed overhead. She shielded her eyes yet felt none of its warmth.

She was back on the walk. "*No.*" The word rushed from her as she got to her feet. The door was closed. Peering through the rain-washed glass, the room showed no sign of their night of passion and the hours they'd spent loving one another. *Had it all been a dream?* No, the floor beyond the door bore a dark water stain.

Jake rose from where he sat against the door. "Lily, what the bloody hell happened?"

"The storm is over. The door's shut again."

"That can't be. Last night…" He raked his hands through his hair.

"The wind shifted again."

"Damn the wind and damn the cursed sunrise," he shouted toward heaven. "I had you in my bloody arms!"

"Maybe this is how it works? Maybe when the winds change and a nor'easter blows, the door opens, and we can be together. I can touch you and feel you. Hold you. Make love to you again."

"What? For just one night?" Jake shoved at the door, rattling the window panes. "Why give us what we had just to take it away again? Are we being punished?"

"Maybe not punished. Maybe we're blessed."

"How is this blessed?" He pounded a fist on the door frame.

"Maybe we don't just get one night. What if we get a thousand and one nights? Two thousand. Three. All of them as wonderful and amazing as last night. As long as the wind is fickle and unpredictable," Lily gazed into Jake's stormy eyes, "and chooses to blow a gale every now and then. Perhaps we can come together again each time. Don't you see, we'll still have each other. We'll still have Fairwinds. Our love can keep us here."

Jake pressed a hand against the glass. "And Fairwinds will still have us."

Lily matched her hand to his on the other side. "Yes, my love, forever."

"Forever, plus one day."

Fairwinds held them and kept them together long after the roses grew tangled, and the great house settled into a long, deep sleep. But every so often, when the sky grows dark with building clouds, and the seas rise with a howling blow, Lily and Jake's eyes lock as the weathervane creaks and *The Phantom* charts a new course in the changing wind.

"Looks like a storm is brewing…."

The End

AUTHOR'S NOTE

As my first experience in working with other authors on a cooperative, I want to give extra thanks and show my great appreciation for Nancy Fraser and Kathryn Hills. It has been a wonderful experience to work with these fine authors, and I was humbled to be asked to participate in this truly unique project.

Widow's Walk was a way for me to play with pirates once again while dipping my toe into the world of the paranormal. I loved it! While challenging to walk with my beloved characters Jake and Lily through their deaths, the promise of keeping them together through eternity made them such special characters to work with. I knew that writing romance, I had to give them their "happily ever after." Even when that "ever after" was in the hereafter.

I think we all have a belief, hope, notion of what awaits us when we die. I have always been a firm believer that true love lives on forever. It gives me a sense of peace believing in something more beyond our knowing.

As always, I want to thank all the sharp eyes that helped edit this work. Especially Theresa who doesn't even like pirates!

Thank you to all my loyal and devoted readers. You are the best!

And last, but by no means least, my amazing family. Surviving the last year without you has been one of the hardest things I've ever done, but we're together again. I will love you all forever…plus one day.

~ Lisa

Cast to the Wind and Waves
(1837)

Best Selling and Award-Winning Author
Kathryn Hills

Cast to the Wind and Waves

A storm is coming to Fairwinds after lifetimes of emptiness. Can love survive when dark secrets are revealed?

A house of mystery and shadows awaits Lucy Ellison on the windswept coast of New England. Neglected and all but forgotten, Fairwinds is the centuries-old estate of her ancestors. Locals know the legend and stay away. Whispered stories of vengeful ghosts and pirate curses. Lucy never imagined she'd experience them firsthand, until her brother banishes her there following the death of their father. The resident spirits, however, are the least of her worries. Her brother's latest scheme includes marrying her off to a stranger. But why?

Nathaniel Bradford arrives at Fairwinds to discover its latest victim on the rocks below the sea cliffs. Unless Nate agrees to step into the dead man's shoes, his mother will be the sole caretaker of the vast estate. His law firm in Boston can spare him for a few weeks, but how can he find a replacement for a man who supposedly left by way of a deadly curse? The unexpected arrival of the beautiful heiress, Lucy Ellison, complicates everything. She's from the dubious family that continues to upend Nate's life. Yet their mutual attraction is as swift and powerful as the waves surrounding them.

Deceptions and dangers abound. Adventure and intrigue loom around each corner, as two lovers are cast into the legend of Fairwinds. Can their bond weather the storm? Or will unknown forces tear them apart?

Dedication

For Theresa

Chapter 1

Fairwinds ~ Autumn, 1837

"He's dead, Mister Bradford," the officer of The Watch yelled. "There's brains dashed all over them there rocks."

Nathaniel Bradford approached the corpse on the beach of Fairwinds. The smell of low tide, mingled with rotting flesh, assaulted his senses. He removed his hat, clutching it in icy fingers, as he said a silent prayer for the poor wretch currently being eaten by crabs.

"How did your mother say the groundskeeper fell from the cliffs?" the officer asked.

Nate rubbed the place between his brows, as if he could somehow wipe the horrid picture from his mind. "She didn't. She has no idea. The man disappeared often, especially when he was drinking. My mother found him this morning. She tends the grave of Lady Lillian. Up there." He motioned to the rocky cliffs above.

"Well…that's another odd one then," the officer proclaimed before raising his eyes toward heaven.

"What are you suggesting that this man's death is suspicious?"

"Not at all, sir," he stated emphatically. "Just that the Fairwinds curse got another one is all. This place is known for *strange happenings*. But I suppose a man, deep in his cups, could've easily fallen. There doesn't appear to have been any struggle at the top. Looks like he just went off the edge."

Nathaniel grimaced. "More than one poor soul has met

their maker on this land. At least according to the legend I've heard."

"Yes, sir. It's a right peculiar place. Townsfolk talk of a *white lady*—a specter—walking the cliffs overlooking Skullery Bay."

"A ghost? Don't be ridiculous," Nate scoffed, though a coldness went straight through him.

Gulls cried—looking to horn in on the crab's meal—and Nate glanced up at the ragged rock face of Fairwinds. With its long, unsettled past, dating back well over a century, the place was now the derelict estate of affluent Bostonians. Also, it was the place where his mother would now serve as the sole caretaker following this man's death.

"Does he have a family?" he asked the Watchman.

"None I'm aware of. He was a drifter from New York until getting the job here. I'll make inquiries around town though."

Nate reached into his pocket and withdrew a few coins. "See to it the man receives a proper burial. I shall be staying if there are further questions. My mother cannot manage such a large property alone. I'm a solicitor in Boston, here on a visit," he added. "I'll take it upon myself to write to the property owner, alerting him of what has transpired."

"Very good, Mr. Bradford," the officer said before signalling to some others to bring a cart around to collect the remains.

Nate was about to leave when he hesitated. "Are those caves?"

"Yes, sir, tidal caves. All but collapsed now under the power of the sea."

Twin black holes, like hollow eyes, stared out to sea. *Odd.* Yet Nate felt drawn to them.

He turned his back on the ominous scene, making his way up the steep trail that led to the back lawns of Fairwinds. Once a finished stairway with railings, not much remained aside from loose rocks and crushed granite. If the groundskeeper truly were intoxicated, this would *not* be the path to take. Even now, with the aid of morning sunlight and all his faculties, it was a perilous hike.

His mother waited at the top, alongside the windswept grave of Lillian Grace Wilder, wife of Captain John Jacob Wilder. The pirate captain who once infamously owned the Fairwinds estate. He'd perished at sea during a storm. Lillian Grace followed him to heaven shortly thereafter.

"What news?" his mother asked, her anxious voice wavering as she clutched the rusty metal fence surrounding the lone grave.

"Just that it is him. As you suspected."

Nate watched his mother tug her shawl tighter around her thin form. "Come, Mum, let's get you warm. There's nothing we can do for the man now. I told the Watchman I will be staying in case he needs anything more."

"But your work," she began to protest.

"I will not leave you here alone. I never liked you staying in this ridiculously secluded place. Even when there was another person here to assist you."

"But this is my home, Nathaniel. It has been for over eight years."

"You do not need the meager income this position provides. I told you, I will always look after you. You can come home with me now, return to Boston, or you will allow me to stay and help you. The choice is yours."

Cora Bradford wrung her hands, and she looked from the

grave to the house and back again. Then she crossed her arms and turned to stare out at the sea.

Nate dropped his head, knowing it was pointless to press her further. "Well then..." He gave a humorless laugh. "I suppose I've been sitting behind a desk far too long. A bit of physical labor won't kill me."

Cora approached him, and she placed her loving hands to his cold cheeks. "Thank you, Nate. We'd best be getting to work then. The groundskeeper's cottage is a filthy mess."

"I can stay in the main house if that's easier. There are rooms aplenty."

"No, that won't do, especially since the weather is turning foul. I can feel it in my old bones."

***

London, England

Lucy Ellison attempted to stifle a yawn. She covered her mouth with her book, grinning when a nearby friend giggled and rolled her eyes.

Their stodgy, old, female instructor at the elite boarding school for ladies droned on, "Strong moral character and Godly values are the foundation of any good marriage. You might enjoy music and dancing. Entertaining things, such as literature and the fine arts. But remember, ladies, it is your solemn duty as a woman to provide a virtuous home for your husband and children."

Lucy sighed. *But what of science and history? Chemistry and math?* All subjects her forward thinking father had taught her long before she'd arrived in London.

A frantic knock sounded on the door, interrupting the

class. An office worker rushed in and handed off a folded message.

The teacher read the note. Clearing her throat, she said, "Miss Ellison...Your presence is required in the headmaster's office.

All heads snapped to Lucy as the energy in the room abruptly transformed into nervous excitement.

"At once, Miss Ellison. Make haste. And take all your things with you."

Foreboding filled Lucy as her footsteps echoed down the long, empty hallways. She paused before the headmaster's door, her knuckles hesitating above the woodgrain. The tiny voice inside her head warned something life altering waited on the other side.

"Come in, Miss Ellison."

She startled at the brusque male voice. Entering the well-appointed office, she closed the door, and asked, "You wanted to see me, Headmaster?"

The portly gentleman behind the desk adjusted his ill-fitting hairpiece, never once looking up from his work. "Your funding is cut off. Pack your things. Your passage home has been arranged."

"But...but...why?" Fear rushed into her. "What has happened to my father?"

"Dead. At least according to the letter, which includes instructions for your immediate return to America."

Dead?

The hideous word swirled in the storm clouds, building in the chaos of her mind.

Father had been ill for some time, but he'd assured her in his last letter his health was holding steady. She'd been hopeful the doctors in Boston were helping him.

Lucy knees became weak, and she wavered on her feet. She worked to swallow the painful lump in her throat, as hot tears threatened.

"Where is my brother?" she dared to ask.

"He's sent a companion to accompany you on the long voyage." As if given some silent cue, another door opened, and a tall, older woman with a severe countenance entered. "This is Mistress Grimes."

Critical eyes assessed Lucy—a slow perusal from head to toe—before focusing on the headmaster. "Mr. Ellison thanks you for the education of his sister. However, it is done, regardless of her course schedule. She is to be married to—"

"Married?" Lucy blurted. "What in heaven's name are you talking about?"

"To my brother," the woman expounded. "A long-standing friend of the Ellison family."

There was only one Grimes Lucy knew of. Her brother's rather unsavory friend and business associate. A man her kind-hearted father despised.

"Come," the frosty woman urged. "We sail for Boston tomorrow."

A mere two hours later, Lucy sat straight as a needle in a coach bound for Liverpool. She did her best to keep from falling apart as her school faded away in the distance. Mere brick and mortar, yet the stately old buildings had been her home-away-from-home for the past two years. All her friends and teachers. Her hopes and dreams to one day make a happy place for herself in the world.

The smug expression on the woman opposite her raised her ire. "Tell me, how is it I am betrothed to a man I've never met?"

Belinda Grimes gave her a tight smile. "Your brother and mine are fast friends. Surely you know as much. Now that your father is dead, your brother is merely looking out for your welfare.

"Lance has never been concerned with anyone's welfare, least of all Father's and mine." Lucy's voice rose in anger. "Surely *you* know as much."

Mistress Grimes' lips pinched together. "Your brother warned me you'd be difficult. That your father had coddled you. Given you far more freedom than any woman deserves. Say good-bye to your days of indulgence, Miss Ellison."

"I hardly consider myself indulged or difficult. I'm simply stating a fact. Do you know anything of Lance's true nature, or has he fooled you too?"

The stubborn woman made a sound like a petulant goose. "I know him well enough, and I think him a fine man for securing you such a good match. Your father should have married you off years ago instead of shipping you to another country to have your head filled with frivolous information. Did you hope to marry some romantic nobleman perhaps? Tsk, tsk, tsk." She shook her head.

"I thought no such thing. I seek only to be valued for who I am. And I do feel I deserve better than to be 'married off' to someone without so much as a waltz between us."

"I think you've spent enough time dancing and reading Latin. You're no spring chicken. It's high time you marry and become a proper wife for a great man of business."

Lucy's hand went to her throbbing temple. *How is any of this happening? Most important, how could Father be gone?* She turned away to stare out the coach window, though her eyes were unseeing. Hadn't her intuition—that tiny voice inside—warned something was terribly wrong? That a great storm was coming?

"I don't want to be anyone's wife," she admitted to herself and the ever-watchful woman staring her down. "Right now, I wish to mourn my beloved father in peace. I'll speak to Lance. Appeal to his brother's heart."

Though that had never worked before.

"I think you should be grateful Edmund is even willing to wed you. After all, there's no fortune to your name. Only that which your enterprising brother has secured through his endeavours."

"You mean his schemes and speculations? They're the cause of my family's financial woes. Lance's careless nature with money, including any inheritance that might have come to me, has no doubt put me in this dreadful situation."

"Mind your tongue, Miss Ellison. I'm charged with reporting everything back to my brother. Do you wish to sour your marriage before it's even begun?"

"You may report anything you like to Mister Grimes, beginning with...I will not marry him," she yelled the last part.

The older woman scowled. "I imagine you'll come round. *If* you have a brain in that pretty little head. You are a penniless woman, Lucy Ellison. Without those two gentlemen you'll end up on the streets. How long do you think soft skin and sweet-smelling curls last there?"

Lucy felt the wind leave her sails at the truth of the woman's words. With Father gone, Lance was her sole guardian, her only immediate family. As such, he could force her to marry whomever he wished. Or turn her out. She could fight and cry, but in the end her only choice would be to run away. Perhaps find work as a governess somewhere. *A distant relation?* Yet all would require time, money, and planning. *In other words, a miracle.*

"You're fussing for no reason," Mistress Grimes remarked as she rummaged through her traveling bag. She produced a small, gilded picture case and passed it to Lucy with a self-righteous smirk. "A likeness of Edmund. A most handsome man, you will see."

Lucy opened the case. The inside was lined with red velvet, and it contained a single image of Edmund Grimes.

It would be a lie to say he was not handsome. He was, indeed. Fair-haired and clean shaven, with just a hint of a smile. His eyes did not hold the sharp coldness of her brother's. Still, she would not give the other woman the satisfaction of praising him.

***

Ship's bells and shouts from the crew above heralded Lucy's time of reckoning. All that remained of their weeks-long voyage was for her and Belinda to disembark.

Lucy raised a small hand mirror to examine her reflection. Pacing the decks for hours on end had darkened her fair complexion and warmed her brown hair to the color of autumn wheat. Despite the efforts of her companion to force her to use a parasol or sit in the shade like a "proper lady," she'd been determined to enjoy every fleeting moment of freedom.

"What matters my appearance if I am already betrothed?" she'd once challenged. *"My cheeks are but kissed by the sun and sea air."*

Belinda had scoffed. *"Kissed by the sun, indeed. Your ridiculous, romantic nature, Lucy Ellison. Couple that with two years of an overpriced education, and my poor brother will need to wrestle you back down to earth.*"

In truth, Lucy's knees buckled with her first steps on dry land, as the chaos of the Boston docks swallowed them up. Belinda went off, hollering at men to collect their luggage, while Lucy floundered alone in a state of utter confusion. She scanned the crowd for her brother's face, yet there was only the mob of strangers.

Someone clasped her elbow, and she spun with a startled cry.

"I beg your pardon. Edmund Grimes, at your service, my lady." The tall man smiled down at her. He removed his stylish hat and bowed his blond head in greeting. "Miss Ellison. *Lucy,* if you'll allow me. You are even more beautiful than I remember."

Shock tangled Lucy's tongue, and she merely blinked up at him.

"Come, take my arm," he insisted. "I'll direct you to my carriage."

Lucy began to leave with him—feeling numb and lost—yet she regained her faculties and slammed to a halt. "Mr. Grimes. Forgive me, sir, but..." She steadied herself to ask the question that had burned in her mind for weeks. "Have we ever met in person? Truth be told, I cannot recall an occasion."

Crimson color spread across Edmund's cheeks, catching her off guard.

"Once, at Christmastime, when you were but twelve or thirteen. I'm sorry you don't remember me, for at twenty-two you've grown to be a goddess. I consider myself a most fortunate man to be standing here with you today."

Lucy squinted up at him in disbelief. *Flowery words?* She

laughed, unable to resist saying, "Forgive me, sir, but I find your words quite amusing. Considering it is *your sister* who accuses me daily of being a hopeless romantic."

Edmund beamed at her, revealing straight, nice teeth. "I mean to impress you. Is it working?"

It was Lucy's turn to blush, and she granted him just a hint of a coy smile.

Yet his smile vanished suddenly when he boldly captured her chin with one gloved hand and raised it until their gazes met. His eyes—blue as the sky above—shone bright with conviction. "I know all this must come as a harsh revelation. Please allow me to offer you my sincerest condolences on the loss of your father."

Lucy stared, feeling at a complete loss for words.

"Well then...there's a good girl. Let us go." Edmund patted her cheek and glanced around. "Where is my sister with the luggage?"

A wave of confusion rippled through her at his abrupt change of demeanor, and she took a full step back from him.

What had Father written in one of his letters? 'Edmund Grimes is a cold, boorish man. The worst sort of influence on your brother.'

"Where is Lance?" she shot back. "Is he here with you?"

Edmund captured her elbow again and began ushering her toward his waiting carriage. "Lance had business to attend to this morning. Truthfully, I was anxious to meet you by myself. We shall see him soon enough."

***

Lucy stood tall when they entered the library of the Ellison family home. Yet inside she cringed at the sight of her brother, sitting like a smug king behind their father's desk.

Lance glanced up from the ledgers before him. "Ah, I see you collected our prize. Lucy, dear sister, welcome home. Tell me, did you recognize old Edmund and rush into his arms?" His familiar, patronizing laughter filled the room.

She took a steadying breath, preparing to unleash the anger bottled up inside her for weeks.

Edmund spoke first. "Have a care, old friend. Your sister is no doubt exhausted from her journey." He looked to Lucy, smiling his support. "She does not remember me, but it is my most fervent wish that we become friends now."

"Yes, of course," Lance said with sudden glee. "Woo the wench. As if she has any say in the matter."

Lucy bristled. "Obviously, you're anxious to be rid of me, Lance. The question is why use your best friend to accomplish the task? I should think you'd auction me off to the highest bidder."

Lance gave her the look he always did. Like a snake about to devour a mouse. "Dear sister, I only have your best interests at heart."

"So everyone tells me. Forgive me if I remain skeptical." Trapped and outnumbered by near strangers, Lucy trembled. Her panicked stare flipped between the Grimes siblings and her brother. "Belinda said she and Edmund have been living here. In our father's house without his blessing, since well before he died," she accused.

Lance shot to his feet. "This is no longer his bloody house," he bellowed, his voice reverberating through the rooms. "It's mine, and I wanted them here."

Edmund cleared his throat. "Allow me to explain." He focused solely on Lucy. "Our home is being renovated. To prepare for you, my dear. Lance offered us lodging until the work is complete. Your father kept to his rooms near the end. We were never in his way. I swear to you."

Lucy met Edmond's unwavering, blue-eyed stare. "You don't know me, sir, nor I you. I loved my father dearly, and I'm confident he loved me. Yet he spoke nothing of me marrying you. I feel this is an utter fabrication on my brother's part, and I don't understand why you'd go along with it. Obviously, you could have any woman your heart desires. So, tell me, why do you wish to marry a complete stranger?"

A muscle ticked in Edmund's clean-shaven jaw. "Because you have just lost your beloved father. I want to look after you, Lucy Ellison. You have no family, no support aside from Lance. I'd hoped you would see me as a worthy benefactor after spending time with my sister. Your 'port in a storm,' so to speak."

"And what about what I want? You grant me no time to even form an attachment to you. How are we to know if we are even remotely compatible?"

Worry lines marred Edmunds attractive face. His gaze dropped dutifully to the carpet. "In time, I hope you will come to care for me, as I know I will you. I already do. I would be most honored if you'd agree to be my wife."

"There, you see, it's all settled. He's proposed," Belinda interjected. She gave Lucy an obnoxiously false smile. "Now you two can wed *before* your trip to New York."

"We're going to…to…New York?" Lucy squeaked, blindsided by yet another sharp turn of events.

"Not you," Lance snapped. "Edmund and I are going to New York. We have investments to look after."

"How long will you be gone?" Lucy demanded, focusing on Edmund.

"It's…unclear," he hedged, tugging at his starched, white collar. "Perhaps a month. Maybe two. Likely more," he ultimately admitted.

Lucy spun and headed for the door. "I'll not even consider your proposal until you've returned. I will not be rushed into making such an important decision. If you care for me at all, Edmund Grimes, your proposal will wait until I've had a chance to properly mourn my father."

"But…but…the wedding is all planned," Belinda stammered.

Lance's vulgar laughter filled the house. "Leave it to Lucy to muck everything up. I've one more twist to add to this ridiculous bit of theatre. I've signed sale papers on this house this very morning. The new owner wishes to occupy it at once."

Lucy let out an audible cry.

"Where do you expect us to live?" Belinda shot back.

All eyes went to Lance, and he grinned, appearing most pleased with himself for being the center of everyone's attention. "Edmund and I are going to New York. You two are going to Fairwinds."

The room fell deathly silent. Only the mantle clock ticked away the tense seconds.

"Fairwinds?" Lucy murmured in disbelief. "The pirate's house? You can't be serious."

"Oh, but I am," her brother sang in perverse delight.

"But no one has been there in years. Father said he could not even let the place because it's so run down."

Belinda pointed an accusing finger at her brother. "You dare ship me off to some God forsaken place? After all I've done for you? We'll be stuck there through the worst of winter. And right after getting off that blasted ship?" she yelled.

"I'll not go," Lucy heaped on Belinda's protests. "You cannot make me."

"I can, dear sister, and I will. I can make you do anything I want. The two of you are leaving tomorrow morning on a coach bound for Fairwinds. Best be ready, or I'll drag you from your beds."

***

"Good afternoon," Nate said upon entering Fairwinds' sunny, warm kitchen. He bent to kiss his mother's upturned cheek.

"Sit yourself down," she ordered. "There's gourd soup to warm your belly."

Nate removed his cap and coat and hung them on a peg near the door. After washing the dirt from his hands, he settled at the long wooden table in the center of the room. "Thank you," he murmured when his mum placed a steaming bowl before him and offered warm bread.

Cora served herself next and sat across from him. "Are all the animals bedded down for the night?"

"Aye, but I need to summon a farrier for the work horse. He threw a shoe today, and the other three don't look far behind. Otherwise, all is well."

"Any word from Mister Ellison yet? There are repairs that must be made, and not much money left to make them."

Nate cocked a brow in annoyance. "No word, which I find exceedingly irresponsible given the weight of the situation. To think...the death of his groundskeeper elicits no response. I'll write again tomorrow. Perhaps even reach out to some of my colleagues in Boston for assistance. It's all I can do, considering no locals wish to hire on permanently to fill the position."

They ate together in silence until the kettle screeched.

"Care for tea?" Cora asked him. When he declined, she removed the pot from the fire and made herself a cup before sitting again.

"Mum…" Nate began slowly. "I found something strange today wedged beneath a baseboard in the cottage." He held the thing up for her to see. It sparkled in the lamplight before he handed it off.

"What's this? A coin?" Cora squinted at the strange markings on the lopsided coin. "It's gold, that's for sure. Spanish, maybe?"

"Do you think it belonged to the previous groundskeeper?"

"I doubt it," she scoffed. "The man would've drunk up every cent of its worth had it been his." She slid the coin across the table to him. "What are you going to do with it?"

"Fix the horse's shoes?" He chuckled and shook his head. "I don't know. I'll likely tuck it away for safekeeping until I've time to learn more about it. Ask some historian, I suppose."

"There are stories about this old place, you know," she said as she took their empty dishes to the washtub. "Pirate treasure hidden somewhere on this property."

"That's all we need. Treasure seekers traipsing about. There are rumors of ghosts and curses, too."

"Well?" It was Cora's turn to raise a dubious brow.

"Aye. A couple of weeks ago I would have said you were daft for believing in such things." Nate grimaced, conceding he'd experienced strange happenings since coming to Fairwinds. "But I prefer to deal in facts."

"What? You don't trust your own eyes and ears? Don't let the Captain be hearing you say that. He might take it as a challenge."

"I don't know what I trust anymore. Fairwinds is a mystery. It...well...it perplexes me, suffice to say." He took a breath and pressed his point again. "I wish you would return to Boston with me. Leave this desolate house of shadows and sadness."

"I'm sorry, Nate, but Fairwinds needs me. I feel it in my bones. I've promised the ghosts that one day love and happiness will return here."

Nate dropped his head, knowing this house—the very land it sat upon—had some sort of mystical hold upon his mother.

"You're a good man for staying to help me, Nathaniel. Loving and kind as the day is long. You remind me of your father, more and more each day."

"I'm afraid you're prejudiced," he said with a weary smile.

"True, but I still don't like you squandering your time or your talents, watching over your old mum. Granted, I'm glad you're not too proud for hard labor, but all those years of schooling...You must return to Boston the moment a replacement is found."

"Trying to be rid of me already? Make up your mind, woman," he teased with a weary smile.

"Of course not, I treasure every moment we're together."

"As do I," he returned softly. Nate stood and donned his heavy coat and cap again. "Fear not, Mum, I've brought a few projects with me. Plus, I've managed to secure work locally with a wealthy ship owner and merchant. Time here will allow me to focus on those things until life gets back to normal for us both. Well...as normal as is possible for Fairwinds."

"Don't you miss your city life? All those lovely ladies back in Boston?" his mother nudged with a twinkle in her eyes. "I'd like to be a grandmother some day. *That* would get me to leave

Fairwinds."

"*That* would be blackmail, Mother." He made his way to the door, kissed the top of her grey-haired head, and stepped out into the encroaching darkness.

Chapter 2

Lucy craned her neck, attempting to catch a glimpse of what lay ahead for them, as they turned onto what appeared to be an old private road. They passed a gatehouse in ruin, its stones tumbled, walls overgrown with vines and brambles. The carriage wobbled and pitched along the rough gravel through a dark forest, until the trees thinned and a wide circular driveway opened before a large house.

"Oh, for the love of all things holy," Belinda moaned. "What have they gotten me into this time?"

The coach rattled to a stop, and Lucy was quick to help herself out. She gaped at the centuries-old Georgian mansion made of grey granite. Fairwinds—like a sleeping giant—stood defiant against the backdrop of menacing clouds.

"Will you look at all these weeds and tall grasses?" Belinda griped as she brushed travel dust from her clothes.

"But the house…" Lucy said with a long sigh. "It's breathtaking."

Belinda gave a scornful laugh. "I'll say. Looks like it took its last breath years ago."

Their baggage was removed from the carriage and carried to a tall entryway framed by white columns. Though the paint was now chalky and chipped, it had likely once been most impressive.

"There's no one here to greet us," Belinda whined.

All at once, one big door creaked open, and a solitary woman stared at them through wary eyes. "May I help you?"

Lucy stepped forward, fearing her companion would be rude. "I'm Lucy Ellison, daughter of Phillip Ellison of Boston."

The older woman dropped into a curtsy. "Miss Ellison. I'd no idea you were coming."

"Obviously." Belinda huffed as dead leaves swirled around them in the cold breeze.

Lucy gave the woman a sympathetic smile. "We've come for an extended stay. If you are unaware...my father has passed away. My brother, Lance, has sent us ahead. I'd hoped he would have sent word to you."

"The younger Mr. Ellison was here a few months ago, miss, with another gentleman. They didn't stay, but rather toured the property with some other men. And the groundskeeper of the time, but..." She hemmed and hawed. "They made no mention of your father being gone."

"I see." Lucy chewed her bottom lip. She looked to Belinda, whose expression was as bleak as the afternoon sky. "This is Mistress Grimes, sister of my brother's closest friend and business associate. We shall both be staying."

"I'm Cora, miss. Cora Bradford. Housekeeper of Fairwinds these past eight years."

"So, you're the one to blame for this mess," Belinda accused.

"No, ma'am, I do my best. There have been no guests for years. Few come, no one stays. There's but a small allowance to keep the place from falling down."

Belinda tossed her hands in disgust. "Wonderful, nothing but the best."

The carriage men grumbled and groaned as they grew impatient, prompting the housekeeper to throw wide the double doors and lead everyone inside.

Lucy stepped across the threshold. A rush of cold air embraced her. She held her breath as the spirit of the old house seeped into her soul.

The tiny voice inside her sprang to life. *Welcome home, Lucy.*

"Remarkable," she whispered, as gooseflesh prickled her skin. *Father...is that you?* She'd longed for a sign from him, yet none had come as yet.

Her gaze wandered the striking foyer. Twin curved staircases joined on the second level. Below the two rises was a doorway made of beautiful stained glass. Floor to ceiling windows allowed waning afternoon light into the rooms on either side of them. A parlor and a library, perhaps?

Loneliness and sorrow...

There it was again. Her tiny, inner voice.

...those are the things trapped within the very walls and windows of this dismal place.

The housekeeper began pulling dust covers from the furnishings, causing everyone to cough.

"Stop," Belinda shouted. "Not until the doors and windows can be properly opened."

Lucy stepped in again, stilling the housekeeper's frantic efforts. "Thank you, Cora, but we are tired from our travels. All we require tonight are rooms to sleep, the warmth of a fire, and a small meal. Can you manage those things for us? If not, I shall assist you."

"Yes, miss, the groundskeeper will help me. We're the only two here. There's a fire in the kitchen. Servant's quarters, you understand, but you're welcome to warm yourselves there while we make ready for you. I've some crusty bread and cheese on the table. Hot water for tea, too."

"That will do nicely. Thank you, Cora."

"Wait one minute," Belinda interrupted. "I want to see those bedrooms before I commit to staying. If the rest of the house looks anything like this…" She pointed to the carriage men. "Wait here until I return. You may be taking us back to that sorry excuse for a town."

The housekeeper lit an oil lamp and led the way up to the second level. "There are bedrooms on either side. Take your pick, ladies." She riffled through a jangling ring of keys, dangling from a chatelaine. Cora unlocked the two doors closest to the landing first.

Lucy wandered down a dark hallway as Belinda inspected the rooms. She hesitated before a closed door, sensing something, *or rather someone*, behind the old wood. "What's in here?" she asked when Cora joined her.

"Another bedchamber, miss. A corner room. Would you like to see?"

"Yes, please."

The housekeeper unlocked the door and stepped aside, allowing Lucy to enter first. She strolled into the space and froze as a flurry of happiness filled her. It felt like butterflies taking flight on a warm summer day. "Oh, my," she whispered, feeling a bit lightheaded.

"This was originally the master bedroom," Cora explained. "Until the house was renovated just about a century ago to convert the top floor into living space."

"A century? It's hard to believe this house has seen so much life."

"Not much life of late, I'm afraid. She's been rented on occasion, but no one has called Fairwinds home in years."

"She?"

"Yes, miss," Cora chuckled. "I like to think of the old girl as one might a fine ship. Silly as that sounds."

Lucy smiled at the charming notion, and she glanced around the room with fresh eyes. *A decent sized bed, side tables, and two chairs before a small fireplace.* Yet what she liked most about the room were the large windows. One facing a side lawn and the forest, the other facing out to the bay and sea beyond.

"This room will do nicely, Cora," she declared with a bright smile. "But first," she added, stopping the housekeeper from leaving. "Tell me, why do you lock the doors if no one is here?"

Cora's lips sealed shut, and she dawdled for a few awkward moments. "Well, you might as well know right off. It's most unnerving to hear when you're alone. The doors open and close by themselves."

Lucy's eyes widened. "So, you lock the doors *because* you're here alone? To stop the doors from moving of their own volition?"

"That was a waste of good time," Belinda spoke from behind, causing them both to startle. "At least this room is a more comfortable size. The others are too small for my liking."

"That's unfortunate," Lucy said, feigning sympathy. "I've already claimed this one for myself."

"Oh." Belinda frowned. "What else have you got?" she pressed the housekeeper. "Surely you've something better to offer. What's upstairs?"

Color drained from Cora's face. "The third floor, ma'am, but no one goes there anymore."

"That's ridiculous. Take me at once."

Cora scurried from the room, and Lucy and Belinda followed, climbing another flight of stairs at the end of the hallway to the top level of the house. A similar hallway—only this one much darker and more mysterious than the one below—led to a bedroom suite.

"Much better," Belinda crooned when the space opened into an airy bedchamber with French doors. "Is that a widow's walk?"

"Yes, ma'am, though we use it as a roof walk these days. To service the chimneys and slates above."

The overbearing woman sauntered about, pausing to gaze out at the impressive view of Skullery Bay. Yet her scrutinizing stare dropped to the floor. "Will you look at this mess? A god-awful stain on the floorboards." She cast an accusing look at the housekeeper. "*Someone* has been careless and left these doors open during a storm."

Cora lips pinched from side to side, as if she fought to hold back her words.

Belinda huffed and rolled her eyes. "Oh, very well, ready this room for me. Stains and all."

"But Mistress Grimes—" Cora began.

"I've made up my mind. I'll not be changing it." Belinda leaned into Lucy and, making no effort to conceal her words, muttered, "This one's obviously a simpleton. She thinks I don't know why she doesn't want me to stay here. It's all those blasted stairs. Lazy thing. You should make quick work of finding a replacement for her."

A heavy door suddenly slammed below them. Another, and then another, until Belinda cried, "What in heaven's name is that?"

"Nothing, ma'am." Cora raised her chin a defiant notch. "Only Fairwinds, bidding you, welcome." With that the housekeeper spun on her heels and left.

Back down in the foyer, Belinda barked more orders, this time at the men with their luggage. Looking to Lucy, she grumbled, "I swear, doesn't anyone understand what's expected of them?"

Lucy took her arm and drew her close. "Have a care, Belinda, it's a hired cab. These men need not bow and scrape to you. Plus, you were extremely rude to Cora upstairs. Don't do that again, or I shall be very cross. None of this is her fault. If anyone is to blame, it's—"

She gasped when a man stepped from the shadows. His bold stare fixed on her and stayed.

Calm, cool, confident... He's annoyed with you, her inner voice decreed.

Lucy busied herself, pretending to be engrossed in the activity surrounding their rooms and bags.

Dare I sneak another glimpse?

She did and felt an instant rush of excitement go through her.

A most mysterious man. Dark haired with a rather dashing mustache.

Lucy could tell his hair was a bit too long beneath his tweed cap. With a heavy coat, blackened by soot and dirt, he looked like a great angry bear ready to gobble her up.

The groundskeeper.

Cora spoke softly with him as he eyed the strangers in Fairwinds' entrance hall. "The father is dead," Lucy overheard her saying. "Ready the northeast corner bedroom and the third floor for the ladies."

A flicker of surprise crossed the man's features, yet he said nothing. He looked to Lucy one last time, making a most daring appraisal of her from head to foot. Then he was gone, as silently as he'd come.

"Cheery fellow. Is he mute?" Belinda queried, earning an elbow to the side from Lucy.

***

Alone in her bedroom that night, Lucy watched firelight dance across the ancient beams of the ceiling as wind whipped around the house. Glancing about, she marveled at where she'd ended up after their long, harrowing journey. *From an ocean crossing to this wonderfully weird, old house. All but forgotten in this isolated place. An anxious housekeeper, a brooding groundskeeper...* It was the stuff of Penny Bloods, the thrilling novels she secretly could not get enough of.

Yet another awful thing about leaving London. No more penny novels.

With a heavy sigh, she admitted it'd been an extremely distressing ordeal to get here.

Of course, thoughts of her father plagued her throughout the trip. The last time they spoke... His final letters... *If only I'd been by his side. What if, what if, what if?*

Lucy rose slowly and trudged to her travelling trunk, tucked in the far corner of the room. Opening the heavy lid, she removed the satchel belonging to her father. She smoothed a loving hand over the worn leather. *Its scent? One I know well and have loved since childhood.*

She'd managed to stuff a few things in the case before being rushed to leave their Boston home. Father's old notes and research. Plans of places he'd longed to explore but never did. However, there was one special item she'd also squirrelled away. Something she kept with her always yet hid from Lance whenever they were together. Knotted up in one of Father's monogrammed handkerchiefs was the secret gift he'd given her when she was a girl.

"*My dear, sweet Lucy,*" he'd said back then, "*this belonged to your mother's people. Now it should be yours.*" He presented her with a heavy golden ring. In its center was an exceptionally large ruby. "*I've a feeling you'll know what to do with this when the time comes. But never show it to your brother,*" he'd cautioned. "*Lance will steal it from you, as he'll try to do everything else.*"

Lucy slipped the antique ring onto her finger for the thousandth time since receiving it. It glistened in the candlelight. Shiny and warm against her skin. A memory of her dear father.

"It's still too big for me, Father," she whispered as if he could hear.

Sorrow filled her heart. "I miss you. So very much. I'm truly alone now that you've gone to your reward." She released a shaky breath and removed the ring from her finger. With great reverence, she wrapped it back in its cloth and returned it to the bag and trunk.

"What advice would you give me if you could?" she continued as she mulled around her strange lodgings, preparing herself for bed. "I can still hear your voice. Sometimes. I imagine you'd say, '*Go to sleep, child. Tomorrow is a new day. Life is short. Make the most of it.*'" She smiled, though her heart was breaking. Truth be told, the sound of her father's voice had begun to fade from memory, and her soul grew heavy as life took its cruel toll again.

Slipping between the cold sheets, she closed her eyes and prayed for peaceful slumber. To escape. To dream of happier days.

The candle on the bedside table sputtered and her eyelids

snapped open. It flickered as if blown by a draft, though there was none. Tiny hairs rose on her skin, and she watched in dismay, as the flame nearly winked out.

"Father?" she whispered. "Please, let it be you."

Yet there was nothing.

Crackling from the fireplace and the ever-present wind around the house was all that answered. Long moments passed until she relaxed again. "Perhaps I've been reading too many horror stories."

The wide pine floorboards creaked behind her, and she bolted up in bed. "Who's there? Show yourself this instant."

Only shadows.

"I'm not afraid of you," she said, lying to herself and whatever was lurking in the dark.

Lucy pressed a hand to her throat, feeling her pulse thump. She eased back down, dragged the covers up to her nose. Squeezing her eyes shut, she prayed for protection.

The sound came again. *Footsteps?*

Lucy sat up in bed and turned to the dark side of the room, nearest the large windows.

"Very well. I know you're there," she announced to the noise. She stared into the darkness, willing whatever it was to materialize. "I'm quite aware of spirits, you know. There was a ghost in my dormitory that would tip things over on occasion. I didn't mind until it was my inkwell, spilled on my favorite book about the Flying Dutchman. I managed to salvage it, but it's forever stained."

Lucy paused and frowned when nothing happened. With a huff, she rolled onto her back to watch the ceiling lights again.

Utter fool...talking to yourself. You're quite on your own. No need to dream up ghosts so as not to be alone.

And yet, somehow, she didn't feel alone anymore. It seemed as if someone was there, silently studying her. Deciding if she was worthy of talking to.

The candle flickered again, nearly snuffing out, and Lucy held her breath.

"What then, you wish to talk after all? Very well, what shall we talk about?" She waited for an answer. "I like your home," she said on a whim. "Thank you for allowing me to stay. I find this room most agreeable. Was it yours?" She turned back to the darkness as if someone—something—might respond. "I find it wonderfully romantic, with its grand view of the water. Although I'm often accused of being too romantic," she revealed with a thoughtful frown.

Wind whistled around the corner of the house, and the image of a man on a ship popped into her head. She closed her eyes, recalling her father's stories. He often began by saying… *"A long time ago, a pirate captain married a lady fair and made Fairwinds their home…"*

"A captain. Is that you, then? Captain John Jacob Wilder?" Lucy paused, listening. "Were you happy here with my ancestor, Lillian Langdon?" she murmured, realizing she truly wished to know.

The candle fluttered as if answering, and excitement zipped through her. Along with a healthy dose of fear.

"Yours must have been a remarkable life. One I should very much like to learn about. Though I've never seen a book about you." She frowned, wishing she knew more of the house's history. No portraits or drawings. No one left to ask. Only bits and pieces of old stories from her father about the infamous, ill-fated couple.

The pacing sounds resumed.

"I shall do my best to stay out of your way," she promised. "This is your house, after all. I'm merely a temporary guest. But...perhaps...you could grant me one small favor tonight. If you would pace somewhere else, I would be eternally grateful." She rubbed her sore, weary eyes. "I shan't admit this to anyone else, but I'm exhausted. And quite heartbroken. I'll tell you why someday if you'd like."

The candle sputtered one last time and then burned as normal.

Lucy closed her eyes and released a contented sigh when the room became still. Whoever the ghost was—the Captain or someone else—she sensed they were gone now. Only the pervasive wind remained. An inextricable part of what was now her home, too.

She was just about to doze off when the sound came again. This time from above. Lucy grinned and whispered, "Thank you," knowing Belinda was now playing host to the ghost.

***

"I couldn't sleep a wink," Belinda complained the following morning at breakfast. Seated in the dining room at the back of the house, she glanced around, grimacing at the dusty china buffet the housekeeper had yet to clean. "It was as if a marching band was touring the entire third floor. It even sounded as if something was moving inside the walls."

"Truly?" Lucy exclaimed, pretending to be astonished. Yet her gaze drifted to the lovely large windows that faced Skullery Bay and the vast ocean beyond. Sun shone brightly, shimmering on the waves. The back lawns of Fairwinds—though browned by the coming winter—beckoned her to explore. Truth be told, she couldn't wait to tour the estate, having been denied freedom for so long.

"Did you even hear a word I said?" Belinda's annoyed voice startled her from her musings.

"Forgive me. I was lost in my thoughts."

"See, I knew it. You didn't sleep well either. Lumpy old mattresses and constant drafts. My candle kept going out, and the fire dwindled to near nothing. I about froze to death." She huffed dramatically. "I said…what are we going to do with ourselves today? Not to mention the next few months? God only knows how long." She took a sip of tea and grimaced, muttering it'd gone cold. "A library with no books. No games to entertain one. We've no needlework. *And* the pianoforte in the ballroom is in desperate need of tuning. There's even a key missing."

"I'm going for a long walk to explore and get some fresh air," Lucy announced with a genuine smile of anticipation. "You're welcome to join me if you'd like."

Belinda scrunched up her nose. "But it's cold and windy out. What's there to see anyway? Trees? Weeds? Run-down old buildings? No, thank you. You are obviously a heartier soul than I."

"Suit yourself."

"I'll borrow one of your books though?"

"Of course. I unpacked them all already. They're on the bookshelf in my bedroom," Lucy fibbed. She'd stashed away her favorite penny booklets, wanting to keep those for herself despite having read them repeatedly. Best Belinda didn't know any more about her soaring imagination.

After a light breakfast, Lucy headed out the doors of the small rotunda onto a stone patio. A stiff ocean breeze had her shivering and drawing her heavy woollen cloak tighter around her. Yet she closed her eyes, savoring the fresh, salted air on her cheeks. She loved the sea and rugged shoreline. There was no denying it.

Strolling to the center of the yard, she turned to study the back of the house. Her gaze snapped to the large widow's walk encircling the entire third floor. Iron fencing made it appear as if Fairwinds wore a pointed black crown. She smiled, envisioning the house as some grand old dame.

Why not? As Cora had said, *ships are considered ladies. Why not houses?*

A dark figure passed before the glass doors that led to the third-floor walkway, and Lucy squinted and raised a hand so she could see. *Belinda?* That was her room. Yet when Lucy left the house only minutes before, the woman was seated before the fireplace in the parlor with a blanket and a book. "Huh," she exclaimed, doubting her own eyes.

Turning, she strode away to inspect what was likely once a most impressive arbor. The thing was massive—easily the length of a ship—its metal ribs now broken or missing altogether. "Roses," she murmured with a whimsical smile. "I bet it held yards and yards of glorious blooms." She took a deep breath, imagining what the scent must have been like.

Something interesting caught her eye next, and she headed toward the edge of the property to investigate. A solitary grave lay encircled by the same style of wrought iron fencing atop the house.

Lucy read the inscription on the weathered headstone. *Lillian Grace.*

"Wife of a Pirate." she murmured. "My father told me stories about you, Lady Lillian. As well as your fine captain. Your sister, Abigail Gibson, was my great, great grandmother." She tapped her chin, thinking. "Perhaps I left off a 'great,' but surely you understand. We are distant kin."

She glanced back at the house, wondering what it must have been like when this woman lived at Fairwinds. "You're lucky to have lived on such a grand estate." She squared her jaw and looked longingly out to sea. "I think I should like to marry a pirate," she admitted because no one could hear. "Instead, a pirate of business wishes to marry me. A most troubling turn of events."

Lucy considered the lonely gravesite. "I wish God, or his angels, or my father…you perhaps…could grant me one wish. *Time.* I need time to decide what to do. Should I marry Mister Edmund Grimes, as my brother insists? Or should I attempt to strike out on my own?" She strolled the rocky edge, peering over to the small beach below. "I find it appalling I'm even considering such a risky venture. My father died, you see, and now my brother plans to marry me off to his business associate. I don't like being forced to do things, simply because I was born a woman. I desire to find my own husband. A love match. Is that too much to ask for?"

She paused, as if waiting for the ghost of her ancestor to reply. If her father wouldn't speak to her, perhaps this woman would.

With a sigh of reluctance, Lucy shook off the heavy mantle of melancholy that had plagued her for months. "Well then…time to explore your lovely estate. Good day to you, Lady Lillian. I shall visit you again soon."

Sunshine warmed her face and shoulders once she left the rocky coastline to follow a well-worn path across the lawn. The ornate weathervane atop Fairwinds—fashioned to look like a sleek ship under full sail—squeaked and groaned noisily high above her. It wavered in an uncertain wind, pointing in no steady direction.

How remarkable, Lucy thought, *that the weathervane should look shiny and new when the rest of the house is falling apart.*

She walked on, attempting to clear her busy mind.

Tiny birds twittered in the treeline as she followed the trail into the woods. Their happy chirps helping to lighten her mood. Scents of damp earth and forest undergrowth rose all around her.

Memories of when she'd first learned their family had inherited a remote estate came back to her. Father had mused when she asked about it, saying, *"It's like an old soul, Lucy. Wise beyond all understanding and ripe with magic. Perhaps you will visit someday."* She smiled at how he carried on.

Yet he was certainly right about one thing. Most of the property remained in its primordial state. Towering trees—oak, maple, chestnut, and pine—blocked out the light in many places. By some miracle, these trees had escaped The Crown's government agents. Unmarked by the three slashes, known as the *King's Broad Arrow,* which designated the tallest for shipbuilding.

Today, it felt to Lucy as if the ancient trees slumbered—much like the mansion itself—as the days grew colder and nights longer with the approaching winter. Still, she sensed, there was something mystical hidden beneath it all.

A slow, rhythmic chopping sound replaced the hush of nature, and Lucy followed the noise. The forest opened to a sunny glen with a little stone cottage covered in jade-green ivy.

The Groundskeeper's Cottage perhaps?

Edging closer, Lucy peeked around the corner of the tiny house. The man she'd crossed paths with last night came into view. He was indeed chopping, with a large pile of firewood already beside him. She pressed a gloved hand to her mouth as she watched him swing a very large axe.

No doubt, he is working to fill the empty woodbins now that we are here.

She could see more of him without his great, bearish coat. Young and strong, his muscles stretched and bunched with each log he split. His dark hair was indeed a tad long and tied back from his face by a strip of leather.

He's handsome. A secretive smile turned her lips. *Not at all the sort of man one expects to find in the middle of nowhere.*

The groundskeeper paused to swipe a sleeve across his brow. It was then he looked up and spotted her. Their gazes locked, and Lucy gave a tiny gasp.

"Good day to you, sir," she rushed to say, forcing a lighthearted tone to cover the fact she'd been caught ogling the man. "I didn't mean to disturb your fine chopping." She approached him, still smiling like a fool, as she navigated wood debris in her cumbersome skirts. "I'm Lucy Ellison. Forgive me, but in all the confusion last night, I neglected to properly introduce myself."

The man buried the heavy axe in the chopping block and wiped his hands on his thighs.

The rugged sight of him—tight britches, tall boots planted firmly in the dirt—caused her to swallow hard. She glanced away, feigning interest in their surroundings.

"My...what a charming little spot you have here. Quiet, secluded, yet still close to..." She let the remainder of her words float away in the presence of his irritated stare. "This *is* the groundskeeper's cottage, is it not? I see it's made of the same granite as the house," she rambled on like a tourist. All she was missing was a guidebook.

Stop rambling, and talk to him, the little voice inside her prodded.

"And you are, sir?"

The man stood tall—a good foot taller than she—yet she came closer and raised her chin a brave notch. Tension around his deep brown eyes eased a bit. One sooty brow arched, and his mustache tipped with a grin. "Nathaniel Bradford," he murmured in a deep, masculine timbre. He dipped his head. "At your service, *Miss* Ellison."

Lucy dropped her gaze as a nervous fluttering sprang to life in her belly. She cleared her throat before meeting his penetrating stare again. "Bradford? Any relation to our Cora?"

"Aye. I'm Cora's son. Here to help until another groundskeeper is hired."

The anxious breath, lodged in Lucy's chest, began to ease a bit. "Your mother is exceedingly kind, considering all we heaped on her last night. As are you," she rushed to add. "Thank you for helping to ready our rooms. And for tending the fires. I imagine it's not easy to warm such a big house."

"You'll have more wood as soon as I can fill a cart, if that's why you're here," he grumbled in a gruff tone.

"No, I'm simply here to…I mean I'm out because…I wanted to see the estate. To explore on this fine autumn day. Fairwinds is like a dream come true for me after being cooped up for so long," she found herself admitting.

Mr. Bradford's broad shoulders relaxed somewhat. "Why have you been 'cooped up,' if I may ask?"

"I recently sailed from England. While it was not a hard crossing, idle time does drag on. Though I found I genuinely enjoyed life at sea," she chattered on as if they were friends at a garden party, rather than strangers, standing in a forest glen. "Forgive me. It's just…I've only had my travel companion for company these many weeks. Suffice to say Mistress Grimes is not an accomplished conversationalist."

Her jab startled a laugh from him, and Lucy grinned.

Strolling to a stone well, he dipped a ladle into a wooden bucket and brought it to his lips. Lucy watched him, captivated by the sight of clear water spilling down his scruffy chin and neck to dampen his blue knitted shirt.

"Is there something I can do for you, miss?" he said, catching her gawking again. "Would you care for water?"

"No, thank you. I must be on my way." She forced a happy tone. "Good day to you, sir."

The man bowed his head but didn't speak. Still, his gaze never left her. The slightest hint of a smile teased the corners of his mouth.

In a flurry of clumsy movements, Lucy bounded through the brush and scurried to the trail. Heat flooded her cheeks. Was he watching her? Laughing? *Oh, dear Lord, I've lost all my wits and sense of decorum. Thank goodness Belinda wasn't here.*

Upon returning to the house, Lucy attempted to sit quietly and read in the parlor. Yet her mind churned over every second of her encounter with the enigmatic groundskeeper, Mister Bradford. *He certainly is pleasing to one's eyes. And well spoken. I wonder if he reads. Do most physical laborers have time to read?* Indeed, thinking such nonsensical thoughts monopolized way too much of her time.

Still, Lucy could see him in her mind's eye, standing in that sunny glen. A lock of chestnut hair falling across his brow.

His cheeks made red by the frosted morning air. More than a day's growth of beard had darkened his rugged jaw, yet she found herself longing to touch his face.

What a contrast…this man compared to the polish and perfume of Edmund Grimes.

She closed her eyes, imagining her hands, holding and caressing Mr. Bradford's manly countenance.

I've never touched a man's face before, other than Father's. Would his skin be soft or prickly?

Edmund Grimes is prickly, she admitted to herself. She'd discovered that unpleasant fact about him the day they'd met on the pier. Perhaps the prettiest man she'd ever encountered—not a hair out of place—yet Edmund made her anxious and itchy all over.

Nathaniel Bradford, on the other hand—though rough and gruff and bearish—was much more intriguing. Tall, strong…

Perhaps he is what Father called a 'man's man?' The sort of man other men admired and looked up to. The type women secretly desired. She blushed at the notion, as she read the same page repeatedly. *Would his mustache tickle if he kissed me? Pressed those frowning lips to mine, and—*

Lucy practically threw her book when Belinda spoke out of nowhere, startling her from her lurid thoughts.

***

It was late afternoon when Lucy sought out Cora, hoping a conversation might turn to the woman's captivating son. "Hello, Cora. Might I keep your company for a bit? Mistress Grimes has dozed off on me again."

"Of course, Miss Lucy," the housekeeper said with a cheery smile as she worked to prepare their evening meal. "I hear you met my boy today." Cora's cheeks turned a deep apple red.

"Listen to me. Nate's all the man now. Grown up, to be sure. But you know how mothers are."

Lucy smiled to herself, pleased their discussion turned so quickly to where she longed to go. "We did meet this morning, while I was out for my walk. How old is your son?" she asked, trying hard not to sound nosy.

"Twenty-seven, miss, and a fine solicitor in Boston. The youngest lawyer in his firm," she shared with obvious pride.

"A solicitor?" Lucy's mind pounced on the new bit of information. "My, how admirable. Yet he's so far from the city now. How did he come to be at Fairwinds?"

Cora's gaze darted to hers. "It's only temporary, miss, I assure you. He's here to help me. The previous man…He…Well. I suppose you might as well know the truth. There's no kind way to say it. He died. Fell from the cliffs out yonder, he did."

"Died? Right here at Fairwinds? That's dreadful."

"Aye, a terrible thing, for sure," Cora agreed. "I was most upset. Thank heaven, Nate was here for a visit, and he stayed on to help me. He worries about his old mum, here in the up-country, all alone. He wrote to your father, straight away, informing him of what happened to the unfortunate man. Nate asked that a replacement be hired at once. Now we know why your father never answered. I am sorry for your loss, miss, though I was too flustered when you arrived to say so."

"Thank you, Cora, that's alright. I'm sorry for the predicament my family has placed you and your son in. Lance should have answered Mr. Bradford's letter immediately."

"I'm sure your brother will be in touch any day now."

Lucy had her doubts, though she didn't say so. Instead, she strolled around the large kitchen, ending up beside the large, rustic hearth where a plump goose sizzled on an iron spit. She took a deep, savoring breath of fragrant air. "This smells divine. I'm famished for the first time in months."

"It's all that good sea air, miss. Nothing like the shore to improve one's constitution. Nate went hunting for us today," Cora chattered on, giving her another proud smile. "There's a fine turkey in the icehouse as well, awaiting your pleasure."

An image of the man, traipsing through the shadowy forest with a long gun, filled Lucy's head and she had to stifle a romantic sigh. *A skilled huntsman? Yet he's a lawyer from Boston? As out of place as this grand house in the wilderness.*

"Is there a lake or freshwater pond on the property?" she asked to stop her mind's wanderings again.

"Aye, miss, a pond the ducks and geese frequent. Fairwinds has its share of deer and rabbits, too, but we haven't had anything as big as a deer in ages. It being only Nate and me."

Lucy returned to the long table, noting freshly baked breads and apple tartlets. "My, you've been busy in this kitchen. May I help?" She peered over Cora's shoulder as she prepared root vegetables.

"That won't do, miss. It's my job to cook the meals."

"But I feel quite useless. And lonely," she confessed to the kind older lady. "May I at least stay and talk with you for a while?"

"Certainly, I'd welcome a bit of feminine conversation." Cora pointed to a chair opposite where she worked, and Lucy sat. "Nate typically comes round for supper. We share a bit o' this and that from our day. That is until you ladies arrived. He'll keep to the cottage now."

"I'm sorry we've upended your lives. Everything was quite

chaotic when we left Boston," she shared a sad sigh, recalling how she'd stuffed anything she could into her luggage, before leaving forever the house she'd grown up in.

"Don't you worry bout a thing, I'm happy to serve. Keeps me young. Fairwinds has been sad and lonely for far too long."

"Why is that, Cora? I should think a beautiful estate, such as this, would have visitors all the time. Those who enjoy the sea or the forest. Hunters, perhaps?"

A shadow of unease flickered across Cora's features. "Oh…I don't know, miss, perhaps it's because we're far from Mystic Point. Or because the weather is so fickle near the bay."

"My father told me about this place. He often called it 'peculiar.' That the house sat empty for long periods of time, only to have someone move in, then leave soon after. He went so far as to say it's because the house is haunted."

Cora dropped the knife she was using, and she scrambled to retrieve it. "Old houses do have their history, Miss Lucy. People talk, make up silly stories. Not your father, mind you, but the townsfolk." She shrugged the notion off, yet Lucy noticed she chopped all the faster. "My room and this kitchen are peaceful, that's all I know."

Lucy sat in silence, watching Cora work, though her curious nature demanded she learn more about the possibility of ghosts, especially after last night. "Mistress Grimes complained of noises again today. Mice, possibly even rats, and not just on the third floor. She swears there's something in the walls throughout the house. She was in the rotunda today when she heard things."

Cora set down her knife. "I had Nathaniel search for rodent droppings when he came today. There were none to be found. As I expected."

Lucy pressed on, sensing she'd struck a nerve. "She also said she caught a chill because of frequent, mysterious drafts. She accuses you of neglecting the fires."

Cora scowled. "I swear to you, we haven't neglected anyone or anything. I go up to her room often to feed the flames. And Nate set a large fire in the parlor, especially for her. I've kept it going all day. You both saw me."

"Yes, we did, Cora. That is precisely why I don't understand what's bothering her. It seems rather unnatural to me."

Considering the experience in her own bedroom, in addition to the slamming doors when they arrived... Lucy thought it most *unnatural,* though she'd yet to hear the doors slam again. *Was a spirit tormenting Belinda? And why did Cora refuse to speak of it?*

"We run a tight ship here," Cora assured her. "The house may be dusty, but it's never dirty. And I'd never ignore a guest. Or a mouse, for that matter. The lady was in quite a dither this morning. I explained Nate would set traps immediately to rule out rodents. We'll know soon enough, but she'll just have to wait."

Lucy pondered for a moment, remembering when there was a mouse infestation in one of her old school buildings. She grinned when an idea popped into her head. "What if we get Mistress Grimes a cat? One to warm her lap *and* guard against marauding rodents."

Cora paused to consider the idea. "I like the way you think, Miss Lucy. You're a most resourceful woman. I believe there are several cats in the stable that would do nicely. She can have her pick," she said with a hearty chuckle.

Lucy laughed along, growing increasingly fond of the

housekeeper's light and friendly disposition. It'd been a long time since she'd felt anything akin to a mother's warmth.

"It's decided then," Lucy said happily. "I shall conduct interviews first thing in the morning. As the current lady of this house, it's my solemn duty."

Chapter 3

Nate was raking leaves in front of the mansion the next day when Lucy Ellison surprised him.

"Mr. Bradford," she sang out cheerfully, causing him to halt his work. "Good morning to you, sir. I'm looking for a cat."

Removing his cap, he dragged a hand through his unruly hair. "Say again? You lost your cat?"

"Not my cat, Mr. Bradford. Actually, no one's cat is missing. Perhaps I should start over? I require a housecat. For Mistress Grimes."

"Rats again." He dropped his head with an exasperated huff.

"Indeed. She swears she cannot rest because of all the commotion."

"There are no bloody rats in this house," he erupted. "I searched everywhere. Again, today. Including the cellars. Plus, I've set the blasted traps. Enough to catch a bloomin' army of vermin."

Lucy's smile vanished, and Nate instantly regretted his outburst and crude words.

Yet she took a step closer to him and leaned forward. "There are basements? Perhaps I should investigate. Just to be certain."

Nate squinted at her.

"I sense Mistress Grimes is quite mistaken about the rats. I have my own theory as to where the noises are coming from.

However, she will not relent. Something has her petticoats in a bunch, and I'm determined to find out what it is."

Nate couldn't help himself. He laughed, hard and long. "A cat, you say?" he finally questioned, blowing out a haggard breath. "Well…you know what? That's bloody brilliant." Setting aside his rake, he began walking, and he motioned for her to follow him. "Come along. I know just the fellow."

A short walk later and they were at the stables. Nate opened one of the large barn doors, allowing Lucy to enter first. The place was cool and quiet, the air filled with the scents of hay and horseflesh.

"Pip," he hollered down the center corridor, causing the horses to poke their heads out of their stalls and nicker. "There's a fine lady here to meet you. Hurry up."

The striped tabby took his sweet time getting there, but he eventually sauntered in to sit in front of them. Pip began cleaning his paws, as if he had not a care in the world.

"Come now, Pip, Miss Ellison has a very important job for you. I know you're the best mouser at Fairwinds. You just need to convince her."

The haughty feline glanced up at Lucy with his striking lime-green eyes and gave a loud, "Meow."

The lady made a sweet sound, like the coo of a dove, and she crouched down to pet the ratty barn cat. Pip nuzzled into her gloved hands without hesitation, purring loudly.

"Good day, Mr. Pip. Aren't you a fine, handsome fellow? How would you like to be an indoor cat for a time? I can promise you bowls of fresh cream and plenty of table scraps. *If you'll serve as my chief mouse hunter. You may even sleep on my bed if you wish. Unless Belinda claims you for herself."

Lucy glanced up at Nate wearing a brilliant smile, and his

insides gave a twist. *Lord have mercy if she isn't the prettiest woman I've seen in ages. Bloody cat gets to sleep in her bed. Lucky bastard.*

Despite Lucy's somber clothes of mourning, Nate suddenly envisioned her in something cheerful. A party dress or a ballgown, with her golden-brown hair done up in ribbons and bows. Instead of strangled into the tight bun she wore now beneath the hood of her dark cloak.

No doubt this stunner has a slew of admirers back in Boston.

"I'd best take him right to my mum. She'll want to bathe him if he's going to be in the house." He gave her a sheepish look. "When I was a lad, she'd take whatever stray I'd dragged home and put it in a tub of soapy water. Fleas would travel to the head, so she could pick them off."

Lucy stood and faced him. "So, you like animals then, Mr. Bradford?"

"Don't you?"

"I do, very much so, but we could never have pets growing up. My brother doesn't like them."

"That's unfortunate. Animals enrich a person's life. Like old Pip here. He keeps me company while I tend the farm animals. I think he likes my whistling. And the bit of cow's milk I spill," he added with a cheeky grin.

Lucy studied him. "You seem to have found your voice today, Mr. Bradford. A most pleasing development." She strolled down the walkway, peeking into each stall.

The cat followed, as if instantly smitten.

Nate followed too, enjoying the soft swish of her skirts and the enchanting way her hips swayed. The sight of a beautiful woman after weeks of being sequestered sent his thoughts into a tailspin.

"This is a very large stable. How many animals do you care for?"

Nate shook his head to clear it. "There's the cow and an old work horse that belong to the estate. Then there's my own horse." He pointed to his sorrel mare, munching hay in the corner stall. "Almost forgot. There are chickens."

"Chickens?" She brightened. "May I see them?"

Though he was surprised by her request, Nate led the way out to the fenced portion of the barnyard with the coop.

"There are so many," she said when they entered. Chickens clucked and scrambled, sending feathers flying in every direction.

"Some for eating, some for laying eggs. Though the egg laying has slowed now that it's cold."

"I'd no idea chickens didn't lay eggs in the winter."

"Some do, just not so many. I've not yet checked this morning. Let's see if there are any to be had." He grabbed a basket and showed her how it was done, working his hand beneath a plump hen.

Lucy giggled at him, rooting around while whistling.

"Your turn," he announced.

"Oh, no, I couldn't." She stepped back, hiding her hands behind her back.

"You can. Remove your gloves. I'll help you."

Balking at first, she eventually came forward, and Nate moved close behind to guide her hand. He couldn't resist taking a deep breath of her perfumed scent.

"Oh, my...I don't know." Apprehension filled her voice. "Ooo...I found one," she cried in triumph. She presented her delicate hand, showing him a nice brown egg.

"There, you see. Try again."

She did so, eagerly this time, and together they collected all the eggs there.

Nate snagged her arm once they were outside, causing her to pause. "You've got a bit of fluff…just there," he said, pointing to a place near her eye. "Allow me." His large hand cupped her cheek. Gently, he brushed the tuft of feather from her face.

"Did you get it?" she asked, as she blinked up at him.

Rosy color warmed her smooth cheeks, and Nate couldn't help but stare. The most adorable little freckles dotted the skin around her nose. Her eyes were hazel, he discovered. A blueish green, much like the ocean on a clear summer's day.

"Aye. I got it," he murmured, making one last sweep of her satiny skin though no feathers remained.

Lucy coyly looked away. "Well then, thank you, Mr. Bradford, for a most enjoyable experience." She smiled at him. "Truthfully, that's the most fun I've had in ages."

Nate found himself grinning like a schoolboy. "I'm glad you liked it. Come by anytime to see me. I mean the animals," he rushed to say.

"Good day then, sir." Lucy strolled away, breaking the spell she'd cast upon him.

Say something, you idiot.

"I'll bring the cat round and have him checked for fleas. No need to worry about the rats." Nate groaned, feeling annoyed with himself. *Cats, rats, fleas. Lawyer, my arse. You're no better than a love-struck lad.*

***

"May the angels have mercy on that woman's soul, because she's about to meet her maker," Cora griped when Nate brought Pip into the kitchen for a scrubbing.

"I'm sorry to add to your workload." He winced when she glared at him. "He's to be a housecat. I thought you'd want him clean."

"Ugh...of course, I want him clean. It's that damn woman. She's driving me mad."

Nathaniel held the squirming, yowling cat to his chest, as it eyed the sudsy water with alarm. "I'm assuming you mean Mistress Grimes."

"None other. She's cold, she's bored, she's hungry. Plus, she's written a heap of letters since arriving, *which* she demands I post immediately. As if there were nothing better for me to do. I should have you hitch up that poor old horse with the lousy shoes then drive myself to town to post her blasted letters."

"I'm going to town to fetch the farrier. I'll bring her 'blasted letters' when I go." He handed off poor Pip, who wailed like he was being murdered.

"Buy more traps then, too, Nathaniel. I'll not listen to another word about us 'mistreating and ignoring her.' I'd like to ignore her. With a stick. This will be a very long winter if that woman isn't appeased."

"Why do you think she's so distressed?"

Cora leveled an irritated stare on him. "You know why, Nathaniel. The Captain is not pleased with her presence in his house. He's been slamming doors all day. My poor nerves. I've had to lock most of them again. Do you know, earlier, I heard her disparaging the Captain? She said, 'Any decent man of the sea would know not to sail into a storm.' As if she'd know a decent captain, or a decent man for that matter, from a hole in the ground. She's a vile, ugly woman. Rude to everyone, including dear Miss Lucy. Who's always trying to be kind to her."

Pip got shoved into the wash basin, and Cora waited a minute before picking the fleas from his furry face. Then she hauled him from the tub and doused him with clean water, earning a blood curdling yowl from the traumatized feline.

"I'll not be responsible for my actions if she says anything awful about her ladyship."

Nate grimaced at the thought. "I expect she'll have more to fear than you if she speaks badly of Lady Lillian. The Captain will keelhaul her."

"One can only hope." Cora handed the wet cat to Nate. Pip flew from his arms and went to hide beneath the chair by the fireplace.

"Miss Lucy brought the eggs you two collected this morning," his mother said, switching topics. She gave him a sideways glance. "That was nice of you…giving her a tour of the barnyard."

Nate strolled to the hearth, pretending to examine the meal his mother was assembling. "She's a rather odd woman. She actually wanted to learn about the animals."

Cora wore a telling grin. "She has a bonny face, too. High time you got around to noticing."

"A man can 'notice' all he wants, Mother. But he should know when to steer clear of dangerous waters. We're from two different worlds."

"Don't underestimate yourself, Nathaniel, you're a fine gentleman. I don't know the lady well, but Miss Lucy doesn't appear to be the pretentious type. In fact, she seems quite level-headed."

"And how many suitors do you think this *level-headed*

woman has waiting back in Boston?"

"Oh, I don't know." His mother made a great show of looking around the empty kitchen. "I see no suitors here at Fairwinds. Besides, she's the one who said they're here for an extended stay. That means there's time for affections to blossom. She doesn't talk like a woman longing to return to a busy social schedule."

"I've a busy schedule myself. Or have you forgotten? Especially now that I'm a groundskeeper as well as a solicitor. I don't need a woman complicating my life anymore than it already is."

"Your choice, my dear boy. I'm just saying, I'm impressed by Miss Lucy thus far. My mother's intuition tells me she's a good soul, looking for a safe place after all she's been through."

"Well then, it's settled. I've no desire to be anyone's 'port in a storm,' so to speak. Especially a woman who's destined to leave in a few short months. Or sooner. I hate to say it, but her family has a reputation for being unreliable. Who knows if the lady is the same as her notorious brother? Perhaps we just haven't seen that side of her, as yet."

"I'm right about Miss Lucy. I know it, Nate. There's more to her situation than meets the eye."

"We shall see," he said, shrugging her off.

Cora wiped her hands before collecting the stack of letters. "Here, take these to town then, will you, love? Give your old mum a bit of peace."

Nate undid the twine binding them, and he riffled through the pile. "New York? Why are these not addressed to Boston?"

"I've no idea. Last thing I'll be doing is asking that woman anything more than, *'When are you leaving?'*"

Nate frowned. "You don't understand. All my

correspondences were sent to the last known address, which is Boston. I doubt we'll hear anything back now if the man isn't even there."

"It's shameful." Cora shook her head. "Young Mr. Ellison appears to have sent his sister to deal with his mess. Doesn't seem right. Sending poor Miss Lucy away when she's just lost her father."

"Hopefully, my colleagues can shed some light on the family's situation."

"Best be off, Nate. Time's a wasting."

"Aye. I'll be back before nightfall."

***

"A cat? That's your solution to all my concerns about this horrible place?" Belinda scolded Lucy that evening at the dinner table. "The creature doesn't even like me."

"That's because you make no effort to befriend Pip, to be kind to him," Lucy reasoned.

"I don't care for animals. Dirty, smelly things."

"Mr. Pip had a bath this morning. Mr. Bradford said so."

"But the way the thing stares at me…I don't like it one bit. But if he's all I'm to get, then let him do his job, and be gone."

Lucy smiled at the cat, reclining like a sultan on a silk pillow by the fireplace. "I quite enjoy having Pip around. Today we played with a bit of string and a seagull feather."

"Honestly, Lucy Ellison." Belinda heaved a dramatic sigh. "Must you always make the best of every situation, no matter how grim? It's as if you're perfectly fine with being abandoned here by our brothers."

Cora came into the room just then, carrying a large tray of food.

Lucy greeted her warmly before turning back to Belinda. "I

am fine with being here. How often does one get to stay in a mansion by the sea? It's the stuff of romantic novels."

"Stuffed quails," the housekeeper announced.

"Mmm...They smell delicious, Cora. Mr. Bradford went hunting for us again?"

"Yes, miss."

Lucy beamed. "Please thank him for his efforts on our behalf."

"He went to town and has not yet returned. Truth be told, I'm worried. The way is dangerous in the dark due to the poor state of the road, plus the cart being so old."

"Is there anything I can do?" Lucy asked.

"Not unless you've brought the allowance promised by your father to make repairs. Or a new cart and horse."

"Sadly, no." Lucy frowned and chewed the corner of her bottom lip.

"If there's nothing else then, miss," the housekeeper began.

"No, thank you, Cora. Go and have some dinner yourself. We shall manage on our own."

Belinda gave a clipped laugh once the housekeeper was gone. "The way you mollycoddle these servants. You behave as if you're actually friends with them. Not to mention I think you've taken a shine to that...that...Bradford fellow. You should keep your distance. It's unseemly for a lady to cavort with strange men, let alone common laborers."

"Cavort?" Lucy laughed in her face. "Gathering chicken eggs and finding a cat to hunt for *your mice* is somehow scandalous behavior? Who knew the country was such a hazard to one's virtue?"

"Mark my words, Lucy Ellison." Belinda pointed a finger

at her. "People talk."

"People, what people?" Lucy demanded, glancing around. "You're jealous, Belinda, and well you should be. Cora is a delight. Today she shared stories about Fairwinds and its previous occupants. I found her most entertaining."

"There's nothing to entertain about this monstrosity of a place. Besides, she doesn't like me either."

"Pip doesn't like you. Cora doesn't like you. I'm sensing a trend. Perhaps it is *you* who does not like others? That *you* struggle with being sociable? Maybe if you'd try to get along—"

"Don't you lecture me, Lucy Ellison. I'm many years your senior. Much more knowledge of the world than you. Silly chit. And to think, I'm stuck in this drafty old dungeon because I'm forced to look after you."

"Look after me? Whatever for? I'm perfectly fine on my own. If you're so miserable here, perhaps you should write to your brother. Have him make alternative living arrangements for you. I've grown tired of your constant badgering and complaining."

"Fine," the other woman snapped. She shot to her feet. "If that's how you're going to treat me, I'm going to my room."

"Fine, indeed. This room could use a good airing out." Lucy listened as her whiny housemate stormed off, stomping up the stairs like a chastised child. She leaned back in the chair, kicked off her slippers, and dove into Cora's delicious meal. When she was finished, she licked her fingers in a most unladylike fashion. "Pip," Lucy sang out. "Come and finish Belinda's dinner, my fine, furry friend."

Later that night, Lucy donned her warmest bed clothes and snuggled beneath her covers, settling with a deep sigh of satisfaction. Belinda had stuck to her room since their fight, providing a peaceful evening for a change.

"How dare she tell me what to do in my own home?" Lucy muttered.

My home?

Rebellious thoughts began circulating in her brain.

Could I make Fairwinds my home?

She glanced around the bedchamber, now dusted and aired. The antique furnishings were even polished, gleaming in the light of a freshly filled oil lamp.

"Huh...most pleasant," she said, making a mental note to thank Cora on the morrow.

Lucy opened a favorite Penny Blood to a well-worn page and went straight to her favorite part. Her eyes devoured the words on the pages. The heroine, alone in a mysterious castle, was about to discover a hidden passageway behind a wall, when—

A terrifying scream shattered the silence.

Lucy shot up in bed.

Belinda?

She raced to the door. Another scream came, and she sped up the staircase, through the dark hallway, to the third-floor bedroom. She found the woman inconsolable in the center of the room, wailing and pointing to the French doors that led to the widow's walk. "What's happened?" she cried.

"A face," the frantic woman screeched. "A white face. Like a corpse, pressed to the...the...glass!"

Thunderous footsteps sounded through the walls, and not a moment later, Nathaniel Bradford burst into the room. Belinda screamed again and swooned in Lucy's arms.

Cora arrived—huffing and puffing and holding her chest—

and she went straight to Lucy's aid. Together they lugged Belinda to the bed.

"What?" he demanded.

"I've no idea," Lucy said, meeting the other's alarmed stares with one of her own. "She said there was a face, pressed to the glass."

Mr. Bradford went to investigate. "There's no one. And the way is barred." He jostled the tightly latched door to prove his point.

Belinda moaned as she began to come around.

"Do you have any smelling salts?" Lucy asked the housekeeper.

"Aye. They're as old as me, but I'll get them."

"I shall require cool water and a cloth as well."

Cora went straight away to fetch the things, but Lucy called after her. "Bring them to my room. Mistress Grimes shall stay with me tonight."

"I can't and I won't," the distraught woman cried.

"Calm yourself, Belinda. You're safe with me," Lucy said in her steadiest tone. "I shall protect you from whatever is tormenting you." She looked to the housekeeper. "Hurry, please, Cora."

"But it was right there," Belinda insisted through her sobs. "A face so white. Like a dead thing. And her eyes glowed red, like hot coals."

"*Her eyes?*"

"Yes, it was a woman," she yelled.

Lucy's stare connected with Nathaniel Bradford's darkening gaze. He checked the door again and shook his head. Helping Belinda from the bed, Lucy wrapped her own bed jacket around her, and started for the doorway. He followed, taking the lamp from the room, and going ahead to guide their steps.

"Wait." He handed the lamp off to Lucy before sweeping the other woman up in his burly arms as if she weighed no more than a child.

A few minutes later, Belinda was tucked safely into Lucy's bed with Cora by her side, administering water and salts.

"Mr. Bradford?" Lucy called softly before he could leave. "Something, or someone, is tormenting Mistress Grimes. Please, can you shed any light on what is happening here?"

Firelight cast the man's troubled face in shadows. "I'd rather not say."

"It was that blasted cat," Belinda accused, overhearing them from the bed. "It hissed at the door. When I looked, there she was, pale as death. Glaring at me with those hideous, red eyes."

Lucy took Mr. Bradford by the arm and led him to the far corner of the room. "I know this house is haunted. Don't try to pretend otherwise with me. This night is most disturbing."

Nate rubbed the bridge of his nose. "Aye."

"Is that all you've got to say for yourself? Now is not the time to stop talking, Mr. Bradford."

He tipped his head toward the women in the bed. "That's all I think you'll be wanting me to say right now. Given the lady's delicate condition."

Lucy grimaced. "I see your point. We must make time to speak in private. Perhaps, tomorrow morning we can—"

"I'm leaving tomorrow," Belinda vowed, talking over them. "I'll not spend another night in this house of horrors."

"But—" Lucy started.

"No buts. That man, servant, whatever he is, is driving me

to Mystic Point as soon as it's light enough to leave. I will find a coach there to take me back to civilization. My mind is made up, Lucy Ellison. Do not try to persuade me otherwise."

Lucy's gaze flipped back to the silent man. "You'd best take her to town. Will she be able to get back to Boston by herself from there?"

Nate rubbed a hand through his disheveled hair. "There's a regular coach. If there's space, I'll make sure she's on it. If not, there's an inn. It's safe and relatively clean. I know the proprietor. He'll look after her if I ask him to."

"Thank you, Mr. Bradford. I've a bit of money saved up."

He gently touched her hand, stopping her. "No need, miss. I'll see to it the lady is safely on her way."

The cat chose that moment to wander into Lucy's bedroom through the cracked door, and Belinda began to scream again.

Nate scooped the credulous cat up. "Off to the kitchen with you, Pip. We've had enough excitement for one night. Come on, Mum, let's leave these ladies to rest. If that's even possible."

The next morning, true to his word, Nathaniel Bradford drove Belinda to town with all her belongings.

Lucy knew her companion was indeed desperate to leave Fairwinds because she hoisted herself up into the wagon without assistance. Quite prepared, was she, to endure the rough road in the run-down, open cart for what promised to be a raw and dismal ride.

Chapter 4

Nathaniel walked silently through the dark halls of Fairwinds, heading for the library. The place his mother said Lucy waited for him.

Memories of her beauty the night before still unsettled him. Long hair undone and falling about her shoulders like a shiny brown curtain. Her naked form, barely visible beneath her nightgown. She'd been a silhouette of curves against the backdrop of the fire's glow. The globes of her breasts, swaying as she adamantly plead her case that Fairwinds was haunted.

Aye, the house is haunted. But dare I speak the truth I've come to know?

Fear that Lucy Ellison would leave Fairwinds like all the rest, once she learned the extent of the hauntings, left a pit in Nate's stomach. Whether he liked it or not, he was powerfully attracted to the new lady of the house.

Approaching the library door, he eased it open to peer inside. Lucy sat before the large, ornate fireplace in one of the old wing-back chairs. She wore a simple grey dress, her hair pinned up and tamed again. *Reserved and distant. Somber in her loss.* About her shoulders was his mother's favorite, thick shawl to ward off the November chill. Pip slumbered in her lap alongside a discarded book.

"Penny for your thoughts," he murmured upon entering.

Lucy startled, yet her gaze warmed when connecting with his.

"I'm sorry I frightened you."

"You didn't." She gave him a weary smile. "I was but lost in my thoughts."

"I see Pip is off duty tonight," he teased.

"Yes, he hasn't found a single thing to interest him in the house, proving my theory. Fairwinds has a ghost problem, not a rodent problem."

Nate sat beside her in a twin chair, and he held his cold hands out to the fire. "My mum said you've been in here for hours. And that you didn't want dinner."

"I'm not hungry." She glanced around them. "I am, though, quite fond of this part of the house. I imagine it was most impressive when these carved, mahogany bookshelves were filled with volumes."

"Like the library at my university. They had a sitting room with a fireplace, tucked away, so it was often empty. It was my favorite place to work."

Lucy gave him an admiring smile, as she stroked the sleepy cat. Nate watched her graceful fingers, transfixed as they glided through Pip's striped fur.

"Thank you for seeing Mistress Grimes safely to town."

"She's onboard a coach bound for Boston already," he explained. "Didn't waste a second looking back."

"Did she say where she would go after Mystic Point? Would she stay in Boston, for example?" Lucy asked, sounding genuinely concerned for the woman, who was often cruel to her.

"She's not one for sharing, especially with the hired help. Didn't utter a word the entire way there. Except to threaten my life should I let anything happen to you."

Lucy tipped her head and frowned. "How very odd. I've the sense Belinda secretly loathes me, yet she worries for my safety?"

"I imagine she'll head to New York, since your brother and hers are purportedly there."

"Cora told me about the letters. Lance said he was going to New York, but I've no further knowledge of his plans." She released a worn-out sigh. "My brother and I have a very strained relationship. More so since he seized our family home—the house we both grew up in—right from under me. That is why I am here at Fairwinds. I've nowhere else to go."

Nate crossed his arms, irritated by what appeared to be more erratic behavior on the part of Lucy's brother. "I jotted down the address. Figure I'll try writing again in hopes of getting an answer. However, I won't be holding my breath."

"I wouldn't. My brother does as he pleases." She set the cat down. "Believe me, I understand, this is all very untoward. I cannot believe any of this is happening. My father always managed to control Lance, at least up until the last few years. Now I fear the worst. Perhaps you and your mother should go. I've no idea when you'll get paid for your service."

"There's no need, miss. We'll manage until arrangements can be made." Nate cleared his throat, recognizing he'd drifted into uncharted waters. The entire way back from town, he'd thought of nothing but remaining close to Lucy, despite being long overdue to return to his law firm. Did he stand a chance with this extraordinary woman? Was it worth the risk to find out?

Lucy smiled as if sensing his thoughts. "Please call me Lucy. I'm tired of formality. I miss hearing my own name spoken in casual conversation." She put on a brave face yet sniffled. "Father and I used to talk for hours. Now I no longer even speak of him."

"Whyever not?" he asked.

Her bravery crumbled as her lips began to quiver. "Because there's no one who wishes to listen."

Nate dug through his pockets, and he handed her his handkerchief.

"Did you know my father was a scholar? He loved researching topics like ancient Greece and Rome. Especially Egypt with it's hidden treasures." She dabbed at her watery eyes. "Lance never got along with Father, but I did. Honestly, I don't think Lance gets along with anyone except the Grimes siblings. Which I cannot comprehend."

"I've never had the pleasure of meeting your brother or Mr. Grimes."

"Consider yourself blessed. Lance sold our home in one day. The very day I returned. Immediately thereafter, Belinda and I were tossed into a coach and unceremoniously deposited here." Lucy gave a bitter laugh. "I did make him drive me to the cemetery first though. I refused to leave without visiting our father's grave. He waited in the carriage. Cowardly knave."

She bowed her head, staring at her tightly clasped hands. "I worry about what my father's life was like in the end. God willing, he's at peace with my mother now. You see…" Her voice hitched on a sob. "Mother died giving me life. Lance has never forgiven me or our father for our parts in her death."

Nate's heart gave a powerful lurch. Family struggles and loss were no strangers to him. Ignoring all propriety, he hauled Lucy into his lap and wrapped sheltering arms around her. She didn't protest. In fact, she thanked him, and wept softly against his chest, with her head tucked beneath his chin.

"Forgive me, I…"

"No, I understand. It's a horrible thing to lose a parent. I feel for you from the depths of my soul. My father was the captain of a merchant vessel. My only brother served alongside him. They died together in a fire at sea."

"Oh, I'm so sorry." She gazed up at him with renewed tears. "How dreadful for you and your poor mother."

"I was a tall, skinny lad when it happened. Mum made me swear I'd never take to the sea as they'd done. Words and numbers—the law—those things became my entire world. I worked hard, finished school, went on to university, and joined a firm with a division specializing in maritime matters. So, I suppose, I still have my connection to the sea. I make a good living as a solicitor. Enough to care for my mother as she deserves. Yet she prefers to live here at Fairwinds."

"Why is that?" Lucy asked, her tears subsiding, as she focused solely on him and his life story.

Nate tightened his protective hold on her. "She grew up in this area and has fond memories. She'll tell you it's because she found peace here when my father and brother died. That caring for this old mansion gave her purpose again. A family in residence—eight or nine years ago now—hired her as a governess for their three children. They left. She remained. It was your father who offered her the permanent position of caretaker."

"I'd no idea our parents knew each other. I'll have to ask Cora about it. But...tell me...how did you end up here?" she inquired.

"Once I'd completed my education, I made a promise to visit. This was my first chance to make the trip. You know the rest." Nate shook his head in disbelief. "Now I'm a lawyer that chops wood and cares for farm animals."

Lucy wriggled from his lap, and she mumbled another

apology before returning to her own chair. "Mr. Bradford, it's high time we speak of these troubling hauntings."

Nate stood and went to the fireplace, stoking the flames with the iron poker. "Only if you'll call me Nathaniel. Or, better yet, Nate." With her quick nod, he took a deep breath and launched into sharing what he knew. "My mother has heard the footsteps for years. Sounds. Like a man marching about on the upper floors. And the doors, slamming. At first, she was frightened, thinking there was an intruder. Yet no one was ever found. Now, she believes it's the ghost of Captain Wilder."

"The pirate captain?"

"Aye, the same. He and his lady love were torn apart over a hundred years ago. He died in a violent storm at sea, she from a broken heart. Or at least that's how the story goes."

"My father told me about them when I was a little girl. We're related to Abigail Langdon, sister to Lillian Langdon, the Captain's wife. Abigail became a Gibson when she married."

"Surely you jest?" Nate gave a surprised laugh. "My mother's kin were Wilders. Descendants of Aiden Wilder, the Captain's only brother." He twisted the ends of his mustache, as he contemplated the new bit of information. "That's an odd twist of fate, don't you think? That the two of us, both with ties to Fairwinds, should end up here at the same time?"

"Most odd. And yet compelling all the same," she revealed with a shy smile.

Even in the low light, Nate sensed Lucy was blushing. Perhaps it was the way she stared at her hands in her lap. Or the way she tilted her head, refusing to meet his gaze. *Could she be attracted to me as well?*

"If Captain Wilder's ghost roams these halls," she began, "then was it he who frightened Belinda into leaving?"

"I don't think so. Legend says Lillian Wilder died on that third-floor widow's walk. Just outside the door to where Belinda said she saw the face."

"So, there are two ghosts to contend with here?"

Nate leaned a shoulder against the mantle. "Well, the lady is buried on those same cliffs, after all." He pointed toward the back of the house. "That's the place folks most often see her ghost. Especially sailors, returning from long voyages. She's called the White Lady of Fairwinds. A specter, white as snow, with eyes, glowing like twin rubies. She's been spied pacing the rocky edge with a lamp. The folktales are at least a century old now."

Lucy's stare fixed on him. She didn't appear to breathe. "Well, what happened next?" she demanded. "How does the story end?"

Nate chuckled at her intensity. "It doesn't, I'm afraid. No one knows what becomes of lost souls. Strange things have occurred at this place for as long as anyone can remember. Because the house sits empty for so long, interest fades, people come and go, and the tales dwindle to nothing more than the tittle tattle of locals. Until something happens again. Such as a man falling to his death from those cliffs."

"Do you think the ghosts had anything to do with his demise?"

"I've no idea."

They were quiet for a few minutes, both staring into the flickering flames. Logs sizzled and popped, as the lonely night settled in around them.

"Why are you so late returning?" Lucy blurted out,

switching subjects. "Your mother was quite concerned."

"Two women, looking after me now? I didn't know they allowed ladies in The Watch," he teased with a wink.

Lucy scoffed. "Forgive me, sir, for considering your welfare."

"Now, now, don't be cross. Don't you want to see the surprise I've brought you?" He watched her straighten in her seat. "There's a shop in Mystic Point that sells goods from old ships. Bits and bobbles. Mostly junk. But sometimes…I find a treasure."

"Fine, torment me, Mr. Bradford," she teased. "I'll not use your Christian name if you behave like this."

"Alright, give a man a chance. When you said you'd been cooped up for a long time, and that you liked being at sea, I thought you might enjoy something I discovered in that shop."

A sassy smile turned her pretty pink lips. "Well, are you going to tell me, or is this some lawyer's tactic? Torturing the jury to death?"

"How about I show you instead?" Nate stood and extended a hand to her. Lucy accepted it without hesitation, slipping her small hand into his.

*Softness against my callused hands…*He closed his eyes for a moment, savoring the pleasant feeling.

Together they walked to the foyer. Nate donned his heavy coat and collected a lantern and a pile of folded blankets.

"Blankets?" She eyed him with suspicion. "What manner of *surprise* is this?"

"You're an impatient lass. Has anyone ever told you that?"

"Often. I'm also accused of being exceedingly romantic and that I read too much. Are there any other vices I should admit to?"

"Well then, I think you'll like my surprise." He led her through the stained-glass doorway to the small rotunda at the back of the house. There they exited onto the stone patio.

Night wind had diminished to a mere breath. In the distance? The rhythmic sounds of the sea. A million stars hung above them, sparkling pinpoints in a cloudless sky.

"Oh, Nate, it's breathtaking." Lucy sighed. "I haven't seen a sky like this since I was aboard ship." She turned to him with a delighted smile. Her gaze shot to the lone chair and the item he'd covered with a dust sheet from the house. "Is that your surprise?"

"Aye." He pulled the sheet, revealing a shiny brass telescope on a wooden tripod.

Lucy's gasp of excitement made the high price he'd paid for the device well worth it. "It supposedly came off a British warship, yet it's been mounted, so it can be used on dry land. Do you like it?"

"Like it?" she exclaimed, "I adore it. May I?"

With an eager nod, he watched as she sat to gaze through the eyepiece. Her long, sooty lashes fluttered until she focused. "Look at them all. They're so close, I feel as if I could reach out and touch them."

"It appears so, yet they're much farther away than you or I could ever imagine. The moon will rise soon," he promised. "Then you'll see something truly amazing."

Nate positioned blankets on Lucy's lap and around her shoulders before pulling a small, worn book from his pocket. "A guide to the heavens," he explained, leaning close to share with her. "My father gave this to me when I was a lad. Said I'd never get lost if I studied the stars."

They stayed outside together until they were both nearly

frozen. Finally, reluctantly, they collected all the things and brought them inside.

Lucy was shivering when Nate accompanied her to the bottom step of the staircase. The house was quiet, and he lingered, enjoying a few more moments of her company.

"Thank you, Nathaniel. I genuinely appreciate your thoughtful surprise. And your company."

"We can do this again. If you'd like," he hedged, trying not to appear too eager.

"I would like that. Very much." She took one step up and hesitated. "Perhaps tomorrow night?"

Nate couldn't hold back a broad smile. "Aye."

Lucy climbed another step. "Of course, we could do something different if it's cloudy." She faced him again with a coy smile. "That is…*if* you have time."

"I'll make time for you," he murmured with a roguish grin.

They stood together. Neither of them speaking. Both fidgeting in place.

On impulse, Nate captured Lucy's hand and brought it to his lips. "Until tomorrow then." He placed a chaste kiss upon her chilled knuckles, lingering a hair's breadth above her skin before adding a second.

In one beat of his hopeful heart, she rushed down the staircase and slipped into his arms. Her palms came to rest on his chest beneath his coat. Wide eyes—filled with wonder—she gazed up at him. Unable to resist, he dipped his head and brushed her lips with his. One kiss, then another. Three to be sure she knew just how much he desired her.

Like a doe startled in the forest, Lucy sprang up the stairs and disappeared down the hallway.

Nate heard her bedroom door click closed before he took

his first full breath. He shook his head, marveling at how life made sudden and dramatic shifts. His entire body hummed with longing for the woman he hadn't known existed a few short days ago.

The entire way back to the cottage, he whistled a happy tune and thought of nothing but seeing Lucy again. Tomorrow could not come soon enough.

***

Lucy sank to the edge of her bed, staring at the hand Nate just kissed. She touched her lips and closed her eyes, as a shiver of delight swept through her.

My first kiss.

She squealed with happiness.

"A lawyer that chops wood and cares for farm animals." She considered his words. "Oh, but you're so much more, Nathaniel Bradford." Flopping back to the bed, she giggled like a schoolgirl. "Is this how it feels to be in love?"

I've never met anyone like Nate. Smart, strong, caring, witty. He even shares my love of books and stargazing.

Lucy let her mind wander to where her heart was already rushing.

Forget about Edmund Grimes and his awful sister. Forget about Lance, and trying to appease him. If she searched her heart for who it truly desired, it was Nate. *How wonderful would it be to stay at Fairwinds with him and Cora? More love, family, and happiness than I dreamed possible.*

But how to do it? How to stay and have her dreams come true?

Lance would never live in such a remote place, she reasoned. *Besides, if I don't marry his best friend, he'll never have a reason to visit. With Belinda gone, might I not be free to do as I wish?*

"I would love to make Fairwinds my home," Lucy admitted out loud, speaking to herself and the presumptive ghost of Captain Wilder. She glanced about the room, hoping for some sign of him. "Would you help me, Captain? Would you and your lady mind very much if I stayed? What if I restored your home to its former glory? I'm not certain how I'll accomplish such a feat, but I'll try my best. And, if I stay, no one will ever bother you. You have my word."

Still nothing. No footsteps. No phantom breezes.

A plan began formulating in Lucy's head.

"What if I use my family heirloom to start the restoration process? It's a remarkable piece—a large ruby ring—worth a small fortune. It's the only thing of value I possess. Sadly, it was a gift from my late father. But perhaps this is what he meant years ago, when he said I shall 'know what to do with it when the time comes?'"

The room suddenly chilled. Gooseflesh spread over Lucy's skin. She sensed a presence—a physical force—in the room with her.

"Good evening, Captain." She attempted a calm tone. Though inside, she was frightened at the prospect of purposefully summoning a ghost to aid her. The candle flickered wildly, and she trembled.

"I don't know if you're in agreement. Or if you'd rather I leave post-haste." She forced a brave smile. "Either way, I'd like to reassure you I have the noblest of intentions. I would never do anything to…for example…extricate you from the premises. I rather like having ghosts about. Odd as this may sound, I feel rather protective of you both and this special place."

Lucy waited for some sort of response or reaction, though none came. Instead, she heard his phantom footsteps above her head, pacing the third floor.

What could it mean?

"Good night then, Captain," she whispered. "I suppose you're right. I've had enough excitement for one day."

Chapter 5

"Good morning, Cora," Lucy said upon entering the sunny kitchen the following morning. She removed her cloak, hat, and gloves before handing off a basket with one lone egg in it.

"You're up early," the older lady replied as she set the kettle to the flame.

"I went for a walk to visit Lady Lillian."

Cora wore a slight frown. "Did you now?"

"I like talking with her, even though I know she doesn't respond quite as readily as the Captain does." Lucy watched the housekeeper's profile, attempting to gauge her reaction to the intentionally provoking statement.

"Tea and scones?" Cora asked.

"Most certainly, but only if I may dine here with you."

The housekeeper paused to study her. She arched one brow. An expression, much like that of her son's.

"I've decided I'd like to take all my meals here with you and Nate."

Cora went back to preparing tea, yet Lucy sensed her thoughts, buzzing like anxious bees. To her credit, the lady revealed no emotion save for a hint of a smile. "Have a seat then, as long as you won't miss dining in the formal room. The kitchen is warmer, I suppose."

"I'm not asking because I wish to be warm. Well, in manner of speaking, I am. I desire friendly conversations here with you and Nate. That would warm my heart better than any stuffy old dining room."

"That's very kind of you, Miss Lucy. I'll set a place for you tonight. And invite Nate back to take his meals."

"Thank you. But there's one more thing I'd like your help with."

"Yes, miss?"

Lucy rubbed her chin. "I shall require an apron, some rags, a bucket of water, and wood polish. I believe that's it for now."

Cora looked puzzled. "That's a mouthful of a list. What've you got in mind, taking over my job?"

"As if I could." Lucy chuckled. "I've never cooked a meal in my life. We'd all starve to death." She sat down with her tea and scones. "I'm going to begin the monumental task of refurbishing Fairwinds. One room at a time, I shall attempt to make this house sparkle and shine again."

Cora beamed. "Well, the old girl will be right pleased about that."

"Old girl? Who exactly do you mean, the house or Lady Lillian?"

"Both."

"And the Captain?" Lucy snuck in. She was met with a smirk and a hands-on-the-hips pose from the housekeeper.

"The Captain, indeed. I suppose he'll be happy enough. Although who am I to speak for the departed? I see Nate's told you about our resident spirits. That's to be expected after all the commotion with Mistress Grimes. Providing he hasn't frightened you too much.

"I'm not frightened. It appears as if you're not either.

"Some of their ghostly antics scare me, but I've got this part of the house all to myself. They never stomp around or show themselves here in the kitchen, for some strange reason." Cora finished what she was doing and turned to Lucy. "There's a bit of strangeness I could use your opinion on now that you know. I discovered it this morning in the rotunda."

"Oh?" Lucy put a hand over her bulging mouth, full of Cora's delicious scones.

"Muddy footprints. I find them on occasion."

"But who do they belong to?"

"Can't say as I know. It's yet another Fairwinds mystery. But given the way the Captain patrols the house...There are no intruders, nothing ever amiss. All the doors and windows are secured. There's just a mess for me to clean up. It's like having boys again, traipsing about the house with their muddy boots."

"Extraordinary," Lucy murmured.

Just as Cora said, there *were* muddy footprints across the compass rose depicted in mosaic tiles on the floor of the rotunda. It was as if someone tracked across the space—passing through the wall—to stand at the window. The prints didn't exit the room. They simply ended.

"But Nathaniel and I were outside last night. Surely, we'd have seen someone standing here," Lucy surmised. At Cora's questioning glance, she added, "He was showing me the stars. He purchased a new telescope and wished to test it."

"Is that so?" the clever woman replied.

Lucy retraced the steps from the wall to the windows and huffed in confusion. Her gaze traveled from the domed ceiling to the faded mural, which replicated a bird's-eye view of Skullery Bay. She pointed to a brass keyhole on the curved wall. "Why is there a keyhole on the wall, and yet no door?"

Nate strolled in at that very moment. "Ah, but there is a door. A *secret door*," he said, grinning. He pressed a spot alongside the keyhole, and a soft click sounded. A hidden doorway creaked open.

Lucy stepped forward. "Upon my soul."

"It's a pressure lock," he explained.

She leaned into the darkness beyond the doorway. Cobwebs cloaked a metal, spiral staircase, which disappeared into hollowness above and below. "Oh, that does look rather ominous. Where does it lead?"

"I've only ventured part of the way," he admitted. "Up leads to a trap door on the third-floor. Down leads to the cellar and beneath the butler's pantry."

Lucy stared at him, wide-eyed. "Are you telling me there are hidden passageways in this house?"

Nate smirked. "I've a sinking feeling I'll come to regret this. But, yes, there are passageways and tunnels. This *was* a pirate's haven, after all. The one from the basement continues, but it ends in a collapse. I could go no further when I tried to investigate."

"Well, let's go then. I want to see these tunnels for myself."

Nate caught her by the arm when she attempted to push past him. "Not so fast, it's dangerous."

Cora chimed in. "Nate's right, it's not safe. Your father warned me about them years ago. They're centuries old, and God only knows what's lurking down there."

Lucy's voice spiked. "My father knew, and he never told me?"

"Probably because he knew you'd try to explore them," Nate countered.

"Like father, like daughter," Cora agreed, shaking her head. "Your father said he'd been down there, and there was nothing to see. I thought he was daft for going alone. He might have died, and no one would've known."

Nate focused on Lucy. "Swear to me you will not go

beyond this door by yourself."

She balked.

"Lucy...please...promise me."

"Oh, very well, fine. I'll not go beyond this door. Unless someone is with me. Even if it's a ghost," she added quickly, earning a dark scowl from both mother and son.

***

"I don't know the legends as well as Mum does," Nate admitted at dinner that night.

"That simply will not do, sir," Lucy declared in mock outrage. "I must know how Lillian Langdon, my great, great, great something aunt, came to marry a notorious pirate. Surely they didn't meet on a crowded dance floor."

"Oh, it's a romantic story," Cora gushed, as she sipped her homemade spiced wine.

Nate rolled his eyes, sensing he'd lost all control of the conversation.

"You see...the lady fell in love with the man, despite her family's objections. When her father tried to separate them, by shipping her off to England, the Captain stormed the lady's ship and whisked her away to Fairwinds. I wish I could say their story ended happily though."

"Nate told me the Captain died not long into their marriage. A shipwreck in a storm?"

"Aye," Nate dove in again. "Alongside his brother, Aiden Wilder. Our distant relation."

Lucy nibbled her lips. "That part of the story is awful. Yet this whole thing is very strange if you ask me. Our relations intertwined around this very place. To think, they walked these halls together, likely even dined here in this room."

"They wouldn't have dined here," Cora clarified. "Of

course, there's always been a kitchen. But the hallway you take to get there was added decades later to connect to the house. And my small bedroom is just there." She pointed to her adjoining quarters. "In the Captain's and Lady Lillian's day, this was an outdoor kitchen. I suppose it kept the heat and noise from the main house."

"I would like to have seen Fairwinds back then," Lucy said with a dreamy look. "The ballroom, for example. You can tell it was spectacular. Two entire walls of windows, with French doors to the patio. The golden trim is all but gone now, but that sky mural on the ceiling…I spent an hour the other day, gazing up at it."

"It's said there were grand parties here at Fairwinds," Cora shared. "Margaretha Langdon, Lillian and Abigail's mother, was a renowned hostess. She was the one who commissioned that hundred-foot arbor. Only the bare bones of the thing remain, but you can imagine it was once a wonder to behold."

"That's odd you mention the arbor," Lucy said. "When I was outside at the grave of Lady Lillian, I swear I smelled roses. It's quite impossible, I know, given it's practically winter. Do you think it has something to do with her ghost? A sign or message, perhaps?"

Nate butt in, attempting to steer the conversation away from ghostly things. "The *Margaretha* was a ship. Dutch. Belonging to Lillian's father, Everett Langdon. I believe it sank."

"What was the name of Captain Wilder's ship?" Lucy asked.

Nate frowned, acknowledging they were right back where they started. Begrudgingly, he muttered, *"The Phantom."*

Everyone fell silent, as if speaking the name of the ill-fated ship deserved their reverence.

"I need to say something." Lucy got a rather fierce, determined look upon her face. "I want to stay here at Fairwinds. It's my intention to make this place my home."

Nate's thoughts spun off in a thousand different directions. He longed to keep Lucy close, to spend time with her, know her better, court her properly. Yet his law firm was losing patience with his prolonged absence. He must return to Boston or face the very real possibility of losing his position.

"That would be delightful. I'll help, miss, any way I can," Cora pledged.

Nate climbed onboard despite his concerns, revealing, "I took a small step in that direction yesterday."

Lucy's gaze shot to him. "How so?"

"Come and have a look." He pushed back from the table.

Lucy sprang to her feet, yet she paused and turned to Cora. "Let's help with these dishes. Your mother's fine cooking should not be rewarded with more work."

"Get out of my kitchen," Cora ordered. "I'm not accustomed to having so many bodies about. Day in and day out, you're both underfoot. Worse than that old barn cat."

Nate kissed his mother's brow and murmured, "Thank you," before escorting Lucy from the room. She freely took his arm, and they walked together down the long hallway.

He captured her hand when they reached the foyer, demanding, "Close your eyes."

Lucy gave him a wary look.

"Did you not enjoy my last surprise?"

"Yes, but whenever my brother said, 'close your eyes,' it meant he intended to put spiders in my hair. Or some other childish nonsense."

"*I* am not your brother, madam. Nor am I a child," he remarked in a haughty tone.

Lucy promptly closed her eyes, allowing him to guide her into the library.

"It feels lovely in here tonight, all warm and welcoming," she said with her eyes still closed.

"I stoked the fire before we ate." He leaned close. Wisps of her soft, perfume-scented hair tickled his face. "You may open your eyes now."

Lucy's frown transformed into a glorious smile when she did. "Oh, Nate," she cried upon seeing stacks and stacks of books arranged around the room. "Wherever did they all come from? There must be hundreds."

Happiness and pride swelled in him. "The same shop where I bought the telescope. Apparently, a wealthy customer no longer wanted them, and he sold the lot."

"It's madness." She spun to take them all in. "To give up such a treasure. There must be an entire library here."

"There are more books in crates in the barn. I couldn't get them all inside without you seeing me. I wanted this to be a surprise."

"It's a wonderful surprise, but the cost. Why would you do this for me?"

"Do they please you?"

"Most assuredly. I'm delighted."

"Then you have your answer." He milled around the books, picking up random volumes to study their covers. "I'd planned to wait until we knew each other better, but since clouds have ruined our stargazing…"

"Nathaniel?" She ambled across the room to stand before

him. "May I ask you something?"

"Of course, anything."

Lucy eased closer to him. "Why did you kiss me last night?"

Nate's attention snapped to her upturned face. Eyes the color of a tumultuous sea stared back at him. The sudden urge to kiss her grew overwhelming. "I couldn't help myself. Did you mind very much?"

"It was my first kiss," she informed him.

Nate dropped his head. "Forgive me. I'd no right to steal it from you."

"What if I ask you to kiss me again?" She slid her hands up his chest to rest over his thudding heart.

He needed no further invitation and pulled Lucy into his arms. He sealed his lips to hers. As she melted against him with a soft womanly moan, he became caught up again in his hunger for her.

Agony. Sweet, sweet torture.

It was the only way he could think to describe the tempest, twisting his insides.

Nate deepened their kiss. Soon the back of his shirt was being bunched up in her anxious hands. Tempting her with the slide of his tongue, she opened her lips for him.

Lucy's mouth was delectable, spiced by the wine they'd both drunk with dinner. Her tongue swirled with his, and he groaned against her sugared lips. Sublime heat shot straight to his groin. His cock responded instantly to the press of her feminine curves.

"Pie, anyone?" Cora called out from the foyer.

Lucy jumped away as if she'd been doused with icy sea water.

"No. Thank you," Nate answered in a rather brusque tone. "I believe we've had enough sweets for one night."

Lucy covered her mouth to smother a giggle.

"Very well. More for me then."

Cora's footsteps echoed down the hallway, and they both dissolved into laughter.

***

Before heading to bed, Lucy returned to the library to extinguish all the lamps. She and Nate had shared passionate kisses on the front steps. So many, in fact, that an anxious, impatient sort of feeling had her craving more time together. More of him, to be precise.

She'd never dreamed kissing could be so thrilling. Nate's first chaste kisses were nothing compared to what they'd shared tonight. Pressed against his strong, hard body…Her blood had boiled.

Other ladies at her school had gossiped about kissing and caressing the way they did tonight. They spoke of elaborate schemes to sneak away to be alone with male admirers. Yet Lucy never understood the appeal of such escapades. Until tonight, that is.

She felt all warm and wonderful inside because of Nate. Truly, she was falling in love with him.

With a frustrated sigh, she picked up the last candlestick and left the library. But instead of going straight to bed, she paused before the glass doorway to the rotunda. With Nate gone, Cora abed, and Pip dozing before the fire, Fairwinds was far too quiet for her liking. Adventure called. A powerful lure she never could resist.

Approaching the secret doorway to the spiral staircase, she shivered with anticipation. *What mysteries lie within this old* house? She wondered as she traced the outline of the old door and felt extreme cold beyond.

"If I was wise, I'd be in bed," she muttered to herself.

Yet one push, and the hidden door opened, revealing a yawning darkness beyond.

Nate's words came rushing back to her. *Swear to me you will not go beyond this door by yourself.*

A promise was a promise, but still...*What harm could come of one, small peek?*

Dank, stale air assaulted her senses the moment she leaned in, causing her breath to catch. The candle sputtered and nearly snuffed out, as she eased onto the metal stairway. The ancient thing quivered and groaned in protest. A jolt of fright shot through her, and she jumped back.

Cora's concerns for her father repeated in her head. *I thought he was daft for going alone. He might have died, and no one would've known.*

The lady was right, of course. And so was Nate. Lucy could feel the danger, oozing from the place. *One lone woman with a candle? Help, if needed, would not come until dawn. If ever.*

Lucy sealed the doorway and turned away from its temptation.

Tomorrow, she vowed. *I'll convince Nate to investigate with me.* But for tonight, she'd keep her word, and leave the secrets of Fairwinds to the ghosts.

She was about to head to bed when the door to the ballroom inched open with a long, drawn-out creak. Tiny hairs bristled on Lucy's skin. "Hello?" she said, as she poked her head inside. "Is anyone there?"

The only answer came from the wind and the rustling leaves upon the patio beyond.

Strolling to the center of the old parquet dance floor, she set her lowly candle down. The single flame withered in the room's vastness. Still, she tried to envision the ballroom ablaze with a thousand lights. Candelabras in front of the once gilded mirrors. The scents of beeswax and smoke, filling the heat-laden air.

She closed her eyes and began to sway from side to side, imagining glorious music playing. *A Waltz – how divine.* Her arms raised, and she smiled, as if she danced with a handsome partner. Of course, it would be with Nate. *What a dashing figure he would be in evening clothes.*

Lucy opened her eyes and slammed to a halt.

The White Lady danced out on the patio—the mirror image of herself.

The ghostly figure paused, as if sensing she'd been discovered. Soulful, dark eyes bore into Lucy through the thin glass of the doors.

"Lady...Lillian...?" Lucy stammered. Her heart hammered painfully in her chest. "I'm...honored t...t...to...meet you."

Mist swirled around the eerie visage. It spread like tendrils, morphing into long, flowing hair and the outline of a dress. The spirit was indeed white, rippling like an icy flame.

Before Lucy could say anything more, the lady dissolved into the night breeze.

Lucy sank to the cold floor with a cry of disbelief. Never had she experienced anything so frightening.

Still, there was no harm done to her.

The ghost woman's face, though unclear, was more than just a vision. It was a memory, seared into Lucy's mind. A thing, not to be unseen or forgotten. The lady wore no grimace. No snarl of rage. Merely a look of utter emptiness and sorrow.

Lucy's heart instantly went out to the dead woman. *Why did she remain at Fairwinds? Merely to stare in at the living? A stranger, dancing in her ballroom?*

If it was indeed the spirit of Lady Lillian Wilder, it seemed the cruelest of fates to be denied heaven. To haunt the home she once loved. Earthbound. Alone, and forgotten.

And yet...was she alone and forgotten? Was not the Captain still here within this house? *And I'm here, too...somehow connected to her.*

Lucy began to tremble in earnest.

Tunnels, hidden passageways, and ghosts. Spirits in the night. No wonder the house remained empty for so long.

Was it a mistake to call Fairwinds home?

***

Long days followed, and Lucy worked tirelessly to fulfil her promise to the Captain and herself, despite her concerns. She told no one about the chilling encounter in the ballroom. Instead, she scrubbed, scraped, and polished the old house.

Some things could not stand up to her efforts, and they would need to be replaced. Others were in desperate need of repairs. And still other parts were already beyond saving.

Yet some amazing features of the grand old mansion rose like a phoenix from the ashes. Shiny and bright once more, coming to life with but a bit of elbow grease.

One such architectural element was the many staircases in the house. Lucy cleaned their mahogany wood until it glowed. Mustiness began to fade, replaced by the scent of fresh polish. All day, she buffed the dowels and rubbed scuffs from their rises. Despite the December chill—especially away from any fireplaces—she toiled on, encouraged by her progress.

Fairwinds was coming to life.

Cora checked on her, taking a break from her own work of cleaning trim and doors. Next would come the polishing of floors. A major undertaking, which would certainly require all three of them to accomplish. Better still, workmen with the proper tools to strip away years of neglect. If money were no object, Lucy would have hired some already.

Intruding thoughts of Lance, and the way he'd abandoned her and this place, spurred Lucy on. Christmas was almost upon them, and still, she'd received no word from him or Edmund. Even Belinda, for that matter. It certainly seemed as if she and Fairwinds were forgotten.

At the end of one exceptionally hard day, Lucy sank to the top step of the third-floor staircase and declared, "Done. The staircases in this house are ship-shape, Captain." She leaned back, smiling at her own silliness.

A frosty draft snaked across her fingers, and she quickly righted herself.

Lucy stared down the dark hallway. At the end there was light, where the large bedchamber opened, and the sun shone in through the doors to the widow's walk. But here, from the top of the stairs up to that point, there was darkness and gloom. A persistent heaviness she could not understand.

The cold breeze came again, and Lucy stretched her hands out, trying to locate its source. She raised the lamp she'd been using to work. A ball of dust tumbled across the wide pine flooring. She watched, as dirty bits rolled from beneath the wall.

What in heaven's name?

Lucy stood with her lamp and went to investigate the spot. Frosty air wafted across her slippers. "Ah ha, I found you," she said to the mystery draft.

Stepping back, she examined the wall with a critical eye. It was covered with faded wallpaper. *An extremely poor job if I'm being honest.* The entire hallway seemed inferior to the rest of the house. Ugly, and a waste of good space. She ran her hands over the wall, feeling many lumps and bumps. As if plaster had been heaved upon the surface instead of smoothed by a craftsman.

A sense of cold, so great it stung her skin, seeped into her hands. She yanked them back with a startled cry.

The tiny voice inside her sprang to life. *Something lingers behind this wall.*

Lucy backed away.

Her mind flew back to the night she and Nate were out on the patio stargazing. In between their many conversations, she'd turned to consider the back of the house. The outside of the Georgian manor was a study in symmetry. Whereas, inside, there were curves and domes. Still, everywhere was harmony and balance. Heavy grey stones squared the building's corners. Windows and doors were placed in perfect alignment. *Except for one place. The third floor.*

Stone appeared to have been added later or changed out. Like an afterthought to cover up something. A wrought iron trellis was bolted over the façade from the third floor to the ground. So out of place, it covered the windows below.

"What's the point of such odd stone and ironwork?" she'd asked Nate back then.

"I've no idea. Perhaps to cover up a bit of ugliness someone wished to hide? Seems peculiar though, I agree."

Lucy had remained puzzled about the trellis ever since, contemplating it each time she visited Lady Lillian's grave.

Did this inside hallway match the location of the trellis outside?

She rushed to the staircase to go see. But she slammed to a halt when a column of dark mist appeared out of nowhere. Watching in fear, the thing transformed into the shadow of a person, marching directly toward her. Long coat, wide-cuffed boots. She couldn't make out a face but knew it was a man. She yelped and leapt to one side when the figure passed. Its phantom footsteps were all too familiar to her.

The ghost man paused where she'd been examining the dust balls. He turned to face her, then he walked straight through the ugly wall.

"It's a room," she whispered under her breath. "Oh my God. Nate…Cora," Lucy bellowed as loud as she could. "I need you, at once. And bring a sledgehammer when you come!"

Chapter 6

"You're certain you want me to do this?" Nate gave Lucy one last chance to call off the demolition of the third-floor hallway wall.

"Yes, most definitely. I believe there's a secret room, hidden behind this wall. It explains why the man, ghost, whatever he was, walked straight through, as if there was a doorway still there. It would also explain the odd stones and iron trellis on the back of the house. They cover up what was once a window."

Nate pushed hair away from his face. "Alright then, stand back." He rubbed his hands together, picked up the heavy hammer, gave her one last dubious look, and took a mighty swing. The iron tool buried itself in the wall, and he had to yank hard to get it free. Blow after blow, bricks and old plaster tumbled and ricocheted in every direction. Stone dust filled the air causing everyone to cough. With one last great whack, the wall gave way, collapsing inward with a crash.

Lucy rushed forward to see what lay beyond. Nate held her back until he could clear away shards of debris. Cora handed him a lantern, and they all leaned into the mysterious darkness.

"It is a hidden room. I knew it," Lucy exclaimed. "I believe the ghost of Captain Wilder showed me the way."

"I'll be damned," Nate said, scratching his head. "What was once a window is bricked up. Be careful," he cautioned when she scrambled past him.

"Oh, no." Lucy pressed her hands over her heart. "Something is not right. This room feels very…sad. It's filled to the brim with sorrow."

"What's in there?" he asked.

Lucy glanced around, coughing and fanning her face. "Boxes, and trunks. Look at this." She held up a saber. "There's also a long rifle, and several pistols. Do you think they belonged to the Captain?"

"Could be, but whatever you do, don't handle them," Nate warned. "There could be old powder and shot. He climbed over the wreckage to join her.

"Help me," she urged, when she spied something tall wrapped in canvas. Together they pulled the thing forward and removed the covering.

Nate raised the light. "It's a painting."

"Do you think it's them? Captain Wilder and Lady Lillian? I've longed to know what they look like."

"Must be," Cora piped in, as she peered in from the hallway. "Perhaps it's their wedding portrait. A popular practice."

Lucy's hands trembled, as she reached out to trace the old brush strokes. "They're lovely together. Perfectly matched. I can feel the love they shared. It's as strong as ever."

"A handsome couple," Nate added.

"How heartbreaking this is all that's left of them." Lucy considered the disaster of a room. Its contents blanketed with a century of dust and cobwebs. "These things have waited a long time to be discovered."

Nate examined the old weaponry. "Looks as if everything was just thrown in here. There's no order. Just piles."

Lucy gasped, and he set aside the guns to go to her.

"Her hand." She pointed to the portrait and the ring upon the lady's finger.

"Looks to be gold with a great hunk of a ruby. She was a pirate's wife, after all," Nate surmised. "Perhaps it was booty from one of the many ships he raided?"

Lucy reached beneath the high neck of her gown and withdrew her necklace. Dangling from the chain was the exact ring.

"Bloody hell," Nate said, shaking his head. "Now where'd you go and get that bit of treasure?"

"My father. He gave it to me years ago." She leaned forward, allowing him to examine it.

"It's the same one, alright. That's a bizarre coincidence."

"Let us have a look," Cora said with excitement from the other side. Lucy went to show her. "My goodness. And to think, a ghost showed you where to find this room and that picture. You know…you resemble the lady a bit."

"You think so?" Lucy asked with a thoughtful frown. "There's something here. I've a knowing, a feeling deep within my soul. My heart aches for the things in this room." She glanced around, then bent to examine a pile of what turned out to be baby things. Layettes tossed in a heap. An unfinished blanket, still in its embroidery hoop. She approached something shoved way in the corner. "It's a cradle, fashioned to look like a ship."

"There's never been mention of any children," Cora said. "They both died before being blessed with wee ones."

"Perhaps not," Lucy said sadly.

"Maybe the lady was with child when she died?" Nate suggested with a grim expression.

"Or perhaps they both died hoping," Lucy guessed as tears

welled in her eyes.

***

The remainder of the day was spent cleaning and organizing the contents of the concealed room. Together they discovered men's clothing, wigs, and jewelry in a seaman's trunk, presumably belonging to the Captain. Boxes filled with crumbling parchments, letters, and maps. A treasure trove of the lost history of Fairwinds and its most notorious owner.

Exhausted and filthy, the three laborers-turned-investigators washed for a light meal, ate, and surrendered to their beds. But first Nathaniel helped Lucy move the portrait into her bedroom.

"You're certain you want this here, with you, and not somewhere else, like in the parlor?" he asked, as they propped it up against the wall facing her bed. "Might it not encourage the ghosts to haunt you?"

"I believe they haunt me regardless of what I or anyone else does. But who am I to question the motives of Fairwinds' ghosts?"

Nate came close, and he picked up the ring that dangled from the chain about her neck. "To begin with, you're the one wearing the lady's ring. I'd say that makes you a bonny big target. Perhaps the ghosts are drawn to you because you have this ring?"

"Oh, I don't know, Nate. This place is filled with mysteries, from top to bottom." Lucy squared her stubborn jaw. "Well, this ring is still too big for my finger. Otherwise, I'd wear it outright for the entire world to see. Including the ghosts. My father gave it to me, so it's a connection to him as well as this house. Something uniquely special to me."

Nate smiled, knowing she spoke the truth. He slid a

protective arm around her waist and drew her close. "Aye, I'm convinced you'd challenge the living and the dead to protect this place. I believe you love Fairwinds as much as they did. Maybe more."

"I do, Nate. I've never felt so passionate about a place. Even my own home growing up. Especially now that Father is gone." She rubbed her sore neck and sighed. "I can't think about all this anymore without getting upset. Despite all the mess and all the work to be done, I feel a sense of hope and belonging here. I long to see Fairwinds happy and whole again. As if somehow this place is a reflection of me and my life. Is that wrong?"

"No, my sweet, it's not wrong." He pressed his lips to her furrowed brow. "I don't understand how, but it appears you and Fairwinds are linked. We all are."

"Perhaps saving this house will make us all happy and whole together?"

Nate knew if he was to help Lucy—fund her dreams and keep them going—he must return to work. The time had come to discuss leaving. "Lucy…I'll help you, any way I can, but there's something I must ask."

"Sell the ring for me, Nate," she cut him off. She hastily removed her necklace and worked the ring from the chain.

"But it's your family heirloom. Likely passed down by Abigail, the sister of Lillian Grace."

"Yes, which is precisely why I must use it to help restore this house," she proclaimed, her voice filled with determination. "It's all I have to give, since my brother holds the purse strings to everything else." She forced the ring into his hand, stepped back, and crossed her arms. "Take it to the shop where you bought the telescope and books. Tell the proprietor who it belonged to—a pirate lord and his lady. Bring the man here to see the portrait if need be. He must be made to understand its historical significance. I want as much as I can get for the thing. There's much to do and not a penny to waste."

Nate's perceptive gaze searched her anxious face. She was hell-bent and refused to listen to reason. Still, he couldn't help thinking Lucy would regret this decision. He already regretted not urging her to listen to what he had to say. Now he saw no clear path forward without hurting her.

"I won't go to town until late morning," he said sadly. "Sleep on it. Come see me if you change your mind."

"I won't. But thank you, Nate, for understanding."

***

It was midday when Nate grudgingly entered the stables, preparing to head into town. Lucy's ring felt like an anchor in his pocket, yet he'd promised he would try to sell it for her.

Making his way into an interior room where he kept his horse's tack, he paused when his boot collided with something that clinked. He knelt to see what it was. "Bloody hell," he muttered when he spied a pile of gold coins, shining bright as the sun from beneath the hay. He looked from side to side as if someone might be there, playing a trick on him. *Tools and sacks of feed. Nothing unusual, and certainly nobody around.* He scooped the coins up and examined them. *Oddly shaped. Just like the one in the cottage. But how?*

Nate closed his fist around the gold and grinned when it warmed in his hand. "Let's see what the shopkeeper has to say about these."

"I'll give you what I think they're worth," the man said, as they quibbled over a price. "They're old, most certainly, but I'm not exactly sure what they're worth. I'll need to consult my antiquities expert before I commit."

"Fair enough. But can you give me an advance?" Nate anxiously fingered Lucy's ring, still deep in his pocket.

Like a gift from the angels, the unexplained coins meant he didn't have to sell her precious heirloom. At least not yet. This gold bought him time to determine how much was needed to make repairs versus how much he could provide once he returned to his law firm.

"You know…" the shrewd man began. "I've only seen one other coin like these. It belonged to another man who worked at Fairwinds. One who ended up dead at the bottom of those cliffs. Come to think of it, it was right about the time you arrived."

Nate's blood ran cold.

"Where did you say you got these?" the man questioned.

"I didn't."

"Looks like pirate gold to me," he remarked with a probing stare.

Nate's pulse hammered in his ears, yet he shrugged the man's statement off with a chuckle. "Now where would I be getting pirate gold?"

***

Nate worked to hold back a smile when he dropped a heavy leather purse into Lucy's outstretched hand later that same afternoon. "They'll be more," he explained. "I'm to visit the shop in a day or so to collect the balance. But I wanted something for you today."

Lucy squealed in delight when she dumped the contents of the bulging bag onto the kitchen table. "Oh, my word, it's more than I'd dreamed. Thank you, Nathaniel. I've lost my ring, but to keep this house and repair it…This means the world to me."

"I know," he murmured, feeling a pang of guilt for lying to her. Heat rushed to his face. *Should I have given her the gold pieces instead? Shared what I uncovered, so she could decide what to do with them?*

The first coin he'd discovered in the groundskeeper's cottage was included in the deal. Knowing Lucy, she'd have sold the entire lot for Fairwinds, including her precious ring. At least this way, she still had that bit of family history.

"What shall we tackle first?" she asked, happily unaware of the turmoil in his mind. "The floors or the ceilings? Refurbish the tile work or the murals? Perhaps we should call in a construction expert and have him help us decide?"

"I can ask around in town." Nate knew many would jump at the chance to work on such a large project, but instinct told him to remain cautious about inviting strangers to the infamous house. The merchant was already suspicious of how he'd come to have such valuable old coins. If word got out there was pirate gold at Fairwinds, there would, no doubt, be a mad dash of bloodthirsty treasure hunters descending upon them. "Winter's not the best time to start some of the projects you have in mind. Perhaps you should wait until spring. In the meantime, I want to—"

"You're absolutely right," she said, interrupting him in her excitement. "In the meantime, we'll do all we can and plan for more work when the weather improves. Maybe we'll even find other valuables in the house to sell." She paused and looked toward heaven. "Apologies, Captain Wilder, but I must fund this great endeavor somehow."

Nate's thoughts hit a brick wall. *Was it the Captain's ghost who'd supplied the golden coins?*

"Besides," Lucy continued to chatter on unaware, "it's almost Christmas. I would love to celebrate. A German-born girl—a student at my school—spoke often of a *Christmas tree,* which her family displayed in their sitting room. They would decorate a fir tree with nuts, and strings of beads, candies, and little trinkets. It all sounded so charming."

"I've seen them," Cora piped in from where she stirred a big pot of stew on the fire. "We could have our own little feast of sorts. Sugary treats? A special pie? I do love a good mince pie. Like the ones I used to make for your father, Nate, remember?"

Nate gave a curt nod. Inside he was beating himself up. He'd posted a reply letter already, assuring his employer he'd return by the twenty-fifth of December. It was his plan to tell Lucy and his mother they must return with him. Bring them all back to the city, where they could then enjoy the holiday and new year.

Without a man at Fairwinds to protect and assist, the two women would be too vulnerable. Utterly at risk with the darkest, harshest days of winter soon to be upon them.

"If we could at least repair the pianoforte by then, I could play for you both," Lucy persisted with an excited smile. Every word she spoke sent Nate deeper into worry and despair.

He'd never planned to fall in love. Certainly, he'd never expected to meet the love of his life in an old, rundown mansion in the middle of nowhere. Yet, here they were, talking about renovating projects and celebrating Christmas together. As if the entire world outside this place didn't exist. And yet it did.

The other looming storm on the horizon was Lucy's

brother. Nate had exchanged letters with a close colleague regarding Lance Ellison and his dubious business partner, Edmund Grimes. Rumor was the two men were deep in debt, associating with all the wrong sorts in New York. Land speculation, gambling establishments, and brothels... According to his associate, it was only a matter of time until the law—or some New York City criminal—caught up with them.

Nate turned away from the cheerful women, and he went to stare out the window. His feelings twisted and tangled into an unyielding knot, settling in the pit of his stomach. Even if he managed to hire someone to help with the estate, leaving now meant it'd likely be spring before he could return. Far too long for his liking.

Steadying himself, he watched as dark clouds encroached upon the late afternoon sun. They whipped across the sky, hinting at troubling times and changes to come.

"I'm going," he tossed out, needing to escape.

"But the stew?" his mother fretted.

"I'll just take some bread. That'll suffice. The animals need feeding and bedding down. Plus, I've work to attend to." A stab of remorse stacked onto his already troubled spirit when Lucy's excitement and happiness withered away.

"Would you like help?" she asked gently. "It's my fault, after all, that you're behind in your chores. I was the one who sent you to town today."

"Thank you, but no." He forced a smile for her benefit. "You ladies enjoy your evening together. Goodnight." With that, he left them.

Once outside, Nate turned back to gaze at the house. Something caught his ear. A loud creaking sound came from the weathervane atop the roof. The thing shifted and swung violently in a gusty wind. Cold ocean air swept in, causing him to tug his coat collar tighter, as he hurried toward the stable.

***

"Nathaniel, wake up," someone said from far away.

Loud banging ensued.

Nate stirred with a groan, and he covered his head with his pillow, attempting to block out the noise.

"Nathaniel Bradford." The voice turned angry. "You open this door at once."

Nate startled awake, and he sprang to his feet. Blinking several times, he rubbed his eyes, and focused on the door. It was then he heard the wind, rattling the old window panes.

Rushing forward, he whipped open the door to find his mother, bundled up in a heavy coat. She stumbled across the threshold.

"A…a…storm," she stammered. "There's a mighty nor'easter rolling in. Miss Lucy—"

"What of Lucy?" he demanded. "Where is she?"

"Still in the house, I believe. But I couldn't find her. I went straight to her room when the gale woke me. She was gone. The ghosts, Nathaniel. You must go and find Lucy, or she'll be driven mad with fright."

Nate hurried to don his shirt and trousers. He grabbed his coat, and commanded, "Stay here. You'll be safe. I'll watch over Lucy."

"Hurry," she urged.

Running the entire way to the mansion, Nate was breathless when he reached the heavy front doors. Inside, the foyer was dark aside from a single lamp. He rushed forward and grabbed it as the glass of the large windows rattled in their casements. The thunderous sound of driving rain came next.

"Lucy," Nate yelled over the commotion. When he received no answer, he took the stairs, two at a time, to search.

Her bedroom was empty.

"Lucy," he shouted again. "Where are you?"

On a hunch, he ran to the third floor. She was there, huddled in a crouched position against the doorframe to the master bedroom suite.

"What are you doing here?" He bellowed over the storm. He squatted and touched her shoulder when she didn't respond, and she startled. "Lucy…We need to go."

Wild eyes finally saw him, and she jumped into his embrace. Pointing into the bedroom, she buried her face in his neck. "Nate, there's something there. Something not of this world."

His gaze snapped to where her trembling hand indicated, and he crept into the room with Lucy clinging to his free arm. The French doors to the widow's walk had blown open. Rain poured in, drenching the flooring and everything within a wide radius of the doors. Seawater, mixed with icy rain, sprayed them both.

Nate started forward to shut the doors, but Lucy held him back.

"Wait, look," she cried, pointing again.

Two fiery balls of light collided at the threshold—one coming from outside, the other manifesting just inside the room. They swirled and whirred, spinning faster and faster, until a great, glowing orb of light formed.

"What is it?" he yelled above the storm sounds.

"I don't know, but it doesn't feel right to be here."

Nate nodded, and they hurried from the room together.

The moment they got to the hallway, the door to the space slammed shut with a force that threatened to bring down the house. When he tried the knob, it was locked.

Lucy scrambled down the staircases, rushing to the front doors. She yanked one side open and balked when faced with the fierceness of the storm.

Deafening sound, like the wind of a cyclone, enveloped them, reverberating through the house. Moaning sounds—cries of joy and wanton abandon—soon added to the terrifying cacophony.

"Where can we go?" Lucy pleaded, covering her ears.

Nate grabbed her hand, and together they dashed for the library. He set aside the lamp and closed and barred the door with a side table. The commotion from above muffled as he backed away.

Lucy trembled by the fireplace. Nate went to her, and he pulled her into his embrace.

"Wha...what's happening? I don't understand," she stammered, stepping away to stare up into his wet face with desperate eyes.

"The ghosts," he began, yet hesitated, not knowing how to explain a thing only God could understand. "They come together somehow. When a gale blows in from just the right direction."

"But how can a storm bring the dead?" she cried.

"I don't know. It's happened for years, according to my mother. A century or more if you consider when the Captain and Lady Lillian perished. If there's a great span of time between such storms—as there's been this year—the intensity reaches a fevered pitch."

"I saw her," Lucy said, her voice hitching on a sob. "The

White Lady was on the widow's walk when the wind began. Like she was waiting for something to happen, with her grey hands pressed against the glass. But she looked whole this time, Nate. A complete person. Even her eyes were different."

"Different how? You've seen her before?" he demanded.

Lucy floundered. "Yes, outside the ballroom the night you brought the books. You left. I went exploring. I didn't tell you because..." She bowed her head. "I'm sorry, but I didn't trust you'd believe me."

"I couldn't tell you either about the things I've witnessed in this house. I hoped I'd never need to." He cupped her frozen cheek, bringing her gaze back to his. "Nay, I *prayed* there'd be no storm, no nor'easter, while you were here. I was afraid the ghosts would scare you away from Fairwinds. Away from me."

"I don't want to be away from you, Nate. Quite the opposite," she admitted.

Nate leaned into her, nuzzling her face.

"Where's Cora?" Lucy suddenly remembered.

"Safe in the cottage. She came for me. To warn of what was about to happen."

"Oh, Nathaniel," Lucy moaned. "How can this be? It's madness. No wonder the house has been empty for so long." Her legs wobbled, and she crumbled against him.

Guiding her to a chair, he pressed his lips to her damp temple. "You're all right. That's all that matters. The storm will pass. It always does."

The fire was nearly out. Nate added kindling to the embers, determined to warm her. Folded blankets, from their night of stargazing, remained on a corner chair. He grabbed those, too, wrapping Lucy in their soft warmth.

Wind continued to howl around the old house as he

worked. Rain battered the windows. Yet soon a golden glow filled the library.

Nate tried to ignore what the storm had forced upon them, as he stared into the building flames. They were cut off from the rest of the world. Alone together until the turmoil around them ended. Likely many hours from now.

Telltale sounds from the third floor persisted, causing the deep hunger he felt for Lucy to gnaw at his resolve. Like water spilled over from a too-full cup, his need for her was overflowing.

When he turned to face her, his breath caught.

Chapter 7

Lucy rose from her chair and went to him. She pressed a loving hand to his tight jaw. "Those sounds above…They make me feel…strange.

"The ghosts," he murmured. "I believe it's why they stay here. To be together. To somehow make love."

"I would," she admitted in a smooth, low tone, as she continued to slowly caress him. "What is heaven—or any other place for that matter—if you're not with the one you love?"

Nate couldn't move. He stilled her hand. "Lucy…these are not your feelings, they're theirs."

"No matter, I've felt them for some time now." She eased her hand from his and her touch drifted to the undone collar of his shirt. "Did you know…" she began with a secretive smile. "I wondered what your skin would feel like when we first met. I was drawn to your rugged appearance, that dark, stubbly jawline. A twist of brown hair and a dashing mustache. Your rough and gruff ways, which you so proudly displayed. Little did I know you were not as you seemed."

Nate looked away.

She inched closer and wound her arms around his neck. Her fingertips teased the edges of his damp hair. "All those hours of conversation…Yet my mind would always wander back to these dark, unruly tresses and what they might feel like, slipping through my fingers." She tipped his chin so he would be forced to look at her. "I've dreamed of these deep, brown eyes, especially after we've engaged in some silly debate. The way you listen to my every word. I'm quite swept away by you."

Nate closed his eyes, leaning into her tender caresses. He shuddered when her fingertips grazed his lips, and she gave his mustache a playful tweak.

"Lucy, I..."

"Don't," she silenced him. "I know what I'm doing, if you have any doubts. There've been so many flirtations between us. Passionate kisses, too, which take my breath away. Tonight, there's a storm brewing inside me. A need so great, I don't know what to do about it."

With a tortured groan, Nate looped his arms around her waist, drawing her fully against him. Her eyelids drifted closed in anticipation of his kiss. As his mouth descended, molten heat filled Lucy's limbs. Their lips met, sliding effortlessly together. She delighted in his tongue. How it swirled with hers in a slow, sensual dance.

Engulfed by reckless abandon, Lucy smoothed her eager hands over Nate's wide back and broad shoulders. He wriggled out of his wet coat, dropping it carelessly to the floor. His body was large—strong, trim. Tight from weeks of hard labor. Like iron against her soft, feminine curves.

Urgent hands roamed her sides and slid down to cup her bottom. Keeping her close as their passion grew. She could feel the rigid length of his manhood, pressed against her abdomen.

Nate's lips grazed her chin and cheek. He nibbled his way to her ear. "Will you lie with me?" he murmured in a raspy tone.

"Aye," she said with a smile, using his favorite word.

Yanking blankets from the chair, he hastily fashioned a place for them. A makeshift bed on the old Persian carpet before the hearth. He sat and reached a hand up to her. With a nervous smile, she settled in the space alongside him and smoothed her skirts.

"No bed clothes tonight?" he asked, the husky timbre of his voice causing a nervous flutter in her stomach.

"I'm not yet dressed for bed. I was reading when the storm came. I often read late into the night. A guilty pleasure I find hard to resist." She worked to slow her rapid breathing, as he stretched out, propping himself on one elbow to study her.

"Guilty pleasure?" he murmured with a hint of amusement. "I've got a few of those myself."

She lay down beside him—*a brazen first step*—yet this stormy night had her throwing caution to the wind. The quivering inside had disappeared, replaced by a rising need to be close to him. To touch and taste. To feel everything, she'd been privately yearning for.

"Tell me," she said. "I long to know such things about you."

Nate gave a light chuckle. His fingers combed through her hair, releasing the few remaining pins. "I dream of touching you," he confessed, as one long, lazy finger trailed the length of her throat to the hollow above her collarbone. "Here." His lips followed. "And here." His feather-light touch drifted down until it hovered just above the swell of her breast. "But most certainly here." He cupped her breast, and she moaned. His thumb dragged across the sensitive nipple. It puckered beneath the bodice of her dress.

Lucy's chest rose and fell rapidly, as she lost her battle to remain calm under his sensual ministrations. She squirmed when the place between her legs began to throb.

Inquisitive fingers drifted lower over the curve of her hip, and she rolled onto her back, granting him access to her tingling body. His hand paused at the apex of her thighs. "This stormy night is filled with the unexpected," he whispered. "Let's explore together." He cupped her sex, massaging through the layers of her skirts until she writhed.

Lucy couldn't hold still anymore. Liquid fire flooded in wherever Nate touched. Her hips moved of their own volition, as if seeking more. His mouth captured hers, plundering, tempting with his tongue. Cool air grazed her legs when he bunched up her skirts. A soft stroke of her inner thighs. A touch behind her knees. The ties of her stocking were quickly undone. She shivered in anticipation when his touch inched higher. He brushed her womanhood, and she gasped.

"Oh," she groaned in protest when he removed his hand. Yet he continued kissing her. Soft, pleading sounds made him smile against her lips.

"Lay back. We're in no rush," he murmured. "The storm has just begun."

Lucy did as Nate said, needing to know what it would feel like to be touched there by him. *Scandalous*. And yet, it was all she could think of. His gentle fingers returned to her hidden curls. She held her breath as he parted them and spread the lips of her sex. His fingertip glided into her slick folds, and she trembled.

"God, you're so wet," he rasped. "Relax. I promise I'll not hurt you."

Nate dipped a finger into her most private of places. Lucy squeezed her eyes shut, shocked by the tantalizing sensation of being caressed in such an intimate fashion. He withdrew, and his wet fingertip swirled over the sensitive pearl within. Again, and again, he stroked her. Tempting, teasing, easing into her only to pull back again. It was sweet, sensual torture. All Lucy could do not to cry out in frustration. An ache formed inside her, building until it demanded anything Nate could give her.

"Do you like this?" he asked in a strained voice.

"Don't stop," was all she could manage.

"As you wish." He sank his entire finger into her, and they both moaned.

Lucy clutched the blankets in her fists, twisting the fabric, as the anxious feelings climbed to staggering new heights. Nate filled her again and again. His touch slow and measured. He pulled back to focus on the sensitive nub of her sex—a delicious slide across the place she wanted him most. One more time, and she splintered into glorious pieces.

"I can't stand it any longer. I need to be inside you," he murmured against her hot cheek before plundering her mouth again. "You're so perfect. Feel my fingers. Imagine if it were I there instead."

"Yes," she answered breathlessly.

Nate brushed hair back from her face. "This part will hurt, but hopefully not for long."

"I want you to do it," she urged him on.

Nate pulled away to open his trousers. Lucy shivered without his warmth. His large form settled over her again—an erotic crush—as he positioned himself between her thighs. The blunt head of his sex pushed against her, yet her untried body resisted.

"Kiss me," he commanded. "Like you've never kissed me before."

Lucy did as he said, putting all her heart and soul into her efforts to seduce him with her mouth. Her body stretched and strained, as he drove deeper. Inch by impossible inch. She broke their kiss and bit her lip, fighting through the pain.

Their panting breath mingled as he stilled.

"I'm sorry. The worst is over." He touched his forehead to hers. "Stay with me."

Lucy gave a quick nod.

Slow, steady. Nate was patient, giving her time to catch up, as he began to move. Every effort he'd made to be gentle—to hold back for her—helped to ease the pain. Her pulse soon quickened along with his pace. She felt every hard inch of him. Invasive, yet oh so titillating all the same. Her inner muscles eased. She breathed and rolled her hips.

Nate groaned in response and smiled against her skin. "Aye, love, that's it. Come with me." He kissed her open mouth, tangling their tongues. His weight shifted to take more pressure off her. So that she could join him in moving freely. He filled her up. Deep, slow presses. Until the pleasure of it was all that remained.

Lucy followed Nate's lead, relishing the power her body had to make him shudder and moan. They both gasped for air as their intensity increased. A few more powerful strokes, and Nate stiffened and cried out, collapsing at her side.

***

Sounds of the wind and rain returned, as Nate's thundering heartbeat eased. He smoothed Lucy's skirts down over her chilled limbs.

"I forgot all about the storm," she said with an astonished laugh.

"Aye," he growled, nuzzling her flushed face. "So much for fearing the tempest." He laid back and drew her tight against his side. She snuggled into him with a soft sigh. Together they listened to the gusts, testing the old timbers of the mansion.

Firewood crackled. A log fell. Time ceased to exist, as their limbs lay tangled, and the storm raged all around them.

"Did you really dream of touching me like that?" Lucy asked. A deep blush spread across her cheeks when she looked up at him.

"Every damn night. And most days," he confessed with a chuckle. "I'm a goner, now that I know what delights lie beneath those plain-colored skirts. More alluring than any siren of the sea, you be, Lucy Ellison."

"Siren of the sea, indeed," she scoffed.

Nate lovingly stroked her hair. "I mean it. I couldn't stop myself, despite swearing I'd be the gentleman you deserve."

"I didn't want you to stop," she said. "What does that say about me?"

"That you are the most beautiful, wondrous woman in the world to me. But that most precious of gifts belongs to your husband."

"Then marry me, Nathaniel Bradford," Lucy proclaimed boldly. "We're perfectly matched, even in the physical sense. We're destined to be together. You said so yourself."

Nate rose and fixed his clothing. He went to the window, though it was too dark and stormy to see. Only his reflection showed in the glass, with torrents of rain rushing down it. "I must tell you something. And I'm not certain how you'll take it."

"Oh?" she said, looking concerned, as she sat up.

"My employer demands I return to Boston."

A worried frown marred her lovely face. "When?"

"I promised to be back by Christmas. I know it's soon. I've done my best to extend. I'll not go without you," he finally revealed.

Lucy rose, shaking her head. "I can't go now. There's still so much to do."

"But it's not safe here for you or my mother to stay alone. It's too isolated. If anything were to happen—"

"The house though, Nate. All our plans." She turned away from him. "Did you even intend to help me?"

Nate went to her, and he clasped her tense shoulders, drawing her back against his chest. "Of course, my love. I'd hoped for more time, but I must work if I'm to support you. I want to marry you, Lucy. More than anything. Make a life for us together. This house can be part of all that, but I must have an income if we're to survive."

"Perhaps we could hire someone?" she rushed to say, grasping at straws.

"Not bloody likely with the ghosts. And with what? Good intentions?

Lucy faced him. She stood tall and squared her stubborn jaw. "Pirate treasure."

***

Lucy held her breath the following day when Nate pressed the magic spot on the rotunda wall. The secret door latch released, and the entrance flew open with a bang. An icy wind rushed into their surprised faces.

"Has that ever happened before?" she asked in a timid voice.

Nate stepped back, grimacing. "No."

Together they peered into the blackness.

Nate shined the lamp. "The stairway goes up to the third floor."

"Cora showed me the trap door there, hidden beneath the carpet."

Nate adjusted the lantern to see the other way. "Down leads to the basement. Which way would you prefer to go?"

"Down, of course," Lucy said in a steadier voice. "Pirates *buried* their treasure, did they not?"

"Quite right. However, this is one time a lady does not go first."

"Spoilsport," she grumbled with a teasing grin.

Nate swiped at sticky, dangling cobwebs, as he led the way down the twisting iron structure. Lucy followed close behind him, their footsteps echoing in the hollow. The old metal groaned and wobbled under their weight.

"Is this safe?" she asked him.

"We'll find out. However, I've never been one of two people on it."

Down they went, until they reached the basement. Beyond was a doorway made of dark, heavy wood, banded by straps of rusted metal.

Nate handed Lucy the lantern and used his full weight to pry it open. "The tunnel lies here."

"Where does it lead?" She handed back the light.

Nate started walking. "Beneath the house and lawn to the stables."

Walls, which had begun as granite, like the house, became wooden beams and stale-smelling earth. Roots protruded everywhere. Nate had to stoop under what appeared to be joining points. Likely additions from over a century earlier. A short offshoot tunnel led to nothing but a dead end.

"What are those?" Lucy asked when they passed iron hooks and rings mounted on the walls.

"Probably for torches or to hang lanterns," he speculated.

"You don't think they were for prisoners, do you?"

"I hope not. Captain Wilder was a gentleman pirate. A deadly scoundrel, to be sure. At least according to legends. But not the torturing sort."

What was once dry floor quickly turned to muck and mire, as water dripped in through the earthen walls. Water wicked up onto Lucy's skirts, making them heavy and clumsy. She clutched Nate's hand for support as they followed the long, claustrophobic passageway.

"Is it seawater?" she asked, her voice filled with concern.

"I don't believe we've gone far enough. It's probably groundwater, seeping in after the storm."

A few more yards, and the tunnel ended at a trap door in a low ceiling. A rickety, wooden ladder led up.

Nate handed off the lantern again, and he climbed and shoved until the hatch opened with the screeching sound of metal on rock. Scents of horses and hay wafted down upon them. A questioning nicker came from somewhere beyond.

"It's the stable," he told her. "We've gone from the house to the barn underneath the lawn."

"This won't do, there's nothing here." Lucy heaved an exasperated sigh. "Let's see if there's more the other way. The tunnel appears to continue to the right."

"Wait for me." Nate dragged the door shut and hurried to catch up to his impatient partner.

"It's no use, we can't go any farther," she groaned when he reached her. "The way is barred by the collapse you spoke of. No wonder my father said there was nothing here. Just filth and muck."

"The same muck in the rotunda?" he suggested.

"I believe you're right. We must find a way through."

Nate examined what they were up against. "The joists

appear to be sound, and the side beams still hold. It's soil and some rather large rocks that have fallen in."

"Can we break through?" She held the lamp to the debris, attempting to see. Its flame flickered. "Did you feel that? A breeze. It must be coming from somewhere outside." A smile lit up her face. "The twin sea caves."

Nate smirked and crossed his arms. "And how would you be knowing about those caves?"

Lucy hiked her chin. "Of course I climbed down to explore the beach and see the caves. I wouldn't be my father's daughter if I didn't."

"But the way is dangerous. A man fell to his death, and he wasn't wearing cumbersome skirts."

"Well, I should hope not," she teased with a cheeky grin, making him groan. "I was perfectly fine, though the caves were not. They're tidal, and as such, impassable much of the day. I'd planned to return at low tide, but I never timed it so I wouldn't get trapped."

Nate gaped at her. "Thank God for small blessings."

"Perhaps we should come back with tools? Shovels and picks, so we can break through here? And we should tell your mother what we've found. I know she's anxious to hear."

"Wonderful. Just what I need, two tenacious women."

***

In the frustrating afternoon that followed, Lucy and Nate shared their findings with Cora. She was excited yet gravely concerned. If a collapse happened once, then it certainly could happen again, especially after such heavy rains. Yet together the three of them devised a plan and gathered what was needed. They also discovered more muddy footprints in the rotunda. But just like before, they provided no further clues and simply vanished.

Following the spiral staircase up to the third floor, they struggled to open the secret trapdoor to the master bedroom suite. A heavy, old rug *did* cover the thing, so entry to the tunnels could only be gained if it were rolled back.

The day sped by without them returning to the tunnels. And before Lucy knew it, she was retiring to her room, feeling downtrodden.

The Captain's phantom footfall paced above her head. He'd been louder than usual, letting his presence be known to them throughout the day.

"I know you're anxious," she said aloud. "I'm anxious, too. I suspect that's why you leave your muddy mess all about, as if to guide us somehow. But the last thing we need is to get stuck down there. Buried alive. This estate has enough ghosts, thank you very much."

Removing the pins from her hair, she joined the Captain in his pacing ritual. She walked the room, brushing snarls from her long curls. "What are we missing?" she asked, hoping the ghost would somehow reveal a clue. "I feel as if there's something more. A better way in, perhaps?"

The phantom walking abruptly ceased.

"Is that it, there's a better way? How?"

Quiet your mind, the tiny voice inside her head whispered.

Lucy sat in the chair before the fireplace and closed her eyes. Breathing slowly and deeply, she asked for guidance and listened for an answer. Only the clock on the mantle spoke to her, ticking away precious time.

She tried again, clearing her thoughts of all the worry and confusion of the day.

The image of her father swirled into focus in her mind's

eye. He sat at his desk in his favorite spot in their Boston home. The library.

Could it be in the library?

Father was writing something.

No…not writing… Sketching.

"A map?" Lucy whispered. "Father…is there a map? Cora said you'd visited Fairwinds and that you'd explored."

The woman's words came rushing back to her. *"Your father said he'd been down there to investigate and there was nothing to see."*

"But what if there was something to see? What if you only said that because you wanted to protect what was down there?"

Lucy suddenly remembered the sound of his voice. *"Clever girl…Think, Lucy, think."*

She sprang to her feet and rushed to her trunk in the corner. Flinging open its lid, she immediately went for her father's old bag. She hurried to the bed and dumped the contents on the counterpane.

"Please be here, please, please, please," she prayed.

Chapter 8

"Nate," Lucy cried as she banged on the door of the cottage. She pounded harder when he didn't answer right away.

The door whipped open, and she pushed past him.

"What are you doing here?" he asked, looking groggy and confused as he rubbed his eyes. "What time is it?"

"Late. But I've discovered something, and there's no way I could wait until morning to show you." She set aside the lantern she'd used to get there and threw off her heavy cloak. Then she pressed her father's satchel into Nate's hands.

"What's this then?" he asked in a gravelly voice.

"My father's things. His personal research and writings. I took them when I left the house in Boston. Look at the top page, Nate," she urged, her voice rising with intensity.

He brought the old, worn case to the tiny table and opened the leather flap. On top was a tattered parchment paper. His eyes widened. "It's a bloody map of the tunnels. My God, your father did explore them on his own."

"Yes, he did," she sang out proudly, "and he's shown us another way in."

Nate scoured the faded ink on the page. "It's here." He sank into the chair. "There's an entrance right here under our noses, if I'm reading this correctly."

Lucy spun, searching the one room cottage. "But where?"

Nate bolted for the cupboard built into the wall. "This is where I found the first coin, wedged beneath the trim board just here, and—" He leaned heavily against the piece, and it shifted.

His stare shot to Lucy.

One hard shove, and it slid aside, revealing a hidden wooden doorway in the floor. Nate yanked the thing open. Cold air rushed up. The smell of damp earth filling the tiny house.

"You've found it," Lucy cried. "You're a genius."

His arm blocked the doorway, holding her back from the abyss. "It smells like an open grave. Take care. We don't want to be the ones interred there."

Grabbing the lantern, he cautiously led the way down a ladder. Water dripped, echoing around them. Cobwebs wavered like grimy curtains, sticking to their heads and clothing.

"Please tell me there are no spiders," Lucy fretted. "I can endure anything but spiders."

"What happened to my fearless explorer?"

"She suddenly feels like a ten-year-old girl again."

"Look here, the floor is different. Perhaps it's newer?" he speculated.

A few steps farther, and they were sinking into inches of sludge. Yet they ventured deeper until they reached a rock ledge. Water ran down the walls like a mini stream, pooling black water around their feet. Gaining a small foothold, Nate hoisted himself up, and Lucy handed him the light.

"What's there? Can you see anything?"

"I think there's a room. This could be it."

"I must see. But I don't think I can climb this slippery rock in wet skirts and ruined shoes. You'll have to go alone."

"Not a chance. We've come this far together. I'll not let you quit now." He reached a hand down, urging, "Take it." When she balked, he added, "Do you trust me?"

Wide-eyed, she stared up at him. "Implicitly."

"Then take it, and let's find your treasure."

Lucy's small hand slid perfectly into Nate's, and he hauled her up the slimy, ragged ledge. Their bodies collided at the top, a rush of breath coming from them both before he kissed her. She clung to him. His wet shirtfront bunched in her tight fists.

"Nate," she managed to say between frantic kisses. "We're here to find something, remember? We shall not find anything this way."

"Says who?" he growled, nipping her neck.

Lucy wriggled in his embrace. "But we're *finally* here. This is what we've been searching for. It could mean the answer to all our prayers."

Dank, stale air and the sound of dripping water surrounded them.

In the distance? The rush of the tide.

"Let's go," he said with a tilted grin. Hopping down, he reached his arms up to assist her.

In one corner of the near-empty room, they found shovels and a dilapidated wheelbarrow. Nate grabbed the sturdiest looking tool, and they pressed on. Once in the tunnel beyond, they came upon an iron gate, sealed with a heavy chain and lock.

"Can you break it?" she asked.

Nate wedged the old shovel handle between the iron and the chain, and he heaved. The links groaned yet held fast. However, the lock broke into pieces. Moments later they were through. They passed an offshoot tunnel, which was filled with what smelled like stagnant seawater.

"We must be near the mouth of the caves," she said, rushing forward.

"Lucy," Nate cried. "Wait."

Double gates barred her from advancing any further.

"This is it then. There's no more," she murmured sadly when he came up behind her. "Skullery Bay is out there. I can see it." She gripped the old iron bars like a prisoner. Closing her eyes, she let the fine mist of sea spray cool her fevered cheeks. "This is the end of our quest, Nate. There's no treasure. Not a single coin. Just some rusty old tools. If there was ever a treasure, it's likely been gone for a very long time."

Lucy sensed Nate close behind her, yet he didn't speak.

"My father was right. There is nothing down here. I'd so...hoped," she whispered, but the words caught in her throat. Her eyes stung with tears.

Nate's footsteps faded away. Disappearing lamp light left her in near darkness. The only light came from the moon and stars above the bay, reflecting off dark waves.

Only vaguely, did her brain register there was banging. A chinking sound of metal on metal. Moments later, the light returned.

"Lucy," Nate murmured in a deep, husky voice. "Come and see, lass."

She turned to face him.

Nate was so dear to her...tall and strong, with a tender smile and an outstretched hand. He pulled her to her feet and led the way down another passageway. Past a second gate, he'd opened like the other. In front of them stood a burly-looking door with metal strapping and a newer-looking padlock.

"What's there?" she asked.

"Perhaps nothing. Although, this door looks far sturdier

than the rest. And the lock is nowhere near a century old."

Hope sparked in her.

Lucy held the lantern while Nate bludgeoned the newer lock with his shovel. After several serious strikes, the thing gave way, and he was able to pry it open.

They stepped across the threshold together and froze. Lantern light spilled over the contents of a storeroom, packed to the rafters. Crates and barrels. Casks marked *Rum*. Weapons of all sorts, including a small cannon on wheels.

Lucy began to tremble. "Please, Nate, tell me it's real. That I'm not dreaming this."

"Aye, my love, it's real." He laughed, the happy sound filling the room. "Your father hid this from the world for you."

Lucy hurried over to a small trunk that sat on top of stacked boxes, and she thrust open its lid. Golden light gleamed into her face.

"The same coins. Some gold, others silver," Nate exclaimed. He opened another and another. "There must be ten...Nay, fifteen boxes filled with coins."

Lucy went to yet another trunk and sprang its lid. Chains of gold and ropes of pearls lay atop a pile of what appeared to have once been bolts of silk. A cloth bag held loose jewels, all kinds.

"There's a fortune here," she cried in disbelief.

"Aye, a pirate's fortune," Nate agreed with a stunned smile. "Enough to repair Fairwinds ten times over."

"Perhaps the Captain *did* lead us here? With the help of my father." She pointed to muddy footprints on the floor.

"Bloody hell," Nate exclaimed. "They're not ours, but there's been no one else down here. At least, not that I've seen."

Lucy pressed a hand to her heart. "We must guard this secret. Lance must never know."

Nate wrapped his arms about her, and he held her as she quivered with emotion. Cool lips pressed to her forehead. "Let's close this up as best we can. We'll return on the morrow, when our heads are clear, and we've a plan of what to do with all this."

"Alright," she said with a weary smile.

Together, they closed the trunks and the doorway and made their way back through the tunnels to the groundskeeper's cottage. Nate sealed the secret entrance again and wiped away the scuff marks on the floor.

"There, it's as if it never happened." He reached for her cloak. "Come, I'll take you home."

Lucy turned away from him before he could place the garment about her shoulders. "I don't want to go back to the house. It did happen, Nate, all of it. Everything feels so different now. Like all my dreams are within reach. And I want to share those dreams. With you."

It seemed like eternity, as she waited for him to speak. Would he hold fast to his convictions? Return to Boston and demand she go with him? Lucy prayed his resolve had weakened like her own. She craved his touch. So much since their stormy night together. She couldn't bear the thought of being apart from him for so long.

Nate's strong, sturdy form came close behind her. She could feel him, sense his inner struggle. Her woollen cloak came around her shoulders, and she released a sad sigh of surrender. She was about to head for the door when he held her in place. Loving arms wrapped around her.

Turning, Lucy gazed up into his troubled face. He closed

his eyes and pressed his forehead to hers. "I don't want to go to Boston alone. Or leave you here. We'll need to find a way forward together. A compromise. So we can both have what we want."

Lucy tipped her head to one side, and she smiled for him. "I love you, Nathaniel Bradford."

"Aye, lass, I love you, too. Marry me?" He tugged the cloak from her shoulders and dropped it to the floor. Then he left a trail of slow, sensual kisses from her cheek to her throat, lingering in the place where her neck met her shoulder. Gentle fingers teased the lace edge of her décolletage.

"I would, but my gown is ruined," she murmured and then giggled.

"I'll buy you a new one. Several. Hundreds. Whatever you want. So long as you take this one off for me," he growled.

***

"I want to see all of you this time. Every glorious inch. Help me," he urged when his fingers fumbled with her many buttons, bows, and layers.

Working together, Lucy's gown and undergarments soon lay strewn across the floor. She stood before him, naked as a goddess. Her rouge-tipped breasts, too lovely to resist. He traced their curves, their perfect, porcelain smoothness. Her nipples tightened when the pads of his rough thumbs circled and brushed repeatedly over them.

Nate swept Lucy up and carried her to his bed. He removed his own clothes, watching as her lazy gaze drifted from his chest down to his erection. Cool hands reached out to caress him, and he sucked in a sharp breath. He guided her movements, revealing the intimate motion that weakened his knees.

It was almost too much when he settled beside her on the bed meant for one. Skin to skin. Her soft naked middle pressed to his stiff cock. He fondled her breasts, licked their tight nipples. Blew softly, before taking turns, sucking each deep into his mouth.

Lucy moaned her approval and writhed against him. He could feel her passion rising. "Nate...love me," she pleaded.

A grin tipped his lips, before he silenced her words with more kisses. He rolled with her, until she was spread beneath him. Her long legs wound around his waist.

Nate closed his eyes, attempting to steal himself against the glorious sensation of sinking deep within her body. Hot, wet. So tight. Sultry silkiness, squeezing around him. He began to move with her. A languid slide. An unhurried roll of their joined hips.

They set a tempo together, a steady, building rhythm. Soon they were both panting and moaning. The next instant, they were frantically hurtling toward climax.

Wave after wave of exquisite pleasure washed over and through him.

Lucy arched and stiffened, and Nate let himself go.

In the quiet aftermath of their lovemaking, he gathered her in his arms and held on tight. A sense of great satisfaction and peace settled in.

Nate closed his eyes, savoring his remarkable lady and the wonderful life, stretching out before them.

***

A rooster crowed somewhere in the distance, rousing Nate. He'd slept sounder than ever before, cradling the woman he loved. His gaze drifted down to Lucy, so soft and sweet, as she snuggled against him with her small hand resting on his chest.

Trailing a lazy finger over her bare shoulder, he grinned when she squirmed. *Does she dream of me?* He wondered, as his mind retraced their steps from the night before. Pirate treasure. Chests filled with gold, silver, and jewels. Enough to fix the house and live comfortably for an exceedingly long time. Yet they'd found an even greater treasure in each other's arms, as they'd made love again, until they were both blissfully spent.

Nate eased from the bed, so as not to wake Lucy. He ambled around the cottage, picking up clothing, adding logs to the fire, and setting the kettle to boil. The fire popped and crackled as he searched the small collection of crockery for tea. Then he went to the tiny table to study Lucy's father's old map.

Quite serendipitous that she should find the very thing we needed. Although wasn't that the way of Fairwinds? Did not the old house and its ghostly inhabitants always find a way to carry on through the ages?

However last night came to be, Lucy would now get her dream. She had a fortune. In the bargain, he got the woman he loved beyond all else. He pondered the things they'd talked about and planned. With an easy smile and a grateful heart, he carefully returned the old parchment paper to the case and secured its flap.

Lucy stirred when the house began to warm, and sun peeked through the shutters. "Good morning," she grumbled from his bed. "I've never been so glad to discover something was *not* a dream."

Nate strolled over to her, and he sat on the edge beside her. Gently, he smoothed tangled hair from her pretty face.

She attempted to sit up, but she winced, and lay back

down again.

"Sore?" he asked with a self-satisfied grin.

"Why do you ask silly questions when you know the answer?" She groaned and gave him a playful shove. "You're a beast of a man."

Nate fondled her bare breasts, bringing their nipples to instant peaks. "I wasn't a beast last night when you were biting my shoulder and digging your fingernails into my arse," he teased.

"I did no such thing," she said in a lofty tone. Yet she frowned. "Did I? I suppose I lost control."

"Lucy, my love," Nate crooned and pulled her close. "There's so much I cannot wait to share with you. Once we're husband and wife, and we're not wearing ourselves out in grimy tunnels. How does a warm bath sound? Perhaps before the fireplace in your room with some spiced wine?"

"So…we're to wear ourselves out in my bigger bed?" she teased him back before kissing her way along his chin. "Only if you'll feed me. I'm absolutely famished this morning. Do you think your mother is awake yet? I don't wish for her to cook, but perhaps we can commandeer her kitchen?"

Nate stood, and he tugged her from the bed. "How about we find some eggs, and I'll make breakfast for us all?" He winked at her. "I've a hearty appetite myself."

"Hearty? That, sir, is an understatement. If I can walk all the way to the barnyard, you shall have your blasted eggs. I'll even help you cook them."

Amusement tugged his lips. "Have no fear, my bonnie bride-to-be. I'll hoist you over my shoulder like any good pirate would."

Ten minutes later, they were collecting eggs together and

laughing as the feathers flew around the coop. Nate plucked some from Lucy's long hair, still undone and snarled from their night of passion. She looked like a woman well loved. A dream come true to him. His fine lady, who wasn't too proud to enjoy the simple pleasures of country life.

Her skirts were stained by at least eight inches of muck and mire from the tunnels, yet her cheeks were glowing, her lips red from his kisses. Lovely, as she smiled for him in the frosty morning air.

"That's all there is," she declared. "Shall we head to the kitchen?"

Nate offered her his arm. "Mum will be overjoyed with the news we have to share with her."

"What, that we discovered treasure?"

"No, woman, are you daft?" he joked, pulling her close and giving her a fierce hug. "That we're getting married. She's been hoping and nudging me for weeks."

"That truly warms my heart," Lucy said with a grin. "I adore your mother. She's a very wise woman."

Yet Nate's smile vanished when they neared the house. "Is that a coach?"

"Who would be coming to Fairwinds at this hour?"

Chapter 9

A shiny black carriage rattled to a stop before the mansion.

"No…" Lucy moaned. She dropped the basket. "It cannot be."

"Who is it?" Nate asked.

"There she is." Belinda Grimes' shrill voice shattered the calm air of the morning. "And that's the one she's taken a shine to." The vile woman exited the carriage, and she looked both Lucy and Nate up and down. "Quite the shine if you ask me. They look as if they just tumbled out of bed."

Nate stepped in front of Lucy.

"Dear sister, how I've missed your smiling face," a well-dressed man exclaimed, his voice dripping sarcasm. He turned back to the coach, holding the door open so another man could exit.

Flamboyant as a peacock, with golden hair and an extravagant royal-blue cape, the second man's eyes widened upon seeing Lucy in what amounted to filthy peasant attire. "Miss Ellison?" he cried in obvious surprise.

Cora was already in the front doorway, wearing a nervous frown, as she repeatedly twisted her apron.

Lucy stepped away from Nate. She walked straight up to the two men, going head-to-head with the first one. "What are you doing here, Lance?"

Lance Ellison's lips twisted into a ruthless smile. "I told you we would come when the time was right." He gave Nate a superficial glance. "Who is this?"

"You'd know if you read your blasted mail," she fired back.

"Ah, the troublesome groundskeeper. Yes, of course." He waved a dismissive hand. "You're fired. I no longer require your services."

"Wait a minute—" Nate started, but he didn't get far when two men jumped down from the back of the carriage. One brandished a pistol. The other needed no weapon, considering he was roughly the size of the coach itself.

"Mr. Minnow and Bill," Lance sang out. "Would you escort this bit of trash from my property?"

"With pleasure," the giant rumbled in a deep voice. He cracked his knuckles and punched his palms as he strolled toward Nate.

"Stop," Lucy cried. "You don't understand."

"Oh, but I do, sister, based on your positively disgusting state of dress. It's obvious you fancy this mongrel. Belinda said as much. Pity, poor you, silly Lucy. And you thought nothing of breaking your betrothed's heart?"

Lucy's horrified stare shot to Nate, and she shook her head.

"If she didn't tell you, *groundskeeper*, my sister is promised to another. She's been engaged to Mr. Grimes for some time now. So, she's led you on. Dallied with your feelings. If you'd hoped to marry an heiress, you lose."

Lucy released a low, pitiful, moan. "No, Nathaniel, it's not true. Don't listen to him."

"Get this *creature* from my sight," the blond dandy piled on before pressing a handkerchief to his nose and mouth.

All at once, Nate was seized by the two thugs, and they began to drag him away. He shook them off and started swinging, connecting with the smaller man's head before the big one caught him in a choke hold.

"Nate," Cora screamed from the doorway.

"Hold off," Nate gasped, stopping the man long enough to plead, "Let me say goodbye to my mother."

"We are not savages," Lance sang above the fray. "Release the man, so he can make his peace."

Nate staggered past Lucy, going straight to Cora. "Don't anger them," he whispered so only she could hear. "I'll bring The Watch when I return."

"But Lucy?" Cora fretted.

Nate gave the woman he loved one last glance.

"She cares for you, Nathaniel, I'm certain of it. Don't believe that dreadful man."

Meaty hands grabbed him from behind before he could say anything more. He was dragged away by his collar.

The bruiser, called Minnow, gave Nate a thorough thrashing before he shoved him through the door of the cottage. "Get your things, farm boy. Be gone in ten minutes, or your mother will be cryin' over your corpse tonight. Hey, Bill," he called to the little man rifling through Nate's personal items. "Don't be pinchin' nothin'. This bloke has had a bad enough mornin'."

Nate hurried to gather his belongings as the two men watched. "I've a horse in the barn."

Minnow snatched up Lucy's father's satchel from the table, and his breath caught. "Get your bleedin' horse and get the hell out." He thrust the bag at Nate.

Despite the growing pain in his body, Nate faced the mountain of a man. "Why do you work for a toady like Ellison?"

Minnow grinned, revealing two golden teeth, right in the

center of his mouth. "I don't. I hate the mealy-mouthed son of a bitch. I'm here to ensure me boss gets his money. But that's none of your damn business."

***

Lucy seethed with anger as she watched Lance stroll through the front rooms of her beloved Fairwinds. Nate was gone, hauled away by her brother's lackeys. Who knew if he was injured? She did know he would fight, and that would only make things worse. She also knew she and Cora were at the mercy of the mad mob as Edmund and Belinda joined them in the foyer.

"It smells odd in here. Damp and musty." Lance glanced about, scrunching up his nose in distaste. "I loath old houses."

"Then why are you here, Lance?" Lucy asked, struggling to remain calm in the face of exceedingly dire circumstances. "I expected you to stay in New York or even to return to Boston. Never to actually come to this remote corner of the world."

"And miss your nuptials to dear ol' Edmund?" he tossed back casually with a chuckle. "To think…he's been dreaming of your wedding night all these weeks. Tsk, tsk, tsk. I never imagined you were such a strumpet. Did they teach you that in school, too?"

"I told you—all of you—I would not consider marrying—"

"As if I care what you'd consider, *sister*," Lance interrupted, sneering the last word. "You are going to marry Edmund. Then he and I are going to level this place and sell off every bit. The timber, the rocks…The very granite stones of this decaying old mansion."

"What?" Lucy cried in disbelief. "Are you mad?"

"Yes, quite mad. At you for attempting to destroy my plans with your whoring ways. To think, we believed you to be an innocent." He snickered as Edmund looked on with a condescending smirk.

"Why bother forcing me to marry anyone? What purpose could that possibly serve if all you want is the estate?"

Lance came close. So close, his spittle sprayed her face when he bellowed, "Because our *stupid father* changed his *stupid will* right before he died. He left Fairwinds to you."

Lucy staggered back. Hope blossomed in her heart. "Fairwinds is...mine?"

"Only through entitlement. If—or rather when—you marry, the estate goes to you through your husband. And *that* is why *you will* marry Edmund Grimes as soon as possible."

"But that's ridiculous. Archaic. We're not living in medieval times. If this house is mine, then it's mine. I'd be delighted to show you all the door."

Something snapped inside her brother then. Lucy saw it in the sudden, murderous glint in his eyes. He drew back his hand and struck her hard across the face. She spun with the force, crying out in pain.

"Lucy," Cora screamed and rushed to her side. "You horrid excuse for a man," she scolded Lance. "May God show you no mercy. All of you."

Just then, the two ruffians returned, waltzing through the front doors as if they owned the place.

"There's a bit o' trouble on your front lawn, governor," the big man, Minnow, said to Lance with a chuckle. "Your former groundskeeper is being taken away by some fellas with guns."

Lucy scrambled to the door and stumbled out onto the steps.

Men of The Watch were hauling a bloodied and bruised Nate from his horse.

"Stop," she cried. "What are you doing to him?"

"He's under arrest, ma'am," the apparent leader of the band spoke up.

Others from inside spilled out around her to witness the disaster unfolding on the driveway.

"Why? What could he possibly have done to warrant such treatment?" Lucy demanded.

"Theft. And possibly the murder of a man right here at Fairwinds. A store owner in town has raised the accusations. He's to be questioned. We'll send word if formal charges are brought."

"But he's done nothing wrong," she yelled, turning frantic.

Punishing hands gripped Lucy's arms, dragging her back. Lance leaned close to mutter in her ear. "You don't even know a good man from a bad one, do you, Lucy? Aligning yourself with a gold digger. I'm the only thief in this family, you stupid, stupid girl. And the spoils all go to me. He'll rot in prison if I have anything to say about it."

Lucy struggled, bucking Lance's painful grip, as Cora wept in earnest.

"You, Bill," her brother barked at the little thug. "Take that serving wench to the kitchen. See that she prepares me something decent to eat. Pillaging always makes me hungry." He turned his attention to the big man. "And you, Minnow, take my sister to her room and lock her up. Your keys, madam," he demanded of Cora.

Cora's chatelaine was ripped from her waist by Belinda, who passed it to Mr. Minnow with a self-righteous smirk. "You won't be needing those anymore," she snarled at the housekeeper.

"Let me go," Lucy hissed and kicked as she was wrestled

inside.

"Don't make me carry you, Miss High and Mighty. I'm known for me butterfingers. Wouldn't want you fallin' from somewhere high now, would we? Your brother needs you."

"Ouch," she shrieked when his brawny hands squeezed her like a vice.

"Lucy, dear," Edmund sang out over the commotion. "I shall visit you later. Once you've calmed down."

"Don't you dare, you arrogant ass," she yelled, as she was forced up the staircase.

***

Lucy paced her bedroom floor, shaking uncontrollably.

How could life be so insanely cruel? One minute, you're happier than you've ever been. The next, everything you love is ripped away from you.

Her immediate concerns were for Nate. *Theft and murder? Impossible.* She refused to even consider such ridiculous charges. The shop owner was wrong. Dead wrong. *Nate is the best of men. A fine gentleman and lawyer. Working tirelessly. Staying here to help me. He even—*

Her thoughts hit a wall.

He even...*sold pirate gold in town, bringing suspicion upon himself because of me.*

Lucy's heart sank to the bottom of the sea. She could still see him, being yanked from his horse. Hollering, with his face swollen and bloodied. His bag and her father's strung across his chest—

Father's bag? The map?

At least it wasn't in the hands of her brother.

She had to do something. *Save Nate. Protect Cora. Nothing else mattered.* But what could she do, locked in a room?

"Captain Wilder…Lady Lillian…Please, I beg you both, help me. Protect those I love. I don't know what ghosts can do to the living, but please try something. Anything."

That evening, Lucy stood like a stone statue in the dining room. Battered, bruised. She'd spent the entire day locked in her bedroom until being summoned. Minnow stuck close to her side. His ever-present vice-grip wrapped painfully around her throbbing wrist.

"What is that infernal banging noise?" Lance demanded as he picked at the food before him. Another door slammed for the hundredth time since they'd arrived.

Belinda flinched with each crash. "It's the ghosts, I tell you. They slam the bloody doors when they're angry. You won't see them do it. But they do."

"Ridiculous," Lance scoffed. "I'll not be made a fool of. Someone…go make it stop."

"No one ever believes me when I tell the truth," Belinda griped.

"That's because you so rarely *do* tell the truth," Edmund countered in a frosty tone. He took a loud snuff of tobacco, disregarding the daggers in his sister's eyes.

"I don't believe in ghosts," Lance said in a smug tone. "Dead is dead. Gone is gone. The ghosts of Fairwinds are merely childish stories. Invented by my father, so I wouldn't come here. Never see the true worth of this place. Pirate ghosts, indeed."

Lucy smirked when the doors on the second floor slammed even harder.

"Oh…I don't like this," Belinda whimpered, her eyes wide with fear. "I know what happened the last time they got mad.

That…that…*thing* outside. It came for me. Likely would've killed me if I didn't leave. Fine if you don't want to believe in them, but I'll not be taunting the dead. It's the curse, I tell you. We need to get out of this mausoleum before something dreadful happens."

"You really should consider a life on the stage, Belinda," Edmund said in a snotty tone as he considered his fingernails. "You've a gift for theater."

"Listen here, you little squint, I've had about enough of this scheme of yours. Just marry the bitch. It's high time we move on anyway."

Edmund's blue-eyed stare snapped to the two thugs, standing guard on either side of Lucy. "Sister…you know the vicar cannot be here until tomorrow. Until then, we must all relax. Make ourselves at home." He plastered on a fake smile, though Lucy saw him give a little shudder. "Everyone will get what they deserve then."

"You can't spend money if you're dead," Belinda countered.

"Everyone?" Lucy's voice spiked with outrage. "What is this so-called scheme then, to divvy up my ancestral home between you three? You cannot force me to marry you, Edmund, and you will not get this house. No man of God would make me marry against my will."

Lance cackled with glee. "You see…that's just the thing…the vicar is on the take, too. I've paid him handsomely to marry you, regardless of what you say. So, dear Lucy, there's no way round the fact that you're to be a bride tomorrow. Unless…"

"Unless what?" she challenged.

"I might be *persuaded* to let you keep this moth-eaten old

mansion. *If* you'll allow me to sell off most of the property."

A chill slid down Lucy's spine. As if the very walls of Fairwinds trembled at her brother's proposal. The slamming sounds ceased. A deadly silence filled its place.

"Marry Edmond, and I'll let you keep your precious Fairwinds. Then we'll go our separate ways."

"But," Edmund cried out in protest, "you said—"

"I said nothing," Lance barked. Yet he settled himself and gave Lucy an unnerving smile. "I'd no idea how much Lucy cared for this place. If she's going to be miserable, then perhaps we should simply find another way to get what we want? A bargain, so to speak. So that everyone wins."

Edmund huffed his displeasure.

"Tell me, Lance, if you're such a successful businessman, why do you need this estate?" Lucy dared ask.

Minnow spoke before he could answer. "Because these scabies are in debt up their eyeballs with me boss. I'm here to collect. So be a good little girl and do what the man says."

"And if I don't?" She taunted her jailer.

The monster grinned down at her. "You don't wanna know, missy. Let's just say if ya have any fondness for yourself, or your brother, you'd better help 'im get his bloomin' money."

Lucy confronted Lance. "I want Fairwinds. All to myself. Outright. Legally. I demand you help me get Nate released, unharmed. Cora must be treated with respect. And I want you all out of this house the second I say, 'I do.'"

Lance strode right up to her face. "Done. Marry Edmund Grimes without incident tomorrow, and you shall have it all. You have my word."

***

"The man's word is rubbish," Nate accused as he

attempted to plead his case to the leader of The Watch.

"That's a fine blinker you've got there, Mr. Bradford. Are you certain it wasn't *you* who did all the instigating?"

Nate fingered his swollen eye. "I fought back if that's what you're asking. But I'm telling you, Lance Ellison has come to Mystic Point with armed cohorts. Dangerous criminals, who are putting Miss Lucy Ellison and my mother at great risk. You're accusing me of crimes when you should be arresting them."

The commander of The Watch huffed. "We don't get involved in private matters. Especially those involving womenfolk. Sticky business, affairs of the heart."

Nate held up a handful of papers and violently shook them at the man. "*This* is a lengthy report from the head of my law firm. Lance Ellison and Edmund Grimes are wanted criminals in New York and three other states, including this one. They're accused of larceny, embezzlement, investment fraud. Hardly 'affairs of the heart.' That Grimes fellow is even worse. He's accused of bigamy, several times over. There are slews of criminal complaints against him made by wealthy families, whose 'womenfolk' married the man only to be robbed blind when he vanishes. He then moves on to defraud other poor victims. Obviously, Lucy Ellison is his next target. With her father dead, and her brother perpetrating the crime, it is our legal and moral duty to protect her. I'm outnumbered, so I need your help."

Hours later, Nate sat hunched over in a dark corner of a public house. The Watch had released him when he offered proof he was a respected attorney in Boston. The accusations were simply that. They held little weight when the local shipping merchant Nate had done work for vouched for him.

He was ordered not to leave the area until the matter was formally put to rest. Obviously, crime and punishment were negotiable in Mystic Point, especially if one had rich benefactors.

Nate stared blankly at the untouched beer before him. He was broken all over, but there was no way he could eat or drink anything knowing Lucy was in the hands of ruffians. He'd sent word to his office of their dire predicament, hopefully escalating the chance Lance Ellison and his motley crew would be apprehended. The law outside this tiny community needed to be brought in.

If only he knew Lucy was all right.

It had killed him to leave her, especially since she now likely wondered if he was a thief or a murderer. If he ever cared for her at all or was simply a gold digger.

He hugged her father's satchel, strapped once more to his side. At least one Ellison family mystery would remain secret until it could be dealt with in a court of law.

In the meantime, Lance Ellison was capable of causing physical harm to both Lucy and his mother. They'd be in even more danger if the man discovered there was pirate gold beneath his feet.

Nate glanced up when a hooded figure approached his table. "News is…you need a gun. Maybe even a *hired gun*," the man muttered before he sat down to negotiate.

***

Lucy rolled over on her bed with a tortured groan. Hours of contemplating her next move, and still she had nothing. She'd been locked up since agreeing to Lance's dubious offer. Now it was late. On the morrow, she was to be married.

Lance was a liar and a swindler. She knew that much. He'd

been so his entire life. But what choice did she have with no one here to help?

Where is Nate? Her broken heart cried out in misery.

The tiny voice in her head was unexpectedly silent, as were the ghosts of Fairwinds. It was as if the winds of fate had turned against her and Nate. After all the joy they'd shared but a day ago. She'd cried every tear she could over how much they'd lost.

She didn't believe for a minute Nate was capable of murder. *But what could he think of me now, after all Lance's poison words? Leading him on…Toying with his emotions, his gentleman's heart.* In part, what Lance said was true. She'd kept Edmund's bizarre proposal of marriage from Nate, because she never intended to accept it. No part of her wanted anything more to do with Grimes siblings. Her heart, and everything she had, belonged to only one man. Nathaniel Bradford.

Lucy said a silent prayer that somehow, some way, she could explain to him, and they could ride out this terrible storm together.

Forcing herself to rise, she went to the large windows to gaze out into the darkness. She gasped when spying a phantom-like woman patrolling the cliffs.

Lady Lillian?

White as snow, the apparition glowed with an internal light all its own. The lady's long hair and gown floated behind her on the night breeze. She carried a lantern, its golden halo seeming to draw Lucy in with its spellbinding light. The ghostly figure turned toward the house and appeared to look directly at her. Then she motioned with one pale, willowy arm. *Come to me, Lucy.*

Dawn was approaching, and the vision vanished like smoke on the building wind.

Lucy listened as gusts swirled around the corners of the old mansion. She returned to her bed and sank to its edge. *Come to her? How can I? I'm locked in.*

Lucy froze and held her breath as footsteps sounded in the hallway. A key slipped into the keyhole, and the old lock tumbled slowly. She sprang from the bed and rushed the door. "Cora," she whispered, as her heart leapt in her chest.

"Your guard has gone to relieve himself," the older woman said.

"How did you get your keys back?"

"I stole them, right from beneath the big man's nose. He's passed out in a kitchen chair." Cora's lips tipped with a smirk. "Might have been that homemade wine I served him. It's quite strong, you know."

"You're so brave. Thank you. But I'm afraid there's nothing we can do. Two women against those brutes."

"Aye, there is. You can hide. They can't force you to marry if they can't find you. Get to the tunnel and wait for Nate."

Lucy's lips trembled. "But why? He's not coming back."

Cora patted her cheek. "He'd never leave you, child. He's in love with you. Nate always finds a way to look after those he loves."

Hot tears spilled from Lucy's swollen eyes.

"Hurry. The trap door on the third floor is your only option since the others are camped out in the parlor. Roll the carpet away. Give it a hard tug just before you close the trapdoor. Hopefully, they won't notice."

Lucy tiptoed out into the dark hallway. Cora locked the door behind them. They squeezed hands and went their separate ways in silence.

Lucy had to feel her way along the hallway, counting doors as she headed for the pitch-black staircase leading to the third floor. Inching her way up, she rounded the corner, and went straight for the trapdoor to the spiral staircase. She rolled back the heavy rug and cursed under her breath when a light shone upon her.

"Well, what have we here? A bloomin' runaway?"

The small thug's voice made her gasp. She dropped the carpet back in place and scrambled to her feet to face him.

"Whatcha doin', missy? Trying to hide from old Bill?" Her pursuer leered when he caught her arm and twisted it painfully behind her back. Lucy went to scream, but his moist, foul-smelling hand clamped over her mouth.

"Can't a man take a piss without you causin' trouble?" He ground his crotch against her hip, and she struggled all the harder. "Oh...I likes all your curves and soft spots. How's about a little poke, since you made me climb all those stairs to find you? Come on, I knows you like it. You was sleepin' with the help." He wrestled her to the bed, shoving her face down into the pillow.

Lucy choked and gulped for air when his full weight fell upon her. Groping hands raised her skirts, and he pinched and clawed at her thighs.

Cold air suddenly struck her skin when the man flew off her with a yelp.

"What the hell do you think your doing?" the one called Minnow growled as he hauled Lucy to her feet and clamped his meaty hand over her mouth. "Dippin' your wick in Grimes' hot tottie? Ellison will have your head, and I'll let him, too."

"We was just havin' a little touch and tickle. I weren't

gonna do nothin' more."

"Don't make me mad, Bill. I've a pain in me melon already. The fact that I can't trust you alone for five minutes…It irritates me somethin' powerful."

Lucy struggled, yet the giant only tightened his grip.

"She's a crafty one, Minnow. I've no idea how she got out of that locked room. What if it was them ghosts, helpin' her?"

"Shut your trap. Tie her tighter this time, or I'll beat your brains in," Minnow threatened. He shoved Lucy into a chair. "I've had enough of these so called *gentle, country folk*."

Chapter 10

Dawn came too quickly for Lucy. Her body hurt all over, and her heart ached all the more when Belinda came to get her dressed for the ceremony.

"You can't be getting married in those filthy clothes. You must look the part of the happy bride for my brother," the despicable woman proclaimed.

"What's the point?" Lucy muttered as she sank into a chair, so Belinda could work the snarls from her hair.

"The point is…this is a very important day for both our brothers. And for me. We've worked hard for this moment."

Lucy gave a humorless laugh. "You act as if this is something to be proud of, an accomplishment, when in fact what you're doing is stealing everything I've ever loved."

"How you carry on, Lucy Ellison. I'd have thought you'd wise up by now." The older woman clicked her tongue and shook her head. "What gown do you wish to wear?"

"The black one. I'm in full mourning," Lucy stated flatly.

"Are you asking to be murdered by Lance? He's considered it, you know," she revealed in a smug tone. "When I told him about the mice and rats here, he said I should have poisoned you with arsenic. Slipped something into your tea when you weren't looking."

"I don't care what my brother said. I don't care what he thinks, or what he wants. He's dead to me. As are all of you."

"Don't you dare be saying such dreadful things," Belinda scolded. "Not in this frightful place. I felt eyes, watching me all night. Even in the parlor, with grown men around me. I was afraid. You can keep this blasted house, for all I care. Good riddance, I say."

"You know Lance would love to see you hang for murder," Lucy countered. "Not because he cares a whit about me. But because it would mean one less person to divide the spoils with. Do you imagine he or your own brother *actually* cares for you? They're both merely using you to get what they want from me. And you think I must 'wise up?'" she added with a bitter laugh.

"Shut up." The vile woman yanked her hair hard. "Wear whatever the hell you want. I'm not your keeper anymore."

Half an hour later, Lucy strode in silence through the halls of Fairwinds. Stiff as an iron rod, her black gloved hands knitted tightly together. She wore her most severe mourning clothes – a heavy black dress with a high lace collar. Atop the tight knot of her hair sat a black hat with a matching veiling to cover her miserable, tear-swollen face.

"Look at her." Edmund sneered when she descended the staircase to meet them in the foyer. The ever-present Mr. Minnow a mere two steps behind her. "She looks like a widow, just come from a graveside, not my bride to be."

Lance clapped with glee. "She's perfect. The embodiment of everything this pitiful place and our family has come to represent. Yet another ghost of Fairwinds."

A knock sounded at the front door, and Cora hurried to open it.

The so-called "man of God" entered with a grunt and a belch. "Let's get this over with. I've a funeral next with a luncheon to follow," the rotund man griped. Yet he slid to a halt when he spied Lucy. "Is *this* the bride?"

Edmund slithered to her side and snatched up her arm. "It is. Isn't she a vision?"

The vicar adjusted his grimy spectacles and heaved a sigh. "Yes...but a vision of what? No matter." He shrugged. "It's none of my business who marries whom. Just point me to where I shall perform the ceremony."

Everyone looked around in confusion. Except for Lucy. Her gaze had fallen to the floor. Words like "the library" and "the parlor" were tossed about between the others.

Yet the tiny voice in Lucy's head finally awoke. And it spoke to her, loud and clear this time. *"The cliffs. Come to me, Lucy."*

"I want the cliffs," Lucy spoke up, surprising everyone.

Edmund gazed down at her, and the strangest expression crossed his features. *Worry? Doubt? Something akin to real fear perhaps?* And yet, he conceded with a nod. "Give Lucy what she wants."

Together, the morbid bridal party made the walk to the edge of the back lawn to stand alongside the grave of Lillian Grace. The wind was brisk and cold there, yet the winter sun shone bright in a crystalline blue sky.

Such a contrast...the beauty of this day to what is happening. Lucy's thoughts wandered aimlessly, as the gruesome proceedings got underway. She didn't listen to the words the purported holy man spoke. *What did they matter?* She was not marrying her true love. Every bit of this wedding was a sham.

"Do you have the ring?"

Those words, and the befuddled conversation that followed, broke through the fog in Lucy's head.

"Who cares if there's a ring?" Lance blurted out in a raised tone.

The vicar appeared to have reached some invisible threshold in the charade. One he refused to cross. "There must be a ring."

"Ridiculous," Lance scoffed. "None of this will matter when I tear the place down. It's merely a formality. Just marry them, dammit."

The cold finger of reality slid down Lucy's spine, and she spun on her brother. "You swore to me you'd leave me this house."

"Well, I lied," he spewed. "You should've known better than to trust me."

Lucy yanked her arm free from Edmund's, her accusatory stare flipping between everyone present. She took several steps back, but Mr. Minnow and Bill blocked her way. The vicar looked on with not a hint of care or remorse. The Grimes siblings—devoid of righteousness, as always—merely watched in stony silence. Yet Cora wept into her apron on the back patio, her cries carrying to Lucy's ears on the wind.

"How could you do this to me?" Lucy pointed an accusing finger at Lance. "I've done everything you've asked. Always. Except for this. I've tried to be a sister to you, only to have you lash out or turn your back on me completely. You've ruined every happiness I could have ever had. Why? What reason could there be for your hateful behavior?"

Lance stared her down, his eyes stone-cold and dead. *The window to his true soul.* A muscle near his eye ticked. "You were simply...born. Isn't that enough?"

Lucy dropped her head. He'd never forgive her for their mother's death. And she would never forgive him for what he'd done to Nate, or what he was forcing on her this day. "Do your worst then. I've nothing left."

An angry wind suddenly swirled up around them. Lucy raised her gaze as an overpowering scent of roses swept in. Belinda screamed when the ghost of Lillian Grace appeared out of nowhere.

This visage of the woman was not sad and broken. It was powerful and enraged. Long hair whipped about her head like the tentacles of an angry sea monster. Eyes—red as burning coals—emanated from her stark-white face. Her grey lips parted, and the spectre shrieked, sending panic through the group.

"God, save me," the holy man cried, begging for salvation.

Lance and the two thugs cried out and scrambled in horror.

Edmund screamed and stumbled backward, away from the terrifying creature. The ground at the edge of the cliff gave way. He teetered, flailing his arms. Belinda lunged for him. But he slipped from her grasp and plunged to the rocks below.

Belinda crumbled to the dirt. Her bloodcurdling wails scattered on the wind.

The spirit vanished just as quickly as it had appeared. And yet justice was swiftly and utterly served.

The vicar bolted, running for his life faster than any could've imagined.

Lance attempted to flee, but Mr. Minnow and Bill caught up to him. "Let me go," he yelled in protest of being manhandled. "Take your filthy hands off me."

"Not on your life," Minnow growled. "I've got me orders."

"But you saw. It's all real," Lance cried. "The ghosts are all real."

"I saw nothin' but your sleazy partner going over the cliff," the giant man reasoned, as if to save his own sanity. "That leaves only you to pay the debt."

"But I don't have that kind of money. Lucy was going to get it for me. Without her I can't—" Lance's panicked gaze flipped to his sister. His expression transformed into one of sheer stunned disbelief.

Minnow grabbed him by the throat. "I'm going to like pulverizing your bones to dust. I'm sick of your shit. And I'm sick of this place. You'll be pig slops by morning."

Bill hurried away with Minnow close behind, his mighty grip now firmly around Lance's wrist like an iron cuff.

"Lucy," Lance screamed over his shoulder. "You can't do this to me!"

Lucy stood her ground—numb and frozen inside. Yet oddly at peace, despite the chaos surrounding her. A shattered woman at her feet, muttering undecipherable words. Criminals, fleeing the scene or being dragged off. Her gloved hands clutched the rusted iron fence surrounding the solitary headstone of the woman who'd defended her grave.

You're safe now, the voice inside her head whispered. *We're all safe.*

She turned to gaze out at Skullery Bay, ignoring her brother's continued pleas for help. All she could think was how lovely the white-tipped waves looked in the morning sunlight. How the gulls cried as they floated on the salted breeze. She smiled as a sense of calm settled into her heart.

"Lucy!"

Someone yelled her name from far away, and she awoke from her trance-like state.

"Lucy, my God," Nathaniel cried when he reached her.

Strong arms crushed her in a protective embrace. Love

and devotion poured into her soul from him.

Nate swept her up when her knees buckled under the weight of it all. "Lucy, darling, are you alright? Are you hurt?"

"She's in shock, Nate."

She heard Cora speaking words, yet she didn't understand.

The house? she wondered as she gazed back at the grave.

It's safe, the voice inside assured her. *"Thank you, Lucy. Be at peace in the place you love."*

"Get her into the house, Nate."

She heard the words but didn't yet understand.

***

Lucy blinked in confusion as she gazed up at the concerned expression on the other's faces.

"Oh...your poor eye," she murmured to Nate.

"Take a sip of water," he urged. "You'll be alright soon."

"What happened?" she mumbled groggily. She attempted to sit up, yet the room tipped and blackened.

"Take your time, dear," Cora chimed in.

Lucy realized she was on the small sofa in the sitting area, her head resting on tasselled pillows. "Edmund...He fell."

"Aye, we saw the whole thing," Nate assured her. "I brought help. The Watch and some others. They saw what happened, too. Though I'm not sure they'll be telling anyone soon. They're retrieving Grimes' remains now."

"The Watch is here?"

Nate gave her a tilted grin. "Apparently, you get action when you threaten to call the governor."

"She knows!" Belinda's screeches shattered the hush of the house. "She knows all about the ghosts of Fairwinds," the crazed woman bellowed as officers struggled to get her out the front doors.

"What's going on?" Lucy asked.

"They're carting her away," Cora said with a wide smile. "Serves her right. She finally lost her mind after witnessing her brother's waltz over the edge."

"That's awful," Lucy said, frowning as she rose and took a few tentative steps. She followed the men leading the mad woman away.

"Tell them about the slamming doors. And the footsteps. The white face in the window," Belinda Grimes commanded as she was wrestled into a straitjacket. "Lucy, tell them," she yelled, as she was hoisted into the back of a prison wagon.

Just before they shut her in, a mouse ran across her shoes and scampered out to safety.

The woman's eyes went wild, and she screamed and screamed, until the heavy doors slammed. The coach pulled away, yet they could still hear her cries.

Epilogue

Fairwinds ~ Summer 1845

"Alice, darling," Lucy called to their oldest child. "Don't play near the edge. You'll give Jonathan bad ideas." She turned to Nathaniel, who lounged on the picnic blanket alongside her on the back lawn of Fairwinds. "Even that iron fence you erected doesn't stop me from worrying."

"Have no fear, my love, I've an eye on her. Alice knows the rules," Nate assured her, as he played with their young son. He tenderly took Lucy's hand and kissed it, fiddling with the ruby ring upon her finger. "Our babies are safe here."

Lucy caressed the swell of her belly. She wore a wistful smile when she considered their now summer home. "Six and a half years spent between here and Boston, and I've loved every minute of it with you."

Their first born bounded over, her lovely, long curls bouncing as she plopped herself down on the blanket. Alice kissed her three-year-old brother on the head, causing him to screech.

"What have you got there?" Nate asked. He leaned over her shoulder to see.

Alice fanned through the pages of a leather-bound journal they'd given her. An old favorite from Lucy's father. "I'm writing a story about Captain Wilder and Lady Lillian," the girl said with obvious pride.

"And how do you know what to write?" Lucy asked.

"Because they tell me," Alice said in a nonchalant tone, causing both parents to lock gazes over her head. "It's a love story, mostly. But bad things happened to them still. Mainly, it's about how much they love each other and this place. And all of us," Alice chirped happily. "I'm writing about you and Father, too. I'll have to interview you both to get it all right," she declared with a thoughtful frown.

"Of course," Nate said with a grin.

"It's to be expected," Lucy agreed, smothering a smile. "All great writers must do their research."

"Will you write about Jonathan and the new baby?" Nate inquired.

"Yes, but they won't do much. They're babies, after all. I'm all grown up at nearly seven."

"What of Nanny Cora?" Lucy prodded. "She does many things around here."

Alice got a distant look about her pretty face. "The ghosts of Fairwinds love Nanny Cora because she looks after them and their house. She was the one who promised the house would be happy again. That there would always be love here, no matter what."

"That's right, darling," Lucy said with tears in her eyes. "Fairwinds is our home."

The End

AUTHOR'S NOTE

Just a little something from me...

How could I not fall in love with Fairwinds? A haunted mansion on the rugged seacoast of New England? It's my dream destination! I hope it becomes yours, too, as we navigate its many twists, turns, mysteries, and romances through the ages together.

This was a different sort of romance for me to write. A shared setting, plus a forever love that endures beyond death. How fascinating and inspiring, all at once! Thank you, dear readers, for joining me on this adventure.

I'd like to also thank my super-talented co-authors and friends, Nancy Fraser and Lisa A. Olech, for this wonderful experience.

~ *Kathryn*

The Bootlegger's Daughter
(1924)

Best Selling & Award-Winning Author
Nancy Fraser

The Bootlegger's Daughter

Can she withstand the disgrace of being a con-man's daughter long enough to restore dignity to her ancestral home?

Mallory McGuire is the daughter of one of New England's most notorious criminals. She's also the legal owner of Fairwinds, the estate left to her by her late mother after Helene McGuire's fall from the cliffs overlooking Skullery Bay.

The many underground tunnels and hidden passages beneath the stately Fairwinds hide even more secrets than they do illegal activity. Then there's also the unusual noises, the strange occurrences within the house itself, that set everyone on edge.

Harry Carter is a disgraced ex-Pinkerton detective, on the lam from his former employer for embezzlement. Now working for Malcolm McGuire, he's charged with being Mallory's bodyguard to protect her from her father's many enemies.

As straight-forward as his unwanted protection assignment should be, things get complicated when he learns the truth about Mallory. She's definitely not what he thought—who he thought—she was. Now that he knows, protecting her has taken on a whole new meaning. And along with his increased protection has come an awareness, a desire that he does his best to deny.

When his desire becomes their desire, will things heat up to the point of no return? And when she discovers he's hiding secrets even bigger than her own, will she be able to forgive him and accept the possibility of a happily-ever-after?

Dedication

For Maddie, Peggy, Lucinda, and Kathy for keeping me sane. Most of the time.

Chapter 1

Law Office of Thaddeus Miller, Esq.
March 1922

Mallory McGuire sat in the huge leather chair in Mr. Miller's austere office, dwarfed by not only the oversized furniture but by the gaggle of men surrounding her—the solicitor, her father, his two largest bodyguards, and a younger man she believed to be Mr. Miller's son-in-law and law partner, Joshua Blake.

She didn't want to be here, yet the attorney for her late mother's estate had insisted.

Mallory's heart ached from missing her beloved mother, dead barely more than a month in a freakish accident, a fall from the icy cliffs at Fairwinds.

Gossip had swirled around the accident and she'd had a difficult time containing her grief, much less handling the horrible thought that her mother had become the most recent victim of the Fairwinds' curse.

As much as her mother loved her ancestral home, Mallory knew the stories couldn't be true. The supposed ghosts of past ancestors wouldn't have taken someone so gentle and kind as her mama to an untimely death.

Miller took his seat behind the desk and motioned for the others to sit as well. "Let's get this meeting started." Nodding in her direction, he added, "Miss Mallory, I know you did not want to attend this reading, but it was one of your mother's last wishes that you be here. As her lawyer for nearly thirty years, I was obligated to honor her request."

Mallory shifted in her seat, pressed the flat of her hand over her plain black jumper and, with trembling fingers, pushed errant strands of her curly red hair behind her ear. "I'm fine, sir, and most grateful for your adherence to my mother's request."

The solicitor gave a nod of his head and began, "We are here today to unseal and review the Last Will and Testament of Helene Elizabeth Bradford McGuire. In the matter of her bank accounts, as outlined in Appendix A…"

Mr. Miller passed a copy of the appendix to both her father and her. She gave it a cursory glance, as he continued to speak. His words ran together, something about money in foreign accounts, investments made by family as far back as the early 1800s. With each new revelation, her father's demeanor changed—flowing from something akin to disbelief to outright glee. And then deflated just as quickly once the solicitor reviewed the myriad of stipulations surrounding the disposition of the accounts.

Had he truly not known the extent of her mother's wealth? And, how would her father deal with receiving only a small portion of her money?

"As to the matter of Fairwinds, the family estate…"

Mallory raised her head, her attention focused solely on the solicitor's next words.

"…the home, and all of its contents, as listed in Appendix B, is hereby bequeathed to Miss Mallory Lillian McGuire, to be held in trust for her until she reaches either her twenty-fifth birthday or enters into a marriage of her own choice, whichever shall come first."

Mallory's hand shook when she reached for the offered paper.

Miller continued, "It is further stipulated, the estate shall not be sold prior to that time, and will be overseen jointly by Helene McGuire's husband, Malcolm McGuire, and Thaddeus

Miller, Esquire, or his designee, until Mallory McGuire comes of age in accordance with this provision. An additional provision is added to stipulate that Miss McGuire not be forced to leave her home for any reason, save by her own choice. Should something happen, either by natural or unnatural means to Mallory McGuire prior to her twenty-fifth birthday, the estate shall be sold at auction and the proceeds distributed evenly among the charities listed in Appendix C. At no time, shall the ownership of Fairwinds pass to Malcolm McGuire, except by written consent of Mallory McGuire."

Again, the attorney pushed a piece of paper in her direction before moving on to read the remainder of her mother's will.

"A trust account has been set aside for the continued maintenance of Fairwinds to be administered by the office of Thaddeus Miller, Esquire. In addition, a trust account has been set up for Mallory McGuire, which will provide a monthly allowance, the balance of said trust to come directly to her with the same provisions as stated for the transfer of Fairwinds."

Fairwinds was hers. Relief filled her heart.

She might be young, sheltered, but she wasn't naïve. She'd overheard her father's plan to sell the estate, to send her to live with his sister—her maiden aunt—and to move his questionable business practices to New York.

He was welcome to go, if that's what he wanted. However, she intended to stay put in her family home until it well and truly belonged to her.

Her first order of business would be to move from her small bedroom, to the larger corner room that faced the cliffs overlooking the ocean. The same room her mother had occupied since leaving her husband's bed four years earlier.

A room fit for the lady of the house.

Fairwinds Estate ~ Mystic Point
September 1923

"Dammit, Mallory," her father shouted. "Can't you see, I'm in a business meeting?"

Mallory stood her ground, her hands pressed to her hips, her lower lip quivering in anger. "I'll get out of your way as soon as you tell me what those workmen are doing at the top of the staircase."

Her father's angry glare might intimidate the men who worked for him, but not her. Over the past eighteen months, she'd faced down his many attempts to steal Fairwinds from her grasp, to trick her into signing over her inheritance. She'd watched in horror as he'd reopened the tunnels and caves closed off by her maternal grandparents, and taken on the business of bootlegging and running questionable goods through the many nooks and crannies beneath the property.

Now, it seemed, he was bent on changing the inside of Fairwinds as well. She could not—would not—allow him to defile her beautiful home any further.

"Fairwinds is mine. I demand to know what the workers are doing."

Malcom McGuire pushed himself to his feet. "Excuse me a moment, gentlemen. Let me deal with this petulant child of mine."

He closed his hand tightly around her arm and ushered her out of the library and into the massive foyer. "Those workmen," he said sternly, pointing in the direction of the massive staircase, "are closing off the third floor."

"But why? What if there are repairs needed? How will the chimney sweep properly clean the dampers and flue?"

"They'll use a ladder and approach from the outside." He

spun her around to face him, and released the grip he'd taken on her arm. "I can't keep reliable staff because of the stories of what happens up there. The noises, the slamming doors. Nobody wants to clean the rooms, so it's just as well they'll be closed off."

"I'll clean the rooms, if no one else will," she insisted. "The noises don't bother me."

He gave her a sour look, his jaw tightening into a menacing expression. "You most certainly will not. Thanks to your mother's wishes, you are the mistress of this house, and you will act accordingly."

"Mother used to clean the rooms," she reminded him. "She preferred to care for the Captain and Lady Lillian's bedroom herself."

"Your mother was a foolish romantic. She truly believed those stupid tales of ghosts and long-lost love."

Mallory raised her head and returned her father's stare. "Mama was not foolish, except possibly when she chose you for her husband."

She recoiled when her father raised his hand. Rather than strike her as she feared, he clenched his fist and shook it at her instead. "You'd best give up on your silly notion of ghosts and start behaving. Now, go find something to do with yourself that won't cause me any more trouble. I need to return to my meeting."

"If you won't reconsider the barricade, I'll use the iron staircase to reach the third floor. Mama said there was an entryway at the top of the stairs."

"You'll do no such thing. *I forbid it*. The stairs going down to the tunnels have been reinforced, they're safe. The stairs going up are not. I'll not have you breaking your neck on some wild goose chase for something that doesn't exist."

"But—"

He turned away, obviously sparing her no more thought.

Two feet short of the threshold to the library, the door slammed shut in his face. His stance stiffened. He clenched and unclenched his fists, no doubt tempering his anger, before reaching for the glass knob.

Mallory stifled the urge to shout in triumph. A breeze wafted across the back of her neck.

Thank you, Captain. Your help is most appreciated.

Later that afternoon, Mallory made her way through the beautiful stained-glass doors leading into the rotunda. This room had been one of her mother's favorites with its compass rose tiled floor and dome-to-floor windows. Helene McGuire had often sat beneath the beautifully decorated ceiling to read. She'd had a favorite spot where she'd curl up beneath a blanket and spend hours with a book.

As a child, Mallory had loved snuggling on her mother's lap while she read fairy tale after fairy tale to her curious daughter. Her mother had also told her stories of Fairwinds and the home's many colorful inhabitants. Mallory realized that the tales were likely more rumor than fact, but she'd loved hearing about the pirates and their ladies. Like her mother, she was a hopeful romantic.

Instead of reading, as her mother had, Mallory preferred to keep a journal and often came into this very room to record her thoughts. To write about her plans to restore Fairwinds' dignity—to rid herself of her father's latest construction project and to remove the remnants of his shady dealings from the tunnels and caves beneath her beautiful home.

However, today wasn't a day for writing in her journal. Today, she'd test the strength of the spiral staircase to see if it was as dangerous as her father claimed.

Pushing aside the brocade settee, she ran her hand over the pressure plate and slid open the door the men used to access the tunnels. Stepping into the void, she reached for one of the handheld torches that hung on pegs by the door.

Skirting the part of the landing that went down into the tunnels, she put her foot on the first riser going up. Then the second. The rickety steps groaned slightly, but didn't move.

So far, so good.

Cobwebs were everywhere, a sure sign no one had ventured up the stairwell in decades. She took another few tentative steps before she realized she'd need to gather some rags and a heavy broom to rid the passageway of years of dirt and neglect. Not to mention possible spiders. She hated spiders.

Cautiously, she retreated. Letting herself out through the sliding door, she pushed the settee back in place and left the rotunda. Surely, the housekeeper's stores would provide her with what she needed.

"There you are," Sully Adams said the moment she entered the storeroom off the kitchen.

Mallory turned to face her latest bodyguard, the man's presence putting a temporary halt to her plan. "Yes, Mr. Adams, here I am. Had you not been hiding in here drinking my father's whiskey you'd have known where I was, and where I've been for the past half hour."

"Your father's gone out for the evening. You're to stay put." His lip curled, his dark eyes narrowing. "He's left me and Gus to manage you for the night."

"Manage me? I do not need managing. What I need is for my father, and his entire cadre of misfits, to be gone from Fairwinds." She retreated through the doorway, not wanting to be alone in the man's repulsive company.

Following her into the kitchen, his evil chortle sent a shiver up her spine. "You've got another four and half years before Fairwinds legally belongs to you, girlie. I've no doubt your papa will take possession of this fine property long before that."

Without warning, the door to the storeroom slammed shut behind them, sending Sully spinning on his heel. He'd no sooner turned toward the sound when a second door leading from the kitchen to hallway closed with an even louder crash.

Despite his previous bravado, the big man paled visibly.

"Surely, you're not afraid of this drafty house, Mr. Adams."

"Get yourself up to your room, Miss Mallory. Or to the library. I'll send someone to get you when Mrs. Vernon has the evening meal prepared."

Any hope she had of testing the staircase further was thwarted when her two jailers refused to let her out of their sight. Fearing her father's wrath, no doubt, they took turns following her around the house until she finally gave up and went to bed.

News had come early the next morning that a delivery was expected at the main gate, and her father's men had gone about their duties of unloading the bootlegged liquor for stockpiling in the underground storage spaces.

If she could avoid her father's many trips between the library and the parlor, she could secure what she would need to clean the spiral staircase.

Anticipation of what she might discover set the trip switch on her pulse.

Easing the settee aside, she pressed her hand to the slight protrusion in the wall panel. The nearly invisible door slid to the side. She stepped through the opening and closed the connection on the torch, illuminating the dark room. Carefully, she pulled the settee flush against the wall and then slid the panel back into place from the inside.

Taking a few steps forward, she used the heavy broom she'd brought with her to sweep away cobwebs as she advanced. Her heart hammered, but she kept going. The higher she climbed, the more the stairs shook, and she wondered if perhaps her father had been right, and that they were as unsafe as they were dusty.

About ten steps up, a sudden chill lifted the hairs on her arms, and caused a tingling along the back of her neck. She spun around, expecting to find someone following her. Yet, no one was there. Swallowing back her fear, she continued her climb until she'd reached the top and came to a trap door. She gave the wooden hatch a push. It refused to budge.

Surely this wasn't the end of her journey?

Mallory drew a deep breath, took another step upward and braced her feet firmly before pressing her hands against the dirty wood and pushing with all her might.

There was obviously something on top of the opening—something heavy but with a small modicum of give. If she could just get a bit more strength…

A thought came to her. A reckless thought, no doubt, but a thought all the same.

Tucking her chin to her knees, she squeezed herself onto the very top stair and pressed her back against the trap door. Then, placing her hands on the wooden trim on each side of the opening, she straightened her legs, using the whole of her back to raise the door far enough that she could wiggle through the opening.

Safely through the open space, she inched her way forward until she was able to pull herself completely through to the other side. The moment she pulled her foot free of the opening, the trap door slammed shut behind her. The smell of old cloth surrounded her. The heavy weight confirmed her first thought, she was covered by a large rug.

If her mama could see her now, oh how she'd laugh. Stretched out across a floor, covered by a huge carpet… she was surely a sight. She gave another wiggle of her hips, a shove of her hands, and then rolled to her side, finally dislodging the carpet from over her supine form.

When she could finally push herself to her feet, her eyes widened in excitement when she realized she'd reached the Captain and Lady Lillian's bedroom. And, as well, her coveted access to the roof and widow's walk.

Not as musty as the long-neglected staircase, the room had obviously not seen a dust rag or mop in the months since her mother had passed. The floor in front of the beautiful French doors was faded, worn by wind and rain.

Crossing the room, she went to the door leading out into the long hallway. Next door was the nursery the Captain had supposedly built for his wife. Never used, it sat as neglected as the huge bedroom. Tears stung her eyes when she realized the import of the history behind this part of her home. At the end of the hallway, the staircase down to the second floor was dark, the entryway onto the lower floor blocked off by the barricade her father had ordered installed.

For all intents and purposes, this floor was an oasis unto itself, totally isolated from the rest of the house. A place she could come to gather her thoughts, write in her journal, and look after Jake and Lily's legacy as it should be.

After making a note of what other supplies she would need to restore order to this extraordinary space, Mallory rolled up the heavy carpet and set it aside. Since she was the only one willing to come up to the third floor, there was no need to hide the opening.

Then, lowering herself through the trap door, she shut it behind her, and made her way back down the stairs.

Chapter 2

Fairwinds Estate ~ Mystic Point
April 1924

Mallory finished primping, pinning her red curls atop her head and securing the unruly mass with gold and rhinestone clips. Donning her elegant evening gown, she smoothed the fine satin material over her hips and thighs.

Her father had planned a lavish party in honor of her twenty-first birthday, and she looked forward to celebrating with her two best friends, Sadie and Will. Of course, she would also have to tolerate her father's many business associates. And, no doubt, he would parade a string of eligible men in front of her in hopes one would catch her eye.

His ridiculous attempts at marrying her off to one of his like-minded cronies amused her and exasperated her in equal measure.

Despite his ulterior motives, she looked forward to the evening's festivities. There would be musical entertainment. Even a tarot and palm reader—all the rage among the well-heeled of Mystic Point. Or at least that was what she'd been told.

Not that she ever escaped her father's watch long enough to find out.

No matter how many times she'd managed to slip her bodyguards, they always tracked her down. Fortunately, none of them were smart enough, or fast enough, to catch up with her before she'd accomplished what she'd set out to do.

More importantly, at least to Mallory, tonight's event marked her passage into adulthood. She could come and go as she pleased, no longer a child in need of her father's oversight. The idea of having her freedom was more than she could fathom.

By nine-thirty, the party was in full swing. She and Will were making the rounds through the many guests, most of them older, rich friends of her father. Respectable businessmen in some cases, no doubt, but still in want of the bootlegged liquor her father continued to sell to the highest bidder.

"Come on," Will urged. "Let Madame Olga read your palm or turn your cards. It's the bee's knees."

Mallory took her seat at the table and laid her hand in the garishly dressed woman's outstretched palm.

"Your lifeline is long," the woman said. "And sturdy. This house holds no ill will toward you."

"That's a relief," she said softly. "Given the history of Fairwinds."

Madame Olga raised her head, meeting Mallory's gaze. "There are still many secrets to discover; secret places that hide stories of the past." Tracing a line on Mallory's palm, she added, "This line tells me you will one day meet the man who will sweep you off your feet and become your true love. You will have children together and be happy."

"When?" she asked, wondering if it were possible to fulfill her mother's stipulation of an early marriage to secure Fairwinds prior to turning twenty-five.

"You will meet him soon, but it will not be love at first sight. It will be a love worth waiting for if you are patient and trusting. Just be wary of those who proclaim their interest but have ulterior motives." The medium swept her gaze over the huge ballroom. "Do not trust what is put before you. Follow your heart."

A shiver ran down Mallory's back when the medium

repeated the very same thought she'd had earlier that evening.

Madame Olga laid the deck of tarot cards on the table. "Cut the cards, please."

Her hand shaking slightly, Mallory split the stack and set the top half to the side. "What do the cards tell you, Madame Olga?"

Turning the first card over, she said, "You've not been away from your home. You've never travelled."

"That's right."

A second card was turned. "Your circumstances will not change any time soon." Then a third card. "You face danger and should be wary."

"I'm not afraid of my father's enemies," she said firmly. "They hate him, not me."

When she turned over a final card, Madame Olga lifted her head and smiled. "I see a protector. A man. Perhaps two men?" she said, looking perplexed.

"Two?" Mallory's voice rose in surprise. "Is one of them the man I'll fall in love with?"

"The cards do not say." The fortune teller leaned forward to whisper. "There are spirits in this house. You know this, yes?"

Mallory nodded.

"They are sometimes angry, sometimes calm, but they mean you no harm. However, they do not hold those around you in the same regard."

"So, how did you enjoy your party?" her father asked once the last guest had departed.

"It was lovely, thank you."

"And what did you think of Mr. Stoles, the banker's son?"

She met her father's smug grin with a narrowed gaze and purposeful frown. "I thought he was a pompous ass, if you must know. Full of himself. A dewdropper who's probably never worked a day in his life."

"He has standing in society, something that's beneficial to us both. How little you know of the workings of the world, child."

"And who's fault is that?" she countered, feeling suddenly bold. "Other than supervised shopping trips and the occasional social event, I've not left this house since my mother died."

"As I've explained numerous times, it is for your own protection. The world is a rough place. Between the men who came home from the war, beaten down and desperate, to the dandies who'd love to avail themselves of a rich, young girl, to the drunks and partygoers. It's not safe out there. Not to mention the other businessmen who would like to destroy everything I've built and use you to do it."

"Built on the money you received from my mother's estate," she felt compelled to point out. "Were she still alive, you'd have not been able to open the tunnels and run your *questionable activities* from here at Fairwinds."

"Like I said, child, you know nothing of how business is done. Nor do you understand why it's been necessary to keep you safe within these walls."

"Oh, I understand completely. If something were to happen to me, Fairwinds would be sold, and you'd be out on your ear with no place to run your business."

He glared at her, and growled, "You're becoming more insolent by the day. It's not an attractive feature for a young woman."

Anchoring her hands on her hips, she returned his glare. "Given I am now an adult in the eyes of the law, I will no longer put up with your overbearing protection. Or that of your host of bodyguards pretending to care about what happens to me."

The grip he took on her upper arm sent a jolt of pain clear

down to her wrist. "You will still be watched, Mallory. Chaperoned for your own protection until I decide otherwise."

"In other words, I'll continue to be a captive in my own home."

The next morning, Mallory dressed in a pair of pleated trousers, a simple blouse, and comfortable shoes. It was time to give the Captain and Lady Lillian's room its monthly cleaning; time to open the French doors and air out the room. She'd found a bottle of oil soap in the housekeeper's pantry and intended to use it to breathe new life into the worn floorboards.

Though she'd been doing little more than dusting and mopping in the nine months since she first tested the safety of the staircase and uncovered the trap door, today she'd give everything a more thorough scrubbing. She'd take down the portrait that hung above the fireplace mantle and give it a good cleaning as well. By the time she finished, her third-floor sanctuary would be as good as new. Well, perhaps not new, but in far better condition than it was in the moment.

She worked for over an hour, dusting, scrubbing, and rubbing the oil into the weather-worn planks of the floor. Even though she'd thought them only stories from her ancestors' imagination, Mallory now believed some of the tales were true.

The floor bore the marks of many a violent nor'easter. The noises she often heard above her head echoed the romantic notion of the beautiful double doors blowing open during the storm to allow Captain Jake and his love, Lily, their time together. She hoped it were true, that their spirits still live on in the house, allowing them to find happiness in some unearthly form.

The one thing she knew for sure was that the storms… and their noises… stirred something deep within her. A longing. They made her body tingle in the most unusual ways. Made her breath catch and hold, and her heart pound, until the last of the storm receded and the noises stilled.

The older she got, the more acute the feelings became. As much as these changes should have frightened her, she'd never once felt threatened but—rather—intrigued by what it all meant.

Her work nearly done, Mallory pushed the corner chair beneath the mantle, climbed onto the seat, and reached for the portrait. Heavier than she expected, she lost her balance and fell backward, dragging the heavy painting from the wall, until she landed in a heap on the floor.

When she looked up, what she saw stilled her rapidly beating heart.

'There are still many secrets to discover; secret places that hide stories of the past.' The medium's words came back to her in a flash.

There, right in front of her, was a gaping hole in the wall that had been covered by the portrait. Setting the painting aside, Mallory pushed herself to her feet, and rubbed her hand across her sore bottom. No doubt she'd have a bruise from her fall. Yet, she had no time to worry about the possibility. Not when she had a new discovery within her line of sight.

Using her dust rag, she pushed thick cobwebs to the side and reached into the hole in the wall, her hand connecting with a solid object. Carefully, she withdrew the wooden chest and carried it across the room to the big bed.

The latch was rusted, the box itself warped most likely from the dampness that seeped into the room during the rains. Hopefully, the contents—whatever they were—had weathered the storms.

Mallory cleaned off the worst of the rust with the oil cloth tucked into the pocket of her trousers before raising the lid. Her eyes widened in surprise and her hands stilled, hovering over the treasure trove she'd uncovered.

Two journals. The first one covered in leather. A second, thicker journal was adorned with a flower drawing. The box also contained two quill pens, a worn pocket purse, and a bottle of dried ink. Excited over her find, she spread everything out across the bed, setting the useless inkwell and quill pens aside.

Lifting the first journal, she carefully pried open the cover. The name inscribed on the inside cover was that of Alice Bradford, printed in a child's hand. The second journal also belonged to Alice Bradford, although the script writing was obviously that of an adult.

Mallory closed her eyes and let the realization sink in. Miss Alice's grave was the second on the cliffs—the first in the family cemetery—following Lady Lillian's lone burial site from 1738.

The urge to turn the pages and begin reading made her fingertips itch. Yet, she knew she couldn't stay hidden much longer without drawing her father's curiosity. Tucking the journals back into the box, she moved on to the small purse, pulling on the string ties until she could dump the contents on the top of the bed.

A gasp escaped, her hands shaking when she lifted a gold coin from the pile. There were eight coins in total, along with a beautiful gold and ruby ring, and a tarnished iron key.

A key to what?

Pushing herself from the bed, she stuffed everything back into the chest and wrapped it in the rags she'd brought for cleaning. She'd take it all to her bedroom and go through the journals, entry by entry, until she'd acquainted herself with the great aunt who'd served as a nurse and died during the Civil War before she'd even had a chance to live.

Chapter 3

The Sneaky Cat ~ Mystic Point
July 1924

Mallory McGuire took a seat at the table directly in front of the stage at Mystic Point's newest, and most hard to access, speakeasy. Her friends, Sadie and Will, were already there, and no doubt into their second or third glass of champagne.

"I was beginning to worry about you, doll," Will said, leaning in her direction. "You really need to be more prompt about your arrivals."

"Have they come looking for me, as yet?" she asked.

"No, but Sadie said she saw them earlier over at the Cork and Barrel. The two big fellows, the one with the flat nose and the one that reeks of garlic."

"Fools," she muttered. "My father's men are as inept as they are ugly."

Sadie plopped herself down in the chair at Mallory's side, her short blonde bob bouncing against her rouged cheeks. "This new place is the cat's pajamas."

"Yes, it is." Mallory agreed. "And the music is divine." Glancing around the noisy room, she turned to Will. "I'm absolutely dusty. Do you suppose you could be a regular joe and get me a drink? The waiters seem to be overwhelmed with the huge crowd."

"Sure thing, sweets." Turning to Sadie, he asked, "How about you, doll face? Another champagne?"

Sadie licked her lips and smiled sweetly. "Definitely."

The latest jazz quintet took to the stage followed by the sultry torch singer, her voice wrapping around the words she sang as snugly as her elegant hands hugged the microphone.

Mallory envied the woman's independence, her ability to express herself in song. No doubt she led a rather charmed life. Totally unlike Mallory's own sheltered existence.

"How was your evening?" Sadie asked. "Which gentleman got your visit tonight?"

"Samuel. He was quite appreciative of my attention. I only wish I didn't have to sneak around. I wish—"

"Hold that thought," Sadie said in a hushed whisper. "I see your father's thugs have arrived."

"Miss Mallory," Teddy O'Brien, her father's right-hand man, said roughly, his tone menacing. "You've led us on quite the roundabout this evening."

"Perhaps you should give up and stop chasing me," she returned. "After all, it's not like you're very good at it."

"Come on," he suggested through a tobacco-stained sneer, his meaty hand clamped firmly around her forearm. "Let's get you back home before your father sends the coppers instead of Gus and me."

"Perhaps he should send the coppers. They'd likely have a better chance of finding me."

"Or you could be a good little girl and stop running."

Mallory pushed to her feet and rested herself from Teddy's clutches. "That's the problem, Teddy. You and my father still think of me as a 'little girl' when, in fact, I'm a fully grown woman."

Gus Tomas, her father's other man, came to stand at her left.

Obviously convinced she posed no threat of escape, Teddy told her, "The day you start acting like a grown woman, Miss Mallory, we'll no longer need to drag you home every night or two."

She cast him a pained look. "Perhaps if my father wouldn't insist that I stay within the walls of Fairwinds, I'd be less inclined to escape my prison."

***

Harry Carter gave a cursory glance around the ornate library, somewhat surprised by the eclectic selection of books. Somehow, he couldn't picture Malcolm McGuire as a reader of great literature.

The door opened and McGuire entered. Teddy O'Brien trailed behind like an obedient lapdog. Albeit a very big, mean dog. "Teddy here tells me you're looking for a job," McGuire said without preamble.

"Yeah, you might say that. Something under the table, so to speak."

"He also said you're on the lam. From Pinkertons, no less. I'm not so sure a former detective for such an upstanding agency would fit in with my operation." McGuire gave him an up-and-down appraisal. "What'd you do to be running from them now?"

A sneer lifted the corner of Harry's mouth, ushering in a deliberately sarcastic response. "Let's just say… I gave myself an unauthorized raise."

Chuckling, McGuire said, "I don't need any more muscle—even though you look like a man who can handle himself in a fight."

"I can," Harry confirmed. Nodding toward McGuire's ever-present bodyguard, he added, "No doubt I could take Teddy down in fast order."

The burly man snorted a laugh. "Not on your best day, Carter."

"Don't kid yourself. Even my worst day is better than your best."

The two men circled one another, like a couple of caged tigers bent on claiming their turf. When Harry feigned a lunge forward, O'Brien backpedaled a few steps.

"Enough," McGuire ordered. "I'll not have the two of you

bleeding all over my fuckin' floor."

"So, have you got something for me, or not?" Harry asked, pushing as much impatience into his voice as he could muster. "If not, I hear the Santori family is looking for help."

"You'd work for Santori?" O'Brien asked. "You must be desperate."

"Not desperate, just antsy to get back to work and make some greenbacks. My stash is running low. Rumor has it, this place... Fairwinds... is a great place to lay low."

"That it is," McGuire confirmed. "My men have their duties. Teddy and Gus take care of my protection. However, there is one task I could use help with, assuming you're interested."

"Like I said, I'm looking for work. If you've got some, I'd be happy to discuss what you need me to do."

"It's my daughter. She needs protection."

Teddy O'Brien snorted another laugh but said nothing.

Harry glanced from one man to the other and asked, "Have you thought of a good, old-fashioned chastity belt?"

McGuire narrowed his gaze, and Harry suspected he'd raised the man's ire. Instead, both McGuire and his squirrely muscle laughed.

"Mallory's virtue is not a matter for discussion. However, she tends to wander, and that puts her at risk from my enemies."

Harry's gut clenched in revulsion. "You keep her captive here at Fairwinds?"

"No, not captive. She's allowed her liberties for shopping or whatever else it is that young girls do. She's just not allowed to sneak out to meet up with her friends."

Harry vaguely remembered something about a child in the information he'd gleaned on McGuire. Never assuming the child would be part of the bargain, he'd not given her a second thought. He gave a quick shake of his head. "Sorry, but I'm nobody's nanny. I came here looking for something a bit more exciting than shepherding some spoiled, little rich girl."

"Oh, Miss Mallory will give you a challenge," Teddy said. At Harry's questioning look, the man added, "She manages to slip her guard at least two or three times a week. We eventually catch up with her—but not before she's given us a run for our money."

"Speaking of her 'slipping her guard', where is she at this moment?" McGuire asked.

"Sully's keeping an eye on her," Teddy confirmed.

"Sully? Shit! She can outrun that fat bastard with her ankles tied together." McGuire shot Teddy a piercing glare. "Go find her. Bring her here."

Once O'Brien left to do the boss's bidding, Harry asked, "Is this an around-the-clock job? Or does the wandering Miss McGuire take a break from time-to-time?"

"When she's on good behavior, she spends her time in the gardens, the library, and in her second-floor bedroom."

"And, when she's behaving badly?" Harry prompted.

"There's no telling where you'll find her then. She's slipped out through the tunnels, among the trees across the far side of the property, even once sneaking out in the back of the local butcher's delivery truck. Squeezed herself in between two sides of beef to get past the gate."

At the mention of the tunnels, Harry's attention piqued. The stories of the Fairwinds' tunnels—and the wealth of ill-gotten goods they held—was one of the reasons he'd come looking for a job in the first place.

"She sounds… adventurous. No doubt a rebellious adolescent." He waited for McGuire to comment. When he didn't, Harry asked, "Just how old is Miss Mallory?" The thought of watching over and detaining a privileged child made his anger rise.

Before McGuire could answer, the door to the library

sprung open. Teddy came through, dragging the 'child' in question across the threshold, his hand clamped around her upper arm.

"Let go of me, you swine," she shouted, wriggling in his grasp.

"Your papa wants to see you. Now."

When O'Brien hauled the girl around to face them both, the air rushed out of Harry's lungs. Mallory McGuire was not a child but, rather, a very beautiful young woman. Of medium height and slim build, her lush breasts pressed against the shiny satin of her fancy dress.

Curly, bright red hair hung in disarray around her shoulders, totally at odds with the short bobs most women wore nowadays. His hand itched with the thought of drawing the silken strands through his grasp and wrapping them around his fingers.

His gaze fell to where Teddy still clutched the woman's arm. He was about to step forward and suggest letting her go, when she raised her foot and stomped on Teddy's instep, sending the big man howling in pain and jumping around like he'd been set on fire.

Harry bit back a smile and the overwhelming urge to laugh.

"Get over here," McGuire ordered, waving his daughter to his side. "I want you to meet your new bodyguard."

Mallory McGuire's gaze shifted from her father to Harry and back again. "Don't you mean my latest jailer?" She paused, then asked, "What happened to the last one? Did he finally give up?"

"He's been reassigned," McGuire admitted. "He claims you're too hard to handle."

A coy smile lifted the corner of her well-shaped lips, causing Harry's breath to catch.

"Or perhaps he feared he'd have a heart attack keeping

up," she countered.

"No matter," her father said. "This is Harry Carter. Assuming we can come to terms, he'll be your new shadow."

She turned in his direction and met his gaze head-on. "Do you think you're up to the task, Harry?"

His smile kicked into place. "I've no doubt of my abilities to wrangle one slight bit of a girl, Miss McGuire. However, my desire to do so is somewhat lacking."

Taking a step closer to where he stood, she raised her head in challenge, her bright green gaze locking with his. "Well, we certainly wouldn't want your 'desire' to be affected. Would we?"

Too late.

His body had already betrayed him. Thankfully, from where he stood safely hidden behind a high back chair, neither the lovely Miss McGuire nor her father could see the extent of his current desire.

***

The next morning, Mallory slipped through the kitchen and out the back door. She needed to walk off the last of her anger at being hauled before her father the night before, only to have him scold her as if she were a child.

And what was it with yet another new bodyguard? Harry-something-or-other. Younger, more fit than her father's other men, if he took the job, he might be harder to shake than the rest. She would need to devise some new escape routes, should he become her jailer.

Making her way across the grounds, she passed beneath the rose arbor, it's fragrant blooms guiding her forward. The ever-present Gus followed at a distance, obviously not willing to let her escape on him for a third time in less than a week.

"If you must follow me, Gus," she called back over her shoulder. "At least don't sulk in the shadows like a common thief."

"Just doing my job, Miss Mallory, and following your father's orders."

"I'm going to the cliffs, so you don't have to wonder."

She could almost picture the big man's shudder. For a bunch of supposed tough guys, her father's men were downright queasy when it came to her visits to the graves of Lady Lillian, Miss Alice, and—now—her sainted mother.

Personally, she found the hallowed ground peaceful; a place to reflect and plan.

Of course, if the rumors were true, the men were also terrified of the caves and tunnels that ran beneath the grounds. The thought made her smile.

No doubt her fearless pirate ancestor, Captain John Jacob Wilder, or rather his ghost, was keeping the vile men on edge. Tales of dumped rum, overturned stores of ill-gotten goods, and freak accidents among the passageways worried her father as well. His concern, however, was aimed at the loss of his bootlegged booze, and illegally obtained wealth, not at some rumored specter.

Her mother would have been appalled by what was happening in the tunnels beneath Fairwinds. As much as she missed her mother, Mallory was at peace knowing Helene McGuire would never experience the indignities heaped upon Fairwinds' legacy.

"Don't take too long, Miss Mallory," Gus called out, happy to leave a good fifty yards between himself and the iron fencing of the graveyard. "There's a storm brewing."

"I'll be along in a few minutes. I'm neither dressed nor shod to run, if you'd like to go back to the house."

"The boss would have my fat arse on a platter if you ran."

"How about I give my word? Surely, you trust my word as a lady."

He gave a slow shake of his head. "Sorry, Miss, but I'm not leaving you to your own devices."

"Fine. I'll need a few minutes." Thunder rolled overhead, signaling—as Gus had said—an impending storm. Absently, she wondered if it would be a simple shower or a stronger nor'easter? The difference between the two was vast and caused her heart to race with anticipation.

She'd just raised herself from her seat on the soft earth next to her mother's grave when the rain began, mere splatters against her shoulders as she made her way back to the house.

Gus stood by the door to the kitchen, holding it open for her as she passed.

"Let my father know I'm going to my room. Then, if you must, you can take your post at the bottom of the staircase."

Chapter 4

Within moments of reaching the privacy of her room, the first crash of thunder sounded overhead. Wrapping herself in a lightweight blanket, Mallory curled up in the chair beside her bed and laid her head on the cushioned arm.

The wind howled and the house shook.

Above her head, the French doors leading to the widow's walk crashed open, as the storm began in earnest.

Welcome, Lady Lillian.

The familiar noises began, slowly as always at first. A loud thump, followed by creaking floorboards. Heavy, booted footsteps.

Lightning flashed, illuminating the otherwise dark sky.

With each subsequent crash of thunder, the sounds from the third floor increased. Louder, softer, louder again... almost as if they were climbing toward a pinnacle—a precipice to be crossed.

The soft moans began, and Mallory's heartbeat gathered speed. Her breath caught and released in time with the strange noises—as if, she too, were searching for something exciting, yet unknown. As if the storm, and the activity it brought, required some sort of climax before it could end.

Squeezing her eyes shut tight, Mallory let the sounds wash over her, through her. From time to time, the noises would cease—almost as they were resting. And, when they did calm, her heart rate would slow, her breath even out. She'd doze off, only to be awakened an hour or so later when the noises began again.

Eventually, the storm ebbed, the noise abated and—with one final crash—the French doors slammed shut again. Jake and Lily's time had come to an end.

Mallory remained in the chair for nearly an hour after the storm ended, the elements receding, leaving nothing but the sweet smell of rain-soaked trees and damp earth in its place.

Pushing herself to her feet, she changed from her simple shirtwaist to a fancier satin dress, and finger-combed her unruly hair into curls around her cheeks. With another half hour before the evening meal, she had just enough time to scope out a weakness in Gus or Sully's patterns for the evening and plan her escape.

Sadie and Will would cover for her until she arrived at their agreed upon destination. As always, she'd allow her father's men to believe they'd actually found her before she could get into any true mischief. *Gullible fools.*

She descended the double-sided staircase slowly, glancing from side-to-side to see which of her father's men waited at the bottom for her arrival, surprised to find neither man there. Without her watchdogs on her heels, she could easily leave through the ballroom doors and across the cobblestone patio. It was only a short distance from there to where Will would be waiting in his Durant to drive her into Mystic Point.

Or perhaps—if the coast wasn't clear—she'd escape through the library window. She'd scope out that route first, under the guise of looking for a book.

"Good evening, Miss McGuire."

The deep voice sank into her senses, putting her on edge. The sight of Harry Carter standing along the far wall of the library, thumbing through a collection of classic literature, put an immediate and unwanted glitch in her plans.

And a surprising level of curiosity in her thoughts.

"You're here. I see my father offered you a handsome enough salary to coax you into selling your soul."

His voice dropped even lower when he laughed. "My soul was placed on the market years before coming to work at

Fairwinds."

"So, should I assume you'll be my shadow for the evening?"

Setting aside the book he'd been holding, he gave a quick nod of his head, the movement drawing her attention to his face, the way he held himself. Far better looking than any of her father's other men, his dark brown hair held a hint of gray at the temples. She guessed his age to be mid-thirties.

"This evening and until you take yourself off to bed for the night, apparently. I trust we can have an uneventful first night together."

"There will be no 'together', Mr. Carter. I will go about my business, and you shall allow me some space. I don't like hovering."

"That's good, because I'm not someone who hovers. I prefer to observe from a distance."

"After supper, I'll likely read for a while. Alone."

He made a show of glancing around the cavernous library. "Fortunately, there'll be plenty of room for both of us right here. Or, if you'd prefer, the parlor."

Feeling a bit at odds with his confident demeanor, the even cadence of his voice, she looked for a way to rile him, to strike out and throw him off guard.

"You read?" Her sarcastic tone drew his lopsided grin. "Most of my father's men prefer the Sunday cartoon strips."

"Yes, Miss McGuire, I read. Quite well, in fact. Although I do enjoy classic comic strips like *Huckleberry Finn* and *Tom Sawyer*."

"No *Buster Brown* or *Little Orphan Annie*?"

A lock of hair fell across his brow when he shook his head. He brushed it back with his hand, drawing her attention to his long fingers. Her pulse fluttered against her wrist—a most unwelcome reaction.

When he used those same long fingers to dig a pocket

watch from his vest, and the brush of his thumb to open the cover, the flutter increased double time.

"I believe we're expected in the dining room." Crossing to where she stood, he asked, "Shall I escort you?"

Defiantly, she shoved at his offered arm, drawing another of his infuriatingly deep chuckles.

"I can find my own way, thank you."

***

Harry took a seat at the table, flanked by Sully and Gus. Malcolm McGuire sat at the head of the table, his daughter to his left.

The young woman had nerve. He'd give her that. She'd made an obvious attempt to upset him. Rather than drive him to anger, it had ratcheted up his attraction. A fact that irritated him. He wasn't there to be charmed by some spoiled young chit.

He was there to do a job. To relieve Malcolm McGuire of his wealth and drive him back into the hole from which he'd come. If watching over the lovely Mallory McGuire was what it took to get him through the door, so be it.

How difficult a job could it be?

After the meal ended, Harry stood and made his way to the end of the table. Drawing back his charge's chair, he asked, "So, is it the library or the parlor, Miss Mallory?"

"The library, *please*."

Her overly polite, if not somewhat sarcastic, response amused him. She'd not fool him the way she had the others. Once she was settled in with her book, Harry removed a first edition of *Gulliver's Travels* from the back shelf and took his place directly across from where she sat.

They'd been reading for over an hour when the huge clock above the mantle chimed eight times. He cast a glance toward the opposite side of the library in time to see Mallory sit up and stretch.

"I'm tired," she announced. "I think I'll retire early."

He set aside his book and raised himself to his feet. "I'll walk you to your room."

"The bottom of the stairs will be fine. It's not like there's a doorway between the staircase and my bedroom."

"How about we compromise? I'll escort you to the top of the stairs."

"What I'd really like is a glass of warm milk to take with me. Could you ask Mrs. Vernon to prepare one for me?"

She was making her move, was she? He'd play along. For the moment.

"I'll go put in the request," he told her. Crossing the room, he stopped at the door and withdrew the skeleton key that hung inside the lock. "If you don't mind, I'll secure the door from the other side." When she shrugged her elegant shoulders, he added, "Just so you don't get the urge to wander."

"Fine with me, Mr. Carter. As I said, I'm rather sleepy."

***

The moment the lock clicked into place, Mallory was out of her seat and on her way to the window. Pulling the ottoman from in front of her father's favored chair and sliding it into place, she threw open the sash and slid her legs over the sill, wiggling her hips through the narrow space.

About to lower herself to the ground, she startled when a warm hand circled her ankle and slipped slowly up the curve of her leg.

"Here, let me help you, Princess. You wouldn't want to fall into this lovely bed of azaleas, would you?"

"What? I mean… how?"

He circled her waist with his hands and lifted her from the sill to the soft ground as if she weighed no more than a sack of flour before releasing her and backing away.

"Like I said, Miss McGuire, I'm not as easily fooled as Gus,

Sully or any of the others. From this moment forward, you will follow *my rules*. I will be that shadow you detest so much. I'll follow you through the garden, the woods, and even the tunnels should you make it that far. However, know this, for every time I have to chase you, you'll lose one day's shopping privileges."

Shooting him an angry glare, she stomped off toward the front of the house, and he followed in her wake.

"You can't do that. My father won't allow it. I won't allow it."

"One of the conditions I gave your father before I accepted the job was that I set the parameters of your protection." He opened the door and waited for her to enter. "And, in case there's any doubt, you can ask him. He was all for the idea."

Mallory made her way across the foyer and climbed the stairs leading to the second floor, Harry a respectful two steps behind. Once she'd reached the landing, she spun around to suggest he should return to the first floor.

He was in the process of removing his suit coat and hanging it on the ornate newel post at the top of the stairs. The linen shirt he wore beneath the finely tailored jacket clung to his broad chest, the sight of his fit body causing a hitch in her ability to breathe.

"Did you need something?" he asked.

"No," she said, shaking her head for emphasis. "I... uh..."

"Good night then, Miss Mallory."

Mallory gave the door to her room a sound slam, her brash action met by the echo of Harry's laughter as it easily slipped beneath the wooden barrier. Quickly, she stripped out of her dress and donned her nightgown and robe before making her way back out into the hallway for the short walk to the bathroom.

Once she completed her evening ritual, she stepped back into the hallway. Glancing in the direction of the staircase, she wasn't surprised to see Harry still sitting there, his back against the wall, his eyes closed. The only sign he was still awake was the tap of his fingertips against his thigh, as if he were counting out the rhythm to a song.

The simple motion stoked her curiosity. Slowly, she edged closer to where he sat.

Without opening his eyes, he asked, "Can I help you, Miss McGuire?"

She swallowed back the sudden lump in her throat. "What are you doing? The tapping against your leg?"

He opened his eyes and gave her a quick up and down perusal, his gaze flaring. Her fingers tightened around the lapels of her dressing gown, the involuntary action drawing his smirk.

"If you must know, I was mentally reciting a verse of iambic pentameter. The tapping helps me keep time."

"Poetry?"

His shrug drew her gaze to his shoulders, their width most impressive.

"Sometimes. Other times just measured verse."

"I'll leave you to it then."

When she turned to walk away, Harry's low voice came at her from all sides.

"Good night, Miss McGuire. Sleep tight."

Back in her bedroom, she turned the lock on the door and discarded her robe. Her flushed skin prickled with a strange awareness. Goosebumps scattered across her arms.

Drat the man, anyway!

He was definitely not going to be easy to fool. Poetry... verse... in iambic pentameter, no less. Harry Carter was head and shoulders above her father's other stooges when it came to smarts.

She was going to have to improve her skills if she were to carry on with her two or three times a week visits to the men who cherished her company. Escaping Harry Carter's watch was definitely going to be a challenge.

Chapter 5

Mallory ran her fingertips across her great-aunt Alice's journal entry, re-reading it for the umpteenth time. While the other pages had enlightened her on quite a bit of family history, this particular entry drew her like a magnet to steel.

'1856, July 9.

Well, my suspicions were confirmed this morning when my dear mother sat me down to discuss the birds and bees. A rather silly name if you ask me. She was talking about relations between men and women, not some silly insects or aviary.'

The noises from the third floor… the ones that shake the house for hours whenever the storm blows. Mama says it's the Captain and Lady Lillian coming together to make love. I knew it had to be something beautiful, romantic. Why else would it make my insides quake, my heart pound?'

Was that what was happening to her? Was she also feeling the emotions shared by the spirits of her ancestors when they came together?

The thought both excited her and frightened her, at the same time.

Setting the journal aside, Mallory dressed quickly and made her way downstairs for breakfast. Harry had left his post at some point during the night, and she wondered if he'd been relieved of duty and gone home.

If so, was there someone he went home to… a wife perhaps? A lover?

With a shake of her head, she admonished herself for thinking of such unimportant things. She needed to maintain her focus, set out a new and better plan.

She'd call Will and apologize for not showing up at their rendezvous point the previous evening. Perhaps, she'd invite Will and Sadie over for lunch in the next day or two, so they could map out some new strategies together.

Her father was already seated at the table when she arrived, Gus and Sully in their usual spots, but no sign of Harry.

"Did you sleep well last night, Mallory?"

She gave her father a smile, and admitted, "Yes, I did, thank you."

"Harry said he never heard a peep out of you after your light went out. He was also grateful for a quiet, non-eventful night."

Harry hadn't mentioned her attempt at escape? If it had been Sully, or Gus, or even Teddy, they'd have given her up before their first cup of coffee.

"I thought I should probably break him in slowly," she said with a smirk. "He'll fall by the wayside just like the others soon enough."

"Where am I falling?"

That damnably deep voice drew her attention. She lifted her head. Harry stood there, framed in the doorway, the sleeves of his shirt rolled up to expose muscular forearms, his hands braced on either side of the door frame.

"With any luck," she spit out, "off the cliff and into Skullery Bay."

"The water's warm enough," he countered. "Although that first step is a doozy."

Mallory blinked back the threat of tears when she realized she'd all but wished him the same fate that had claimed her mother. Shame flushed her cheeks.

She raised her chin a notch and met his steely gaze. "Or, perhaps, you can just get lost in the maze of tunnels beneath Fairwinds."

"Entirely possible." Glancing from her father to her, he suggested, "Perhaps, I should have someone give me a guided tour, the lay of the land. Assuming your father has no objections, I'd appreciate it if you could show me the way around, Miss Mallory."

His focus on his morning newspaper, Malcolm gave a brush of his hand, as if neither agreeing nor dismissing the idea.

"Really?" She turned her head to confirm her father's approval. "You're usually so adamant about my staying out of the tunnels."

Her father breathed a long sigh. "It's not as if you listen to me anyway. If you want to venture down there and show Harry the route all the way to the gates, I'm not going to stop you. At least it will keep you out of trouble for a while. Plus, you can spin your tales of non-existent pirate fortune and ghosts to a new audience. Heaven knows, the rest of us are tired of hearing them."

The idea of possibly losing Harry in the tunnels was not without merit.

"Okay, Harry, I'll take you into the tunnels. Later this afternoon, then?"

The grin he shot her sent a flutter to her pulse.

"I look forward to it, Miss McGuire."

***

At half-past two, Harry entered the library in search of his somewhat surprised but agreeable escort for a tour of the secretive Fairwinds tunnels. Dressed in a pair of denim work trousers, flannel shirt and sturdy shoes, he looked forward to walking the length of the underground maze.

"You're dressed like the gardener," she said simply, her perusal moving over him from head to toe.

He drew a breath and willed his body to ignore the sweep of her emerald gaze. "And you look as if you're dressed for a party, Princess. Hardly reasonable attire for trudging through damp and dusty tunnels."

She glanced down at her shirtwaist dress and buckle shoes. She probably should have changed, but she'd not give him the satisfaction of admitting as much.

"I have no intention of getting dirty. And don't call me Princess."

Sweeping his arm in a wide motion, he told her, "Lead the way, Mallory."

She stopped short, and he almost ran into her from behind, the near miss sending a jolt of awareness straight to his loins. Cautiously, he laid his hand against her shoulder to steady them both.

"I'd prefer you refer to me as either Miss McGuire or Miss Mallory." Her order given, she was on the move again, her forward motion breaking the contact that was causing his fingertips to tingle.

As badly as he wanted to explore the tunnels, he had a sense this wasn't going to work out as he'd hoped. He should have asked Gus or Sully for a look-see, rather than suggest the lovely Miss McGuire be his guide.

"Whatever you say, *Princess*."

"Oh, for heaven's sake. Let's just get this stupid tour over and done with so I can get back to my reading."

They crossed the foyer and entered the rotunda.

"Are we crossing the grounds?"

"No."

Stopping at the settee, she leaned her hip against the frame and gave it a shove. Then, sliding her hand across a small, almost indistinguishable keyhole, she opened a sliding door, and stepped through.

"I'll be dam… darned, a hidden door."

"Follow me."

When she started down the stairs, Harry pointed to the

upper staircase and asked, "Where do those stairs go?"

"Up."

His snicker drew an unexpected smile from his guide. "Up where?"

"The stairs dead end at the third floor."

"Is this the only hidden door in the house?"

"Yes, inside the house proper. There are two outside entrances to the tunnels. One in the old groundskeeper's cottage and another in the stables."

"What can you tell me about the history of the tunnels?"

"While there were always tunnels under the property, they were extended and built up in 1737 by Captain John Jacob Wilder, a pirate who plied the waters in and around Skullery Bay, as a place to store his stolen treasure. He supposedly won both the home and the right to marry the love of his life, Lillian Langdon, from her father in a game of chance."

Once they'd reached the ground floor, they went through a heavy wooden doorway into an anteroom, and Mallory pointed to a room off to the right. "This is the only room underground with electricity. My father had the wires run down here to use this room as a lockable storeroom. It has some sort of security as well."

She went through another doorway and entered the first open passageway, Harry right behind. A short tunnel branched off to the left.

"What's in that direction?"

"Nothing important. Just a room we never use." Within minutes, they'd reached the main artery of the tunnel and gone another few hundred or so feet, when Mallory motioned at the hatch above her head. "This doorway leads up to the stables. It's rumored my sixth-back grandfather used to sneak his whores down from the stable, then through the tunnels and up to a third-floor loft."

"Whores?" He gave a purposeful chuckle. "A man after my

own heart." Nodding toward a tunnel to the right, he asked, "What's in that direction?"

"That tunnel leads to a large storeroom, specifically one the men have dubbed 'the captain's room', and then ends at the other exit in the cottage."

"Why 'the captain's room'?"

Her soft laugh tickled his senses, and he drew a breath to calm another surge of unwanted desire.

"Rumor has it, that was the room where Jake Wilder stored his most precious booty. Jewelry, gold coins. When my father first began reopening the tunnels, the workers stored cases of bootlegged rum in there. It was their attempt at humor befitting a pirate, I suppose. However, when the rum was found poured out in the dirt, or missing entirely, they moved the cases into one of the storage rooms closer to the house."

"Any idea who was dumping the goods?" It didn't really matter, he supposed. He just liked hearing the honey-and-whisky tone of her voice.

"According to more than a few of my father's men, the ghost of the Captain. Two of them claimed to have seen an apparition they swore was him. Neither of the men work here any longer."

"Your father fired them?"

She gave a shake of her head, her red curls brushing her narrow shoulders and bobbing against her flushed cheeks. "One of the men left of his own accord, claiming he didn't hire on to cross paths with ghosts."

"And the other?"

"He… uh… died in an accident. He fell from the cliffs… two months after my—"

Harry raised his hand, cutting off the rest of her softly whispered words. "It's okay. I already know what happened to your mum." Reaching out, he lifted her chin on the tips of his fingers, his gaze meeting her tear-filled one. "I'm sorry." She took a step back and he dropped his hand to his side.

"Let's keep going. There's still quite a distance to where the caves open out to the shoreline."

"Gus told me that Fairwinds is yours to inherit when you turn twenty-five. Will you keep it? Or have you had your fill of pirates and supposed ghosts?"

"There's no question I'll keep Fairwinds. I've already made plans for changes as soon as Fairwinds is mine to control."

Although his plans for Fairwinds or—more specifically—her father likely didn't match hers, he asked anyway, "What kind of plans?"

"I'm not so sure it's safe to share my thoughts with someone on my father's payroll."

"Fair enough. Although, my only stake in your father's business is in protecting you. So, once you've turned twenty-five, I'm fairly certain I'll be out of a job anyway."

"That you will, Mr. Carter. That you will."

He bit back on the urge to laugh, her honesty a refreshing change from those who surrounded her on a daily basis.

"So, what about the tall tales and ghost stories your father says you're so fond of telling?"

"They're not tales, or rumors, Harry. They're documented facts. My mother shared some of the Fairwinds legends with me. I've read journal entries from my ancestors that confirm what she told me."

"Have you ever actually seen a ghost?"

Her quick nod drew his keen interest.

"Yes. Once. I was sixteen at the time. My mother had taken me with her to clean the third-floor room that once belonged to the Captain and Lady Lillian. Just as she doused the candle to leave the room, I glanced back at the doors leading to the roof. I saw Lady Lillian. She looked so sad it nearly brought me to tears."

"Did your mother see her too?"

"I'm not sure. She didn't say anything. Perhaps she thought I'd be frightened."

They stopped at the end of another long passageway, and she turned to face him. "My mother is likely rolling in her grave with what my father's done to Fairwinds. She'd never have allowed him to use her home for his ill-gotten gains. Prior to her death, whatever he'd been involved in always took place off of Fairwinds' property. Yet not a month after she was gone, he sent his men in to remove the padlocks from the sea gates, reopen the doors, and unseal the many tunnels and storage rooms."

She bowed her head and drew a breath. "The one thing—the one change—that should have been done years ago was the replacement of the worn and damaged fencing along the cliffs. Had those repairs been made, perhaps both my mother and that unfortunate worker might still be alive."

"I take it, that's one of the changes you have in mind." He paused, then added, "If you'd like, I can make the repairs for you now. There's no reason to wait, is there?"

"I suppose not. Repairing the fencing won't interfere with my father's business."

"Sully tells me you often go to the cliffs to visit your mother's grave. If we can procure the supplies, I'd be happy to work a bit at a time, while you pay your respects."

"Why, Harry?"

"Why, what?"

"Why are you being so nice to me?"

Rather than tilt her chin as he'd done before, he threaded his fingers through her curls and cupped the back of her head. When she met his gaze, he offered her a smile. "Is there any reason I shouldn't be nice to you, Miss McGuire?"

She turned away from him, pulling out of his gentle hold. "Yes, there is."

"And what would that be?"

"Because it will make it all the more difficult for me to escape your watch. Something I fully intend to do every possible chance I get."

Ah… there… The defiant Princess was back, her confident remark drawing his broad grin. "I look forward to the challenge."

"As you should. Now, let's finish this blasted tour."

He followed behind her, enjoying the sway of her hips far more than he should have.

Within minutes, they'd reached the end of the line. Two heavy steel gates were propped open and lashed to the inner walls of the cave. Fifty feet out, water lapped lazily at the rocks and across the sand.

"How far inland does the water reach at high tide?" he asked.

"It depends on the time of year, of course, but usually ten to fifteen feet inside the cave. This far in, the water rarely gets above the ankle. However, it does create a lot of muddy footprints. A fact our housekeeper is always grumbling about."

"Are you ready to head back to the house, Princess?"

She spun around, her gaze flaring, no doubt ready to admonish him for calling her 'Princess.' Yet, before she could get the words out, she slipped. Her feet flew out from beneath her and she landed flat on her backside in a puddle of mud.

Harry did his best to stifle an outright laugh but couldn't contain his teasing chuckle. "What was it you said about not getting dirty?"

Holding out her hand, she waited for him to pull her to her feet. The temptation to turn and leave her there to wallow in the wet earth was almost too much to ignore. Yet, his more gentlemanly side prevailed, and he offered her his hand.

"Took you long enough," she groused. "I suppose you were considering leaving me here in the dirt."

Once she'd gained her footing, she brushed her open palms over the mud-covered skirt of her dress and started back through the tunnel, leaving him to catch up. As they walked, he made a secondary scan of his surroundings, committing to memory each turn, each visible room, and the passageways that led to yet another trap-door exit. Given the lovely Miss McGuire knew each and every nook and cranny, he had no doubt she'd use them to her advantage at some point or other.

It was his job to make sure she would be thwarted at every attempt. As he'd told her earlier, he looked forward to the challenge.

Chapter 6

As she did nearly every morning, Mallory withdrew Alice's journal from where she'd hidden it beneath her mattress. Rather than search for a specific date, she let the book fall open at will.

What adventure would her great-aunt take her on today?

'1859, October 16th

Today is my twenty-first birthday and my parents are planning a wonderful celebration. I shall wear my amethyst ball gown and have Millicent adorn my hair with the dried flowers she has pressed from my mother's garden. This morning, they gave me my birthday present, a beautiful gold and ruby ring that once belonged to Lady Lillian. I shall cherish it forever.

I am hoping Mister Garrett will be in attendance this evening. He is the most handsome man in all of Mystic Point. When I look at him, I get those same feelings, the quickening of my heartbeat, the restlessness I get when the Captain and Lady Lillian come together during the storms.

My breath catches when he smiles at me. Should he ask for a dance, I would likely swoon. Could this be what love feels like?

Mallory pulled the journal to her breast and leaned back against her pillow, letting Alice's words sink in.

Would she herself ever find a love like the Captain's and Lily's? Like Alice felt for the unknown Mister Garrett? At her own twenty-first, Madame Olga had spoken of her destiny as fait accompli.

Patience had never been one of her better qualities. Yet, for the sake of her future happiness, for the sake of Fairwinds, she would hold out as long as she must.

"Shopping today, Miss Mallory?" Sully asked, once breakfast was complete. "Or will you be staying in?"

"Are you my company today, Sully? Rather than Harry?"

"Harry's gone into Mystic Point with Gus on an errand for your father."

What had happened to Harry's claim that his only part of her father's business was her protection?

No doubt he'd jumped at the chance to do her father's bidding. She'd held out hope he was a better man than the others. Obviously, she'd misread his kindness and his honesty.

"No shopping today, Sully," she told him, finally responding to his initial question. "Sadie and Will are coming over for lunch on the terrace."

"Hopefully, you're not planning to leave with them when they go."

"I wasn't... but now that you've given me the idea—"

The big man chortled. "Assuming you wait until after lunch is done, you won't be my problem any longer."

"I'm sure you're relieved."

"I am." He took a few steps toward the door before stopping and turning back to face her. "May I ask you something, Miss Mallory?"

She met the man's gaze, surprised by his request. "I suppose."

"Why have you been so easy on Harry? He's been here nearly a week, and you've not set foot off the grounds. If I remember correctly, you ran out on me my first night on duty."

She'd not admit to her first thwarted attempt. Or to the fact she'd not yet found a suitable plan of escape. Instead, she told him, "I've not had any place I've wanted to go. When I leave the grounds, it's not just to rile my father, or to lead you fellows on a chase—although I do love doing that—it's because I can't stand being a captive. Even in the home I love with all my heart and soul."

"The boys and me have a wager on when you'll run, and how long it will take Harry to find you. I'm hoping to win a tidy sum if you can keep him on the hook for at least four hours whenever you make your first escape."

Stifling her urge to laugh, she gave a short nod of her head and a smile. "I'll do my best to fatten your purse, Sully. I truly will."

Sadie and Will arrived promptly at noon, and she and her shadow, Sully, met them at the front door.

"Come on in," she greeted. "Lunch isn't for a half hour, but I've got everything set up in the library."

The three of them hurried ahead, Sully a few feet behind. Once they'd taken their seats, Mallory gathered up the wooden planchette and placed it in the center of the talking board. "What will we ask first?"

Sadie laid her fingertips against one side of the three-sided diviner. "I'd like to know when I'm going to meet the man I'll marry."

"That's the same question you ask every time," Will reminded her with a smirk. "So far, the board isn't saying. Perhaps, you've already met him and just don't realize it yet."

Mallory bit her lip to keep from smiling. It was no secret to anyone but Sadie that Will was head-over-heels in love with her.

"I'm asking anyway," Sadie insisted. "And then Mallory should do the same. After all, she has far more riding on marrying than I do. If she marries, she gets Fairwinds sooner rather than later."

The moment Mallory laid her fingertips to the planchette, the lights flickered. The window, previously opened to allow a breeze off the bay, slammed shut.

Not now, Captain. Please.

"Come on, Will," Sadie coaxed. "Join us."

Somewhat reluctantly, it seemed, Will laid his fingertips on the third side of the triangle. Mallory wondered if he feared Sadie would finally get an answer to her question, and he'd be left out in the cold.

The moment the planchette slid to the side of the board, Sully—for all his bravery—left the room. Perhaps all she needed to do to rid herself of her watchdogs was to carry the Ouija board with her everywhere she went.

The thought drew her smile.

"You go first," she told Sadie. "See what the spirits have to tell you."

Sadie sucked in a deep breath and began. "When will I meet my true love?"

The diviner didn't budge, the obvious stillness drawing Will's low breath.

"Am I ever going to marry?" Sadie asked, taking a different approach. The diviner slid to the bottom of the board and hovered over the word 'yes', the response drawing Sadie's sigh of relief. "Your turn, Mally."

Mallory glanced from one friend to the other, and then asked, "Will I meet my true love soon?"

The planchette slid back to 'yes', and she dared to ask, "When?"

Her fingertips began to tingle, a breeze wafted over her the back of her neck. The diviner began moving.

"N," Sadie said softly.

"O," Will added.

After a moment's stall, the planchette moved again.

"W," Mallory read. "Now?"

No sooner had the word escaped her lips when the door to the library opened. Looking up, her gaze widened when Harry stepped into the room.

"I was sent to tell you that lunch is ready on the terrace," he said, a frown playing across his handsome features—as if being sent on such a trivial errand irked him.

"Thank you, Mr. Carter."

As soon as the door closed behind his retreating form, Sadie asked, "Is that your new bodyguard?"

"Yes," Mallory confirmed. "Harry Carter."

Sadie's vampish giggle echoed across the width of the room. "No wonder you haven't attempted to run. He's keen."

"What he is," Mallory complained, "is a decently educated boor. Which, unfortunately, makes him ten times smarter than the rest. And, harder to fool. Which is why I want the two of you to help me devise some other methods of escape."

"We'll do our best," Will promised. "But first, let's eat. I'm absolutely empty."

Later that evening, Mallory took a seat in the library, a copy of *Little Women* opened to the middle chapters, but not holding her attention. Instead of immersing herself in Alcott's prose, she was watching Harry—as slyly as possible, of course.

He was facing the far wall, perusing a shelf of first edition classics. Books added over the past hundred years or more by various members of her family. His movements were slow, measured, the shift of his tall, lithe body drawing her focus.

The sight of his firm buttocks, swathed in fine woolen trousers, drew her gaze and made heart beat faster. His waist was trim and rose in a v shape up his back to very wide shoulders. Thick, dark hair clipped the collar of his linen shirt. All-in-all, he was very pleasing to look at.

"Is there something you want, Princess?"

The man also had a sixth sense. Even without turning, he knew she'd been watching him.

"Excuse me, Harry, did you say something?"

He turned around and met her gaze, his amber eyes widening, darkening. "You know damn well I did. It would be hard to miss, with you staring at me."

"Conceit does not become you, Mr. Carter. I was not staring. I was deep in thought."

His chuckle set her nerves on edge.

"No doubt plotting another attempt at slipping my guard. Or, were your thoughts on something the board told you earlier?"

"I don't put a lot of stock in what the Ouija board says. As was proved by the ridiculous answer it gave me to my questions."

"Those things are useless, as are so-called mediums, fortune tellers."

"You're a non-believer," she said simply. "What about ghosts? Spirits?"

"More malarky," he responded smugly. "Fanciful drivel to scam people out of their hard-earned dough."

If ever the Captain or Lady Lillian were to make an appearance, she wished it would be at that very moment. Unfortunately, they seemed to be nowhere in sight. Or sound.

"I'm ready for bed," she announced, wondering if he'd offer to walk her all the way to her bedroom door.

"Shall I fetch you some warm milk?"

"No, it won't be necessary."

Harry replaced the book he'd been holding in its allotted slot, and accompanied Mallory to the foot of the staircase.

"I suppose you'll be following me."

"Not tonight, Miss McGuire. I'm sure you can find your way all on your own."

"Yes," she responded sharply. "I can."

She began her climb up the grand staircase, stopping on the third riser when he responded.

"I'll be nearby, so I'd suggest you not make a run for it."

"I wouldn't think of it, Harry. Wednesday nights in Mystic Point are dreadfully boring."

***

As desperately as he wanted to walk Mallory to her bedroom door, if only to tease her about staring at him, he couldn't. Not without running the risk of her finding out how easily she affected him.

It wouldn't do for her to realize she had even a small modicum of control over the man who was supposed to be guarding her, overseeing her whereabouts and every move.

He'd felt the heat of her stare as surely as he breathed. The urge to confront her had come quickly, yet he'd stalled. Waited. The realization she'd been watching him set off his basest instincts. His hunger.

Predictably, he'd been as hard as a flagpole.

Given he was still uncertain as to her level of experience, or innocence, the state of his desire was not something he felt like sharing with the young Miss McGuire.

It was nights like this that made him question his life choices, decisions that had taken him from the comfort of his family's Oklahoma ranch, to New Haven and an expensive education.

For all the research he'd done on McGuire and his operation, the one thing he'd not counted on was Mallory McGuire. Her honesty, her obstinance, and her intelligence were playing havoc with his carefully devised plan, as well as his emotions.

He needed a diversion, almost to the point that he wished she'd make a run for it. Provide him with a challenge that would take his mind off her undeniably sexy body and beautiful green eyes.

Chapter 7

Mallory opened Alice's journal. She'd been avoiding this final page forever. Her mother had told her the stories of her great-aunt's fate. A nurse, Alice went to serve the Union Army on the front lines, losing her life in a particularly bloody siege.

Biting her lip to keep her emotions at bay, Mallory focused on Alice's final entry.

'1862, April 25

Today will be my last entry for a short while. I am to report to the Union Army headquarters in Boston for assignment to one of the field hospitals. While I am anxious to work alongside the doctors and brave soldiers, I will miss my mother, and father, and even my pesky brothers and little sister. Yet, I feel I must do my duty and use the skills I have acquired to help where I can.

Until I return, I leave this diary and a few of my most treasured possessions in the care of the Captain and Lady Lillian, tucked safely behind their beautiful wedding portrait.'

Mallory's tears flowed freely down her cheeks. She was certain her grandparents had been devastated by their loss. Even now, over half a century later, Mallory felt their pain; shared their grief.

Much like the sadness that had enveloped her earlier, the day was dark and gloomy. The winds howled outside, the gusts rattling the windows, shaking the very foundation of Fairwinds. No doubt another nor'easter was headed their way and would arrive at any moment. Almost as if the storm itself was driving her thoughts, her emotions.

Mallory excused herself from the breakfast table and made

her way to her second-floor bedroom. She still wasn't sure why but, whenever it stormed, she felt safest in her bed, away from everyone. Or at least those who were of flesh and blood.

Frantically, she pulled at her linen drop-waist and kicked out of her T-strap shoes. Discarding her dress on the chair beside her bed, she slid beneath the covers wearing nothing but her thin brassiere, silk bloomers, and stockings.

The heavy quilt atop her bed encased her in warmth, welcoming her into its safe cocoon. She stretched out and waited, for she knew what was to come next.

As if on cue, the wind picked up and the rain began falling in sheets outside her window. Her breath came and went in time with the weather's assault; her heart rate picked up speed. Anticipation sizzled through her veins.

She jumped as a crash sounded above her head—the French doors off the widow's walk being blown open, marking Lady Lillian's arrival. The sound of heavy footsteps pounded across the floorboards. *Captain Jake.*

Mallory ran her hands up and down her arms in an effort to calm the excitement raging within her body... her soul.

The moans began, low, slow, building ever so slightly. The creak of the floorboards increased, now a loud, rhythmic thumping. A whimper, a deeper moan, as if something other than the storm was brewing.

Restless, yet driven by the primal sounds, Mallory slipped her hand across her chest, pushing frantically at the tingles overtaking her body, making her ache. The urge to run her flattened palms over her stomach, her hips, and then across her most private parts had her clenching the material of her brassiere tightly in her grasp.

The pace above her head quickened, increasing the race of her pulse.

She stroked her breasts with trembling fingers, the tips drawn tight beneath her touch. A shiver overtook her entire being.

The cries above her were at their peak, as was her own arousal. Her breath labored, her heart thumping, she cupped her womanly mound in her hand and held tight, waiting for this unusual stirring… this ache… to pass.

As the activity above her subsided, Mallory's breathing calmed, the ache in her body eased one small increment at a time, leaving her oddly at peace.

Her own reaction—her desire—was becoming more intense each time she experienced the storm. Ever since she'd read the diaries and learned of the tales of what was happening right above her head.

And, as much as she disliked the foul weather, the more she longed for it to happen over and over again.

Soon.

***

Harry leaned back against the sturdy newel post at the top of the stairs and closed his eyes. The storm raged outside, rain pounding the windows and heavy panes of glass adorning the top of the rotunda.

Off in the distance, toward the far end of the hall, he could hear the noises the other men had only spoken about in hushed whispers. Rumors of fornicating ghosts had him questioning the sanity of those who both worked and resided at Fairwinds. The supposed specters that sent grown men into hiding.

Yet, unlike the others, Mallory chose to go toward the sounds, to take up refuge in her bedroom. He had to admit, he was curious about what was causing the noises, and why the young Miss McGuire felt the need to be alone when they came.

Perhaps the next time the storm threatened, he'd watch from a better vantage point. Outside maybe? Or, better yet, from the third floor.

In the meantime, he'd relax back and let the deluge of rain

and wind surround him.

So much for relaxing.

The noises increased, the tempo a steady thump, thump, thump, raising his awareness, driving the race of his pulse. He drew a deep draft of air and squeezed his eyes shut tight. Immediately, Mallory's image popped into his head, etched itself on the back of his eyelids.

The pink flush of her flawless skin, the softness of her red curls, the sheen of her lower lip when she coated it with the swift dart of her tongue.

"Shit!" He shifted, making room for his growing arousal.

The storm raged on for what seemed like hours. Then, just when he'd finally accepted the fact that it was either tolerate the arousal, or stick himself in a cold bath, the weather calmed, the third-floor noises culminating in one final, loud crash. Immediately, his pulse calmed, his breathing evened out. Almost as if he'd climaxed.

Fornicating ghosts. Jeezus H. This place was making him as squirrely as the rest of them.

Harry circled the house and made his way to where the trees came right up to the front gate. Off in the distance, he could see the dim headlights of a car—no doubt Will Baker's fancy Durant.

He wondered how long the young man would wait tonight before he figured out Mallory wasn't going to be joining him for an evening on the town.

As if on cue, a rustling began among the bushes that lined the driveway. He closed the distance between himself and the woman who'd tried at least three times this week alone to leave the grounds.

Within ten steps of where he waited, the foliage parted and Mallory backed out onto the drive, her perfectly shaped bottom wrapped in an expensive silk dress.

"As tempting as it would be to give that backside of yours a solid smack, I don't think your father would appreciate me man-handling the merchandise."

She turned on him, her green eyes flaring, her cheeks flushing a bright pink even in the dim light of the half moon.

"Harry. I should have realized going behind the rose arbor and then through the trees was too easy a route."

"Come on," he said, tipping his head toward the house. "Let's go."

"Couldn't you let me leave? Just this once. Pretend you didn't find me. Or, better yet, let them think I've already gone to bed."

"And risk this well-paying job? I don't think so. Besides, they'd figure it out when you had to sneak back in." He paused until he had her full attention, and then asked, "Have you ever had to sneak back in? Or are you always discovered and brought home?"

"They've always come for me. That's why this would be perfect. I could go out with my friends, you could have a quiet, easy night of it. If you leave the ballroom door unlocked, I can come back across the patio."

"No can do. Sorry."

"How about you let me go with my friends, and I'll tell you where to pick me up in… say… four hours?"

"And let Sully win the pool? Ruin my perfect record?" He held out his hand. "If you go back to the house without further argument, I won't dock you a shopping trip."

Turning her back on him, she started up the driveway. "You know, Harry, you are the most infuriating man I've ever met."

"Thank you."

"It wasn't meant as a compliment."

"I gathered that."

"One of these days, Harry, I will get the better of you. I will escape, and I'll make it so difficult for you to find me, my father will fire you on the spot."

"As I've told you, at least a dozen times, I look forward to your continued attempts. It keeps the boredom from setting in."

The following Friday, Harry stood at the foot of the staircase and watched as Mallory made her way down. Dressed to the nines, she took his breath away.

"You look rather lovely tonight, Princess."

She reached up to straighten the bejeweled headband holding her curls in place. Grudgingly, he suspected, she offered him a smile and said, "Thank you, Harry. You're quite turned out yourself, for the hired help."

The obvious dig drew his chuckle. "I've been told I clean up nice." Offering her his hand once she'd reached the bottom step, he asked, "Are you looking forward to your trip to the cinema? I understand this new Buster Keaton film is quite entertaining."

"I'd much prefer something more dramatic. Slapstick—I believe that's what it's called—doesn't seem funny to me. Getting hit on the head for a laugh is stupid."

"I assume it's meant as satire, rather than true comedy."

"How about you, Harry? Are you looking forward to a night at the movies?"

"I'm afraid I'll have to hear about it later. I've been relegated to waiting by the car. Perhaps you could give me your review on the drive home."

"You won't be inside with me?"

He could almost smell the smoke, as the wheels began turning in her agile brain. She was going to make a dash for it. He could sense it. Feel it.

"Sorry, but no. Your father insists you'll be safe with him in Mr. Cousins' private box." When she didn't respond, he leaned closer and whispered, "I believe Mr. Cousins' youngest son will be attending as well. It would seem your papa is matchmaking again."

"I've known Alexander Cousins since we attended school together. I've no interest in him, or his father's wealth."

"Much to your father's chagrin, I'm sure."

Nearly three hours later, Harry raised his head at the sound of pounding footsteps coming across the pavement from the front of the theater. Teddy O'Brien was on the run, his fancy evening shoes sliding across the road as if he were on ice rather than dry land.

"She's gone. Slipped right out of the fucking box while we were watching the film. I haven't got the foggiest idea how long ago. When the movie ended, I looked up, and she wasn't in her seat."

"Well, she didn't come by me, so she must have gone out the back. Let Sully take the boss home. You and I will split up and go looking. You take the second car and drive down to the far end of town. I'll start here on foot. We'll meet up at the Cork and Barrel. If you find her, bring her there and wait for me to arrive."

"I shouldn't just take her home?"

"And leave me to walk back to Fairwinds? I think not."

For such a small town, Mystic Point had far too many nightspots, some legal, others not so much. While prohibition had put a damper on the rowdier establishments, supper clubs and fine dining were still the rage. Plus, given the town's proximity to Boston proper, it made for a steady influx of customers.

Speakeasies, although raided often, offered the well-heeled a place to obtain illegal drink and entertainment. While he understood why Mallory chose to escape rather than be confined, he wasn't clear about why she chose seedy establishments, like the Shore Club, to frequent.

Harry slipped into the dingy waterfront property unnoticed and made his way from one booth to the next. People of every ilk filled the crowded floor. If this was where Mallory chose to spend her time, he'd be hard pressed not to turn her over his knee for a sound spanking.

As delightful as spanking Miss McGuire's fine ass seemed, doing it as punishment held no excitement for him. Doing it for pleasure was another matter altogether.

By the time he eliminated two other rather questionable stops, he'd about given up hope of finding her. With only the Cork and Barrel left, it was either here or—perhaps—she was already in Teddy's care.

The lights were dim, but serviceable, making it easy to scour the speakeasy from wall-to-wall. Much cleaner than the previous stops, Harry made his way from table to booth, finally coming to a stop to the left of the stage.

"Oh, look, Sadie. My personal jailer has arrived to haul me home."

The wide, mocking grin she shot him rankled his patience.

"Miss Sadie," he said, bowing his head slightly. "Will." Rather than pull her to her feet as he'd seen both Gus and Sully do on occasion, he offered Mallory his hand. "Miss McGuire, if you'll come with me, please."

She hesitated—no doubt thrown off by his calm approach—something he truly wasn't feeling at the moment. Finally, she laid her hand in his and rose to her feet, meeting him toe-to-toe. "If I must."

He raised his opposite hand slightly, surprised when she flinched. His stomach lurched at the thought she'd been hit before, or that she thought he meant to strike her. With slow movements, he lifted his fingertips to her headband, righting the side that had gone askew. "There," he said, lowering his hand back to his side. "Perfect. We wouldn't want a hair out of place when you're returned to your father."

By the time they'd reached the front door, Teddy was pulling the car into place. "Just in time, I see," Teddy shouted over the rough cadence of the Model T's engine. "Your father is going to have my head, Miss Mallory. I hope it was worth it."

Chapter 8

Harry hefted the last case of whiskey from the rolling cart and set it in the corner of storage room five, just to the left of the main tunnel leading away from the gates. Pressed into service when both Sully and Gus had come down with some wretched stomach ailment, covering for them gave him another perspective of the tunnels. Another accounting of the vast stores of both booze and stolen goods kept by McGuire.

This new knowledge of McGuire's intricate dealings would serve him well when he was ready to bring the man's business empire crashing down. Harry's only concern before putting his plan into place was the effect it would have on Mallory, and on the home she loved so dearly.

He wondered how Teddy was faring with Miss McGuire's weekly shopping expedition. Something told him the rough-edged O'Brien was not accustomed to following a young woman into the dressmaker's shop or—heaven forbid—the rather risqué shop specializing in women's underpinnings.

More importantly, he wondered if Mallory would shake Teddy's watch and hightail it off with her friends again. That is, until Malcolm McGuire would demand Harry *'go find my fanciful brat'*.

If he'd only give his daughter some liberty, perhaps McGuire wouldn't have to worry about her breaking her leash.

There were days when he actually felt sorry for Mallory—for the tight rein her father kept on her. For the way the other men saw her as a chore, rather than for the intelligent young woman she was. No wonder she could fool them so easily. They never gave her credit for being smarter than they'd ever be.

His thoughts on Mallory, rather than on the job at hand, it was a moment or two before he realized he wasn't alone in the dank corridor.

"O'Brien?" When no answer came, he called out again, "Miss Mallory?" A shadow crossed between him and the row of lanterns that hung from the wooden braces. "Who's there?"

The crash of breaking glass drew him from the storeroom and out into the main tunnel. Another shadow flickered farther down the passageway. Withdrawing the Luger pistol from his ankle holster, he edged his way forward until he'd reached the turnoff that led to the next row of stockrooms.

At the entryway to room eight, a pile of broken glass greeted him, the distinct smell of spilled rum assaulting his senses. When he bent to retrieve the top portion of the bottle from the ground, a cold breeze wafted across the back of his neck.

"Listen, whomever the fuck you are, I'm not playing games here. I'll shoot you where you're rooted."

The closest lantern flickered, drawing his gaze. He could have sworn he heard the echo of a man's laughter. A dark, shapeless figure shone against the wall beneath the lamp just as the light went out completely.

What the bloody hell?

He'd obviously been listening to far too many of Mallory's tales of specters and curses. Why else would he be wondering if he'd just crossed paths with the ghost of Captain John Jacob Wilder?

***

Mallory slipped up the iron staircase and let herself into the third-floor bedroom. Ever since she'd been coming to the hideaway, and read Alice's journal entries about its origins, she'd been fascinated by the legend of her scoundrel pirate ancestor, and his love for his wife. Theirs was such a tragic ending, yet it spoke to the romantic in her.

The thought of being loved, cherished, the way Jake had loved Lily, made Mallory's heart race. However, now was not the time to think of such things. Now was the time to put the beautiful widow's walk to use as a new means of escape.

Ever since that odious Harry Carter had been appointed her jailer, she'd found it almost impossible to sneak out at night to meet with her friends—to do what she must during these trying times. The man was everywhere, his gaze always on her, his presence close… just short of hovering. His serious regard made her skin tingle and her breath catch.

She didn't like the way he made her feel. Not at all.

As quickly as she could, without making undue noise, she crossed the room and reached for the brass handle on the beveled French doors that led to the roof, not surprised to discover a spray of water on the floor. No doubt caused by the previous night's storm. *The Captain's and Lily's time together… when they made love.*

Pulling a dust cover from one of the nearby chairs, Mallory bent down and wiped up the water. She couldn't—wouldn't—let Jake and Lily's bedroom become ruined by a storm and whatever occurred at the time. Their legacy deserved care. Her continued care.

Once she'd reached the widow's walk, she stopped to admire the ornate weathervane, a gift from Lily to her husband. A huge sailing ship, a beacon to bring him safely home from the sea.

Mallory made her way to the railing on the side of the house where the ivy vines had finally reached the roof. The iron trellis she'd often climbed as a child was less than five feet below the roof's edge. All she needed was a good foothold among the vines, a secure grip on the roof's trim, and she could lower herself to the trellis and make her escape. Peering over the edge to the ground below, she drew a deep breath, slid her trouser clad leg over the top of the railing, and clung to the decorative trim for dear life. Slowly, she lowered herself down the side of the house, testing the strength of the interwoven vines beneath her feet. Certain it was safe, she took another step, and then another, her foot finally meeting the top of the trellis.

Thank the saints. She'd made it to the safety of the crisscross ironwork.

Taking another downward step, the soles of her sensible oxfords slipped on the wet slats. Her grip tightened around the trellis; her breath held until she'd regained her footing.

The pounding of her heart underscored the danger of her plan. Releasing a long breath to calm her nerves, she eased herself downward. The ground was coming up to meet her, less than twenty feet separating her from freedom.

Another step, then another. The trellis shook beneath her weight, reminding her she was no longer a skinny, ten-year-old girl.

There was no going back now. She lowered herself to the next rung only to have the iron crossbar break beneath her foot. Mallory fell backward, her arms windmilling in a frantic search for something to grab onto.

Tears stung her eyes, and she accepted the irony that she was about to land, injured or dead, in the recently tilled earth of her late mother's precious flower garden.

"Gotcha, Princess," a deep voice growled against her ear.

Mallory opened her eyes. She'd not landed on the cold, unforgiving ground but in a man's strong embrace. *His embrace.*

"Dammit, Harry, put me down."

His mouth kicked up in what could best be described as a self-righteous smirk. Slowly, he lowered her down the length of his body, her soft curves sliding over his much harder angles.

"As you wish, Princess." He glanced around, and then back

up at the path she'd taken down the side of the house. "Mighty lucky I happened to be in the right place, at the most opportune time, isn't it?"

Mallory laid her hands against his chest, his muscles jumping and bunching beneath her touch, and pushed out of his lingering grip. Her knees wobbled, and he grasped her shoulders in his strong hands to keep her from falling.

She straightened her stance and took a step back, freeing herself from his hold.

"Just how did you happen to be here? Right now?"

As it always did, his deep chuckle set her nerves on edge.

"When are you going to accept the fact, Miss McGuire, that you're not going to sneak out on me? You might have the rest of your father's men either fooled, or wrapped around that elegant little finger of yours, but I'm not as easily dismissed."

Mallory was beginning to think she'd never see the outside of Fairwinds again. Harry was just that good. It has been three days since the fiasco on the trellis, and her fingertips still tingled with the memory of the way his muscles had moved beneath her touch; of the way it had felt being held in his arms.

She didn't want to be attracted to Harry Carter. Yet, she was.

Like all her father's men, he was a thug. A pile of hired muscle intent on following a bad man's orders no matter who it hurts.

She despised all of them. Even Harry.

When she arrived in the dining room for the evening meal, she was surprised to see only her father at the table. No Gus, no Teddy. No Harry.

"Where is everyone? Surely you didn't give them all the night off."

"They're lurking about somewhere," her father said. "I

thought we might have some time, just the two of us."

Although she was suspicious—perhaps he was making another play to steal Fairwinds from her—she couldn't help but admit she missed the father he used to be. Before he became so enamored of wealth and whatever means it took to obtain it.

"The quiet is much appreciated for sure," she admitted. "Was there something you wanted to discuss?"

"I wanted to tell you how proud I am that you've given up your running ways. Harry's been a good influence on you. Other than the time you left my company at the movie theater, the men haven't had to chase after you."

It still amazed her that Harry never let on about the dozen or so attempts she'd made to skip out on him.

"I'll be sure to thank Harry for providing me with such a great example," she said, infusing as much sarcasm into her words as she could fit and not choke on them.

"Your thanks will have to wait until Saturday. He's taking a few days off to deal with some family issues that came up before his arrival at Fairwinds. I trust we can count on your continued good behavior in his absence."

"I'll do my best."

Garden or library or through the ballroom doors and onto the patio. So many options, and only three days to try them out.

***

"He'll see you now, Mr. Barclay."

Simon pushed to his feet, dragging himself and his alter-ego Harry Carter, in front of the director of the Boston office of the Federal Bureau of Investigation.

"So, Barclay, what have you got for us? Is it enough to take down Malcolm McGuire's illegal activities?"

He laid his notebook on Jefferson Whitmer's desk. "It's all there, save for a few items that McGuire keeps locked in a safe in the library."

"The daughter, the one you've been spending so much time with, she hasn't given you any idea what's stored in there?"

"I honestly don't think she knows what her father's hiding. I've never seen her anywhere near the safe. I only stumbled on it when I was mapping out Miss McGuire's favorite escape routes."

"Escape routes?" Whitmer asked.

"Her father keeps her on a tight leash—which was what got me in the door in the first place. From what I gather, he's overprotective because of some clause in the late wife's will. If something should happen to her before she inherits at twenty-five, he'd have to leave the house and all its advantages behind. I don't think it has anything to do with truly wanting to protect her, just her hold on the estate."

"Are you sure she's as innocent of his crimes as she appears?"

Simon gave a shrug. "She's as intelligent as sin, far more so than McGuire or his men. I've no doubt my absence has sent them into a tailspin. I imagine she's made at least one break from the house, if not more. As for her innocence... She's definitely aware of her father's illegal activities and she deplores them. It's her intention to send him packing as soon as she inherits legally."

"What does she do when she takes off? Where does she go?"

"Out with friends to the local speakeasies, as far as I can tell. That's the only place she's been found when the men have gone searching for her."

"When are you due back?"

"Saturday morning. My shift begins at eight. I'm there for five straight days, around the clock, before getting another day away."

"How much longer do you think you'll need before we can go in?"

"Another week or two, a month, tops. However, I do have a request. I want to get Miss McGuire out of the house before you begin the raid." He hesitated, before adding, "Also, the estate isn't part of his ill-gotten property, so if they can do as little damage as possible, that would be great."

"I can't promise anything if trouble breaks out between our guys and McGuire's men, but I'll see what we can do about minimizing the damage."

"I'd appreciate that, sir."

"You care for this young woman, don't you?"

Again, Simon's shoulders lifted and fell in a noncommittal shrug. "She's not part of this. She doesn't deserve to suffer for her father's greed and dishonesty."

"Just make sure you're thinking with your head, not your cock."

This time, he chuckled. "I'm still trying to figure her out, but feel fairly confident Miss McGuire has even less experience with men than she does with her father's illegal businesses. Definitely not the kind of woman I go for when I let my cock do the thinking."

Chapter 9

Mallory tested the door to her room, pleasantly surprised to find it unlocked.

"Good morning, Miss McGuire."

"You're back, Harry," she said, as she made her way from her room to where he waited at the top of the stairs. "I assume it's you I have to thank for being able to leave my room again."

His smirk drew her gaze to his face, his well-shaped mouth.

"How many times did you break out?"

"Just twice. Wednesday and then again on Thursday. After that, they locked me in my room."

A frown stole his half-smile. His jaw twitched, and he lowered his gaze to the carpeted hallway. Was he upset over her treatment in his absence? Or, angry she'd successfully returned to her wandering the moment he was out of sight?

"Now that you've been sprung, how about we move those supplies out to the cliffs? I cleared away the old fencing before I left on Tuesday, so I could get started on the repairs today."

"I'd like that, Harry. Thank you. Perhaps, afterward, we can take a drive into town? The dressmaker has some items ready to be picked up."

"Sure, why not. Even watching you shop beats hanging around the house on such a beautiful day."

As she had for the past hour, Mallory sat on the blanket she'd spread out between the fences of Lady Lillian's grave and the family cemetery. The spot gave her a panoramic view of Skullery Bay, the beautiful stretch of beach along the shoreline, and at least one other interesting sight.

Harry worked less than twenty feet away. He'd removed his shirt, his chest covered by the thin undershirt he wore. His muscles glistened with hard-earned sweat as he lifted the heavy pieces of iron fencing into place.

Mallory's throat went dry at the sight of Harry's firm body, lightly bronzed by the late-August sun. The sensations she usually only equated with the storms shot across the surface of her skin, increasing her heart rate ten-fold.

"That's enough for today," he said, tugging on his shirt as he came toward her. "Give me a couple of minutes to clean up and we'll head into town."

Reaching out, he offered her his hand to pull her to her feet. When their fingers touched, sparks skittered over the back of her hand, causing her to pull free of his grasp as soon as she'd gained her balance.

"Yes. I need to change as well. It wouldn't do to go to the dressmaker wearing trousers, would it?"

Mallory moved from one counter to the next, running the expensive fabrics through her fingers, before going on to the next.

Harry stood off to the side, his gaze constantly scanning the large mercantile, always coming back to her.

Gus and the others hated her shopping trips. They hated having to wait while she purposely took her time looking at each and every new item Mrs. Willows had procured for her store.

"What do you think, Mr. Carter?" she asked, holding up a bolt of pink silk. "Would this make a good evening dress?"

Rather than recoil in horror at being asked an opinion on 'lady things' as Gus called them, Harry took a step closer. Reaching out, he ran his fingertips over the soft material. "It's nice, but the pink will clash with your hair."

Her breath caught. How would it be, she wondered, to

have his fingers stroking her cheeks, her throat, her breasts, in the same manner?

"Perhaps," she hedged. "I do love the color though."

"The royal blue, in the same fabric would be better."

"I didn't realize you had experience as a couturier, Mr. Carter."

"I have experience with a number of things, Miss McGuire."

She drew a breath and gave him a quick up and down appraisal, her bold action drawing his outright grin. "Of that, Mr. Carter, I have no doubt."

***

Later that afternoon, Harry entered the parlor moments behind Sully and Gus, all of them summoned by a most irate Malcolm McGuire. When all four men were assembled, McGuire raised his gaze and slammed his fist down on the top of the ornate table at his side.

"What the fuck am I paying you clowns for?"

Gus and Sully traded glances, backpedaling a few steps. Even Teddy took a cautious step backward.

Not to be bullied, Harry chose to move forward. "I don't know about these layabouts, but you pay me to watch that stubborn daughter of yours."

"Well, you obviously haven't been doing your job." Shaking a single piece of paper in his fist, he continued. "This is a note from one of my daughter's—apparently—many admirers."

"A note?"

"Mallory received a delivery earlier today, while you and she were in town. Flowers. Not very expensive ones, two single roses, along with this note."

Harry glanced down at the torn envelope that lay atop the table and then back at Malcolm McGuire's beet red face.

"You opened the note addressed to your daughter?"

Malcolm shot him a glare, yet he refused to back down. "Yes, I did. As her father, it's my business to know who might be courting her."

"I'd hardly call two roses courting," Harry felt compelled to point out. What he really wanted to do was rail at McGuire for invading Mallory's privacy.

"That's not the point. I couldn't care one bent nickel about the fuckin' flowers." Shoving the note into Harry's hands, he ordered, "Read this, and then tell me exactly how good you are at watching over my daughter?"

Harry passed the note back unread. "I'll not invade Miss Mallory's privacy. I know for a fact, the only time she slipped my watch was the night she went with you to the theater, and I was told to wait by the car, that she was 'handled'. It took Teddy and me nearly two hours to track her down, but she was safe and sound with her friends at the Cork and Barrel."

"What about this past Thursday?" Malcolm argued.

Harry could almost feel the room vibrating, as both Gus and Sully moved toward the door.

"Not my watch," Harry said. "Not my screw up."

"Gus!" McGuire shouted. "Get over here."

The burly man inched forward. When Malcolm thrust the note forward again, Gus took it in shaking hands.

"I don't want to read it either," Gus admitted. "Sir."

McGuire snatched the note back. Unfolding the paper, he began to read.

'*Dearest Mallory, it was so wonderful to spend time with you again. I've missed you terribly but the night before last was one I'll not soon forget. Bobby and Jeff can't wait to be graced with your favor again, as well. We're all in awe of that thing you do with your...*'

McGuire's words stalled and he drew a breath. '*...with your mouth. It is most fun. Sincerely, Trevor.*' I don't know who this fuckin' Trevor is, but I intend to cut off his cock and shove it down his throat when I find him."

Harry's heart clenched. Was she truly not as innocent as she seemed? Not that he himself had any room to judge, given the company he'd kept over the years, as opposed to settling down with a wife and family.

Still, the realization that the one woman to whom he'd found himself both physically and emotionally attracted, might not be what he thought her to be was upsetting.

Perhaps it was time to allow her to slip his watch, and then follow her to see if this note had any credence. To find Trevor so he could kill the bastard himself before McGuire found him and cut off his dick.

Chapter 10

Malcolm McGuire raised his head and met Harry's gaze, the man's bushy brows furrowing in surprise. "You want to do what?" McGuire asked.

"I want to let her slip out on her own. Tomorrow night. I'll tail her and find out where she goes. See if I can figure out who this Trevor fellow is."

"She doesn't even try to run when you're on duty. What makes you so sure she will this time."

"Tell her I've got the night off," he suggested. "Let her think Gus or Sully will be on duty. She'll be out of here before either of those stupid bastards can make it down the driveway."

"Why would I want to give her the chance to meet up with this guy when I can count on you keeping her here?"

He knew he was treading on dangerous territory, but he decided to voice what he'd been thinking ever since his first night on duty. "Have you ever thought of giving her some leeway? A few nights with her friends, with one of us at a distance of course."

"It's not up for discussion," McGuire said firmly. "She'd be a bargaining chip for my enemies if they got their hands on her."

"For all the times she's snuck out on you, she's never once been put in danger. At least not that we've seen. What makes you so sure she's even in your competition's sights."

Pulling the drawer of his desk open, McGuire fisted a handful of papers and pushed them across the polished mahogany surface. "Threats. A half dozen of them."

Harry lifted the notes from top of the desk and scanned

them quickly. Perhaps it wasn't just McGuire's fear of losing access to Fairwinds that caused him to guard Mallory so closely, but also concern for his daughter.

As much as he wanted to believe McGuire's fatherly worry was heartfelt, he couldn't discount the fact that the man was still a criminal. Possibly a murderer.

"I give you my word she'll be safe." He drew a breath and asked, "Aren't you the least bit curious where she goes? What she might be doing?"

McGuire's eyes narrowed to mere slits as he gave Harry an up and down appraisal. "You seem to be more interested in finding this Trevor character than I am."

"My only concern is that these men may be working for one of your many supposed enemies and only befriending her to get close. Either for information, or to follow through on one of these threats." Pushing himself away from the corner of McGuire's desk, he added, "You made it my job to protect your daughter. I can't do that properly if I don't know all the players."

"Fine," McGuire finally conceded. "Work it out with Teddy and Gus. Just make sure you don't lose her, or it'll be your privates on the chopping block."

"Don't worry, boss. I'll be within a hundred feet of her at all times. She'll never know I'm there."

The next afternoon, Harry went in search of Mallory, finding her in the library, curled up in her favorite chair.

"Behave," he warned, giving Mallory his sternest expression. "I need to follow up on my business from last week. I'd hate to return in the morning and find you locked in your room again."

She met his gaze, a coy smile lifting the corners of her full, ruby red lips. "I'll do my best, Harry."

He loved it when his plans came to fruition. She'd be gone

by nine at the latest.

By eight that evening, Harry had positioned his car in among the overgrown trees about a mile down the road leading into Mystic Point. At eight-thirty, Will's fancy Durant went whizzing by on its way to Fairwinds. At eight-forty, he pulled out of his secluded spot and followed them into town.

Rather than turn toward the main street, where most of the entertainment was located, Will made a right onto the route leading into an area of older, somewhat shabby homes.

Where the hell were they going?

His temper rose with each turn they made, the route taking them into the seedier part of town.

Finally, Will drew to a stop in front of an enormous four-story home. Painted recently, the house wasn't as bad as he'd expected. The yard was bordered by shrubs, rows of late summer plants, and appeared well tended.

Mallory slipped out of the front seat of the Durant sedan, leaned over to talk to Will, and then shut the door. Thankfully, Will waited until she'd reached the wrap-around veranda and gone inside before driving away.

The moment Will turned the corner out of sight, Harry jumped out of the auto and moved cautiously up the walkway. Lights shone from nearly every window on the first floor and dotted the windows on the second and third. The fourth floor was dark, possibly an attic.

Once he'd reached the porch, he turned his attention to the neatly painted sign nailed to the shingles beside the door.

Hansen House.

He thought about barging in, demanding to know where Mallory had gone. Instead, he decided to walk around the grounds and see what he could find without revealing his presence. Turning on his heel, he came to an immediate stop when he noticed a woman making her way up the steps.

"Can I help you?" she asked.

He looked down from the porch and met her gaze. She was older—mid-sixties maybe—wearing a white uniform.

"I'm sorry, I must have the wrong address," he said quickly. "I thought this was a private home."

"No, it's not," she said, offering him a friendly smile. "Hansen House is a home for veterans."

"War veterans?"

"Yes, we house men who came home handicapped but have no family to help care for them."

"Very commendable of you," he said honestly. "Is there a large staff?"

"We have two doctors and six nurses on staff. However, we'd be lost without our wonderful patrons. They help with meals, they read to those who've lost their sight. Sometimes, they just sit with those who are lonely."

"I'm sorry if I'm being nosey, but I never knew this place existed."

"Most don't. These men are forgotten time and again. We receive government funding, of course, but we also rely on donations. Unfortunately, we lost our largest benefactor a couple of years ago in a tragic accident."

"Really? That must have been tough."

"Yes, Mrs. McGuire was a godsend. Hansen House still gets a yearly donation from her estate, and her lovely daughter volunteers her time whenever she can, but the men miss the hours Mrs. McGuire would spend with them. Especially Phillip."

"Phillip?"

"He was Helene's beau years ago, long before she married."

"I'd better let you get to work then," he said, stepping back so she could go inside.

"Would you like to meet some of our residents?" the woman asked.

He gave a quick shake of his head. "I'm afraid I can't tonight. I need to figure out where I went wrong on the original house number and get to where I'm supposed to be."

"Are you sure? Miss Mallory called to say she'd be here tonight to entertain the men with her silly bird calls. It's a wonderful laugh for them."

Bird calls? A sense of relief washed over him, drawing his smile.

"Maybe another time."

"My name's Mabel. Just ask for me when you come back."

He held out his hand. "My name's Simon. Simon Barclay."

"Nice to meet you, Simon."

"You too, Mabel."

It was another hour and a half before Mallory came out of Hansen House. A hired car was there waiting to whisk her away to meet up with her friends. He'd follow behind and then give her an hour before he went in to get her.

As long as there were no shady looking characters going in or out, there was no reason she couldn't enjoy the rest of her evening.

He wasn't sure which thought pleased him more—the idea she was carrying on her mother's legacy of kindness—or that the 'thing' she was doing with her mouth was nothing more than bird calls.

***

Mallory slid into the seat beside Sadie and leaned back against the plush upholstery. "Any sign of Gus or Sully?"

"Nope," Sadie said. "Not here or earlier at the Cork and Barrel."

"I'm sure it won't be long before they show." Waving for the passing waiter, she added, "No doubt, I'll need to down an entire bottle in order to put up with my father's tirade."

The music at the Sneaky Cat was divine as always. She'd

actually been able to enjoy two full sets without interruption. The evening had been such a wonderful success, she was half tempted to call it a night and ask Will to drive her home.

"Uh… oh," Sadie whispered. "Here comes the hired muscle. Ooo… and such nice muscles."

Mallory spun in her chair, turning in time to see Harry walking in her direction, his long legs eating up the floor like a man with purpose.

"Miss Mallory," he said, his jaw twitching in what she'd come to know as his attempt to fight back a grin. "Miss Sadie. Will."

"I thought you had the night off."

His shrug—those impossibly broad shoulders—set her pulse racing.

"I got done early. When I found out you'd taken off, I volunteered to come fetch you."

She made a show of rolling her eyes and shooting him a frown. "Well, then, I suppose we should go."

"I wouldn't mind a drink," he said before sliding into the chair at her side. "As long as you're buying, of course."

"Me?"

"You're the heiress with the hefty allowance, aren't you? I'm just the paid help—as you often like to point out."

Mallory raised her hand and waved for the hovering waiter. "Sadie and I will have another champagne. Will?"

"Same for me, doll face."

"Three champagnes and a beer."

Before the waiter could escape, Harry called him back. "I'll have a glass of your finest red rather than a beer, thank you."

"Wine? Really? You don't look like a wine drinker."

"I'm not a fan of bootlegged beer," he said, his gaze locking on hers. "And champagne bubbles don't agree with me."

By the time their drinks arrived, the jazz ensemble had returned to the stage, along with their newest singer. Sadie and Will bolted for the dance floor, leaving her alone in Harry's irritating company.

"I can see why you like this place," Harry said halfway through the first song. "The music's good. That singer is one sexy dame."

"Perhaps you should ask her out," Mallory suggested. Her breath caught tight in her chest while she waited for his response.

"Maybe I will. Assuming I ever get another night off. No doubt I'll pay for Gus and Sully's lapse in protection with extra shifts."

"She looks like your type of woman."

"I didn't realize I had a type," he said, chuckling.

"Every man has a type." Nodding toward the stage, she added, "Sultry, sexy, I think you said, low cut dress, heavy on the makeup, bright red lipstick."

Without warning, Harry raised his hand to her cheek and rubbed his thumb across her lower lip before holding it up to the candle in the middle of the table.

"That ain't pink, Princess."

Every nerve-ending she possessed sizzled with awareness. Meeting his gaze, she told him as firmly as she could manage, "Don't call me Princess."

"Whatever you say, *sweetheart*."

Chapter 11

Mallory accepted Harry's offered arm and followed at his side when they left the speakeasy. When he led her to an expensive looking auto, she asked, "Whose car is this?"

"Mine." Once he'd closed her door and circled the car, he settled into the driver's seat, and continued. "Embezzlement… whether it's true or not. Even though I came to Fairwinds to stay out of the limelight, I still prefer to enjoy at least a few of my supposed ill-gotten gains."

She should have expected as much. After all, a reputable man wouldn't be working for her father. Still, she'd held out hope that Harry was different, more honorable than the thugs her father usually hired.

"I suppose you're going to turn me into my father when we get back to Fairwinds."

"And why would I do that, Mallory? You're not a child who needs to be punished, are you?"

"No, I'm not. A fact neither my father nor his goons seem to realize. If it had been Teddy or Gus who'd come for me, they'd be manhandling me right to my father's desk."

"I don't believe…"

His words stopped short, as if he was rethinking what he wanted to say, his pause making her all the more curious.

"You don't believe what, Harry?"

Broad shoulders lifted and fell on a sigh. "I don't believe a woman should be roughed up, manhandled, under any circumstances. To do it as a form of containment or punishment is despicable."

She let his words sink in, this true contradiction of a man. Intelligent, stubborn, and undeniably handsome. *And kind?*

"Can I ask you something, Harry?"

"As long as it's not going to cost me my life or my job."

"It is about your job, but nothing life threatening."

"Then, go ahead. Ask."

"Why are you working for my father? You're a hundred times smarter than the rest of his men, you're understanding… kind even."

"I need to lay low for a bit, earn some dough free of public scrutiny. To be honest, when your father first laid out the job, my instinct was to say, 'no thanks'. But then when Teddy hauled you into the room, his hand wrapped tightly around your arm, I realized I needed to say, 'yes' if only to protect you from yourself."

"From myself?"

His deep chuckle ratcheted her pulse up another notch.

"It was obvious to me, when you stomped on Teddy's foot, you weren't going to give up your impulse to run, to escape. I figured if I took the job, you'd be less likely to get away and, even if you did, you wouldn't have to be forcibly returned."

"So, you'd never 'force' me?"

"I prefer to show you respect. Allow you to realize you are going home—like it or not—and might as well do so peacefully."

"Thank you, Harry. I appreciate you saying so."

"Just so we're clear though, Princess. If you didn't accept my show of respect, I'd still have no qualms about hoisting you over my shoulder and carrying you out like a sack of well-dressed potatoes."

The idea of being hoisted over Harry's broad shoulder and carried off was not without appeal.

"I'll keep that in mind, Harry, for the next time I escape your clutches."

The next morning, Mallory withdrew her great aunt's diary

from beneath her mattress and opened it to a random page. She needed something to grasp onto, something to get her mind off of Harry, his devilish smile, and the kindness she appreciated but didn't want to enjoy.

It wouldn't do to let her guard down around any of her father's men, even those who seemed to hold her in higher regard than the others.

Laying the journal on her lap, she began to read...

'1861, October 29

The Union army suffered its worst defeat just this month. Ball's Bluff, where nearly one-thousand Unions soldiers lost their lives, along with over one hundred Confederates. This war has gone on for over six months now with no end in sight. They are calling for medical help.

My parents do not want me to go, but I cannot ignore the training I was afforded. I must look into joining up and helping where I can.'

Mallory closed the journal and laid it aside. Perhaps today, if she could find an opportunity, she'd spend some time on the third floor.

***

Harry took a cautious step closer to doorway. Out of sight.

What the devil was she up to now?

He'd cut her a wide berth all morning, allowing Mallory to come and go between her bedroom, the library, the rose arbor, and then back to her room.

Watching her from a distance was both a blessing and a curse.

While it helped build trust between them, it also caused him more than one or two bouts of attraction. Desire. At a distance, there was no need to fight back his longing. No need to pretend an indifference he surely didn't feel. Despite all his best intentions, and the secrets he kept, he'd fallen for Mallory McGuire.

Malcolm McGuire had been right about one thing. His own concern for Mallory's well-being far outweighed that of her father, or any of her father's men.

So, here he stood at the library door and watched as she crossed from the bottom of the curved staircase, through the double doors, to the opposite side of the rotunda to go through the hidden doorway, a bouquet of fresh-cut roses clutched tightly in her hand.

Glancing from side-to-side, as if on the lookout, she shifted her weight and used her hip to shove the lounging chair to the side. A moment later, the concealed doorway sprung open, and Mallory stepped into the dark void. No doubt using all her strength, and weight, she poked her hand through the opening and tugged the settee back into place before sliding the door shut from the inside.

Why would she be going into the tunnels at this time of day? And, why was she carrying flowers?

He gave her a short head start and then followed her into the passageway. He was about to head to the tunnels when he heard a noise from above. She'd gone up, not down.

The stairs going upward were less sturdy than the reinforced ones that went to the ground floor. He took a tentative step, and then another, the wrought iron railing cold beneath his hand.

At the top, there was a trap door. He was about to shove it open and climb through, when the sound of Mallory's voice seeped through the wooden barrier.

"I wish I could talk to you," she said softly. "All of you. Not just my dear mama, but the Captain, Lady Lillian, my dear great aunt Alice."

He waited, wondering what she'd say next. Taking a seat at the top of the stairs, he shamelessly listened in on her private conversation with her ancestors.

"I know all of your spirits are here somewhere. I've seen

the signs in the way the Captain loses his temper and slams the doors. My mother spoke of seeing Lady Lillian on the roof top just before a storm and, again, on the patio during one of her many parties. I'm certain I saw Lady Lillian that one time myself."

She drew a breath, the long, laborious sound drawing on his heartstrings.

"I'm doing what I can to keep Fairwinds together, despite my father's shady business dealings. It's why I come here from time-to-time to care for the room, to leave fresh flowers in the vase atop the dresser, and to talk. When I'm especially in need of your company, I read Alice's journal and revel in her stories. I've kept Lady Lillian's beautiful wedding ring safe, as well as the eight pieces of the Captain's gold."

Captain's gold? Closing his eyes, he let Mallory's words sink in.

Was there more to the legends of Fairwinds than met the eye?

"I have to go now," she said, sadness filling her voice. "They'll be looking for me soon enough. Harry and the others. I'll be back to clean after the next storm. I promise."

The sound of shuffling on the other side of the trap door set him in motion. Taking the stairs down two at a time, he made it through the hidden doorway just as he heard the hatch slam shut.

Then, taking a spot out of her line of sight, he waited until Mallory had made her way into the rotunda, righted the settee, and bolted up the circular stairs toward her bedroom. Climbing the stairs moments behind her, he settled onto the top riser and leaned back against the newel post to wait. No doubt she'd come out of her room in a few minutes and demand to know why he was keeping such close tabs on her, and insist he stop.

He needed to keep his focus where the lovely Miss

McGuire was concerned; keep his head in the game, and take her father down while still protecting her from both her family and the government. Without getting emotionally involved.

Not entirely possible, given how this game of cat and mouse with the Princess was more fun—and far more enticing—than he could have ever predicted.

Chapter 12

Mallory stood at the top of the staircase, and nudged Harry's foot with the toe of her T-strap slippers. "Harry, are you sleeping? Or, just hoping I won't notice you lurking about."

He shifted and stretched, and opened one eye, gazing up at her. "Cat nap. I figure I need my rest in case you want to try to run away later this evening."

"As much as I'd love to go out with my friends, I don't hold much hope of my father agreeing, or my escaping your overprotective watch. Plus, there's a storm coming. I prefer to stay at home when a nor'easter blows through."

"That's what I've heard." He pushed himself to his feet and motioned for her to go down the stairs ahead of him. "Your father says you're afraid of the thunder and lightning, so you hide in your room."

"My father doesn't know anything about why I choose to be alone during the storms."

"So then, you're not afraid of the elements?"

"No, as a matter of fact, I find them relaxing. Which is why I go to my room. To relax."

"Storms put most people on edge," he pointed out. "How is it, they relax you?"

She spun on him, bringing them toe-to-toe. Immediately, she regretted the impulse. He made her wary enough when he was ten feet away. Being this close rankled her nerves, set her heart beating in an uneven rhythm.

Yet, rather than back down, she raised her head, met his gaze, and explained. "In case you haven't noticed, I'm not 'most' people."

He lifted his hand and chucked her beneath the chin, his touch making her skin burn.

"Ah... Princess, I've definitely noticed."

The winds began slowly, picking up momentum with each moment that passed. Mallory pushed herself from the soft leather chair and left the library with the first rumble of thunder.

When Harry fell into step behind her, she called back over her shoulder. "I don't need an escort. I'm going to my room, as I said I would."

"Not to worry, Miss McGuire. The moment you're behind closed doors, I'll find something to occupy my time. Maybe I'll go outside and watch the storm up close."

"Don't be ridiculous," she scolded. "You'll get wet, not to mention running the risk of being hit by... uh... go ahead if you want."

"You wound me, Mallory. Not the least bit concerned for my safety? Encouraging my risky behavior, in fact?"

"I hear there's great viewing from underneath the shelter of a big tree."

His laugh crossed the air between them. "Now you're just being cruel."

They'd reached the door to her room, and she stopped to turn around and meet his gaze. "Good night, Harry. Enjoy your evening's respite."

He dipped his head in a quick nod. "Good evening, Princess. Enjoy your storm and—assuming you're as relaxed as you claim—a good night's sleep."

Rather than back through her bedroom door, she took a step closer, drawn forward by the brooding stare of his dark amber eyes. When she licked her lips, Harry sucked in a sudden breath.

"I will," she said, her attention never leaving his mouth, or the scruff of his evening beard. "Enjoy the storm, that is." When he didn't back away, she asked, "What do you enjoy, Harry?"

"This."

Leaning forward, he pressed his lips to hers, stealing her breath and her very sanity with the slight pressure of his mouth. She laid her hands flat against his chest, intent on pushing him away. Instead, her fingers curled around his shirt front until she could tug him forward, putting them chest to chest, breath to breath.

"You shouldn't have done that," she said, the weakness of her resolve little match for the heat she could see in Harry's gaze.

"Then, let me go."

She licked her lips again, tasting Harry's kiss on the tip of her tongue. "I can't."

He lowered his head, returning to the kiss, pressing himself against her body, drawing her gasp. When he slipped his tongue between her parted lips, she groaned. She tasted the coffee he'd had with supper, the peppermint he'd enjoyed afterward. The warmth of his wet mouth.

Finally breaking the kiss, he took a step back. Grasping her wrists in his hands, he removed her grip from his shirt. "Get in your room, Princess. Now."

"But—"

"Now!"

Backpedaling across the threshold, she shut the door between them, and turned the key in the lock. Moving quickly across the room, she collapsed on her bed, every nerve ending in her body tingling beyond anything she'd ever felt—even during the most violent of the storms. Even when the Captain and Lady Lillian made love above her head.

The crackle of lightning announced the arrival of the storm she'd been anticipating for the past half hour. The wind, lazy before, had picked up significantly. Scrambling out of her clothes, she donned her thin cotton gown and slid beneath the covers.

Between the third-floor activities of her ghostly ancestors, and the tumultuous feelings Harry had raised within her, she had no doubt this was going to be a perfect storm.

***

Jeezus H, you stupid bastard. What the fuck were you thinking?

Obviously, I wasn't, he responded silently, wishing his damning conscience back into the corner of his innermost thoughts.

Kissing Mallory McGuire had been a huge—albeit delightful—mistake. A mistake he couldn't afford to make again. For the sake of his assignment, and his own sanity.

She was sassy perfection.

He was not much better than the lowlife criminals he sought to bring to justice. He was living a lie, one that would soon come crashing down around them all, beginning with Malcolm McGuire's arrest. Ending when Mallory found out he wasn't who he claimed to be. She no doubt believed the worst of her father's sins to be greed in the form of illegal activities. He believed it to be worse. Much worse.

The late Mrs. McGuire's attorney had been the one to turn Malcolm McGuire into the Feds, not for his business activities, but for Helene McGuire's murder. The solicitor felt certain McGuire had paid off one of his men to facilitate the woman's fall from the cliffs. And, while they had a paper trail of a huge cash withdrawal less than a week after her death, they still didn't know who pushed her over the edge and out onto the beachfront where her body was found.

He had less than two weeks to complete his investigation, formulate a plan, and to come up with an excuse to get Mallory away from Fairwinds on the day of the FBI's intended raid.

And he had to do it from a relatively safe distance.

Otherwise, he knew he'd be unable to stop with just a kiss. Especially when he wanted so much more.

Thursday arrived sunny and hot as blazes, making his mood even more foul than it had been since he'd kissed Mallory two days earlier.

He needed a diversion. Something that took him away from her unsettling presence. Unfortunately, the remainder of the fencing supplies arrived earlier that morning, and he had no excuse that would keep him from finishing the repairs to the ironwork at the top of the cliffs.

"Harry, are you ready?" Mallory asked. "I had Mrs. Vernon pack us a light lunch and some cold drinks."

"You don't have to come with me, if you don't want to. It's got to be ninety-five degrees out there. I'm sure you'll be much more comfortable here in the house."

"I don't mind," she said, hesitating slightly. "After all, you're doing all this as a favor to me. The least I can do is keep you company. Besides, I've not been to my mother's grave in a few days."

"We could pick some roses from the arbor on the way," he suggested. "If you'd like."

"I would, very much."

Lunch basket, gardening gloves, and clippers in hand, they left the house and stepped out onto the cobblestone path that wound its way toward the overflowing rose arbor.

He stood back and watched as Mallory made her way around the beautiful flowers, eyeing each section before making her final selection. She reached up to gather the first bunch and stuck her finger on a thorn.

When she sucked her fingertip into her mouth, his breath lodged in his throat, and his body responded predictably, an ache shooting through his groin, settling hard as a rock between his legs.

"Here," he said, extending the gloves and clippers in her direction. "Take these rather than prick your fingers."

She took the offering from his grasp, her brilliant green eyes lighting with obvious excitement. "Thank you."

***

Mallory bit back the urge to curse. She was struggling with her ever-changing reaction to Harry. Her first instinct was to dislike him, or at least be distrustful, as she was with her father's other men.

She'd thought of trying another escape from the roof—if only to be caught in his arms if she fell.

And... his kisses... they took her breath away.

The moment they reached the cliffs, Harry made his way to where the last six feet of fencing would be placed. He rolled up his shirt sleeves, the sight of his bronzed muscles making her insides quiver.

Rather than be caught staring, she went to the family cemetery and took a seat on the ground in front of her mother's grave. What she wouldn't give, she realized, to be able to ask her mother for advice—especially where the enigmatic Harry Carter was concerned. She could imagine her mother's response. *'If you want to know something, just ask. Better to pose a question than continue uninformed.'*

In her youth, she'd been an endless stream of questions. And her mother had never failed to answer, had always shown patience, and never laughed at her childish naïveté.

Lost in her memories, it was a moment or two before she realized Harry had taken a seat less than five feet away. Leaning back against the iron fencing that surrounded the family burial plots, he reached for the basket, no doubt in search of a cold drink.

"Do you have the evening off?" she asked. "It is Thursday, after all."

He swallowed back a mouthful of lemonade and chuckled. "Planning your escape already?"

She shot him a glare. "If I get the chance, you can bet your last dollar I'll be out of here for the night."

"I have a better idea," he said, lifting one of the sandwiches from inside the basket. "Your father has gone to Boston on a business trip. He won't be back until Friday evening, or possibly not until Saturday. How about I have Gus and Sully let you out for the night? Your friend Will can pick you up at the door, rather than somewhere between here and town."

"I don't think either of them will risk my father's wrath just because you say so."

"They will if I guarantee your safe return," he countered.

"And how do you propose to do that?"

"It's part of my conditions for having the boys look the other way. You can go without having to sneak out provided you're waiting for me at the Sneaky Cat by eleven."

Rather than respond to his offer, she chose to follow through on her earlier thoughts. "May I ask a personal question?"

His expression clouded over, a frown rearranging his handsome face. "You can ask. I can't guarantee I'll answer."

"Are you married?"

"No, I'm not."

"Where do you go every Thursday night? Do you have a girlfriend that you visit?"

"As I explained to your father, I have family obligations on Thursday evening. Obligations I'm neither required, nor inclined, to share."

"What about the girlfriend?"

He pushed himself to his feet, and she thought he wouldn't answer when he finally said, "No lady friend, at the moment. Why the sudden interest in my personal life, Princess?"

Because I can't get our kiss out of my head. She shrugged, hoping the simple lift of her shoulders would convey indifference—even though she was anything but disinterested. "I just assumed most single men your age would have lady friends."

"My age?" He met her gaze, his eyes sparking with humor. "I don't think age has anything to do with having a wife, girlfriend, or even a mistress."

Mallory swallowed back the sudden constriction in her throat. "A mistress?"

"A woman used for... uh... carnal activities."

Heat rose in her cheeks that had nothing to do with the warm weather.

"I suppose you have one of those."

"We've now reached the point in our conversation where I decline to answer."

"Fine. There's nothing else I need to know. However, I will take you up on your offer to meet me at the Sneaky Cat at eleven."

"I'll talk to Gus and Sully when we get back to the house."

"Thank you."

He took a few steps toward the last of the fence repairs, before turning to respond. "You're welcome, Princess." His smile widening, he admitted, "No mistress, either. At the moment."

It was another hour or so before Harry finished the last of the fencing. Mallory kept herself busy weeding the area around Lady Lillian's grave, then moved on to the spot where her mother and great aunt Alice were buried. Finally, she divided up the bouquet of roses and laid them on each of the three graves.

"You do a great job of caring for their final resting place."

The deep tenor of Harry's voice sank into her senses, pulling her attention to where he stood above her, the sun backlighting his stance. His feet were spread for balance, his hands rested on narrow hips. Were the sun not making it difficult to see his face, she imagined he was sharing his crooked smile.

"The gardener is squeamish about attending the gravesites. And, as for my father's men, they scare easily when it comes to the possibility of encountering a ghost."

"The possibility doesn't seem to bother you."

"I constantly feel their presence, and I've heard them—"

"Heard them?"

She drew a breath, her pulse racing at the memory of the goings-on above her bedroom. "Yes, during the storms. It's said that when a nor'easter blows the doors open leading from the roof to their bedroom, Lady Lillian can come inside. They meet there, and… and… they make love."

"And you believe the stories?" Harry asked.

"Yes, I do. My mother did, as well."

He lowered himself to sit beside her on the ground before taking a drink of the lukewarm lemonade he'd not finished earlier.

"You don't talk about your mother very often."

"It makes me sad to realize she died so young, and so violently."

"Were you home on the day she fell?"

"Yes, I was reading in the library when my father came to tell me about the accident." She paused, drawing a breath. "The gossip going around was that she was a victim of the Fairwinds' curse."

"But you don't believe it, do you?"

She tossed her head from side-to-side, her long, red curls sliding across her shoulders. "No. My mother was kind, gentle, and she loved Fairwinds and its colorful history. Neither the Captain nor Lady Lillian would have reason to harm her."

"So, she was alone when she fell?"

"Yes, as far as anyone knows. She'd had an appointment earlier in the day with her attorney. My father was in town up until a few minutes before he came to get me."

"Where were the others, if you don't mind my asking?"

"At that point, there were no others—at least not here at the house. My father didn't start running his business from Fairwinds until after my mother died. The only people in the house during the day were the cook, the gardener—he was the one who found … who found …"

When her tears threatened, she dashed them back with her fingertips.

"That's enough, Mallory. There's no reason to relive that horrible day on my account. I'm sorry I upset you."

His words were followed by the gentle sweep of his hand across her cheek, the touch of his fingers against her trembling lips.

She turned slightly and nuzzled into the palm of his hand, needing Harry's warmth, his caress.

His breath caught and held. He stroked her lower lip with the pad of his thumb before releasing her and pushing himself to stand. "We'd better get back to the house, Princess. I've got to clean up before I go into town, and you need to make arrangements for Will to pick you up later this evening."

Chapter 13

Mallory seated herself at her dressing table, taking special care with her appearance. When she'd called Hansen House to let them know she'd be coming in, they'd informed her of their most urgent cases.

Tonight, she'd been told, could easily be Phillip Hurley's last. She intended to spend as much time as possible with the man her mother had always favored.

Will called for her at eight. And, as promised, Sully and Gus watched from the doorway as she climbed into Will's auto and rode off toward town.

"I can't believe they're letting you out," Will commented when he pulled onto the road in front of Fairwinds. "It's not like them to defy your father's orders."

"Harry cut a deal with them. He'll be the one to pick me up at eleven at the Sneaky Cat. Knowing Gus and Sully, they'll welcome the night off."

"This Carter fellow seems like a regular joe. Nothing like your father's usual goons."

"He is very considerate. And fair."

"You don't even try to run when he's there," Will pointed out.

His comment drew her laugh. "Oh, I've tried. All those times I didn't show at our scheduled rendezvous, it wasn't because I chose not to leave. It was because Harry caught me before I even got to the gate."

"In other words, he's smarter than the others."

"Yes, by leaps and bounds." She paused, then added, "He's never once told my father about my attempts to escape. Even the time when I fell from the trellis on the side of the house.

Had he not been there to literally 'catch' me, I'd have probably broken something."

"So, he's smart, strong, doesn't look like a creep or smell of garlic or booze. What's he doing working for your father when he could, obviously, be working anywhere else?"

"I'm not sure. According to the house gossip, and the little he's shared with me, he's on the lam from Pinkertons."

Will pulled up in front of Hansen House. "Be careful, doll face. Both here, and with this Harry fellow. Something's not adding up about him."

"What do you mean?"

"Hiding out from Pinkertons by working for one of the area's most questionable businessmen? You'd think associating with your father would put him directly in Pinkerton's line of sight."

***

At half-past eight that same evening, Simon entered the four-story brick building on Main Street and climbed two flights of stairs in search of Mr. Miller's office.

This would be his first official meeting with the solicitor who'd prompted the Bureau's investigation of Malcolm McGuire with little more than a telephone call. Tapping on the locked office door, he waited semi-patiently for someone to answer.

When the door opened, Simon produced his government-issued identification. A man who appeared to be in his late sixties stepped back, allowing him to enter.

"You're Barclay? I was expecting someone older," the man said.

"I get that a lot. Everyone expects a G-man to be in his forties or fifties, to look more mature."

Sticking out his hand, the older man confirmed, "I'm Thaddeus Miller, attorney for the estate of Helene McGuire." Nodding across the width of the room where another man stood, he added, "This is my law partner, and son-in-law, Joshua Blake."

Simon shook Miller's hand and gave a short nod in Blake's direction.

"I spoke with the Boston office earlier," Simon began. "And I was hoping you could clarify a few things for me."

"We'll do what we can," Miller confirmed. "Rest assured, if Malcolm McGuire is guilty of murder, we want to see him brought to justice."

Taking the seat Miller offered, Simon withdrew a small notebook from the inside pocket of his suit coat. "Does the name Rick Temple mean anything to either of you?"

"The name is vaguely familiar," Blake said. "Give me a minute to go through my records."

When Blake left the outer office, Miller asked, "Do you suspect this Temple fellow of something related to Mrs. McGuire's death?"

"His name came up in relation to the large cash withdrawal McGuire made shortly after his wife's death. It appears this Temple character was an employee of McGuire's import company when they were housed in Boston. When the Bureau did a cursory check of McGuire's known associates, they found a large deposit in Temple's bank account, made the day after McGuire's withdrawal."

"Here it is," Blake declared loudly, as he came back into the main office. "Rick Temple. Miss Mallory McGuire directed us to pay for Mr. Temple's burial expenses from the Fairwinds business account."

"Burial expense?" Simon asked. "Why would she do that?"

"Seems Temple died in a fall from the cliffs at Fairwinds, a month or so after Helene McGuire's death. Miss McGuire felt responsible for the man's passing and wanted to cover the cost of his funeral rather than leave the expense for his brother."

"She told me—or, should I say, she told Harry Carter—

about the accident when she gave me a tour of the tunnels beneath Fairwinds."

"How's the undercover work going?" Blake asked. "I honestly didn't think it would work when your boss first suggested it."

"They're an off bunch, that's for sure. Fortunately, most of them are as stupid as they are strange. All it takes is a couple of shots of whiskey to get the hired help singing like a bunch of canaries."

"So, you have enough to take them down without it affecting Miss McGuire?" Miller asked, his concern for Mallory evident in his tone.

"For his illegal business practices, for sure. As for Mrs. McGuire's death, we're still investigating. However, the cash transaction looks like a pretty solid link between Temple and McGuire and Mrs. McGuire's death." Simon leaned back in the chair, and admitted, "However, with Temple dead as well, it's not going to be an easy case to make."

"Any idea if this Temple fellow really fell? Or was he murdered too?"

Simon gave an honest shake of his head. "I'll have to take a look at the police report, and autopsy if there was one, to be sure. However, if the police deemed it an accident right from the get-go, there may be nothing to find."

"So, no way to prove McGuire was involved," Miller said, a long sigh sealing his thoughts.

"Not yet, but I'm not giving up." Simon shifted in his seat, preparing himself for the one question he had to ask. "Miss McGuire mentioned you met with her mother the morning of her death. What was the purpose of the meeting?"

"We were reviewing her annual charitable contributions," Miller confirmed. "She wanted to raise her donation to two of her favorite charities."

"And you went there, instead of her coming here?"

"I often did that," Miller told him. "She'd invite me out for brunch, and we'd spend the morning talking about family. I knew her father and mother quite well."

"And nothing seemed out of the ordinary that day?"

"She was a bit under the weather. A cold coming on, I think she said." Miller gave a slow shake of his head. "That was one of the things that bothered me after I heard she'd fallen from the cliffs. Why would she have gone out there on such a blustery day when she wasn't feeling well? Unless she was lured there. Or, forced to go."

"I agree. It does seem odd." Pushing himself to his feet, Simon told them, "I'll be in touch if I have any more questions. Thank you for agreeing to meet me so late in the evening."

"Anything we can do to help," Blake offered. "We want what's best for Miss McGuire. No young woman should lose her mother so early in life."

Once he'd left Miller's office Simon went straight to the police station and picked up a copy of the report on Temple's death. Exiting the station, he tucked the report into his suit coat pocket so he could read it in greater detail later.

It was getting late and, no doubt, Mallory was wondering when he'd arrive to claim her. He glanced at his watch. Ten-thirty. Time to put his Harry Carter façade back in place and meet Mallory at the designated location.

***

Mallory cast her gaze across the width and length of the Sneaky Cat in anticipation of Harry's arrival. It was nearly eleven and she was getting nervous. Will and Sadie had left a half hour earlier on their way to a party and she'd assured them she'd be fine on her own. Yet, she felt anything but fine.

No sooner had her friends left when she'd sensed someone watching her. The hairs on her arms stood up, an uncomfortable shiver skimmed the length of her back. Her father's many words of caution came back to haunt her, warning her about his business enemies, and how they'd like nothing more than to bring him down by threatening her.

"Good evening, beautiful lady."

Mallory turned at the sound of the unknown man's thick voice, her gaze lifting to his dark and menacing stare. "Please go away. I'm waiting for someone."

"Aw, come on now, Miss McGuire," he continued. "You know those dull toadies of your father's are useless. Slow as winter molasses." Motioning to the two men standing six feet or so behind him he told her, "Me and the boys here can take much better care of you, if you'll just come with us all peaceful like."

"And if I don't?"

"What 'ya think, little missy? It's noisy here. Me and the boys can just snatch you up and carry you out and nobody'd be the wiser."

"That's what you'll have to do, then. I'm not going anywhere peacefully."

His deep, evil chortle made her insides churn. Perhaps if she upchucked all over the floor, she'd draw attention to herself and send them scurrying for anonymity.

The horrid man grasped her wrist in his meaty hand, only to release her within seconds before falling to a heap on the floor, writhing in pain.

Harry leaned over the man, his fingers pinching the side of the man's neck.

"There are two others," she said quickly. "Not far away."

"They're taken care of," Harry responded in a calm, reassuring voice. "And in the capable hands of the supper club's security."

Harry dragged the wailing young man to his feet, his grip still firm against the man's throat. "The coppers are on the way," Harry warned. "Assuming your boss chooses to bail your sorry asses out of jail, you can give him a message for me."

"Yeah, what?" the man managed to spit out between grimaces.

Harry tightened his grip, sending him back to his knees. "Tell him if I ever catch any of you within a five-mile radius of Miss McGuire, you'll have to answer to me. I won't be so gentle next time."

The moment the man was hauled away by one of the Sneaky Cat's bouncers, Mallory bolted from her seat and threw herself into Harry's arms.

"Thank heaven you arrived when you did." She pulled in a calming breath and laid her head against his chest. "I thought you'd never get here." Pushing back slightly so she could meet his gaze, she asked, "Why were you late?"

His chuckle lifted her spirits, replacing the fear she'd felt only moments earlier.

"I'm not late, Mallory. It's ten minutes of. So, technically, I'm early."

A shudder took hold of her, and she snuggled back into his arms. "Late, early, right on time. It doesn't matter now because you're here, and I'm safe again."

"As I always will be, Princess. For as long as you're my responsibility. Whenever you need me."

Mallory settled into the front seat of Harry's car and closed her eyes, releasing a long breath. "Thank you, Harry."

"For the tenth time—at least—you're welcome." Before he shut the passenger door, he removed his suit coat and laid it across her shoulders. "I'll have you home before you know it."

He eased the door closed and then circled the car and slipped behind the wheel.

"I always thought my father was trying to scare me in order to keep me from taking off. I never truly believed I was in any real danger."

"There have been threats over the years," he confirmed. "However, none ever resulted in any action. I'm not sure why it happened tonight, but I intend to find out."

"I'm glad it was you who was there to come to my aid. I doubt Gus or Sully could have taken those men down. Teddy… maybe."

"Where were Will and Sadie?"

"We'd been invited to a party, but I declined. I didn't want to be a flat tire, so I told them to go on without me."

"It's quite possible you'd never been bothered before because you were always in the company of others. They waited for you to be on your own."

Harry pulled into the circle driveway in front of Fairwinds, drew to a stop at the front door, and killed the engine. Circling the car, he opened her door and offered her his hand.

She slid from the car but, when she tried to stand, she couldn't. The import of what almost happened turned her bones to jelly.

Within a heartbeat, Harry scooped her up into his arms and carried her into the house.

"What happened?" Sully asked the moment they cleared the doorway. "Is Miss Mallory all right?"

"Yes," Harry confirmed, starting toward the staircase. "She's fine. I'll be back down once I have her settled in. Grab Gus and meet me in the library in a half hour."

Mallory sank into Harry's arms, confident in his strength—his ability to climb the flight of stairs bearing the extra weight of her numb form. Once he'd reached her bedroom door, he loosened his hold long enough to turn the knob. With a nudge of his foot, the door sprung open, and he carried her across the threshold.

"I can go the rest of the way on my own," she assured him.

"Sure, you can, Princess. I set you down, and you're going to melt into a puddle on this expensive Persian rug."

"Just put me down. I can manage."

His deep chuckle warmed her cheek. His next words slid

easily beneath the curtain of her hair.

"I'm not going to ravish you, Mallory, if that's what you're worried about."

She tossed her head from side-to-side, her cheek brushing his. "Not worried, Harry. Terrified."

Harry sat her on the bed and removed his suit coat from around her shoulders. "You've nothing to be terrified of any longer. You're safe here at home."

"What nearly happened tonight isn't what scares me, Harry." She lifted her hand to his cheek. "What terrifies me is you… the feelings I have when I'm with you. The realization that I wouldn't try to stop you if you did… ravish me."

He dropped to the floor to kneel in front of her. Reaching for her foot, he carefully removed first one shoe, and then the other, caressing her instep with his big hand.

She held her breath, waiting for him to acknowledge what she'd just told him.

As if he could sense her impatience, he pushed himself to his feet and stared down at her. "If things were different, I'd like nothing better than to make love to you. With you."

"What things?"

"I'm not the right kind of man for you, Mallory. While I might not be as questionable as your father's other hired thugs, I'm far from perfect."

"I don't care about that," she assured him. "I know I should, but I don't."

"It's the emotions of the evening talking, Princess. I came to your rescue tonight, that's all. I'm no saint, no knight in shining armor."

"Dammit, Harry. I know what I want."

"I tell you what. If you'll agree to settle in and try and get some sleep, we'll spend the day together tomorrow and see where things go. I'll even let you bore me with some of your favorite ghost stories."

Chapter 14

Harry took a seat in his usual spot at the top of the stairs. With another fifteen minutes before he needed to be in the library, he was hesitant to leave Mallory until he was sure she'd settled in for the night.

Withdrawing the police report on Temple's death, he scanned the findings.

Subject had been drinking, although did not appear to be in excess.

Jacket covered in white dust, later identified as outdated brass polish.

Discovered on rocks at the base of Fairwinds' cliffs.

Coroner ruled the possibility of a heart attack given rigid facial features.

Final disposition: Ruled accidental with possible medical complications.

Outdated brass polish? Possible heart attack? He closed his eyes and released a long sigh. Something seemed off about Temple's death. Perhaps it was time to share a few tongue-loosening shots of hooch with the boys.

"So, what happened to Miss Mallory?" Sully asked the moment Harry entered the library, a bottle of whiskey and three glasses clutched in his hands.

If you want info, you have to give a bit. Even if it's a lie.

"A couple of low-life jerks were giving her a hard time, that's all. It scared her. Not surprising given all the tales her father has spun about his supposed enemies."

"It wasn't one of Sartori or O'Malley's men, then?" Gus questioned.

"No, I don't think so. The club had them arrested for

harassment. They've probably already been sprung." He swallowed back a mouthful of whiskey and posed his first question. "One guy was mumbling something about someone named Temple. Either of you know who he was talking about?"

The two men shared a glance but didn't respond.

Pouring another round of drinks, he added, "He claimed Temple died here at Fairwinds."

"A lot of people have died at Fairwinds," Gus said, downing the contents of his glass in a single swig. "Ain't you heard the stories?"

"Yeah. The Fairwinds curse." Shooting them both a lopsided grin, he filled his voice with a measure of sarcasm. "All that ghost bullshit, Miss McGuire's so fond of spouting."

He poured both men another drink.

"Temple worked for the boss in Boston for a while. Rick, his name was. He had a brother named Pete," Sully said. "When we moved operations here to Fairwinds, they came along. They didn't do much, that I remember. Fuckin' lazy, they were."

"Always bragging on how they did special work for the boss," Gus added. "Pete did some time in the tunnels but kept goin' on about how he'd seen the captain's ghost. I think the boss was getting tired of his bellyaching."

"What happened the night Temple died?" he asked, adding a deceptive slur to his words.

Sully shifted in his seat and reached for the bottle. "It wasn't long—maybe a couple months—after Mrs. McGuire died. A bad nor'easter had blown through the night before. There was ice everywhere. We were all sitting around the fire here in the library. Miss Mallory had already gone to bed."

"Where was the boss?"

Gus snorted a laugh and then let loose a belch. "Off fuckin his Boston whore."

"He had a mistress?"

Gus laughed again, louder this time. "Naw, just a whore. A mistress is usually kept all nice like. Prissy was just a two-bit tramp he dallied with from time to time."

"So, if the weather was so bad, what was Temple doing anywhere near the cliffs?"

Sully gave a shake of his head. "Beats me. He and Pete had been arguing over Pete wanting to quit and go back to Boston. Rick pulled on his jacket and stormed out. Pete waited for a few minutes, thinking he'd cool off. When he didn't, Pete followed him as far as the driveway, then came back to the house screaming like a crazy person."

"Screaming about what?"

"Claims he saw the ghost. Not the usual floating lady some claim to see, but big and scary like, with red glowing eyes."

"In other words," Gus inserted, "bullshit. Despite the bad roads, Pete hopped in his brother's car and hightailed it out of here as fast as he could. We never saw him again."

"Maybe he was the one who pushed his brother off the cliff, and he was running."

Sully swallowed back another mouthful of booze and shook his head. "Don't think so. He didn't have enough time to make it to the cliffs. He wasn't gone more than thirty, forty seconds tops, before he came back yelling his fool head off."

"When Rick hadn't returned by the next morning, we went out looking. That's when we found him dead on the rocks below the cliffs."

Sliding the half-empty bottle across the table, Harry pushed his chair back and stood. "It's been a long day. I'm going to grab a couple hours of sleep. No doubt, Miss Mallory will be up and demanding my attention earlier than I'd like."

"She's a handful, that one," Sully agreed. "As much trouble as she can be, deep down she's a good kid."

"Goodnight, boys. See you in the morning."

"Night, Harry. Don't get too comfortable," Gus said, his thick laugh echoing through the room.

"Don't worry," he confirmed. "I know better than to let my guard down around the troublesome Miss McGuire."

***

Mallory awoke the next morning still wearing her silk sheath. Her headband lay atop her pillow. She gave a long, luxurious stretch, unfurling like a lazy cat.

Immediately, the memory of Harry carrying her to her bed, carefully removing her shoes, caressing her instep, drew her gasp, made her toes curl.

Had she truly admitted desiring him? Her cheeks flushed with embarrassment.

No doubt he thought her a foolish child for being so eager to accept his claim of wanting to make love to her. With her.

The flush was back, stronger than before. Warmer.

Stripping out of her clothes, she pulled her dressing gown around her naked body, grabbed a basket of scented soaps, and made her way to the bathroom across the hall. She needed a soak. A long, reviving bath.

The moment she turned the lock on the bathroom door, she sank back against the solid frame and let loose a ragged breath. She'd expected to see Harry in his usual place at the top of the stairs.

What she hadn't expected were the wisps of hair falling across his brow, or the rumpled, half-opened shirt that exposed the bare skin of his throat. The day-old stubble of his beard gave him a positively rakish appearance.

Obviously sound asleep, his long sable lashes feathered across chiseled cheekbones. His impressive chest rose and fell with his steady breathing.

Desire coiled within her, making her heart race.

He'd said they'd spend the day together. She looked forward to sharing a few of Fairwinds secrets with the only man she'd ever truly trusted.

"Where are we off too, if I might ask?"

Harry followed on her heels as she made her way from the dining room and into the rotunda.

"Since you seem rather amused by my ramblings on Fairwinds history, I thought I'd share a few of the family secrets. Assuming, of course, you're interested."

His full lips lifted in a smile that made her pulse thrum against her wrist.

"I'm always interested in learning something new. Whether I take it as fact or fiction will depend on what I see."

When she stopped beside the brocade settee, he came to a halt at her side. She pressed her hip to the side and shoved, uncovering the doorway.

"You'd better not share what I'm about to show you with a soul, do you understand?"

"The door to the tunnel?"

She shook her head. "Not the tunnel. Promise you won't tell."

Long fingers slid across his mouth like one of those fancy zippers that were all the rage in men's clothes. "My lips are sealed, Princess."

"Then, follow me."

The moment the hidden door sprung open, she stepped across the threshold, Harry following closely behind. Rather than wait for her instruction, he reached through the opening and pulled the settee flush to the wall.

When the door slid back into place, he asked, "Where to now, Mallory?"

She pointed skyward, and told him, "Up. We're going up."

He followed behind her on the precarious staircase. When the ironwork groaned beneath them, she gave a moment's pause to the fact that perhaps it wasn't built for the weight of two.

"How much farther?"

"Another flight. We're going to the third floor."

"I thought your father sealed off that part of the house."

"He did. Or, at least, the main staircase." Once she'd come to a stop at the very top, she added, "Fairwinds still has a few hidden passageways."

"Sounds intriguing. Lead the way."

"I could use your help with the trap door," she suggested.

Taking his hand in hers, she tugged, drawing him to her side on the third riser from the top. The moment Harry's chest met hers, Mallory's breath caught.

"Let me… get that for you."

Harry pressed his hand against the solid surface and pushed, easily dislodging the heavy door and pushing it wide open.

"Thank you," she said, moving forward on shaky legs.

The moment she'd cleared the opening, Harry was right there at her side.

"So… this is the infamous bedroom of the pirate and his lady."

"Yes, Captain John Jacob Wilder and Lady Lillian," she confirmed. "That's their wedding portrait leaning against the wall."

"Why is it not mounted above the fireplace, as it should be?"

A warm flush rose to her cheeks when she admitted, "I took it down to dust it, but it was too heavy to lift back into place."

"Oh, I get it," he said, laughing. "You've brought me here to do your heavy work."

She gave an adamant shake of her head, her curls tossing wildly around her cheeks. "No. I brought you here to share Fairwinds' secrets. To show you the beauty hidden behind the legend."

Harry made a show of glancing around the room, taking in the many appointments, his gaze lingering on the huge bed. When his attention returned to her, he smiled.

"The room isn't the only beautiful thing to be seen."

She swallowed, wishing away the sudden dryness that had taken possession of her throat. "It's not?"

He raised his hand and fingered a lock of her curls. "No, Mallory, it's not."

She held her breath, waiting most impatiently for his kiss.

And waited.

"Harry?"

"The doors leading to the widow's walk are quite lovely, as well."

Embarrassment flooded her cheeks and she moved to turn away when—quite quickly—he grasped her chin in the cup of his hand. Raising her head so that their gazes met, he pressed his lips to hers.

His delicious kiss sent shards of electricity skating across the surface of her skin. Yet the sensation ended far too quickly when he lifted his warm lips from hers and took a step backward.

"That was nice," she said softly.

A smile tugged playfully at the corner of his mouth. "Perhaps, after your tour of the Captain's third-floor hideaway, we could share another."

"Maybe," she teased.

They toured the widow's walk and she showed him where she'd gained access to the trellis the night she'd nearly fallen.

"Of all your escape plans, that was undoubtedly the least thought out," he reminded her. "You could have broken something. Or had you lost your grip earlier, you could have been killed."

"I rather enjoyed being caught in your arms." She shifted

slightly until she faced him directly, then laid her open palm against his cheek.

"You realize, Princess, you're making it very difficult for me to remain a gentleman."

"Perhaps—"

"How about we finish the tour? I'm anxious to hear about the other secrets hiding in Fairwinds' walls."

Mallory led the way to the middle of the roof, stopping beneath the gabled roof that held the ornate brass weathervane. "This was a gift from Lady Lillian to Captain Jake. It was intended to guide him home safely from the sea."

"You keep it very well preserved, given the beating it must take from the elements."

"Not me," she said. "I've never had to polish it." She paused, before suggesting, "I believe Lady Lillian's ghost cares for the weathervane."

"Mallory... this notion of ghosts—"

"It's not a notion. I know it's real—that they're real."

She stepped away and went back into the bedroom, waiting for Harry to follow and secure the French doors. Once he'd come to her side, she took his hand and led him to the fireplace.

"You want to show me a hole in the wall?"

"This is where I found a wooden chest with my great-aunt's journals, Lady Lillian's wedding ring, and eight pieces of pirate's gold. There was also a key, but I've not yet determined what the key unlocks."

"Show me," he insisted.

"The box, and its contents, are hidden in my bedroom. I'll be happy to show everything to you if you promise to not tell my father."

"That's an easy promise to make, Princess. Those items are part of Fairwinds history and therefore, as the rightful owner, they belong to you. But perhaps your treasures would be safer here behind the portrait than in a room anyone can get to."

"You may be right. After all, the box was safely stored for decades before I accidentally stumbled upon it."

"Why don't you go and get everything? I'll go to the pantry and grab some tools. You can put everything back where you found it, and then I'll rehang the portrait and anchor it so it can't be moved."

"I'm not sure… I mean… I've enjoyed reading Alice's musings."

"Once you've formally inherited Fairwinds, you can retrieve everything and do with it as you wish."

She offered him a grateful smile. "Yes, that's what I'll do."

He glanced across the width of the room. "And perhaps we should also put that heavy carpet over the trap door. Just in case."

"But then I can't open the trap," she felt compelled to point out. "At least not without a lot of hard work."

"I'll be here to open it for you, should you be in the mood to do some visting."

Chapter 15

Mallory had been right about the value of her treasure trove. He held the gold doubloons in his grasp, fingered the rough edges of the coins, and mentally measured their worth in the twentieth century. No doubt priceless to the right collector.

And best hidden as far away from Malcolm McGuire's greed as they could get.

"Is this everything?"

Placing the items back into the wooden chest, she nodded. "Yes. Two journals, the coin purse with the gold and key. Even the dried-out ink and quills."

"You've kept the ring, as I suggested?"

"Yes." Tugging on the chain around her neck, she pulled the gold and ruby heirloom from within her bodice. "Safe and sound."

Once the box was tucked away, he climbed on the chair and set the portrait back where it belonged. Then, using the screwdriver and metal shims he'd procured from the storeroom, he fashioned anchors and secured them on each of the four corners.

"That should do it," he said, stepping down to the floor. "No one will get past this painting without removing the anchors or tearing it from the wall with a sledgehammer."

"Thank you."

He gathered up the tools and put them back in the canvas bag he'd used to bring everything up the iron staircase. "If you're ready to go now, I'll set the rug in place so I can use the tassels to tug it over the opening once we're safely through the door."

Mallory stepped through the trap door and lowered herself down a couple of steps and waited while he positioned the heavy carpet.

About to close the lid, he spared one last glance around the open room, his perusal stopping on the French doors. His heartbeat skipped when his gaze fell upon the woman. Ethereal, dressed in white, her skin as pale as the gown she wore. Her sad countenance stole the breath from his lungs.

Lady Lillian.

Her head bobbed up and down once, as if she approved of them returning everything to its rightful place.

"Harry? Are you done?"

The sound of Mallory's voice broke through his thoughts, drawing him back to reality.

"Yeah, Princess. I'm done."

As much as he'd looked forward to sharing a few more kisses with the lovely Miss McGuire, as promised, their arrival back on the first floor was nearly witnessed by Sully. Harry had managed to shove the settee back in place just as the other man came through the double doors of the rotunda.

"There you two are. The boss is back and has been looking all over for you."

"We're right here," he said, a touch of sarcasm added for effect. "We were out in the rose arbor, and then went to cliffs to visit Mrs. McGuire's gravesite. Then—"

"I don't give a shit where you were," Sully responded, his big hand pressed to his forehead, no doubt aching from the booze he'd imbibed the night before. "Just get to the library before the boss has another fit."

Mallory went through the door ahead of him and planted herself in front of her father's desk. "You were looking for me?"

"I'm hosting a dinner party Thursday evening for some

business associates. Given that's usually Harry's night off, I want to make sure you understand I expect you to be here. No sneaking out."

"I can stay in," Harry offered. "All I need is an hour or so to check in with my family. I could even do that on Wednesday, if need be."

"Take the time you need, but be back before my guests arrive. You're better at managing Mallory than the others."

Harry released a long sigh. "Perhaps that's because I don't 'manage' her. I treat her like the adult she is."

McGuire gave a dismissive wave of his hand. "I don't give a damn how you do it, just keep her here so she can perform her duties as my hostess."

Mallory opened her mouth to say something—no doubt wanting to comment on being given a 'duty' to perform—but changed her mind when Harry gave a quick shake of his head.

"Is there anything else?" she asked.

"No. The dinner party will be formal, as befitting the wealth of my guests. If you need a new dress, have Harry take you shopping."

"Come on, Miss McGuire," he coaxed. "Let's take a drive into town. Even if you don't require a new dress, it'll give us something to do for the afternoon."

***

Mallory shifted in the front seat of Harry's car, every nerve ending she possessed throbbing in anger.

"Damn him," she cursed. "He knows I hate feigning a smile for his awful cohorts. And Thursday, of all nights. I bet he chose that night on purpose, because he knows it's the one night I really want to go out."

"Perhaps you could arrange to visit Hansen House on Wednesday instead," Harry suggested.

It took a moment for his words to sink in. When they did, she turned to face him. "What did you say?"

The corner of his mouth lifted slightly. "I said—"

"Dammit, Harry, I know what you said. How do you know about Hansen House?"

Slowing the car, he pulled onto the side of the road and turned the engine off. Then, swiveling in the driver's seat, he met her confused gaze. "I know a lot more than you give me credit for, Mallory. You didn't really think I'd leave your wellbeing to Sully and Gus, did you?"

"But, how?"

"Simple. I followed you. The very first Thursday night, and every night since. I sat outside of Hansen House until you came out and got in your hired car to go to the Sneaky Cat. Then, I sat outside the Cat for an hour or so to allow you some time with your friends. The one night I didn't follow you nearly ended in disaster, for which I'm still berating myself."

"I don't know whether to thank you or slap your face."

"I'd prefer the thank you," he admitted. "Or perhaps another kiss. We never did get around to it after we left the captain's hideaway."

"I suppose we could… I mean… I do enjoy your kisses."

"I'm too old to neck in a car, Princess. Perhaps, once we return to Fairwinds, we could take a walk around the property. You can show me more of the captain's secrets."

"I'd like that. I've still not shown you the stables."

"I tell you what. You attend your father's fancy dinner party and put on a happy face. Then, on Friday, you and I will take a drive to Boston. You can shop to your heart's content. We'll have fish and chips on the wharf."

"Are you asking me out on a date, Harry?"

"Would you accept, if I were?"

"Yes, Harry, I would."

"Good. Then I'm officially asking."

Mallory was up bright and early the next morning. She slid

her hand beneath her mattress, only then remembering she'd tucked Alice's journals away for safekeeping. She'd read her great aunt's missives so many times, no doubt she could quote most of them verbatim.

Still, there was something comforting about reading and rereading accounts of her family's history. Up until reading Alice's journals, she had no idea just how many ancestors she truly had, or how Fairwinds had passed from one person to the next.

The stories of Alice's mother, Lucy, and how hard she'd fought to keep Fairwinds from the clutches of her evil brother read like a mystery. The love Lucy and Grandpa Nate had shared while restoring Fairwinds was so romantic.

Was love what she herself felt for Harry? She certainly felt something. Given her sheltered life and limited experience, she truly had no idea what romantic love was like.

Perhaps today's tour of the remainder of Fairwinds property, combined with Harry's wonderful kisses, would give her the answers she sought.

Dressed and ready to get started on her day, she made her way down the stairs, surprised there was no one waiting for her. No doubt, Harry was already in the dining room, or the library.

"Good morning, father," she greeted once she'd taken her seat at the breakfast table.

"You're up early," he commented, peeking over the edge of his newspaper. "Were you able to find yourself a new dress for Thursday?"

"Yes. The dressmaker is making a few alterations. Harry's going to take me into town to pick it up later today."

Her father gave a shake of his head. "You'll have to ask Gus or Sully for a drive. I sent Harry and Teddy on an errand."

"What kind of an errand?"

"That's not for you to worry about, Mallory."

"But why Harry? He's supposed to be my bodyguard, not your errand boy." She bit back on her anger. She truly hated the thought that Harry might be as involved in her father's shady dealings as the others.

"Harry is on my payroll. He does what he's told."

"Surely Gus or—"

"That's enough." He paused, shot her a frown, and asked, "Why so concerned about which of my men takes you on your errands?"

"It's just that neither Gus nor Sully have the patience for a trip to the dressmaker. They do nothing but grumble. Harry stands there like a gentleman, without complaint, while keeping an eye on everything and everyone." She drew a breath. "I feel safer with Harry than I do a bunch of middle-aged, overweight thugs."

"Which is exactly why I sent him with Teddy. They've been dispatched to bring back some very valuable cargo. I wanted my two best men for the pickup."

"When will they be back?"

"Around suppertime, most likely. So, if you're plotting an escape, it will need to be an early one."

"I'm not planning on going anywhere. At the moment."

"That's good to know," he said with a chuckle. "I've got work to do before my dinner party. I've not got time to worry about whether you're sneaking out for a night with your friends."

"I would like to go out tomorrow night, if possible. Harry has agreed to chaperone me." She drew a breath. "He's also offered to drive me to Boston for a shopping trip on Friday."

"As long as he's with you, I have no problem with you going out Wednesday or Friday. Providing I can count on both of you for Thursday."

She smiled broadly and gave her father a girlish giggle. "Given what you paid for my new dress, it's the least I can do."

Chapter 16

Harry threw the last canvas bag in the trunk of Malcolm McGuire's fancy Nash roadster and slammed it shut.

"That's the last of it," he said, sparing a sideward glance at Teddy.

"We best get on the road then. It took us way too long to gather the lot. The boss is probably thinking we've snuck off with the goods."

"I still need to make a call to let my family know I'm not going to be there on Thursday. Why don't we grab some grub for the road? I'm fuckin' starved."

Teddy gave a nod toward the dingy diner across the road.

"There's likely a public phone in there. Why don't you go in, order us some sandwiches and drinks, and make your call while they're getting the food ready? I'll stay here and guard the car."

"Sounds like a plan," he agreed.

Teddy pulled across the street and cut the engine. "I'll take a roast beef with mustard on rye and a root beer."

"No real beer?" he joked.

"Not when I'm driving the boss' car. He'd have my nuts if I put a dent in his prized auto."

Stepping out onto the curb, Harry held out his hand. "Keys, please."

"What?"

"It's not that I don't trust you, O'Brien. Okay, I don't trust you, but it'd be my balls on the chopping block if you hightailed it off with the boss' stash."

Grudgingly, Teddy thrust the keys out. "Get some cookies, too."

After putting in their order, Harry made his way to the public phone booth at the back of the diner. A sign above the black call box read: *Private line, direct dialing available.*

He breathed a sigh of relief, grateful there'd be no operator necessary—so nobody to eavesdrop. Dropping a nickel in the slot, he dialed his supervisor's number.

The phone rang twice before the nondescript voice responded. "Whitmer."

"It's Simon. Friday is set. McGuire's hosting a party on Thursday night with guests coming from as far away as New York. McGuire's got me and O'Brien transporting enough goods and cash to Fairwinds that you'll hit the jackpot the next day."

"You've arranged to get the girl away from the house by nine?"

"Yes. We'll be gone the entire day."

"We should be there by ten." Jefferson Whitmer pulled in a deep breath, and then asked, "Do you intend to tell her who you are before you get back to Mystic Point?"

"I'm not sure. I've been going between telling her the truth, or just leaving. After all, it'll look like Harry got lucky by not being caught up in the raid. There's no need for him to hang around after her father and his other men have been taken into custody."

"I'll confirm our plan with the higher-ups. Assuming we get the final approval, and everything goes as planned, we'll be out of the way before you return, so whether you fess up or not is up to you," Whitmer said.

"I'd better go. Teddy O'Brien's out in the car and, no doubt, getting antsy waiting for me to return with his cookies."

"Cookies? Never mind, I don't want to know. If anything changes, call me right away."

"Yes, sir. I'll see you on Monday for a case review."

"Take care, Simon."

"You too. Be careful on Friday. McGuire's men will be armed and they're just stupid enough to be dangerous."

Wednesday morning, he reached the dining room just as Mallory was taking her seat at the table.

"Good morning, Miss McGuire."

"Morning, Harry. You and Teddy must have been really late getting back last night. Father was pacing so much, I got bored and went to bed early."

"I was just grateful I didn't have to go out looking for you when we finally got here." He shot her a broad smile. "Thank you for taking it easy on Sully and Gus."

Her elegant shoulders rose and fell on a sigh. "It was the least I could do after Sully took me into town to get my dress. Besides, I had nowhere to go. I have made arrangements to meet my friends tonight, as we talked about."

"And our shopping trip on Friday?"

Her coy smile raised his heart rate. "Yes, Friday is still on my calendar."

"It sounds as if the rest of the week is worked out, then. Other than the tour of the grounds we keep putting off."

After taking a sip of her tea, she raised her head and met his gaze. "We've got all day and nothing else planned."

"It's going to storm. We should probably take our walk right after breakfast."

***

Once they left the house, she led the way down to the cliffs to make a brief visit to her mother's grave. Harry gave her a respectful amount of space, choosing instead to clear the leaves around Lady Lillian's grave while he waited.

"The cement you poured around the metal fence posts appears to have hardened completely. I'm certain even the worst nor'easter won't be able to knock the wall down."

"Speaking of nor'easters, the clouds are rolling in earlier

than expected. Maybe we should head back to the house. I know how you like to hole up in your room."

"I'm in no hurry today," she said, her shoulders lifting in a carefree shrug. "I've still not shown you the stables."

"Let's go then. Nothing says cool, fall day like the smell of old hay."

"The stables are another change I'm going to make when I turn twenty-five. I intend to bring horses back to Fairwinds. Chickens maybe."

"I have no doubt whatever changes you choose to make will only enhance Fairwinds."

His kind words warmed her heart. "That's nice of you to say, Harry."

The first crack of thunder sounded shortly after they entered the huge, empty, stables. When she startled, Harry put his arm around her shoulders and pulled her to his side.

Peering through one of the large, open windows, she snuggled into his light embrace when the rain began. Lightly at first but picking up more quickly than usual.

"So, should we make a run for it in the rain?" she asked. "Or, go through the hatch and into the tunnel?"

"We could wait it out here," he suggested. Giving an upward nod of his head, he added, "The hayloft will give us a great view of the house. I know, personally, I'd love to watch the supposed activity on the third floor from here. If you're willing, of course."

Mallory was torn. She had to admit a certain curiosity. Yet, she'd always considered the storms as Jake and Lily's special time together. "I'm not sure."

"It's up to you, Princess." Glancing toward the ladder that led to the loft. "I'd imagine it's nice and cozy up there. Not to mention, private."

It wasn't just the idea of spying on the captain and his lady that made her hesitate. What if her reaction to the storms was the same, even out here in the stables? What would happen if, while she and Harry were together, her thoughts... the unusual feelings... overcame her?

A chance not taken, is an opportunity wasted. Her beloved mother's words echoed in her thoughts, giving her a welcome boost of courage.

"I guess it would be okay."

"That a girl." Giving her a gentle push, he told her, "Up the ladder you go, Princess."

Once they'd reached the loft, Harry made quick work of opening the wooden shutter on the window facing Fairwinds, anchoring it on the hooks so that it stayed open. Then, he shoved two bales of hay to the middle of the space to give them something to lean against.

She knew a moment's hesitation when Harry lowered himself to the loft floor, leaned back against the bales, and motioned for her to take a seat in front of him. Drawing a breath for strength she would surely need, she sat down and leaned back against Harry's broad chest.

When he slid his arms around her and drew her close, tingles tracked across her entire being. When he nuzzled beneath the curtain of her hair and kissed the spot directly behind her ear, she stiffened.

"Don't worry, Mallory, you're safe with me. I'm not going to press you for anything other than a few kisses."

"I trust—"

Her words, her thoughts, were rudely interrupted by a rumble of thunder, and a flash of lightning that looked as if it were going to land directly on Fairwinds' roof.

The ground beneath the stables shook. The sound of heavy footsteps echoed from floor to peaked roof, as if someone were in a hurry to get through the underground passages.

"That was strange," Harry commented. "Maybe it was Gus or Sully taking stock to the storerooms."

She shook her head and twisted in Harry's embrace to meet his gaze. "No. It's the Captain on his way to meet Lily. I'm sure of it."

Another clap of thunder shook the entire building. The sky lit with a bright light.

"Look," he said, his voice hoarse with obvious surprise. Stretching out his arm, he pointed to the roof, in the direction of the French doors. "There."

Mallory turned in time to see a white figure—Lady Lillian—rise up and float toward the double doors leading to the third-floor sanctuary. The vision lifted her arms slowly, a gust of wind blew from the bay, across the grounds, passed the stables, and then over the widow's walk, swirling like an ominous cloud of dust.

The double doors crashed open, and Lily floated across the threshold before coming to a stop.

Thunder rumbled and lightning rent the sky.

"Oh... my... word," Mallory mumbled.

Harry's breath caught. "What the devil?"

A ball of bright light spun in circles around the bedroom, swinging from side-to-side in a flurry of frantic motion.

Mallory's pulse raced, keeping time with the light show in front of them. Against her hip, she could feel the rapid change in Harry's body. Tight, hard, aroused.

"They're making love," she said simply, softly. "It's their time together. Only during the storms."

The brush of Harry's hands along her arms was all it took to coax her into turning in his embrace. When he lowered his head, she met his mouth in a crushing kiss. When he nipped at her lower lip, she parted her lips and welcomed the slow, sweet invasion of his tongue.

The thought of spying on Captain Jake and Lady Lillian was the farthest thing from her mind, her entire attention given to the man whose very heartbeat hammered against the palm of her trembling hand.

"I want you so badly, I ache," he mumbled against her mouth. "Yet, I can't. Not now, and definitely not here."

"I want you too, Harry. I'm willing—"

"No, Princess. Kisses, a few touches, it's all we've got."

"Touches?"

He eased her off his chest and reached for the hem of her blouse. "Yes, Princess, touches. For you, at least." He eased her blouse up and over her head until he'd uncovered her modest brassiere. "First here," he whispered, drawing the tips of his fingers across the swell of her breast above the lacy edges of her undergarment. "Then, maybe here," he continued, rubbing his thumb across the tight peak aching for his attention.

When he lowered his head and pressed his lips against her skin, Mallory thought she might burst from the exquisite feel of it all.

"I need to touch you too, Harry." She skimmed her fingers over his shirt and twisted the buttons free of their holes.

"That might not be a wise idea," he said, a growl escaping his throat. Yet, he did nothing to stop her slow, deliberate unveiling of his bare chest.

"You have such nice muscles," she said, her palm grazing his taut skin. When she leaned forward and pressed a kiss to his chest, Harry sucked in a deep breath, and shivered.

"May I uncover you as well?"

Despite her nervousness, she nodded.

Within moments, he'd managed to loosen the hooks on the back of her brassiere until he could peel it away from her body, leaving her bare to his gaze. Once he'd shrugged out of his shirt, he raised his hand and laid it against her breast, cupping her gently.

A deft twist of his strong body was all it took to switch their positions, stretching them out across the scattered hay, until they lay body-to-body, their ragged breathing echoing through the cavernous loft.

Harry eased her onto her back and hovered over her, pressing his lips to hers for another deep, passionate kiss. When he lifted his lips from hers, she wanted to beg for another. Yet, the very words stuck in her throat, as lowered himself down her body and took her breast into his mouth. The flick of his tongue against the tightly drawn crest drew her whimper.

He bit her gently, and she swallowed back the urge to cry out.

He shifted slightly, paying the same wonderful attention to her opposite breast while his fingertips skimmed down the middle of her chest, teasing the waistline of her linen trousers, but going no farther.

Her lady parts ached, more so than ever before. When Harry pressed his open mouth to the goose-fleshed skin of her midriff, something burst within her.

"Harry, please. Like you, I ache."

"I can help with that if you'd like. But I can't... I won't... take you completely."

"Why not? Don't you want to?"

He took hold of her hand and slid it between their bodies, guiding her fingers around the hard ridge beneath the surface of his pants. "Yes, Princess. I want you. To the point of near agony." Pulling her hand away from his arousal, he splayed her fingers across his chest.

His smaller, rigid nipple poked her palm. As he'd done to her, she stroked the tiny nub with her thumb. When he groaned, she repeated the caress then pinched him between her thumb and forefinger, drawing a deep growl from his throat.

"Do you like that, Harry?"

"Yes, very much. Almost as much as I like sliding my tongue into your sweet mouth." He followed his words with action, initiating another heart stopping kiss.

As exciting as his kisses were, her attention was focused on Harry's hands. They were everywhere, stroking her breasts, taunting her middle with feather-like teases of his fingertips. When he reached for the buttons at the waistband of her trousers, she pulled in a breath and held it. Her heart hammered in wanton anticipation.

The first brush of Harry's fingertips beneath the edge of her silky panties drew her gasp. Frantically, she reached for his hand and clutched his wrist in her grasp.

"Relax, sweetheart," he coaxed. "I won't hurt you. If anything, I'm going to ease the ache between your legs."

She released the breath she'd caught and let go of his wrist. "I trust you, Harry. More than anyone I've ever known."

Chapter 17

Jeezus. What the bloody hell was he doing? A question he seemed to ask himself often where Mallory was concerned.

Her trust in him was absolute. Overwhelming. She deserved so much better than a man who'd been deceiving her since the day they met.

A good man, an honorable man, would restore order to her clothing, and escort her back to the safety of Fairwinds.

At the moment, he felt anything but honorable. His fingers tingled with the thought of touching her, bringing her pleasure.

"Are you sure about this, Princess?"

Laying her hand atop his, she urged him to continue. "Yes, Harry. I'm positive."

Pressing his lips to hers, he took her mouth in another deep, wet kiss. The tension in her body relaxed and she snuggled into his chest.

He slid his hand lower until the tips of his fingers tangled in the soft curls at the juncture of her thighs. He pulled back on the kiss, teasing her lips with gentle bites, before thrusting forward again, burying his tongue deeply inside her mouth.

She returned the favor, trading tastes, driving him insane with desire.

There'd be no going back now. Despite all logic, he'd done the unthinkable.

He'd fallen in love.

Easing his hand lower, he slipped his finger across the tiny pearl at the edge of her sex. Her legs parted slightly, the unconscious movement offering him easier access to her delights.

"Oh..."

Her soft gasp spurred him on. He rocked his hand back and forth, sliding across the damp button. Off in the distance, thunder rumbled.

Encouraged by the elements, he picked up the pace, and reveled in the quickening of her breath, the soft whimpers muffled by their joined mouths.

Her hips rose and fell in time with his stroke, her lush bottom bouncing against the hay-covered slats of the loft.

"Harry... please..." she whispered against his lips. "Make it stop, please."

He pulled in a deep breath and deepened his caress, sliding his finger into her heat, and his tongue into her mouth.

***

Dear saints in heaven, she was dying from the excitement of it all.

Harry had taken possession of her most private parts and was driving her crazy, unraveling every one of her senses. The very surface of her skin tingled. One stroke, two, a half dozen more and her body began trembling.

An enormous wave of pleasure consumed the whole of her body, her soul.

Harry cupped her gently, then slowly withdrew his hand from within her trousers. He pulled her into his arms, pillowing her head on his broad shoulder, allowing her time to recoup her wits.

Sheltered in Harry's embrace, she must have dozed off. When she awoke, she could sense Harry at her side. His breath came and went in ragged puffs of air.

"Harry?"

"Yes, Princess?"

"How long was I asleep?"

"An hour, maybe a while longer."

"I'm sorry, I was just so relaxed."

"Apparently, the captain and his lady were taking a break as well. However, it appears they've begun again. The lights have been flashing for ten minutes or so."

"I can tell," she whispered, her lips pressed to the side of Harry's throat. "My heart rate picks up, my body tingles, in time with their lovemaking."

"As does mine," he said. "I've been laying here in agony since they began again."

"Is there something we can do about that? I mean—"

"I'll be okay. Eventually." Skimming his fingertips across her bare midriff. "However, if you'd like another release, I'd be more than happy to oblige."

Just the suggestion of Harry touching her again, as he had before, set butterflies loose in her middle. "It wouldn't be fair... I mean..."

Her words drifted off when he moved his hand lower to slide beneath her panties, across the throbbing button of her sex. As he'd done before, he slid his hand back and forth until the exquisite pressure sent her entire body into a frenzy of excitement.

"A bit farther this time, Princess," he whispered.

When he slipped his finger inside her body, her hips rose to meet his hand.

"Oh... god..."

"You like that, Princess?"

"Yes, very, very much."

"That's the idea, sweetheart. How about we see if I can make it feel even better."

"Better?"

She couldn't imagine how it could get any better than the way she felt at that very moment. Yet, when Harry pulled his hand back and doubled his caress, she nearly shot up in the air.

One stroke, two. Her insides quivered. Harry closed his

lips over hers and thrust his tongue into her mouth, mimicking the penetration of his fingers with the stroke of his tongue.

"Stop… please…"

His throaty chuckle filled her mouth. He picked up the pace of his hand, nearly withdrawing before sliding forward again.

Her hips thrust skyward, her back bowed. Her insides quivered. And, even more powerful than before, her body burst forth with a release that threatened to stop her heart.

"That's it, Mallory. Just like that." As he'd done earlier, he cupped her womanly mound in his hand for a moment or two before withdrawing his hand from inside her panties. With a twist of his nimble fingers, he refastened the button at the waistband of her trousers.

Her breathing slowed in time with the rainfall. The storm, both outside and within her body, was coming to a conclusion. A final crash of lightning rent the sky, illuminating the loft of the barn as surely as if someone had turned on a hundred electric torches at once.

She raised herself up and glanced out the window in the direction of the widow's walk. What she saw drew her gasp and caused Harry to rise up as well.

The woman in white was pulled back through the open doors, as if sucked out by an unknown force. The doors slammed shut, and her form sank to the rooftop. Captain Jake's ghost stood just inside the bedroom. His handsome, bearded face contorted by sadness, his arms outstretched, Jake bid his sweet Lily goodbye until the next storm.

Overcome by emotion, tears streamed down Mallory's cheeks, her heart aching for her ancestors and their tragic love story.

"It's okay, Princess. Let it out."

"I never realized… I mean, I knew what was happening. I didn't expect the sadness, the finality of it all."

"It must be horrible for them, knowing they can only be together at the whim of the unpredictable weather, an uncontrollable force." He paused long enough to press a chaste kiss to her lips. "You have to wonder why they're not at rest."

"According to the writings in Alice's journals, she believed it was because they never got the chance to say 'goodbye'. Captain Jake never returned from the sea, and Lily died of a broken heart."

"I can't imagine a more devastating ending to such a deep love."

Easing her off his shoulder, he pushed himself to stand and offered her his hand.

Most suddenly, she was overcome with a flush of embarrassment. When she crossed one arm over her bare breasts, Harry's mouth kicked up at the corners. To his credit, he didn't comment on her show of modesty.

"Harry, about what happened—"

"Shh, Princess. We can talk about it later." He lifted their discarded clothing from the floor and handed hers off. Giving a short nod toward the open loft window, he added, "It looks as if the storm has knocked out the electricity. The house is pitch black."

"We should probably make our way back. My father will be wondering where we got to."

Fumbling with the catches of her brassiere, she let out a sigh of frustration.

This time, Harry did laugh. "Would you like some help getting dressed?"

"If you wouldn't mind. These dratted hooks and eyes are difficult enough at the best of times. I'm afraid my hands are still trembling far too much to manage them."

Laying his hands on her shoulders, he turned her around to face away from him. Rather than begin on the difficult closures, he drew her back against his chest and wrapped his arms around her middle.

"You're an exasperating woman, Mallory McGuire. Yet, all I want to do is hold you, kiss you, stroke your soft body."

"And I want you to do those things, but... I mean... you still didn't..."

"I'm fine," he assured her. "Still as aroused as a penned-up stud horse, but I'll survive. It's not the first time you've left me in this condition."

"It's not?"

"No, it's not. That very first night we met, I said something like 'not having the desire to babysit a spoiled woman', and—"

"And I responded, 'we wouldn't want your desire to be affected'."

"Little did you know, standing behind that big wingback chair in the library, I was as hard as rock."

Boldly, she slid her hand between them and enclosed his hard shaft.

"Are you sure—?"

"Don't tempt me, Princess. My more righteous, gentlemanly side is telling me to push you away, and take you back to the safety of Fairwinds."

Stepping back, he put distance between them. She dropped her hand to her side, her skin still tingling from the feel of Harry's arousal pressed against her palm.

"Perhaps when we go away on Friday, we could find some privacy, do more."

"Count on it, Mallory."

Her trousers straightened, her brassiere and blouse in place, she reached for the last two buttons on Harry's shirt. "Here, let me. It's the least I can do given how quickly you refastened my underpinnings."

His deep chuckle did its usual dance across her emotions.

"It was that or be tempted to return to those luscious breasts of yours for another thorough tasting."

His husky admission made her knees weak to the point where they were threatening to buckle beneath her.

"We'd better go then. Before I tear my clothes off again myself."

He gave an exaggerated roll of his eyes and pursed his lips to hold in an outright laugh. "Ah, Princess, you are going to be the death of me."

***

By the time they'd made their way back to the house, dusk had settled in, made even darker by the clouds that still hung above the grounds. Harry opened the door leading to the kitchen so they could cut through there to the rest of the house.

As he'd assumed, the house itself was dark, the only illumination the candles placed strategically around the various rooms and the glow from the cook's wood-burning stove.

They located McGuire, Teddy, and Gus in the library huddled around the fireplace, a bottle of whiskey and three glasses on the table in front of them.

"Where the hell have you two been?" Malcolm demanded.

"We got caught in the downpour coming back from the cliffs and decided to ride out the storm in the stables," he explained.

"You spent nearly three hours in the stables?" Teddy asked sarcastically, his gaze shifting between him and Mallory, obviously trying to get a read on Harry's honesty.

"It was that or risk getting hit by lightning," Mallory said, meeting Teddy's gaze head-on.

"You could have come through the tunnels," Gus suggested.

"We could have," Mallory agreed. "But someone forgot to return the electric torches to the wall pegs, and there was no way I was going to risk twisting my ankle in the pitch black of the shaft going down into the tunnel."

"Well, you're here now," Malcolm groused. "I need to talk to Harry. Alone. You, Teddy, and Gus go to the kitchen and rustle us up something to eat."

"Wasn't this Mrs. Vernon's day to come in and cook?" Mallory asked.

Teddy gave a snort. "Power's out in Mystic Point, too. Plus, she couldn't get a ride to work. Apparently, her whole fuckin' family is afraid to come to Fairwinds during a storm."

As soon as the door closed behind the three of them, Harry asked, "What's up, boss?"

"Take a seat, Harry."

He took the chair opposite McGuire, his back toward the wall so he could see the entire room, including the door. "Okay, I'm seated."

"First off, Teddy tells me you don't trust him. He said you made him give you the keys to the auto when you went into the diner to pick up a food order."

Harry met the older man's gaze. "Should I trust him?"

McGuire snorted a laugh. "Hell, no. It's best to not trust anyone, not even me."

"I definitely don't trust you," he confirmed. "I'd be an idiot if I did."

"You're no idiot, are you, Harry? Which is why you're sitting here and not Teddy, or Gus and definitely not Sully."

What was McGuire up to? Did he suspect Harry Carter was more than what he seemed? A sense of unease swept through him, and he asked, "What do you need me to do, boss?"

"Assuming they get these damned light poles fixed, I'm still planning on my big dinner party tomorrow. Hell, I'm having the fuckin' party, lights or no lights. I've got too much riding on it to cancel."

"Are the phones still working?" he asked, suddenly aware

that if McGuire's plans changed, he'd have to find a way to call it in.

"For what I pay for a private line, they'd better be." Chuckling, he admitted, "I honestly haven't checked."

"We won't have to worry about that if the lights come back. If they don't, you may have to make a few calls to let your guests know the party's still on."

"Right now, my biggest concern is the safety of all those goods you fellows brought in from my warehouse and the safe deposit boxes."

"Isn't everything stored in the safe room?" Harry asked.

"It is," McGuire confirmed. "However, I was down there doing a second inventory of the items you and Teddy brought in when the lights went out. Since the door lock runs on electricity—the only place on the ground level where we ran lines—I wasn't able to set the lock."

"So, it's virtually a wide-open bank vault."

"That's the problem. The cash, of course, is locked in my wall safe, but the artwork, the jewelry, the imported booze, and the antiques are up for grabs."

"Yet, they're not guarded at the moment," he pointed out.

"Why do you think I had those jackasses in here drinking my booze? I'd like to think I could trust them all, but temptation has taken down many a loyal man."

"And you trust me?"

McGuire shook his head. "No, but I figure you've got more scruples than the others. And, given that expensive car you drive, I'm guessing you're not hard up for money."

"I'll go grab myself a sandwich, a thermos of coffee, and head down to the storeroom," he confirmed. "If you'd like, you can send the others down in two hour shifts just to keep me honest."

"If the lights come back on, you'll know it because the switch is still flipped. Just set the lock and come back up."

"Will do, boss."

He stood to leave, stopping short when McGuire spoke again.

"I supposed I'd be remiss if I didn't ask—"

"Ask what?"

"Are you fucking my daughter, Harry?"

Well, there it was. The question that should have come before business.

"No, I'm not. As lovely as Miss Mallory is, she's only a child. She may be legally an adult, but I'm ten years her senior and not into robbing the cradle."

McGuire gave a quick nod. "See that you keep it that way. I'd hate to have to off a good employee because he couldn't keep it in his pants."

Chapter 18

Having to pay penance in the cellar was a fitting punishment for his lapse of judgement where Mallory was concerned.

The realization that she expected—wanted—to do more on Friday had him rethinking his plans. As badly as he wanted her, he couldn't be totally intimate with her until she knew the truth.

He wasn't even sure if it would be possible then.

She'd no doubt want something permanent, deserved something permanent. A love like the Captain and Lady Lillian shared. He'd never been a permanent kind of man.

Besides, according to the scuttlebutt going around the Boston field office, they were looking for additional agents to send to Chicago to deal with the rival gangs run by Capone and Bugsy Malone.

Director Hoover, with the approval of the Attorney General, was determined to take both leaders down, even if it took every man the Bureau had available. And, according to Whitmer, 'Simon Barclay's name was at the top of the list.'

He'd been all for the transfer, a possible promotion, until now. Until an opinionated, obstinate, and totally infuriating slip of woman made his heart race, and his unruly body respond with no more than the toss of her wild red curls.

He was about to consult his pocket watch for probably the hundredth time when the lights came back on, the single bulb hanging from the ceiling of the storeroom shining in his eyes.

Eager to reach a soft bed for whatever was left of the night, he flipped off the light switch, engaged the lock, and shut the door behind him. There'd be no need to cancel the party or alter the Bureau's plans to relieve Malcolm McGuire of his ill-gotten gains, and his freedom.

While Mallory made no bones about her hatred of her father's business practices, he was still her father. Simon couldn't help but wonder how she'd react when she returned on Friday evening to an empty house.

***

Mallory swept into the dining room the next morning, eager to get this day over with so they could get to Friday, and to her trip to Boston with Harry.

As much as she'd tried to fight it, she couldn't ignore the fact that Harry's good qualities far outweighed his bad. She trusted him—something that didn't come easy to someone who'd spent so much time living among criminals.

Harry was different. Special. He was considerate, gentle, and he made her feel something she'd never felt before, save for her sainted mother.

Love. She'd fallen in love with Harry Carter.

"Good morning, Miss Mallory," Sully greeted before taking a seat at the opposite end of the table.

"How was your evening off, Sully?"

"Wet. My car broke down halfway to Mystic Point, and I had to walk the rest of the way home in the rain."

"Still, I bet your wife was happy to see you."

"You'd think," he grumbled. "Instead, she harped at me for dragging mud in on me boots from those damn tunnels."

"Well, you're back now, and we've got a grand party to prepare for, don't we?"

"I suppose. Although, I'll likely be assigned to the driveway to organize the parking."

She offered the big bear of a man a smile. "We'll have to make sure to pack you a basket of Mrs. Vernon's homemade bread, some roasted pheasant, and a flask of father's finest whiskey. Just don't say it was me who gave it to you."

"Perhaps being off on my own won't be that bad after all," he conceded.

Her father arrived next, followed by Gus and Teddy.

"Where's Harry?" Her question drew another look from Teddy. "Did you give him the day off after all?" She gave her father a sly smile. Let him think she was going to run out on his party.

"He was up all night at my request," Malcolm said. "No doubt he's catching a few hours of sleep."

"We're going to need his help setting up the merchandise," Teddy said quickly. "He'd better not plan to sleep all day."

Mallory saw the exchange of glances between her father and Teddy, sensing tension between the two men who'd been thick as thieves for the past few years.

"I'm sure if you fellows put your backs into it, you could get the job done on your own. I have another, more important, job for Harry."

Mallory's heart sank. *Was Harry to become her father's new right-hand man?*

By noon, the housekeeping staff were busy polishing, mopping, and wiping down every surface on the main floor, and scrubbing the bathroom on the second. Mrs. Vernon had brought her daughters along to help out, assigning Edna, her eldest, to work in the kitchen. The gardener was busy clearing away the fallen leaves and trimming the bushes.

Harry had joined the others in the tunnels by eleven, bringing up twice the amount of goods as the others in half the time.

She'd caught her father and Harry huddled in conversation. The phone had rung constantly all day, most often guests confirming arrival times, or suppliers double-checking their orders.

Mrs. Vernon's younger daughter, Rebecca, had been given

the task of minding the phone and confirming with the callers that the party was still on and, when necessary, taking down names of anyone who cancelled.

The entire household was running like clockwork. Mallory looked forward to keeping them all on once Fairwinds was hers to control.

At half-past four, Mallory set aside the list of tasks her father had insisted she attend to, a checkmark next to each item. As much as she hated being part of her father's sordid affairs, she couldn't stand by and do nothing while Harry and the others were working so hard.

It was time to don her beautiful new evening gown, her mother's diamonds, and do something fancy with her often-stubborn hair.

"Rebecca," she called out as she passed the parlor door, "do you think you could give me a hand getting ready? The phone has finally stopped ringing."

"I'd love to, Miss, if you're sure it'll be all right with my mama."

After a quick bubble bath, Mallory slipped on her expensive French lingerie and slid her arms through the sleeves of her dressing gown. Taking a seat at her dressing table, she sat patiently while Rebecca wrestled her curls into a sleek chignon at the back of her head.

"This beautiful rhinestone clip will hold everything in place," the young girl said. Giving a tug to her handiwork, she proclaimed, "Tight as a drum, Miss. You can dance the night away and not have to worry about a thing."

"Thank you, Rebecca. Now, if I can get your help shimmying into this tight dress, I'll be ready to add a bit of rouge and lipstick and make my way downstairs."

"You'll be the most beautiful woman there, Miss Mallory."

"How sweet of you to say so." Standing, she dropped her

robe to the floor and reached for the elegant satin evening gown that lay across her bed.

The sleek, midnight black design cost her father a fortune, as well it should, given she was his hostess for a night she'd rather not be part of in the first place.

"This is the most beautiful dress I've ever seen, miss. It fits your body like a glove."

"A tight glove," Mallory acknowledged, drawing in a breath so she could adjust the bodice to cover a bit more cleavage.

"You'll have all the men drooling, for sure."

There was only one man she wanted drooling over her. Assuming, of course, her father hadn't assigned him a job away from the party.

***

Spending what would amount to his last night as Harry Carter, Simon slid his arms through the tailored tuxedo jacket and gave his black tie and extra tug to secure its angle.

At six o'clock sharp, he entered the foyer and went in search of his assignment.

'*Keep her close*', McGuire had ordered. '*Some of these men, while wealthy, are pigs. I don't want their grubby paws anywhere near my daughter.*'

Even though he'd feigned disappointment at being assigned as Mallory's well-dressed babysitter, there's nowhere else among these swells that he'd rather be.

"Have you seen Miss Mallory?" he asked once he'd reached the main floor.

Teddy looked up from the guest list he'd been reviewing. "She's in the ballroom, I think. She said she needed a moment of quiet before the chaos."

"And you didn't think she might be taking off on you?"

Teddy coughed out a laugh. "She ain't climbing a fence in that piece of nothing she's wearing."

Really? He rushed forward, eager to see this 'piece of nothing' for himself.

When he arrived at the French doors leading into the grand ballroom, she was standing in front of one of the floor-to-ceiling windows and gazing out over the garden.

The room was dark but for the candles atop the mantle, their glow bouncing off the shadowed corners of the room.

She was perfect.

From the top of her sleek coif, down the length of her curvaceous body, to the tips of her jewel trimmed slippers.

His mouth watered at the thought of kissing her, his fingers tingled at the memory of touching her intimately.

"Hello, Harry," she said without turning.

He closed the distance between them and pulled her backward into his embrace. After glancing toward the doorway to assure himself they wouldn't be seen, he slid the tips of his fingers up and down her bare arms. When she trembled, his heartbeat gathered speed.

Against the length of her elegant neck, he whispered, "You look absolutely stunning."

She turned in his arms and took a step back, her gaze raking him from head-to-toe. "You're pretty well turned out yourself, Harry. Elegant, in fact."

"Well then, we should make a very attractive couple for this fancy shindig."

"You'll be with me throughout the night, then?"

"Yes, Princess. My orders are to not let you out of my sight. A job, I assure you, I take most seriously."

"Well then, I suppose we should get ready to welcome my father's guests."

People milled around everywhere. Simon's plan was to keep a close eye on Mallory, and never let her get more than five feet from his side.

He recognized a number of McGuire's guests. Some from the society pages, others from wanted posters passed between the local law enforcement and the FBI. The richest of the rich, the lowest of the low. It didn't seem to matter to McGuire, as long as he sold his stash to the highest bidder.

Mallory stepped away from a particularly annoying man and threaded her arm through his. "Do you mind if we go in and check on the dinner table? I want to make sure it's set up properly?"

"Gladly," he agreed. "Anything to get away from the cigar smoke and loud chatter."

They entered the dining room where the main table had been extended to hold twenty. The fine dinnerware gleamed in the overhead light. All the trappings of wealth and privilege.

Mrs. Vernon's daughters stood off to the side, ready to begin service as soon as the guests were seated.

"What do you think, Harry?" Mallory asked. "Will there be room?"

"Harry?" Rebecca repeated. "You're Harry Carter?"

He turned to the girl. "Yes, I am. Why?"

"I took a message for you earlier. I asked a couple of times, but the other men didn't know where you were." She dropped her gaze to the floor. "I hope it wasn't important."

"Don't worry. I'm sure it's not urgent."

When she handed him the scrap of paper, he unfolded it and read the short message, his heartbeat coming to a full-stop at what it said.

'Your family called. Your uncle is arriving tonight, instead of tomorrow. His bus gets in at eight. He plans to gather up the entire family. Hopefully, you can get away in time to say hello.'

Jeezus H. Some idiot had changed the day and time of the raid. They were not only targeting McGuire and his men, but the party guests as well.

"Is everything all right, Harry?" Mallory asked.

He nodded. "Just a change in family plans."

Once she'd turned back to the last of the meal preparations, he checked his pocket watch. *Seven-twenty.* He had little more than a half hour to get Mallory out of the house and to safety.

The guests began filtering into dinner, taking their seats at the designated spot. Mallory stood off to the side, waiting to be seated once everyone else was in place.

At seven-forty, Simon pulled back her chair and then eased her closer to the table, before taking his spot along the wall.

Twenty fucking minutes. Think, Simon, think.

He was about to resort to the half-assed idea of spilling wine on her dress, so she'd have to leave the table, when Sully burst into the room, out of breath.

"Boss, you gotta see this," the big man choked out between ragged breaths. "There's a whole line of black cars coming down the road, lights flashing."

"Shit," McGuire hollered, his panicked gaze shifting from side-to-side. "It's a raid!"

The guests scattered quickly, running toward the dining room doors, eager to escape across the patio and out over the grounds.

Grabbing her hand, Simon ordered, "Come with me, Mallory."

"What's going on?" she asked, her words frantic.

"Like your father said, we're being raided."

"But I've done nothing—"

"It won't matter. They'll arrest first, ask questions later."

"I'm staying. This is my home."

"Dammit, Mallory." Pulling her to her feet, he wrapped his arms under her hips and hoisted her over his shoulder.

They made it through the foyer as the first of the police

cars arrived in the circle drive. No doubt, the unmarked cars belonging to the FBI wouldn't be far behind.

With everyone headed in the opposite direction, he slipped through the doors of the rotunda and headed straight for the hidden door that led to the third floor.

Shoving the settee aside, he hit the pressure plate and stooped to clear the narrow opening.

"Put me down, Harry. Right now."

"Not until we're safe. Now, quit wiggling or I'm going to smack that fine bottom of yours. Or drop you, whichever comes first."

The moment he'd pulled the furniture back in place, he shut the door, leaving them in total darkness.

Slowly, he lowered her over his body, until she'd gained her footing.

"I don't intend to stay here forever," she said. "Fairwinds is mine, and I need to make sure those men know it."

Steering them to the foot of the staircase, he coaxed her to sit.

"They're not here for Fairwinds, Mallory. They're here for the bootlegged hooch, stolen art, jewels, and antiques."

"Who's 'they'? And how do you know what they want?"

He was about to string a line of bull until he could get her out of this musty corridor, when a volley of gunshots rang out.

"Shit." Taking her hand, he led her up the staircase until they'd reached the top step. "I need to see what's going on but I can't—we can't—go back out there."

Giving the trap door a hard shove, he dislodged the edge of the rug, stepped into the third-floor bedroom and lifted Mallory in after him.

"Shouldn't you be down there helping my father and the others?"

"You're my primary responsibility. Your father, Teddy, Gus and Sully can take care of themselves. Besides, your father brought this on himself. It's not like he wasn't going to get caught at some point."

"I feel so guilty," she admitted. "I've often wished they'd arrest him for his deeds, get him away from Fairwinds. But I never intended on it being in a raid. Or, that there would be guns. He may be a criminal, but he's also my father. I don't want him killed."

"Sit here," he ordered, pushing her down onto the big four-poster bed. "Do not attempt to leave this room."

"Where are you going?"

"Out onto the widow's walk to get a look around the grounds." He pulled the doors open and turned back for one last warning. "I mean it, Mallory. Stay put."

She shot him a dark glare. "And, if I don't."

"I'll tie you to the fucking bed." He paused, released a long, calming breath, and added, "Please, Princess, don't test me."

Simon made his way out onto the roof and circled the perimeter until he could see the black paddy wagons, assorted police cars, and plain brown autos belonging to the Bureau.

Sully and Gus were sitting on the side of the drive, cuffed and ready for transport. Teddy sat on the back bumper of one of the wagons, holding a blood-soaked cloth to his shoulder. Simon was about to move to the other side of the roof when Mallory came to his side.

"Come quick. Someone's trying to break through the barrier my father had built to block off the third floor."

He took off his jacket and wrapped it around her shoulders. "You stay here on the walk but remain close to the chimney, so you won't be seen. I'll be back for you."

"I'm scared," she whispered, her voice choked with fear.

"We'll get out of this. I promise."

He'd barely cleared the doorway into the bedroom when a scream rent the air, pulling him back out onto the roof. "What is it?"

She shook her head. "That wasn't me." Pointing to the far side of the grounds, she said, "It came from that direction."

He made his way to the edge of the widow's walk, Mallory clinging to the back of his shirt. A loud screech of pain filled the cool night.

"Son of a bitch," he muttered. "Look at that—Lady Lillian is about to scare the crap out of them all."

"Good for you, Lily," Mallory whispered.

A bright light shone over the entire yard, as Lily's ghost rose in anger, her eyes glowing as red as fire, her screams sending chills down his spine and sending the men and women on the ground scurrying for cover.

Every low life that had fled toward the cliffs was now running to the front lawn of Fairwinds, literally begging to be arrested and taken away.

"Come on, let's get back inside so I can deal with whomever is in the stairwell."

More noise, more muttered oaths filled the space below them. Heavy footsteps pounded across the floor. The walls shook. Doors slammed. The sound of a man's deep laughter filled the entire house. The efforts to break through the barrier at the bottom of the stairs stopped abruptly.

From the other side of the wall, an anonymous voice called out to someone nearby. "Did you hear that? What the hell? I don't give a shit about the orders to clear the third floor. I'm getting my arse outta here."

Two sets of footsteps fled down the hallway, no doubt on their way to the staircase leading down to the main floor.

Satisfied for the moment they were in no danger, Simon returned to the bedroom. "It seems the Captain has arrived to help as well."

"There are definitely some advantages to having resident ghosts."

"I think it's safe to go back onto the widow's walk and

watch what's going on. We just have to be careful not to be seen."

Placing her hand in his, she followed him out onto the roof. He swallowed back a lump in his throat when he thought of how easily she trusted him. How she likely wouldn't the moment he confessed his part in her father's downfall.

Chapter 19

At half past twelve, Mallory sat on the rooftop, wrapped in a combination of blankets from the bed, and Harry's strong embrace.

The last of the police cars had pulled out of the driveway only moments before. Three paddy wagons had left earlier, filled to the brim with her father's well-heeled, but nefarious, guests. The house staff had been taken in for statements but were afforded the courtesy of the backseat of two of the plain brown vehicles.

"Is it horrible of me to be grateful you dragged me up here to safety?"

"It was what I was charged to do, Miss McGuire."

She turned in his arms until she could meet his dark gaze. "Miss McGuire, is it?"

He nodded but didn't respond.

"I suppose I should be grateful my father gave you such an important assignment."

"He wasn't the one who ordered me to get you out of sight."

"He wasn't? Then, who?"

"He told me to stick to your side, all right, but that was to keep his guests from getting too close. But I'm sure he never imagined what was to transpire this evening."

"Then who, Harry? I surely don't remember anyone speaking up in the initial chaos."

"My assignment came from my *real* boss, not your father."

"Your real boss? Please, Harry, don't tell me you work for Sartori or O'Malley. They're as crooked as my father. Or worse."

"No, Miss McGuire, I work for the Federal Bureau of Investigation. I'm a government agent."

Her wide-eyed gaze scanned him from head to toe. A frown played across her lips, sending a sharp pain to his heart.

"The FBI? So, this was all a setup? You came to work for my father, to watch over me, so you could get close enough to turn him in?"

"Yes, that was the intent. Although, I'd not counted on being assigned as your bodyguard. You were a glitch in my original plan."

"A glitch?" Pushing her way out of his arms, she jumped to her feet. "Dammit, Harry, how could you? I mean, I thought I meant something to you, but you were just stringing me along to get to my father?"

"No, that's not how it is. Maybe in the beginning, as a way to get through the door, but it took no more than a few days to realize you were nothing like your father. Nothing like the spoiled little girl they made you out to be. My feelings for you were—are—real."

"How can I believe you, when you've been lying to me all along?"

"I might lie about a lot of things in my line of work—necessary lies—but I'd never lie about how much I've grown to care for you."

"I'd like to believe you, but... I can't..." She drew a breath. "At least not until I've had time to put my life back in order. Time to think things through. If you truly care for me, Harry, you'll give me that time—time to come to grips with the fact my father will likely be going to prison, time to rebuild my trust in you."

"Dammit all, I know I just asked you to trust me, but I have one more confession I need to make."

Mallory wasn't sure she could take another revelation. If he were to be so bold as to tell her he loved her, she wasn't sure she could send him away. Yet, she must.

"Yes? I'm waiting."

"My name's not really Harry Carter. It's Simon. Simon Barclay."

She drew in a long, sustaining breath and prayed for strength. "Tell me something, Mr. Barclay. Did you know about the raid ahead of time?"

He nodded. "Yes, I did. Although, it wasn't supposed to be tonight. It was scheduled for tomorrow morning, which was why I'd planned our trip to Boston. That way, you wouldn't be here when it happened."

"Our trip... our chance to be alone... was just another ruse?"

"In the beginning... yes. However, the more I got to know you, the more I realized how special you are—especially to me. You're a warm, compassionate and giving woman. I fully intended to confess everything while we were in Boston. And, beg your forgiveness. Then, if you still wanted me, I would have gladly been with you."

Her lower lip trembled; her entire body ached with sadness. She wanted desperately to believe him... she loved him that much. Yet, she'd been lied to so often, by so many, she questioned her own judgement. As badly as she wanted him, she couldn't. Not yet, anyway.

Shaking her head, she crossed the room and flipped open the trap door. "Go, Harry... Simon... whatever the hell your name is."

"Miss McGuire... Mallory—"

"Just go. Now."

Without another word, or backward glance, he lowered himself through the opening and onto the iron staircase. The moment he started down the stairs, she slammed the lid shut, threw herself on the bed, and dissolved into a puddle of tears.

Fairwinds Estate
Late November 1924

It had been nearly two months since the raid on Fairwinds, and Mallory had finally managed to untangle the mess her father had created. Thankfully, there'd been very little physical damage to Fairwinds, other than one wall leading into the dining room, and the partition at the top of the staircase—which she'd intended to tear down anyway.

"Miss Mallory, can I get you some breakfast?"

She raised her gaze from the legal papers Mr. Blake had dropped off the day before. "Thank you, Edna, but I'm fine. I will have another pot of tea, if you don't mind."

"My mother will have my hide if I don't get you to eat something. She's worried about you."

"I haven't had much of an appetite lately, but I will have a couple of her delicious biscuits and jam if she has some made."

"I'll see to it."

Returning her attention to the court filings, Mallory skimmed the first page and went directly to the judge's decision. Thanks to Mr. Miller and Mr. Blake, the court had accepted her petition to allow her access to her inheritance earlier than stipulated in her mother's will.

While the judge hadn't given in completely, he had ordered the right of inheritance be lowered from twenty-five years of age, to twenty-three. Mr. Miller would continue to administer the estate for another fourteen months.

Her father had been sentenced to thirty years in prison for bootlegging, possession, and sale of stolen goods, and in a surprising turn, counterfeiting. Teddy had received twenty years, Sully and Gus five. Additionally, a charge had been laid against her father in her mother's death. The court had refused to hear the case until more proof could be offered. He'd surely face the chair if he was found guilty. However, if it were true, she'd regretfully accept whatever sentence he was given, if only to get justice for her mother.

The FBI had emptied the tunnels of all ill-gotten goods and alcohol. The safe in the library had been emptied as well. They'd taken possession of cash, bonds, and—much to Mallory's surprise—her mother's wedding rings.

Mr. Miller had petitioned for the return of the rings, making the case that they were not part of her father's business dealings but, rather, part of Mallory's estate. She hoped to hear any day of the outcome.

"Here you go, Miss Mallory," Edna said, setting the biscuits and fresh pot of tea in front of her.

"You and your family have been a godsend these past weeks. Even Mr. Piper has stopped complaining about the size of the grounds he must keep tidy."

"I'm pretty sure he's just happy to be working for you, instead of your father, Miss."

"Have we heard anything about my plans to go out later?"

"Another driving lesson, Miss?"

"Yes. They may have taken away all my father's fancy autos but there's no reason I can't buy one of my own once I learn how to operate the blasted beast."

"I'm sorry but Mr. Collier called to say he can't be here. He claims you scared him to within an inch of his life when you swerved to avoid that cat in the middle of the road."

"I couldn't very well run over the poor thing. How was I to know the road would be so slippery?"

Edna stifled a laugh. "It is the onset of winter, and the road was nothing but ice, after all."

"I suppose. I'll just have to find another teacher who won't balk at a bit of sliding around."

"According to Mr. Collier, the sliding was two complete circles ending against a tree trunk." Edna gave her shy smile.

"Perhaps it would be best to wait until spring to learn how to drive."

"I truly don't know who's worse about fussing over me—you or your mother."

"We care about you, Miss Mallory." The young woman gave a shy smile. "Can I ask you something personal?"

"I suppose."

"Whatever happened to that handsome fellow… Harry? My mama said he wasn't who he said he was, and that he actually worked for the government."

"That he did." She paused, sparing a thought for Harry… Simon. Something she was doing a lot lately, despite not wanting to. "I saw him—briefly and from a distance—right after the raid. Then, he was gone. The last I'd heard from Mr. Miller was that Mr. Barclay wouldn't be attending my father's trial because he'd been transferred to Chicago."

"Mama also said that she thought there was something going on with you and him. That you looked at each other like two people in love."

"Your mother obviously needs to have a doctor look at her eyes."

"So, we just imagined all that crying, and cursing his name—both his names?"

"Oh, there were plenty of tears, and swearing, mostly because I couldn't believe how gullible I was, how easily fooled by a few kisses." She sighed. "They were very nice kisses."

"He definitely looked like a good kisser," Edna agreed.

"Miss Mallory," Mrs. Vernon said from the doorway. "Mr. Miller just called. He said to tell you the police have released your mother's rings from custody. They're having them delivered later this morning."

"That's wonderful."

"Everything's about right now," Mrs. Vernon said. "The house is in good repair, the tunnels sealed off again, just as they were before your mother passed, rest her soul. Even the Captain has stopped banging around and leaving muddy footprints in my kitchen."

"If it weren't for the occasional nor'easter, we'd never know they're here," Mallory added. "Truth be told, I kind of miss them."

"Not me," Mrs. Vernon said. "I like the peace and quiet. Especially now that Edna and I take turns staying over nights."

"I do appreciate your efforts to make sure I'm not alone. I'm thinking of inviting my friend Sadie to come live with me."

"That won't last long," Edna said. "I heard through the gossip mill, that she's finally come around and realized how much she cares for Will Baker."

"I guess that means we've no use for the Ouija board any longer."

Edna gave a giggle. "I'd better get back to my chores. I'll let you know when the police arrive with your parcel."

"I'd appreciate it. I'm going upstairs to work on the floor. The clerk at the hardware store gave me a new wax to try. It's supposed to soak right into the wood to protect it."

"You shouldn't be waxing the floors, Miss. I can do it or, when Sally comes to clean on Tuesdays, she could do it."

"Nonsense. I'm not some gilded bird in a cage. Besides, I love taking care of the Captain and Lily's room."

"Okay, just don't let my mama see you down on your hands and knees waxing floors."

"I'll do my best to avoid her."

Mallory was nearly finished applying the wax, when Edna appeared at the doorway of the third-floor bedroom. "Your package has arrived."

"Please place it in the desk drawer in the library."

"I can't… I mean… he says you have to be the one to sign for it."

"I'm almost done with this floor. I can't stop now, or the wax will dry unevenly."

"He says he's willing to bring it up to you."

"Good God. I only have another couple of feet to go. Very well."

"Yes, Miss."

Edna bolted for the stairs. Mallory could have sworn she heard the young woman's laughter as she left.

It would take the man a few minutes to reach the third floor. Turning her back to the door, she returned to the task at hand.

"That's still one fine ass you got there, lady. Almost makes me want to give it a love tap or two."

Mallory froze. Simon Barclay's deep baritone filled her senses, easily slipping past her defenses. Without looking up, she responded. "What are you doing here, *Simon?*"

"Delivering your package, Miss McGuire."

"I didn't think the FBI were errand boys, or the ones who'd taken custody of my mother's rings. They told Mr. Miller, the local police had them."

"They did."

"Then how did you get them?"

"I'm on an assignment for Pinkertons, who loaned me out to the local coppers for a special case."

She raised herself from the floor and wiped her hands on a clean rag. "You quit the FBI?"

He nodded. "I refused an assignment, and they didn't take kindly to it. They offered me a transfer to some god-forsaken town in Montana. The alternative was to tender my resignation."

"I take it, you weren't really 'on the lam' from Pinkertons."

"No, I wasn't. It was all a fabricated story they agreed to put out there in cooperation with the Bureau."

"And now you're here in Mystic Point. For how long this

time?"

"Well, that depends on you."

"Me?"

When he reached for her hand, she desperately wanted to pull away. Yet, she couldn't. At least not until she'd heard what he had to say.

He led her to the bed and set her down on the edge before taking a seat beside her. "Don't worry, I'm not here to ravish you."

"Where have I heard that line before?"

His chuckle lifted her heart.

"Unless, of course, you'd still like to be ravished."

"How about you tell me why I should be the one to decide how long you stay in Mystic Point?"

"I'm thinking of ditching Pinkertons now that the job is done. Of course, if I do, I'll be looking for work. I understand you'll be needing someone to manage the stables you hope to fill this coming spring."

"I need someone who knows horses," she insisted.

"Then you're in luck. I wasn't always an East Coaster, Miss McGuire. As a matter of fact, I was raised in Oklahoma on my family's ranch. I started riding horses when I was four."

"Your family has a ranch?"

"Yep. Cattle, horses, a few random oil wells."

Random oil wells?

"I suppose I could give you a formal interview. Assuming you meet the qualifications, I might consider you. The job pays a fair wage and comes with a very nice cottage. You can live in it if you want."

His lips twitched.

"Well, before we draw up an employment agreement, I should probably tell you about the special case I was assigned."

"Does it have something to do with me?"

"Not you. Your father. Your mother."

Her breath caught. A fine tremble shook her entire body.

"I finally tracked down Pete Temple, the brother of the man we suspected of murdering your mother."

"The man they thought my father hired to push her off the cliffs."

"Yes. It turns out, your father did give Rick Temple money, but it wasn't to kill your mother. It was because he'd arranged to hire a counterfeiter to reproduce artwork. The first forgery your father sold netted him a big sum and he gave Temple a cut."

"Then, what happened to my mother? And why did Temple die?"

"Rick Temple did kill your mother, but not at your father's behest. I truly believe your father thought her fall was real, at least until the rumors started after Temple's death."

Her father wasn't a murderer after all. Tears of relief rolled freely down her cheeks. When Simon reached for her, she went slowly, but willingly, into his arms.

"It seems Temple had been here looking for your father. He'd been drinking, as usual, and when your mother asked him to leave, he chose to wander out onto the grounds toward the cliffs. Even though she'd not been feeling well that day, she followed him to demand he leave Fairwinds completely. They argued over her refusal to give your father and his men access to the tunnels. He swore at her, and she slapped him. He shoved her and she stumbled backward and tripped over the damaged fencing, falling over the edge of the cliff."

"And Temple's death a month or so later?"

"Temple and the others had settled in here at Fairwinds, he and his brother had words and Temple took off toward the cliffs in a fit of anger. According to his brother—who'd gone looking for him—Lady Lillian rose from her grave and scared him to death, causing his fall over the cliffs, just as your mother had died. Ordinarily, I'd have called the white ambulance to take Pete Temple to the sanitarium. However, given the things I saw while I was here, I have no doubt it happened exactly as he said."

"It's over," she said, her words ending in a hiccup.

"Yes, it's over. Everything's neatly tied up." He paused, then lifted her chin with the tips of his fingers, meeting her tear-filled gaze. "Other than you're still in need of a horseman."

"I've missed you," she admitted. "It would be nice to have you around to run the stables and to teach me to drive."

"You want to learn to drive?"

"Yes, I do. I hired a man from town to teach me, but he didn't fare too well."

"Oh yeah, the icy road incident. I heard all about it."

She took a playful swat at his arm. "Have you been spying on me, Simon Barclay?"

"Not spying. Protecting, as I said I always would. And, just so you know, I love it when you say my name—my real name."

"I spent a good month cursing it, after you left."

"You mean, after you threw me out?"

"Yes, I suppose I did, didn't I?"

"I don't suppose you'd invite me back? Not just as your stable hand, but as something a bit more... uh... personal."

"More personal?"

He pressed a kiss to her lips, and she welcomed the warmth of his mouth against hers.

"Yes, something close by, but not the cottage. Although I'm certain you've done a wonderful job of fixing it up." He kissed her again, before adding, "I'd like a position that allows me to live in Fairwinds. Preferably in your room."

"That is personal, but I'll consider it. Assuming of course, you can pass the interview."

"I'm pretty sure Mrs. Vernon and her daughter have gone

into town. I saw the gardener loading them into his car as I was coming up the stairs."

"So, we're alone?"

"Yes, we could start on that interview any time you'd like."

She spread her hand across the heavy brocade bedspread. "Not here. This is their room."

He stood and scooped her up in his arms. "I know just the place."

"It's too cold for the stables."

"No, not the stables." He started toward the stairs before adding, "I spent far too many nights leaning against that damned newel post at the top of the stairs, wishing for an invite into that fancy corner bedroom of yours. Other than the one night I carried you to bed, I never breached the door, no matter how badly I wanted to."

"Well then, I guess it's time for a guided tour."

"Yes, sweetheart, it is."

Chapter 20

They'd just reached her bedroom door, when Mallory spoke up. "Before we do this, I need to make one thing clear."

Simon came to a dead stop and lowered her to the floor. When he met her gaze, his intense stare pierced clear through to her soul.

"Whatever you want, Princess."

"Honesty. I demand it. No more secrets between us. Ever."

He released a long sigh, the reaction making her heart skip a beat.

Was there still more to be told?

"I must confess, while I'm more than willing to help you find and purchase some fine horses, I'm not overly fond of chickens."

She pursed her lips, holding in her outright laugh.

"Too bad. While the local poultry shop's chickens produce fine eggs, there's nothing quite as nice as one fresh from the hen's nest."

"And you'd know this how?"

"I read it. In my great-aunt Alice's journal. Apparently, her mother was quite fond of gathering the eggs."

"Okay, enough discussion about the merits of chickens and their eggs. Let's get down to some serious kissing."

"Oh, yes. I have definitely missed your kisses," she admitted, raising herself up to accept the first of what she hoped would be many.

Simon lowered his head and pressed his mouth to hers, dusting her lower lip with his tongue. Most willingly, she parted her lips to allow him entrance.

When he reached past her to open the bedroom door, she

backpedaled across the threshold, pulling him with her, never once breaking the delicious joining of their mouths, the dueling of their slick tongues.

"Princess," he whispered against her mouth. "I've missed this... you..."

"As I, you, Simon. I admit, I regretted sending you away almost immediately."

"Seeing you at your father's preliminary hearings tore me up. Knowing you hated me for what I'd done."

She shook her head. "I never hated you, not once."

"You refused to speak to me."

"Only because I was afraid that I'd end up begging you to come back to Fairwinds."

"I'd have gladly accepted. However, I'm pretty sure the 'begging' would have been mine, not yours."

Lifting her off her feet, he carried her to the bed and laid her gently atop the quilt.

Mallory's heart raced with the import of what they were about to do. What she'd been longing for since their brief time together in the hay loft.

Simon knelt beside the bed, removing her soft slippers and tossing them aside. When he reached for her stockings and rolled them down her legs, it was all she could do to keep from screaming out in anticipation.

He reached for the waistband of her simple cotton skirt and slipped the buttons from their holes until he could peel the thin garment across her hips, easing it beneath her bottom, and down her legs.

Her skin flushed when uncovered to both the air and his intense gaze. He lifted her into a seated position and gathered the hem of her blouse in his hands. Drawing it up over her shoulders and tossing it on the nearby chair, he left her in only her bandeau bra and lacy undershorts.

"My God but you are beautiful." His whispered words

came out husky, filled with emotion.

She made a very unladylike show of perusing his form up and down. "And one of us is grossly overdressed."

"A fact I'm more than happy to remedy."

She'd never seen anyone move as fast as Simon did to strip out of his shirt and trousers, leaving him nearly naked in a pair of tight boxer shorts. The obvious bulge in the front made her throat tighten.

When he came to lay beside her on the bed, butterflies swarmed her stomach, her pulse raced.

"We'll take this slow. Easy. If you ever want me to stop, Mallory, just say so."

She reached out and pressed her hand to his chest, toyed with his nipples. "I've no intention of asking you to stop. I've been dreaming of this, imagining this, for months."

"Months?"

A quick nod of her head drew his smile. "Ever since that night you caught me when I fell from the trellis. The feel of my body pressed against yours when you lowered me to the ground… it was like nothing I'd ever felt before."

"I hope to recreate that feeling for you and go far beyond."

He lowered his head and took her mouth in another mind-boggling kiss. With the twist of his fingers and gentle sweep of his hand, he removed her bra. Enclosing her breast in his hand, he snagged the very peak between his fingers.

When he deepened the kiss, she sucked his tongue into her mouth, drawing his groan.

His body pressed firm to hers, his arousal flush against her hip, Simon slid his hand from her breast to the waistband of her panties and then beneath until he could cup her intimately.

Memories of the last time he'd touched her there came flooding back and she parted her legs in willing surrender.

He managed to brush her panties over her hips, across her

bottom, and down her legs without breaking the contact of the bodies, leaving the scrap of silk and lace dangling around her ankles. Restlessly, she wiggled her feet until the garment fell away to land at the foot of her bed.

"I'm going to touch you now," he told her. "As I did before."

"I remember. It was heavenly."

Her hips rose to meet his hand, her body trembling with the first onslaught of feeling. An enticing pressure built within her, slowly at first, then picking up speed when he slipped his touch inside her body. His thumb plied the tiny button at the edge of her lady parts in time with the plummet of his finger.

Mallory clutched at the bedclothes beneath her, crumpling them up in her fists as the first wave of deliciousness flowed through her.

"Simon… oh…"

Her entire being convulsed in one spasm after another until Simon withdrew from inside her and pulled her tight against his side. His sex throbbed against her hip.

"Are you okay?"

"I've never been this okay in my entire life. I don't believe anything could feel as wonderful as this."

His chuckle reverberated between them. "I can promise you, that's only the beginning."

Holding her close, he managed to shimmy his way out of his underwear. When he guided her hand to his arousal, her breath caught.

She wrapped her hand around his thick shaft, and he enclosed her grip with his larger one, moving her hand up and down, teaching her how to stroke his flesh.

Within mere moments, she'd proudly mastered the technique, enjoying the feel of his body swelling even more with each pump of her hand.

"Enough," he said, his words coming out in a ragged rush

of air. "Or I'm going to explode."

Laying her back against the pillows, he hovered over her. "I can't promise this won't hurt, but I'll do my best to be gentle."

"I trust you, Simon. I've always trusted you."

He stole her words on a kiss, his tongue dancing across her lips, sweeping her mouth from side-to side, while his thigh slid between her legs, spreading them wide enough to accommodate his fit.

"I love you, Princess." His softly spoken admission was followed by the slow thrust of his hips, as he entered her.

Mallory's entire being melted around him, welcoming him inside her body. A small pinch drew her gasp, and Simon swallowed it up with his mouth.

Once he'd breached the final barrier of her innocence, he began moving. Slowly at first, filling her in cautious increments.

She slid her hands to his firm buttocks and urged him forward, deeper. Eagerly it seemed, he picked up his pace and acquiesced to her demand.

"Well, what did you think, Princess? Was it all you imagined?"

Mallory settled in at his side, fully spent, and welcomed the warmth of his embrace, the cushion of his shoulder beneath her head.

"Are you fishing for a compliment, Simon Barclay?"

"No, just making sure you were satisfied."

"Most satisfied, I assure you." She twirled her fingers through the fine hairs on his chest. "And, assuming you've nowhere else to be, I'd like to be satisfied again. Soon."

"I'll do my best." He kissed the top of her head before adding, "And just to be clear, I've nowhere else to be for the next fifty or more years."

"Good, me either. And, as long as we're being 'clear', I love you too, Simon Barclay."

"Thank heaven," he said with a laugh. "I was worried you only wanted me for my body."

She pressed a kiss to his slightly stubbled cheek. "That too, darling. That too."

Epilogue

Fairwinds Estate
May 1926

Simon waved to his wife, the love of his life, as she made her way across the paddock on her way to the stables to see their newest delivery, a fine colt, fathered by their champion sire, by way of a regal bay mare. The horse would be magnificent.

"He's most handsome," Mallory said, snuggling in at Simon's side. "What shall we name him?"

He laid his hand against Mallory's swollen belly. "Anything you'd like as long as it's not Stephen. That's reserved for my son."

"Don't be ridiculous," she chided. "Stephen would be a strange name for a horse. Or a daughter."

"Son," he insisted. "The next can be a daughter. Or the one after."

"Aren't you ambitious," she teased. "Let's not forget who has to carry these babies."

"And you're even more beautiful for the effort, Princess."

"You are so full of yourself, Mr. Barclay. I have half a mind to name this horse Simon."

He shook his head. "Nope."

"I know," she said suddenly. "We shall name him Sir Galahad." Smoothing her hand over his forearm, she gave him a smile, "That way he'll still be named after you—my knight in shining armor."

The End

Jilly's Dilemma
(Present Day)

Best Selling & Award-Winning Author
Nancy Fraser

Jilly's Dilemma

Having a stuffy old professor invade her home is the last thing she wants. However, once he shows up on her doorstep, he turns out to be exactly what she needs.

When Jillian Barclay inherits the family estate of Fairwinds from her father, it comes with the two unforeseen problems. First, she must live there for a minimum of three years before she can sell the property. She grew up at Fairwinds, so she's more than aware of the strange occurrences, the presence of the ghosts of Captain John Jacob Wilder and Lillian Wilder—the infamous 18th century pirate and his beloved wife. As a matter of fact, Jilly talks to them on a regular basis.

Nicholas Martin, PhD is about to become Jilly's other problem. An associate professor of history, Nicholas has been granted five days' access to Fairwinds to study the home's history as part of a research project for Harvard University's history museum.

Expecting a stodgy old professor, when Jilly meets the professor, she's wishing he was there to model for her rather than to study her home. Younger, and far sexier, than she'd pictured, she's immediately drawn to the handsome professor.

Nicholas has spent the previous month-and-a-half studying five other homes on the list of historical New England homes, all of which were inhabited by octogenarian, cat-loving spinsters. He has no reason to believe Fairwinds will be any different. Yet, the young woman with the wild red curls and penchant for talking to spirits is the last thing he expected, and the one thing his usually buttoned-up personality needs. Desperately.

Will opposites really attract? Or is it just the unusual effects of the ghostly carnal encounters that drives them into one another's arms? And when they can no longer resist their desires, will they be able to find a working compromise to his professional career and her legal commitments?

Dedication

For Lisa A. Olech and Kathryn Hills who had to talk me down off the ledge more than once during this project and this book!
Love you ladies.

Prologue

*Fairwinds, Mystic Point
Present Day*

Jillian Barclay took a seat in the middle of the third-floor bedroom, settling herself atop the thick Persian rug. Resting her forehead on her drawn-up knees, she took a breath and let it seep out slowly. When she finally raised her head, she scanned the entire room from the beautiful French doors leading to the roof to the closed bedroom door.

"Okay, I know you're both here," she said, her voice firm with conviction. "I heard the Captain stomp his way up the stairs, and felt the breeze sweep beneath the closed double doors."

Another gust blew across the floor. The bulb in the bedside lamp dimmed and then went out entirely.

"Are you both done fooling around? If so, it's time for a 'Come to Jilly' moment." She paused, waiting for another sign she wasn't alone. An ornate brass candlestick fell from the mantle.

"Yes, I'm back. Whether you like it or not. I won't be intimidated the way I was in my teens. While I put up with the two of you scaring the crap out of every boyfriend I had in both high school and college, I won't have my choices questioned any longer. I'm a grown woman, and deserve to be treated as such."

The faint sound of a man's laughter echoed through the room.

"Don't start with me, John Jacob Wilder. I didn't

appreciate you chasing off my visitor the other night. He was a perfectly nice man. If the two of you keep this up, I'll die single and alone." She paused, drew another breath, and continued, "Thanks to the provisions in my father's will, I'm now the owner of this ghost-riddled home, at least for a minimum of three years. And, as such, that makes me—Jillian Mallory Barclay—the mistress of the house."

The doors to the widow's walk rattled but didn't open.

"Yeah, yeah, I know it's *your* house; *your* bedroom; *your* little love nest. But— legally—it belongs to me. Your tenth or eleventh removed granddaughter. So, suck it up."

Pushing herself to her feet, she picked up the candlestick and returned it to its rightful place. "And, one other thing that's probably going to get your breeches in a bunch, my father signed an agreement with Harvard University before he died. It allows them to come here to Fairwinds and go through our books, papers, journals, anything and nearly everything, to catalog the history of this property for their museum. As much as I'm not looking forward to some stodgy old professor poking around my home, I am legally obligated to honor the agreement. I would appreciate your cooperation. Unless, of course, he's a pain in my ass, in which case you're free to send him packing."

Chapter 1

Checking the directions in his notes a second time, Nicholas Martin, turned off the feeder highway from Boston on his way through the town of Mystic Point. He'd have much preferred the anonymous voice of his GPS to guide him to the last destination on his list, but—apparently—Fairwinds was so far off the side roads, the route wasn't mapped.

He'd been collecting data for five weeks now, since the end of his second year as an associate professor. So far, he'd not been impressed with the assigned project. However, when one is working toward tenure, you do what's asked of you; go where you're told.

The History of New England's Oldest Homes. Whomever had come up with that title should be soundly thrashed. Or, they should have taken on the task of interviewing little old cat ladies and perusing dust-covered shelves of worthless books on their own.

Nicholas made a mental note to himself: come up with a less boring title for the project. Soon. He'd much rather have spent his summer diving off the coast in search of sunken ships and, supposed, pirate treasure. Now *that* would be a research paper worth writing.

Any time now. How far out of town was this blasted place anyway?

The private road leading to Fairwinds was coming to a dead end a quarter mile in the distance. If he didn't find a driveway soon, he'd end up at the water's edge of Skullery Bay.

Less than a hundred yards from the shoreline, an iron gate appeared out of nowhere. Open, thankfully, it led up a long, winding driveway. Gripping the steering wheel tightly in his hands, he made the left turn and, within twenty feet, came to a sudden stop.

There at the far end of the drive was the most magnificent house he'd seen so far. Two full stories high, with an unusually shaped third floor, the Georgian era mansion commanded attention; respect. An ornate widow's walk sat atop the entire home, circling the structure like a black crown. Lifting his camera from the passenger seat of his SUV, he adjusted the telephoto lens and snapped a half-dozen shots of the house. Then, panning to the right, he took another dozen or so of the grounds and cliff overlooking the ocean.

Off in the distance, at the edge of the property sat two fenced plots of land, the larger one no doubt a family cemetery. The other, a single grave off on its own. His scholar's curiosity was definitely piqued.

Eager to see if the inside of Fairwinds was as stately and intriguing as the outside, he set his camera aside and continued up the drive, parking his car on the curve of the circle drive at the front of the house.

A somewhat beat up, mud spattered four-wheel drive sat off to the side, and he wondered who owned the sporty vehicle. Surely not another octogenarian who doted on their spoiled felines.

Grabbing his briefcase, he made his way to the door and lifted the ornate brass knocker, letting it fall into place.

***

"Dammit all," Jilly groused, setting aside her trowel and thin-edged knife. Glancing at the grandfather clock on the far wall of her studio, she grabbed a rag and wiped the worst of the clay from her hands. As usual, she'd become engrossed in her work and lost track of time. "Coming," she called out as she crossed through the rotunda, and out into the foyer.

Pulling the door open with a hard yank, she raised her head and met the gaze of a young man, his black-rimmed glasses unable to disguise his beautiful sea blue eyes. The rest of him wasn't half bad either—once you got past the rumpled jacket and button-down oxford shirt.

"May I help you?" she asked. Obviously, this wasn't the company she was expecting, but a definite upgrade. Absently, she wondered if one of her artsy-fartsy friends had sent her an Adonis to model for her next project.

And, would he be willing to pose nude?

"I'm Dr. Nicholas Martin," he responded, his deep voice sending a flutter to her pulse. "I have an appointment with Miss Jillian Barclay. If you wouldn't mind letting her know I'm here, I'd appreciate it."

Jilly stepped back and motioned him inside. "I'm—" she began, stopping short when he looked past her and toward the double doors leading to the rotunda.

"No doubt you've got work to get back to," he said, his tone all but dismissing her. "I don't want to take up too much of your time."

Oh, this was perfect. He thought she was the help.

"That's okay, I don't mind." Giving her hands another swipe across the front of her clay-crusted apron, she tilted her head to the right. "If you wouldn't mind waiting in the library." She pushed the door open, and offered, "Feel free to browse while you wait."

"Thank you." He turned, his gaze slowly scanning the

many books before coming back to her. His very nice smile spread in obvious appreciation. "I will definitely have a look around while I'm waiting."

Jilly exited the library and made a dash for the first-floor powder room. The least she could do was wash her face, discard the apron, and comb her hair for such distinguished company.

Distinguished, my ass. You think he's hot–in a geeky sort of way.

Off in the distance, the parlor door slammed with a resounding crash, followed by the dining room door, and then the door leading to the kitchen.

Beneath her breath, she mumbled, "Back off, Jake. At least let the man get comfortable before you drive him away."

***

Nicholas ran his hands across the leather-bound, first edition classics lining the back wall of the Fairwinds library. An outstanding collection. Lifting a gold-leaf trimmed copy of *Gulliver's Travels* from the shelf, he skimmed his fingertips across the raised lettering, admiring the exquisite attention to detail.

This was the type of history he lived for; devoted his entire academic career—as new as it was—toward. All the previous stops on his information gathering tour shifted to the back of his mind.

Fairwinds was the holy grail of this entire project.

He'd read the sketchy research already gathered on the place, the tales of the pirate owner and reports of ghost sightings. Although he questioned a good portion of the writings, he'd reserve judgement until his visit was concluded. Assuming the spinster Barclay wasn't senile, he looked forward to learning all there was to know about the home and its colorful history.

And what was with the housekeeper anyway? With her dirty apron, unkempt red curls flying around her face, and the way she'd slammed the doors on her way to announce his arrival. He was pretty sure she was angered at having her duties interrupted by his presence.

The initial agreement called for him to stay at Fairwinds for a minimum of five days, which included a room and meals. Absently, he wondered if the young woman with the mud-crusted nails was also the cook.

He hoped not.

The door opened and Nicholas turned from the wall where he'd been studying a collection of framed maritime charts, their renderings more detailed than any he'd seen before.

The redhead was back, a tray of tea and cookies balanced on her slender arm.

She'd changed out of her apron and jeans, made a somewhat successful attempt at taming her wild curls, and now wore a pair of casual slacks and pale pink sweater.

"I thought you might like tea, Professor."

He swallowed back the sudden dryness in his throat, her smoky, honey-and-whiskey voice a stark contrast to her clipped conversation earlier.

Was she flirting? Did it matter? Especially, when he couldn't seem to take his eyes off her porcelain complexion and her—

"Is something wrong?" she asked, drawing him from his scattered thoughts.

"No, nothing. When the door opened, I was expecting Miss

Barclay."

She gave him a smile that made his breath catch.

"I owe you an apology," she said. "I should have properly introduced myself earlier. I'm Jillian Barclay."

"You're the spinster Barclay?" He immediately regretted the presumptive words.

"Well, I wouldn't go quite that far," she responded, her warm amber gaze narrowing, a frown rearranging her attractive features. "True, I'm pushing thirty with a vengeance, but I'm not sure I'd classify myself a spinster just yet."

He couldn't hold back his chuckle. "Now it's me who needs to apologize. It's just that the previous five homes I've visited for this project all belonged to never-married, cat-loving women in their later years. I made a thoroughly improper assumption. I'm sorry."

"No harm, no foul, Nick," she said, offering him a forgiving smile. "I can call you Nick, can't I?"

He sucked in breath and shook his head. "No, you can't."

"Professor? Mr. Martin?"

"Nicholas is fine," he confirmed. "But not Nick. I detest that name."

She rolled her huge eyes around for obvious emphasis. "Well, okay then, *Nicholas*."

Once they'd seated themselves in the two wingback chairs closest to the fireplace and she'd poured their tea, he began, "So, Miss Barclay—"

"Jillian, or just Jilly," she corrected.

"Jillian. What can you tell me about Fairwinds?"

She shot him a quizzical look, as if he'd asked a difficult question.

"Nick... ah, Nicholas. I can tell you *everything*. Where

would you like to start?"

Chapter 2

Jillian sank back in the brocade-covered chair and drew her cup of tea to her lips, hopefully hiding her amusement behind the rising steam. Professor Nicholas—but not Nick—Martin's bright blue gaze flared appreciatively when she'd offered to tell him everything there was to know about Fairwinds.

"Would you mind if I recorded our conversation?"

"I suppose it would be okay."

She waited while he took a worn notebook from his jacket pocket and clicked the top of his gold-plated ink pen. Sliding the tips of his fingers across the screen of his cell, he pulled up the voice recorder and hit the *start* button before laying the device on the table between them.

"Day one, Thursday, one-thirty." Nodding in her direction, he asked, "How about we start from the beginning?"

Drawing a deep breath, she told him, "That would be 1737, when Captain John Jacob Wilder won Fairwinds and the hand of his lady love, Lillian Grace Langdon, in a game of chance."

"A game of chance?" he repeated, scribbling frantically in his notebook.

"Yes. There was no love lost between Captain Jake and Everett Langdon, a wealthy merchant and Lily's father. As a matter of fact, Jake and his twin brother Aiden often set sail on Jake's ship, *The Phantom*, with the express intention of raiding one of Mister Langdon's many vessels."

"Fascinating," he mumbled, adding to his notes.

"Jake and Aiden perished on the ship during a violent storm. Aiden left behind a wife, Primrose Gimbly Wilder, and a young daughter named Pearl. No more than a few months after the shipwreck, Lily died of a broken heart."

He made another note and then raised his head to meet her gaze. "In the bits and pieces of history I've read, former residents and employees have said Fairwinds is haunted by the ghosts of Captain Wilder and his wife. As the owner of Fairwinds, how do you deal with these fanciful tales?"

Go ahead, tell him. He won't believe you anyway. Nobody ever does until they witness it for themselves.

"Very carefully, and with a smile," she chose instead.

He gave a quick nod. "No doubt. I'm surprised you're not overrun by tourists or bogus ghost chasers."

"My father had many requests for access by various paranormal investigators over the years. However, neither he nor I intend to make a spectacle of our home. The only reason he agreed to the university's request is because he's an alumna, and he respects the institution's integrity."

"And we appreciate his willingness to participate in the research." Pausing briefly, he added, "My condolences on his passing."

"Thank you."

"What happened to Fairwinds after Lillian Wilder's death? Did her father regain possession?"

"No. The home went to Lily's sister Abigail who hated the house and what it had done to her sister's health in the final months. After burying Lady Lillian in a grave above her beloved cliffs, Abigail closed up the house. She was married to Mister Alister Gibson and they had two children. The older child, a son, wanted nothing to do with Fairwinds, so it fell to the daughter, Prudence. She married a man by the name of William Ellison. Her son, William Jr. took over responsibility for the house, but never really did much with it other than general maintenance. When William, Jr. died, it passed to Prudence's grandson, Phillip."

"It sounds as if there was a long period of time between occupants. A shame for such a magnificent property."

"Phillip Ellison did try to put money and effort into keeping the property up. In a rather weird twist, he hired a caretaker by the name of Cora Bradford who happened to be a descendant of Primrose and Pearl Wilder. The property had renters over the years, but never anyone who stayed very long."

"Chased off by the ghosts, *were they*?"

Rather than respond to his sarcasm, she only lifted her shoulders in a shrug. "After Phillip Ellison's death, the house would have normally passed to his first-born son, Lance—an absolute jackass of man. Fortunately, Lucy Ellison—my third or fourth back grandparent—ended up taking possession of the property and began the many, many renovations that have made Fairwinds into the beautiful home it is now."

"I've read there are tunnels beneath the property. Is that true?"

Rather than answer outright, she suggested, "Why don't we plan a short tour of the property for tomorrow? In the meantime, I've brought out the business ledgers, some personal journals, and other written materials for your review. I have them sorted by century. Perhaps you'd like to get comfortable here in the library and go over them."

"I was enjoying your verbal recounting. However, if you'd rather, I can hit the books—so to speak."

"It's just that I have a job—a commission—that's due to the gallery next week. And, let's just say, my artistic muse is being a bitch at the moment."

"You're an artist?"

"Sculptor, actually. I work mostly in clay. As you saw earlier when you arrived."

His deep chuckle surprised her and sent goosebumps skittering across her arms.

"I thought you were the housekeeper when I first arrived."

"I know."

"I have to admit, after seeing your dirty apron and hands, I was hoping you weren't also the cook."

"Oh, I am definitely the cook. However, I promise to wash my hands before I start the evening meal."

"You don't have a regular staff?" he asked. "For a house as big as Fairwinds?"

"Even after I graduated and moved away, my father kept a cook and a full-time housekeeper on staff, whether he needed them or not. He didn't have the heart to put anyone out of work."

"But you did?"

Purposely, she narrowed her gaze, measuring his expression. Was he being sarcastic? Or, just rude?

"The cook, a wonderful woman in her mid-sixties, retired after working here for over forty years. The housekeeper, who now works part time, chose to cut back on her hours. Now, she comes in twice a week to tidy up. On Saturday mornings, she bakes for the next week."

The look she'd given him, and her tone, obviously registered, and he shot her a sheepish grin. "I'm sorry if my question sounded like an insult. I didn't intend it that way."

"Now that it's just me, I prefer to be on my own. Both of those women hovered over the motherless little girl when I was growing up. That's the last thing I need when I'm trying to work."

"Duly noted. I promise to stay out of your way."

"I didn't mean—"

"*Yes, you did.* Also, I realize the agreement with the university was your father's, and you're just honoring his wishes, but I'll do my best to be as unobtrusive as possible." Glancing toward the stack of books on the desk across the room, he added, "I'm perfectly comfortable with my nose stuck in a book."

"That's good, because I need to get back to my dirty old clay."

He reached for his cell and stopped recording. Then, pushing himself to his feet, he took a step or two toward the desk before turning back. "I did enjoy your recount of Fairwinds' history, so I'd prefer to not read any farther in the journals than where you left off. Then, when you have the time, perhaps you could tell me more."

"Why not? We've got five days. Supper will be at six, if that's okay. I'd planned on making eggplant parmigiana." She paused, gauging his reaction. "By the way, I suppose I should point out, I'm a vegetarian."

The corner of his lips lifted slightly, a half quirk. "I can live with it. For five days anyway."

"If you get to the point where you're craving a big, juicy burger, Molly's Café is a few miles down the road going into Mystic Point."

"I'll keep that in mind." He made a shooing motion with his hand. "Go. Work. I'll immerse myself in this stack of facts and figures about Fairwinds." Glancing back at the far wall, he commented, "Or, perhaps, I'll read *Gulliver's Travels*. Again."

***

Nicholas took a seat behind the rich mahogany desk and pulled the first stack of ledgers across the desk. He'd have much preferred Jillian's storytelling, if for no other reason than the sound of her husky voice was calming and filled with a passion for her family's history.

She certainly cleaned up nice—literally. Her tangle of curls looked as soft as spun silk, the unruly mass held in place by a single clip shaped like an antique cutlass—no doubt in homage to her ancestor, the legendary pirate. Rubbing his fingers together to dispel a sudden tingle, he reached for the first journal marked "Shipping Logs" and opened the cover.

It wouldn't do to be thinking about Jillian Barclay's silken hair when he had far more important things to look into.

Closing the cover on the third journal, this one belonging to William Ellison Sr., Nicholas spared a glance at the mantle clock, surprised to see it was nearly seven.

What happened to supper at six? Obviously, his hostess felt no need to cater to him. Perhaps she was hoping he'd make that drive into town and fend for himself.

He stood and stretched, working out the kinks in his back from sitting for far too long. He'd find the kitchen and see if there were leftovers. Or, if he'd need to drive to Mystic Point for a meal...

When he reached the kitchen, two things became immediately apparent. First, there were no leftovers. And, second, the ingredients for the promised meal were still sitting on the top of the counter.

He hated artists. They were all self-absorbed, scatterbrained, and oblivious to anyone not among their creative circle. This was going to be a long five days.

Would you have preferred the cloyingly attentive octogenarian spinsters and their smelly cats?

Ignoring the taunt of his inner-voice, he searched the cupboards for the necessary pans, bowls, and utensils. Everything set, he reached for the first of two eggplants and began slicing.

Chapter 3

Jilly ran a damp rag across her hands, removing the worst of the clay that clung to her fingers like glue. She'd wash up quickly and get supper started before checking on her unwanted—albeit interesting—guest.

Interesting in what way? Intelligent? Sexy as hell—even with those glasses and habit of biting his lower lip when he's thinking? I suppose you'd like to take a bite yourself? And, since when did nerdy college professors have such broad shoulders?

Mentally shushing her inner voice, she picked up her pace.

The closer she came to the kitchen, the more her nose twitched, the heavenly aroma of roasting tomatoes assaulting her senses. Behind her, the entryway clock chimed eight times.

"Son of a biscuit," she muttered. She'd been so engrossed in her work that she'd completely lost track of time. As usual.

The moment she reached her destination, Jilly drew to a complete and quite sudden stop, nearly losing her balance on the slick tile floor.

"There you are," the professor said, his tone teasing rather than upset. "I was beginning to think I'd need to make that drive to Mystic Point."

"I'm so sorry. I have a show coming up in Boston in less than two weeks, and was engrossed in a new idea for my sculpture. I... I..."

Her words faltered when she suddenly realized there was a sexy man standing in her kitchen, dressed in a gingham apron, stray locks of his light brown hair teasing his forehead, and a smudge of flour coating his cheek.

Clenching her hands into her fists at her sides, she fought the urge to lift her hand and wipe away the trail of white dust.

"I assumed you were engrossed in your work. I get the same way with my research." Offering her a broad smile, he admitted, "Until my stomach starts to rumble."

"Again, I'm sorry." Tilting her head toward the oven, she told him, "That smells fantastic."

"I'm not a cook by any means and, without a recipe, I was flying by the seat of my pants. I assumed the items you had set out on the counter were what I'd need. I hope you don't mind, but I also threw in a sprig of basil from the herbs above the sink."

"No, I don't mind at all."

"Oh, by the way, you might want to have a handyman come in and take a look at the drawer where you keep the utensils."

"Really?"

"No matter how many times I closed it, firmly, it kept sliding open. I must have run into it half a dozen times going back and forth to the sink."

Jilly closed her eyes briefly and drew a breath. *Stop it, Jake. Now.*

"I'll be sure to have it looked after."

"Our eggplant surprise should be ready in another ten minutes. I wasn't sure how to set the timer on your stove, so I've been watching the clock."

"Not eggplant parmigiana, as I'd planned?"

He chuckled, the deep growl of his voice sending a swarm of butterflies rushing her stomach.

"Not the way I cook. With me at the stove, everything is a *surprise*."

She matched his laugh with one of her own. "How about I set out some wine to have with our meal?" When he nodded, she asked, "White or red? That's the beauty of being a veggie-freak, you're not tied to the old adage of red for meat, white for chicken and fish."

"I prefer red," he told her, his attention directed behind her, over her shoulder. "Although, whatever you have handy is fine."

Don't you dare, Jake. It's too soon. She turned, ready to confront the ghost of John Jacob Wilder, only to find nothing—no one—there.

"Red it is, then." Intending to step around him to grab a corkscrew, she found herself overcome with the urge to stop. When she lifted her hand to his cheek, he grabbed her wrist, his eyes widening. "Smudge," she said, embarrassed by her boldness. "Flour... on your cheek."

He nodded and released the light hold he'd taken on her wrist. "Thank you. I thought I'd noticed something in my reflection on the oven door but I wasn't sure."

A bit more slowly than necessary, she lowered her hand. "How about I set the table and decant the wine," she suggested, "while you get our meal out of the oven?"

"Sounds like a solid plan. I'm starving."

She met his gaze, and said softly, "Me, too."

Jilly pushed her plate away and lifted her wine glass in salute. "The meal was delicious."

He grinned and straightened his already impossibly broad shoulders. "Thank you, I was honestly surprised it turned out so well. But, glad that it did."

"So, tell me Nicholas, what other hidden skills do you possess?" The moment the question was out, she wished she could pull it back. Given her inquisitive nature had often been mistaken for flirting, she wasn't yet ready to send the professor running for the hills on her own. That job was usually reserved for Lily and Jake.

Apparently, he took no offense, because he responded without hesitation. "I scuba dive—most often in search of sunken ships off the coast. I play an absolutely atrocious trombone. And, according to my mother, I'm a passable ballroom dancer." He shot her a grin and asked, "How about you? Hidden talents?"

She shot him a broad grin, her imagination easily picturing the professor in a tux and escorting a woman in a flowing gown around the dance floor.

"I obviously can't claim time management as a skill. However, I do crochet, thanks to unwanted lessons from my Grandma Susan, and I play the piano. I have two left feet though, so no dancing."

"You mentioned growing up motherless. Pardon me if I'm being nosey, but I didn't realize your father was a widower."

"Information for your research?"

The slow shake of his head dislodged the already errant lock of hair, sending it to hang rather enticingly across his brow.

"No, just curious."

"He wasn't a widower. My mother was—shall we say—a child of the eighties. Independent, a bit reckless. She tried to settle down, but it didn't take. Not long after I was born, she ran off with a bass guitarist from a post-grunge band. My father waited for her to grow up but, when she didn't, he divorced her."

"That must have been difficult, growing up without a mother's influence."

"I had 'mothers', so to speak. Remember… the housekeeper and the cook."

"Ah, yes, the surrogate smotherers."

"Besides, I'm pretty sure my mother's influence wasn't something I should have welcomed."

"Your father never considered remarrying?"

"No, his medical career became his love, his life. How about you? Brothers, sisters?"

"Yes, to both. One brother and two very annoying sisters."

"I have to say, you're definitely not the stodgy old professor I was expecting. How long have you been teaching?"

"A couple of years. I spent my first two post graduate years as a toady for Professor Collins. He was as impressed as the old goat can get and, when he retired, the position for an associate professor of history came open. Thankfully, he wrote me a very complimentary letter of recommendation."

"Those are some heavy-duty credentials. You must be a real brainiac."

"Hardly. I got into Harvard on a football scholarship, but I fully intended to get an education, a viable degree."

"You were a jock?"

"Don't sound so shocked. Not all jocks are poor students, especially in the Ivy League. We were expected to maintain at least a 3.0 average and no special favors were given when it came to grading. Not even to the star running back."

"Modest, I see."

He let the snarky comment slide, but asked, "So, where did

you go to school?"

"After two very, very boring years at Brown, I convinced my father I wasn't cut out for either the corporate or medical fields, so I switched to the New York College of Art."

"How did he take the about face in your curriculum?"

"He was hesitant. No doubt he was worried I was following in my mother's free spirit footsteps. However, after I won a prestigious competition with one of my earliest pieces, he accepted that I was exactly where I was meant to be."

Jilly pushed herself to her feet and gathered up their dishes.

"I can give you a hand," he suggested. "I load a mean dishwasher."

"Sure. I'll appreciate the company while I straighten up. Housework, like time management, is not one of my strong suits."

"Are you done working for the night?"

"I've got to take a few pictures to email to Sam—the gallery manager—but, otherwise, I'm done."

"May I tag along? Assuming you're not one of those artists who doesn't want to show their work until it's done."

"I'm not. Although, I'd have thought you'd want to spend more time with the Fairwinds papers."

"What I'd like, if it's okay, is to see the widow's walk. I read through the plans and cost estimates in one of the first journals. It sounds as if Captain Wilder was very deliberate in what he wanted done."

"Captain Jake was very deliberate about a lot of things," she said firmly. "However, he could also be a pain in the butt about others."

Her comment drew another laugh from the professor.

"You sound as if you're angry with him for his past transgressions."

Past, present. Same difference.

"Not angry, but I sometimes get very frustrated."

"Well then, I guess it's a good thing he's been dead and gone for nearly three hundred years."

Dead, yes. Gone... not so much.

Chapter 4

Nicholas turned full circle in the huge ballroom, now converted to Jillian's studio, and took in the ornate crystal chandeliers and massive French doors leading to the patio.

"This room must have been magnificent in its day," he commented. "If I close my eyes, I can picture the fancy balls, the women in their elegant gowns, the men in their silk breeches and waistcoats."

"You really are a history geek, aren't you?"

He opened his eyes slowly, his gaze meshing with hers. "You bet. Grade A, certified, history nerd."

"I'm pretty sure the last time this ballroom was put into service was for my high school graduation party. My dad pulled out all the stops. Catered teen-friendly food, a local, but talented, rock band, and a mock casino with some very generous prizes for the winners."

"It's a shame it's not been used since then. At least not for what it was intended."

She gave a soft chuckle, drawing his attention to her full lips.

"I'm pretty sure he always intended to throw a lavish wedding reception here someday as well. Much to his dismay, the opportunity never presented itself."

"No serious relationships?"

"His? Or, mine?"

"Yours," he said honestly, suddenly wanting to know more about Jillian than he'd intended.

She gave him a rather quizzical look, as if he'd crossed a line with his question. Just when he thought she wouldn't answer, she admitted, "A couple of possibilities, but they fizzled out before getting to the proposal stage."

He pulled in a breath, and redirected the conversation. "Can I see the work-in-progress?"

"As long as you're not moonlighting as an art critic, I guess it would be okay." Pulling back the plastic wrapping, she waved her hand. "Meet Stanley. My interpretation of a modern-day chimney sweep."

"He doesn't look like a 'Stanley.'" Circling the huge lump of clay, he suggested, "He looks more like a Charles. A distinguished sweep, no doubt."

"Perhaps. We'll see when he's finished."

Nodding toward a taller piece, the entire sculpture covered in layers of plastic, he asked, "What's this? May I see?"

She gave a shake of her head, her red curls flying across her shoulders, the loose tendrils teasing her lightly flushed cheeks.

"It's nothing important, just something I've been working on a bit at a time for the past four or five months."

Without warning, the patio door blew open.

"That must have been some gust of wind," he said, making his way forward to shut the door.

"It happens sometimes. Usually when it's *most unwelcome*."

"How about you get those pictures and then, perhaps, you could give me an inside tour? Assuming you don't mind, of course."

"Sure, why not? After all, it is *my home* to show, isn't it?"

He wasn't quite sure why she felt the need to put emphasis

on her wording, but he found her enthusiasm most interesting—in a quirky, artistic sort of way.

Once she'd taken a few pictures from different angles, he waited while she washed her tools and straightened up for the night. After locking the patio doors, she motioned toward the door that led into the rotunda and connected the downstairs rooms.

"You've seen the library already. The formal parlor is over here."

He stepped through the doorway, close on her heels, immediately drawn to the warmly decorated room. A fireplace with an intricately carved mantle took up at least half of the far wall, at the side there was an antique poker and shovel set.

Brocade covered settees, tall wingback chairs, and ornate rocking chairs were scattered around the room. Warm mahogany side tables with tiffany lamps and assorted glassware sat in corners, beside the chairs, and against walls.

Original landscapes hung on the walls. The room was a showcase of eighteenth and early nineteenth century history.

A true find for anyone who treasured either history or antiques.

"I take it this room isn't used very often either," he said, the thought drawing his frown.

"Only when we entertained. So, not in some time, for sure. My father used to love to sit in front of the fireplace and have evening tea. It was—what he called—his recovery time from his busy medical practice."

Sparing one last glance around the room, he asked, "Shall we move on?"

Jillian made her way toward the back of the house. Twin staircases rose up in half-circles toward the second floor. In the middle was a set of double doors that led back into a glass enclosed rotunda.

Skirting the doors, Jillian continued the tour. "There's an open seating area here. I imagine it was used for overflow during balls and large dinner parties. I know we haven't gotten to this part of Fairwinds history yet, but I can tell you this wall leading into the dining room required extensive repairs after a very dramatic shootout between the FBI and one of the residents in the mid-1920s."

"Now, there's a story I'm looking forward to hearing—in great detail."

Leading him forward, she explained, "This is—obviously—the dining room."

His chuckle drew her smile. "Yes, I remember."

"The butler's pantry is through there," she said, nodding to her left. "Finally, we're back in the kitchen—where all your culinary expertise was on full and welcome display."

She exited back through the dining room, returning to the main foyer. He willingly followed on her heels.

"Is that it for the first floor?"

"Other than a closer look at the rotunda." Opening the French doors, she stepped across the threshold. "The rotunda has been a favorite of many of Fairwinds' residents, myself included. On any given night, you can stand here and gaze at the stars through the dome ceiling and feel as if you're standing in the middle of the open sky."

He glanced down at the mosaic tile flooring. "This compass rose inlay is beautifully preserved."

"Yes, it's definitely one of the more cared-after parts of the house. I've read it was one of Lady Lillian's favorites."

"No doubt. It's exquisite."

She shot him a look of surprise. "Yes, it is."

"You know, history isn't just significant dates and places. It's also about changes in the surroundings, architecture, and habits."

The nod of her head tossed her curls across her shoulders, and he found himself fighting back the sudden urge to reach out and gather the loose strands in his fingers.

"Perhaps I just took the wrong history requirements in college. My classes were all boring wars and politics."

"Or, you didn't have the right teacher."

His breath caught when she darted her tongue out to sweep across her bottom lip.

"Perhaps you're right about that... Professor."

"How about we finish the tour?" he suggested, needing a diversion from her wide-eyed stare and freshly dampened lips.

"Right this way."

He followed her out of the rotunda and up the stairs, his gaze immediately drawn to the sway of her hips. Swallowing back the dryness in his throat, he blinked to dispel the arousing image. Unfortunately, it wouldn't leave.

From somewhere behind them, a door slammed.

Jillian turned on the stairs and glanced toward the sound. "Draft. It happens from time to time."

"For such a well-constructed home, Fairwinds has quite a few drafts."

"Or a *pest problem*, perhaps."

There it was again, her emphasis on certain words—almost as if she were having a private conversation with someone other than him. His lips twitched with the urge to ask if there were 'pests' big enough to slam doors. Instead, he opted for a compliment. "The double staircase suits the house perfectly.

Grand, sweeping."

"It used to drive my father crazy, especially when he was trying to catch me to braid my hair for school and I was running away." Once they'd reached the second floor, she waved her hand toward the end of the hall. "The master suite is there. That's where you'll sleep. My father had an ensuite installed about ten years ago, so you'll have privacy."

"You don't use the master suite?"

"No, I'm at the opposite end. It's the bedroom I grew up in, and I've no reason to change. There are two other bedrooms and a bathroom on this floor as well."

"And those stairs?" he said, nodding to the end of the hall closest to the master bedroom.

"They lead to the third floor. We don't use the third floor, other than to reach the roof for chimney cleaning and repairs."

"And access to the widow's walk, I presume."

"Yes. We can go up there before you leave, if you'd like."

"I'd love to see it after dark, as well, if possible. I'd imagine, on a clear night, the stars would be extraordinary."

"Maybe tomorrow, after our tour of the grounds, we can get a look at the cliffs during the day. As for a night-time viewing, there's a new moon on Monday, so no interference for your stargazing. I'm pretty sure we have an antique telescope around here somewhere. We could take it with us."

"I'd intended to head back to Boston late Saturday, and then return Monday morning, so that should work out perfectly. Assuming everything remains on schedule, I'll be out of your hair by Tuesday afternoon."

"Perfect."

He wasn't sure why, but it irked him that she was so agreeable to his leaving.

Chapter 5

Jillian waited in the hallway until Nicholas went into his room and shut the door. Then, closing herself inside her own bedroom, she slipped the lock into place and collapsed on her bed.

Footsteps sounded above her head. Not the usual stomping of a petulant ghost but, rather, the more considerate footfalls of a spirit who had no immediate reason to act out. Or, perhaps, the Captain had grown weary of the waiting for another storm, another chance to be with Lily.

The late spring and early summer had been unusually dry and sunny, the last nor'easter in late April. No doubt, Jake and Lily were getting restless.

Jilly had actually welcomed the reprieve. The storms, and the activity they brought, always made her anxious. Knowing what was going on in the third-floor retreat only added to her own sexual frustration, making her as on edge as Fairwinds' ghostly lovers.

If they could just get through the next few days without incident, then her own frustration be damned. She'd welcome a string of heavy storms, if only to appease the spirits who both exasperated her—and enthralled her—with their devotion toward one another.

She was up early the next morning thanks to a quiet and uneventful night. Dressed in her usual uniform of yoga pants and T-shirt, she made her way out into the hallway.

Even as early as she was, it was apparent the professor was also awake, the door to the master bedroom open. She ventured farther down the hall.

Calling out from the doorway, she asked, "Anyone in here?"

When no one answered, she peeked inside. The bed had been made, the professor's duffle sat on the nearby chair, his expensive camera on top of the dresser.

The smell of freshly brewed coffee drew her from the foot of the staircase toward the kitchen.

"Good morning, Jillian."

Nicholas stood there behind her kitchen counter, a cup of coffee cradled in his hands, drawing her gaze to his long fingers and well-kept nails. Self-consciously, she tucked her own work-weary hands behind her back.

When this latest sculpture was complete, she fully intended to treat herself to a manicure. Not that it would last any longer than her next moment of inspiration.

"Good morning, Nicholas." A smirk escaped, drawing his frown. "Why the aversion to being called Nick? Is it a real hatred for the name, or just an attempt at being an Ivy League professional?"

His shoulders lifted and fell on a shrug. Beneath the open-collar shirt he wore, she could see tanned skin, the tease of light hair on his chest. Her throat tightened around a sudden knot of awareness.

"Let's just say, there were far too many versions of 'Nick' floating around campus and the fraternity house that I'd just as soon forget."

His comment drew her outright grin. "How about 'Nicky' then?"

This time his blue gaze flared, the corner of his full lips lifting in a half-smile. "Only if you have a desire to sound like my mother."

"Well, then, Nicholas it is."

"I was going to take my coffee into the library and hit the books again. I assume you'd like to work for a while before the promised tour."

"No breakfast? I was going to make chopped veggies and vegan cream cheese on croissants."

"I had a glass of juice. I'm fine until lunch."

"Suit yourself. Personally, I work better on a full stomach."

Another of his warm chuckles filled the space between them. "I don't picture a veggie sandwich filling anyone's stomach."

"You're probably right. But at least it's something. How about I come and get you in an hour or so for the tour."

"Really? I've no doubt, you'll start working and forget all about me. I'll come and get you instead."

While he was probably right about her getting engrossed in her work, it was highly unlikely she'd forget all about Nicholas Martin any time soon.

***

Nicholas let himself into the library and made a beeline for the desk, eager to get back to the final set of navigational charts hand drawn sometime in the early eighteenth century. Could it have been Captain Wilder who'd drawn them? Or, perhaps, one of his men?

He took a sip of his coffee and set the cup on a nearby table, close enough to reach, but nowhere near the valuable papers. Time to get to work and unravel all the history behind Fairwinds and its legends of pirates, questionable inhabitants.

And… dare he say it… ghosts?

"If you're here, ghosts of Fairwinds," he joked, his gaze scanning the room. "Show yourself."

"What are you doing?"

The sound of Jillian's voice coming from the open doorway nearly gave him a heart attack.

"I… uh…"

"You were summoning the ghosts of Fairwinds?"

His breath came out in a sigh of relief. "Just joking around. I thought maybe I could conjure up some of the legendary spirits I've read about." He paused, taking in her obvious displeasure. "I didn't mean to be offensive. I'm sure you're very protective of Fairwinds' history."

Her shoulders lifted and fell on a sigh, and he wondered how many times others had made jokes at the expense of her home and it's supposed inhabitants. He was about to extend a further apology, when she met his gaze and smiled. A silent show of forgiveness, perhaps?

"I just realized, the supplies I need for the next step in my project haven't yet arrived. I thought we'd do the tour now, before you get too far into the ledgers. With any luck, the package I'm waiting for will be here by the time we get back."

He pushed away from the desk and came around to meet her. "Gladly. Where do we start?"

"Drop your coffee cup off in the kitchen and we'll begin."

"May I grab my camera from the bedroom?"

"Yes, as long as we have an agreement that you won't publish any picture you take without me seeing it first and giving written permission."

"Agreed. And, I might add, very smart on your part."

"Thank you."

"I may be a history nerd, but I also believe we should honor the wishes of those who share the historical information. Especially when privacy is an issue."

Once he'd retrieved his camera from the guestroom, Jillian led the way across the foyer until they stood at the double doors leading to the rotunda. "I couldn't agree more about the privacy. As an example, what I'm about to show you is a secret that's been kept between the occupants of the house since the 1920s."

Stopping in front of an antique brocade settee, she gave the heavy piece of furniture a nudge to the side until she'd uncovered a small brass keyhole. When she pressed the flat of her hand against the wall, an invisible door slid to the side.

"Damn! A hidden passageway." He stopped for a moment and turned full circle in the room, in an effort to get a sense of the construction that must have gone into the structure to hide such a gem in plain sight.

Once she'd stepped into the dark void, he followed quickly behind.

"Here, take this," she ordered, handing him one of the high-powered flashlights that hung just inside the entryway. "There's no electricity down here any longer. There was one room at the base of the stairs wired for light and security, but the wiring has since been removed."

"Back to basics, so to speak?"

"It was my great-grandmother Mallory's wish to get back to the original design of the tunnels, and away from her father's bootlegging and other crimes."

"You mentioned last night about the brother of one of the inhabitants being… uh… a…"

She came to an abrupt halt, nearly causing him to run into

her from behind. Despite the darkness surrounding them, he could picture her expression, the firm set of her full lips.

"Jackass. I called him a jackass."

"How so? What was so bad about him?"

"He was evil. He hated his younger sister. He dealt with criminal types from New York. His business partner—and only friend—was a snake who tried to claim Lucy for his bride. Thankfully, that fell through. Literally."

"He backed out?"

"Yes, all the way off the cliffs in the middle of their wedding."

"Details. Please."

Rather than respond to his request, she led them through another door and into the main corridor of the tunnels. "This is the first section of what little remains open." Motioning to her right, she told him, "The storage rooms through there are closed off with barricades."

"How many entry hatches are there?"

"Two. One in the stables, and one in what used to be the groundskeeper's cottage. Both trap doors are still viable, but I rarely go into the tunnels, so I have no reason to use them."

"Aren't you afraid someone will use the hatches to gain access to the house?"

"I'm doubtful anyone, other than a very few trusted employees—and now you—even know of their existence. You aren't planning to sneak into Fairwinds in the dead of night, are you, Professor?"

He shot her another grin. "I hadn't planned on it."

Once they reached the first turn-off to the left, she gave a nod and told him, "The stable access is about fifty feet farther down this way. We'll get to the stables when we do the above ground tour."

They continued through the narrow tunnel, the occasional breeze wafting in around them, despite the confined space. The smell of saltwater permeated the entire tunnel, adding to the ominous feel. Off in the distance, a light flickered, and he wondered if someone had left a dying flashlight or lantern hanging on one of the wall pegs.

They'd gone another thirty or so yards, when she motioned toward a passageway to the right.

"What's down in this direction?"

"The only room that's not been opened in over three hundred years."

He couldn't stifle his curiosity and took a step into the corridor. "Why not?"

"A couple of reasons, I suppose. First off, it's locked and for the longest time nobody knew where the key was. Yet, there's a peephole, so you can look inside."

"Can we?"

"Sure, why not? There's nothing much to see but cobwebs but have at it."

He ventured forward until he came to a heavy wooden door, soundly secured with an iron lock. "This lock is definitely late seventeenth, early eighteenth century."

"How can you be so sure?"

"I've spent the past four summers diving for sunken ships, treasure. I've scavenged my fair share of artifacts for the university's collection. You can tell by the ironwork, especially around the keyhole."

"That would definitely match the notations in some of the earlier journals from the Langdon family. Pre-Captain Wilder."

He had to force the sliding window open but, with a bit of elbow grease, it finally gave way. Shining the flashlight into the dark room, he waved the beam from side-to-side. "Are those shackles anchored into the walls?"

Her long sigh had him turning to face her.

"Yes, they are. Fortunately, for my peace of mind and that of my ancestors, they were never put to use by our family. However, Lady Lillian's grandfather was known to keep both slaves and people who wronged him in business against their will. We assume this is where they were kept."

"Why wouldn't someone from the past have removed the lock and emptied the room?"

"My father had a theory. Despite the many renovations, the tunnel closings and openings, this room was kept intact as a reminder of the atrocities of the past. While they're not sins of my family's past, they are part of Fairwinds' history."

He raised his camera but waited for her permission. "May I?"

"The lock, the window, but no more than two shots of the interior."

Nicholas nodded, and took the four pictures before lowering the camera to his side.

"Was the key ever found?"

"Yes, by my third-back grandparents, Lucy and Nathaniel Bradford. Then, it disappeared again until the early twentieth century, when my great-grandma Mallory found it."

"Where?"

Shaking her head, she dislodged a few of the curls she'd tucked behind her ear, the disarray sending a distinct skip to his heartbeat.

"That's a story for when you reach the 1920s in your

reading."

"Fair enough. I'm a patient—or, at least semi-patient—man."

She shot him a coy smile that ratcheted up his heart rate another notch.

"Good to know, Professor. Patience is a definite virtue in any man. Or woman."

Chapter 6

Jillian led the way closer to the locked gates that closed off the oceanfront caves. She really needed to watch what she said, even in jest, to the professor. Her off-hand comment about patience had sent a very intriguing flush to his cheeks, and darkened his usually light gaze.

It wouldn't do to form any type of attachment, friendship or otherwise, to a man who'd be gone in four more days. Assuming the Captain didn't send him running for the city sooner.

"The corridor leading to the second hatch is to the right. Also, what's fondly been dubbed the 'captain's room'. According to journals from the early 1800s, it was the room where Captain Jake kept his most valuable treasure."

"No doubt quickly accessible by the hatch, but not so close to the house that it could be easily reached."

His comment drew her smile. *Nicholas Martin would have made a great pirate. He was smart, handsome, and as sexy as her dashing ancestor, Captain Jake.*

"You said you've been diving for relics. Have you found anything valuable?"

"A few nice pieces. Some gold doubloons, a sextant from a ship believed to belong to a mid-1700's merchant. Pieces of a shattered cannon. One nearly complete gangplank. They're all on display in the history wing at the university. If you're in Boston sometime after the semester starts, I'd be happy to show you around."

"So, the university finances your dives?"

He hesitated, but then confirmed. "Nine times out ten, yes. Occasionally, I pay my own way."

"Have you ever found anything valuable while diving on your own dime?"

His shrug amped up her curiosity.

"Maybe. Although, without the university's corroboration, it would be hard to put a value on any of the random pieces."

"I scuba off the coastline here, occasionally venturing into the caverns beyond Fairwinds, but I've never considered cave or deep-sea diving. It must be exciting."

"Exciting and dangerous." He paused, then suggested. "Perhaps when I come back on Monday, I'll bring my scuba gear with me. We could go for a dive. You can show me the caverns."

"That would be great. Assuming I've finished my project." Starting off toward the far end of the tunnel, she added, "Speaking of which, we should get a move on, so I can get back to work, and you can get back to your reading."

***

Nicholas' heart beat faster with every piece of history Jillian willingly shared. He'd been so caught up in her vivid descriptions, he'd nearly forgotten to engage the recorder on his phone. Not that he was about to forget anything he'd seen.

"Why don't we exit back through the door in the stables?" she suggested. "Then we can take in some of the grounds before we reach the house."

"Would it bother you if I asked to go to the cliffs to see the family cemetery?"

"Perhaps later in the day, if you don't mind. I've really got to get back to work."

"I could go alone, if that's okay."

She shrugged, the motion knocking loose the clip she'd used to secure her hair at her nape. The red curls fell free of the confining adornment, dusted her shoulders, and sent a sudden rush of arousal to his most predictable places.

He drew a breath to slow the sudden racing of his pulse. He couldn't afford to be attracted to Jillian Barclay—no matter how much he longed to be. She'd been hesitant enough about honoring her father's agreement. No doubt, she'd be happy to be rid of him.

'*Perfect*'—wasn't that what she'd said when he claimed he'd be gone by Tuesday evening?

"To be honest, I haven't been as attentive to the family plots as I should have been. The gardener only comes once every two weeks, so I try to check on them in between. I'm not sure what state they're in."

"Don't worry. I won't take any pictures that would compromise their true beauty."

She raised her head and met his gaze, her expression filled with worry. "Okay. Just… please… don't go past the iron fencing along the edge of the cliff."

He thought briefly of the lore surrounding the deaths on Fairwinds' property, and realized she needed reassurance. "I won't. I promise."

Once they'd exited the tunnels, Jillian took him on a brief tour of the expansive rose arbor. "This was a favorite spot of my grandmother's and, from what I've been told, also *all* my female ancestors."

"I can understand why," he told her honestly. "There are some very unusual roses among the standard American Beauties."

"Imported from all over the world, at least throughout the past century." She paused, offering him a smile as beautiful as any of the roses. "Personally, the only thing I know about roses is they smell nice and the thorns hurt like a bitch if you stick yourself."

His chuckle drew another of her coveted smiles. "That they do, Jillian. That they do."

They parted ways at the edge of the vegetable garden. While Jillian turned toward her studio, he started off in the direction of the cemetery.

Her warning about the cliffs had been expected. According to everything he'd read so far, both before arriving at Fairwinds, and throughout the first day, there were at least a half dozen or more documented deaths in falls from the cliffs. The victims ranged from hired staff to members of the family, including Jillian's fourth-back grandmother, Helene Bradford McGuire.

He stopped at the single grave, the headstone reading simply, *'Lillian Grace—Wife of a Pirate'*. After gathering up a few stray scraps of fallen leaves, he moved on to the larger, family graveyard. Seven plots were spaced out across the grounds, Jillian's father the latest addition to the site.

Twigs, a few stray pieces of paper, and some browned foliage littered the grounds around the headstones. As he'd done at Lady Lillian's grave, he gathered the refuse and stuffed everything in the outside pocket of his camera case. Then, choosing his shots carefully, he documented each burial spot for his research.

A sudden wind came up, blowing off the water. The ground vibrated beneath his feet, as if something were moving below the earth itself.

A shiver ran up his back. Shaking off the strange feeling, he bowed his head, paid his silent respects to the dead, and started toward the patio doors. He'd let Jillian know he was back, and then return to the library to continue his review of the inventory lists from Captain John Jacob Wilder's ship, *The Phantom*.

He was about to reach for the handle of the French doors leading from the patio to Jillian's workshop, when he heard her raised voice, admonishing someone for their carelessness. He realized he shouldn't eavesdrop, but her next words caused his breath to catch.

"Dammit, Jake. Stop pounding through the tunnels like a spoiled child. I heard you down there while we were in the stables. Thankfully, our guest didn't seem to notice your childish rattling of the gate chains."

No response came to her scolding. Not that he expected one.

"I know you're here as well, M'Lady. I saw your shadow hovering over your tombstone while we were in the arbor. If the professor would have turned around, no doubt he'd have seen you too."

Nicholas backed away, retreating from the patio to circle the house and enter through the front door. *Was she really talking to the spirits of Jake and Lily Wilder?* Jillian wasn't just an eccentric artist, but possibly off her pretty little rocker too.

Perhaps a review of the supposed ghost sightings deserved a second glance and not just an automatic dismissal. Surely, they couldn't all have been certifiable loons.

Or, could they?

***

Jillian put the finishing touches on her newly named sculpture. *Charles* definitely fit her modern-day chimney sweep. As usual, she'd worked through lunch and had gratefully accepted the salad and iced tea Nicholas had delivered to the workshop. Glancing at the clock on the far wall, she was happy to see she'd finished in plenty of time to clean up and make a decent evening meal.

Knocking first, she pushed the library door open and poked her head inside. "Dinner is at six. It's already on the stove."

He looked up from his work, removed his glasses and pinched the bridge of his nose, as if warding off a headache. "Do you have time to talk? Or, are you needed in the kitchen?"

"I've got a few minutes. Did you have a question?"

"After my trip to the cliffs, I decided to review the records of those who'd died here at Fairwinds. I found some very interesting accounts."

She took a seat opposite the desk, and said simply, "It's a slippery slope of truth and myth."

"From what I've read, it seems like a lot of myths. The stories are sketchy between the time of Lillian Wilder's death up until the early 1800s. The relatives you mentioned the other day." He paused and referred to his notes. "Lucy Ellison, who later became a Bradford. You said she was supposed to marry one of her brother's business associates. Edmund Grimes, right?"

"Yes. During the ceremony out on the cliffs, he was startled by what they suspected was the loud caw of a seagull. He lost his balance and fell over the cliff."

"Grimes' sister, who was later committed to a sanitarium, claimed it was Lady Lillian's ghost."

"I don't know what to say. After all, she was committed. That should explain it, shouldn't it."

"What happened to Lucy's brother? The... uh... jackass?"

"Rumor had it, he was killed by his rather unsavory business associates. However, no proof was ever found. Of course, neither was he."

"The accidents seem to stop until 1922 when Helene Bradford McGuire fell to her death. The police thought her husband murdered her to get control of Fairwinds for his bootlegging business."

"Yes, but it turned out it was one of his employees who'd argued with Helene."

"And, less than two months later, the actual murderer also fell off the cliffs. The eventual report on his death was classified by the FBI, by the same agent who ended up marrying Mallory McGuire."

"Yes, my great-grandpa, Simon Barclay."

"Then, the deaths stopped again until the mid-1950s when two men who tried to breach the caves along the shoreline were found drowned on the beach. Their boat was moored safely, so no chance they'd capsized. The investigation was inconclusive, but it appeared they'd actually made it into the mouth of the caves before their bodies washed out with the tide."

"Those gates leading into the cave and tunnels have been locked since the late-twenties, so I'm pretty sure the report was incorrect."

"But—"

She held up her hand, interrupting his next question. Pushing herself to her feet, she told him, "I do have to get back to the kitchen. Maybe we can talk about this later?"

His quick nod sent her scurrying for the door, her escape halted when Nicholas spoke again.

"Jillian, may I ask you a question?"

"If I said 'no', would you still ask?"

"Yes, probably," he responded, a half-smile lighting his handsome face.

"Then, go ahead and ask."

"Do you believe the ghosts of Captain John Jacob Wilder and Lady Lillian haunt Fairwinds?"

She closed her hand around the doorknob and hesitated before she met his gaze again. Drawing a deep breath, she told him, "I don't 'believe', Professor. I *know* they're here." Glancing around the room, she added, "No doubt, Jake's got his sights on you as we speak."

Chapter 7

Well, that went better than she'd expected. He hadn't packed up his briefcase and hightailed it away from Fairwinds. Plus, he hadn't called for the doctor and straitjacket, at least not yet.

"What smells so good?"

Jillian lifted her head and met Nicholas' gaze across the kitchen island. His eyes sparkled beneath the lens of his glasses. His smile, while not broad, hitched up the corners of his thoroughly kissable lips.

Her own lips tingled at the possibility of sharing a kiss with the professor.

"Mushroom risotto. One of my personal favorites."

His smile spread. "I like risotto. I haven't had any success making it though."

"There's also a cucumber and tomato salad, and some of Vera's homemade rolls."

"Do you ever eat meat or chicken?"

"No, at least not for the past couple of years. I occasionally have fresh seafood, in the spring when it's at its most irresistible."

"There's nothing like a New England clam bake."

He gathered the plates she'd set out on the counter and carried them to the small table in the corner of the kitchen, rather than the formal dining room.

"Thank you."

"You're welcome. I'm curious, what led you to a vegetarian

lifestyle? Personally, I can't imagine I'd ever give up a good T-bone steak."

"Stone Parker."

"Stone?"

"He's an on-again, off-again friend. Mostly off. He runs a health and wellness yoga studio in Boston."

"So, a modern-day hippie."

"Sort of. The 'my body is a temple' type."

"And, was it?" His gaze narrowed in on her mouth, increasing the tingle.

"Was it what?"

"Was his body a 'stone' temple?"

She couldn't stifle her outright snicker. "Only in his own mind."

The timer dinged on the stove, giving her an excuse to turn away from his close perusal of her face. The flush of her cheeks had nothing to do with the warmth of the steam when she lifted the lid from the stock pot to stir their meal.

"Is it ready?"

"I think so. At least it's creamy enough and the liquid is all absorbed, so that's a good sign."

She met him at the table with a full serving bowl, happy to see he'd already poured the wine. Something told her she was going to need at least a small amount of liquid fortification to get through their tour of the widow's walk.

Once they'd finished their meal and loaded the dishwasher, Jillian realized she couldn't put off the inevitable any longer.

"Are you ready for your tour of the third floor?"

"Yes, definitely. Lead the way."

They made the climb up the main staircase, followed by the narrow set of stairs that took them to the top floor and, eventually, the roof and widow's walk.

Nodding to her left, she told him, "This room was built by Jake as a nursery for their planned children. Unfortunately, it never happened for them. The room was discovered in eighteen thirty-seven, plastered over and the window blocked with bricks."

"I see it's been reopened," he said, peeking inside the neatly kept room.

"Lucy and Nate had it cleaned up and the furnishings repaired. I don't know if it was ever used for their children, but rather kept as it was in Lily and Jake's honor. I know my nursery was on the second floor, the room next to the master. At least until I moved to the end room when I was ten."

"It must have been exciting growing up in a home with so much history behind it?"

"Sometimes," she admitted. "Other times, it became a pain. Especially when so-called friends were more interested in seeing a ghost than actually being a friend."

His gaze narrowed, as if he were reading between the lines of her statement.

"I take it that it happened on more than one occasion."

"Many more." Shrugging, she added, "I got used to it after a while. At some point, I just stopped inviting people over except on occasions like graduation."

When she pushed the door open leading to the bedroom, she stepped back and let the professor enter first.

"So, this is the infamous bedroom belonging to a pirate and his lady."

"Yes, it is. We keep it cleaned, the floors are tended, but

nobody sleeps here."

"Ever?"

"Never. It's their room."

"Oh, right. You're a believer."

She tucked her lower lip in between her teeth and nodded. "Yes, I am. You would be too, if you'd seen what I've seen."

"Right now, what I'd like to see is the widow's walk."

They'd just reached the French doors, when the door to the bedroom slammed shut. The candlestick—Jake's favorite toy—hit the floor.

"This way," she said, pushing the double doors open wide. When Nicholas swept his gaze over the room behind them, she assured him, "Don't worry, Professor, he can't follow us outside."

***

Nicholas wasn't sure what the hell was going on, but he doubted it was spirits of any kind. He stepped across the threshold and out onto the roof, his attention immediately drawn to the peak of the roof where a brass weathervane in the shape of a pirate ship at full sail stood proudly on display.

"The weathervane is beautiful," he commented. "And so well preserved."

"A gift from Lily to Jake. It's said she had it made by a local craftsman who also made sextants and other brass objects often found on the ships in the area. If we could get closer, you'd be able to see the man's initials etched into the keel, along with Jake's personal monogram."

"His personal monogram?"

Jilly nodded. "J.J.W. and *The Phantom*. He demanded it be placed on everything used on the ship. Some thought it was a form of conceit on his part. Others believed it was his way of marking his hard-earned success. If anyone were to ever board them, they'd know exactly who they were dealing with, and—if they were smart—they'd turn tail and run."

They made a circle of the roof, stopping every so often for him to take a picture of the bay, and the grounds surrounding the house. "This is quite the view." Peering over the side of the roof, he added, "And, a long way down."

"A fact my great-grandma discovered, nearly with disastrous results."

"How so?"

"She had a habit of escaping her father's tight rein. Once she attempted to leave by climbing down the ivy vines and trellis. About ten feet above the ground, she lost her hold and fell."

"What happened?"

"Simon caught her. According to what's been written in the journals, that was when she—literally—'fell' in love with him."

Despite the warm night, a strong breeze blew across the roof, sending a chill down Nicholas' back. He glanced toward the nearby trees, their branches and leaves unmoving.

"Did you feel that?"

"We should probably go back inside," she suggested. "It's getting late, and you said you wanted to spend another hour or so on the journals."

When he stepped forward, so did she, and they collided. Automatically, he raised his hand to her waist to steady them.

"Sorry," he said. His attention fell to her mouth, her lips parted on a gasp of surprise. The thought of kissing her, of sweeping her mouth with his tongue, was almost too much to resist.

"I... uh... we..."

He lowered his head and pressed his lips to hers.

When she darted her tongue out to wet her lower lip, he drew her close to his chest and deepened the kiss. She tasted perfect, a hint of the cabernet they'd shared over dinner clinging to her mouth.

Grasping his upper arms in her hands, she sank her fingers into the bare skin beneath the short sleeve shirt he wore.

"Jilly," he whispered against her mouth. "Forgive me—"

Inching forward, she told him, "Shut up, Nick, and kiss me."

Perhaps it was the intoxication of her kisses, or the desire he could feel pulsing through his entire body, but he'd not even minded her calling him 'Nick'. Right now, all he wanted was another kiss. And then maybe a few more after that.

Off in the distance, heat lightning streaked across the sky.

Jillian pressed her hands flat against his chest, her short fingernails flexing against his muscles, before she stepped back and put a safe distance between them.

"We should get back inside," she repeated softly.

"It's only heat lightning, not a storm."

"Yes, unfortunately."

When she started toward the door, he followed in her wake. "Unfortunately?"

"Lightning, but no real storm, can get very, very frustrating and cause emotions to flare."

Once she'd secured the French doors, she stooped to pick up the fallen candlestick. Rather than set it back on the mantle, she laid it down on the nearby chair.

"Jillian, about what just happened—"

She held up her hand. "It's this place, this room, nothing more. How about we get back to your research? I think we were about to close in on the Roaring Twenties."

"Sure, why not?" Drawing a breath to calm the desire raging through his body, he admitted, "A good dose of gangsters and bootlegged whiskey is exactly what I need at the moment."

***

Jillian felt horrible about pushing Nick away, especially given how badly she wanted him for more than a few—albeit perfect—kisses. However, knowing how the humid night was going to affect the Captain's already foul mood, she needed to get Nick as far away from the third floor as possible.

Perhaps, she'd even turn on some music to detract from what was sure to be a major temper tantrum from both Jake and Lady Lillian.

Once they were back in the relative safety of the library, she took a seat across from the desk and asked, "So, where were we?"

Nick raised his head and met her gaze, his narrowing and falling to the top of the desk.

"It's getting late. I've got another half a journal to read before I actually make it to the early 1900s. If you don't mind, maybe we can put off our discussion until tomorrow, before I leave for the weekend."

"If that's what you want," she agreed half-heartedly. "I'll get out of your way then."

He gave a short nod. "Thanks, I'd appreciate it."

The moment she'd shut the library door between them, Jillian sank back against the foyer wall and let out a long sigh.

Apparently, Captain Jake didn't have a monopoly on fits of

frustration.

Chapter 8

Nick rolled over in the bed and punched the pillow into submission. Sleep was not going to come easily, especially given his pent-up sexual frustration.

Damn her, and this weird house. Not for the first time, he found himself wishing Jillian Barclay had been a spinster with an armload of cats. Or, even one of the brief relationships he'd indulged in over the past few years.

Something simple, quickly dismissed. Somehow, he doubted Jilly would be so easily forgotten.

The wind off the bay must have picked up, not that you could tell from his room on the far side of the house. The sound of rattling glass was getting louder, as if someone were shaking the crap out of the French doors on the third floor.

Combined with the sound of heavy footsteps pacing the length of the hallway above his head, he was on the verge of buying into the idea that Fairwinds was, well and truly, haunted.

The noises only seemed to add to his frustration. You'd think they'd be distracting, but they weren't. If anything, they were making it worse. The urge to go in search of Jillian and pull her back into his arms, take her to his bed, was overwhelming.

He needed to get the hell out of this house and back to his Boston home, to finishing this project, so he could take a long, much needed, swim in the cold, unforgiving ocean.

"Dammit, Captain Jake," he swore beneath his breath.

"Stop already. Take pity on another frustrated man."

Pulling the pillow up around his ears, he closed his eyes and concentrated on lowering his heart rate. Breathe. In and out. Think of it as decompression after a dive.

A light, bright enough to penetrate his closed eyelids, flashed across the double windows on the wall opposite his bed. When he lowered the pillow, he realized the rattling and the footsteps had stopped.

Maybe all he'd had to do was ask?

Pushing the ridiculous thought aside, he rolled over in search of sleep.

***

"Well, that was quite the display," Jilly admonished. "You've definitely put me in an awkward position here and caused me quite a dilemma. I've no doubt the professor is going to have questions tomorrow. How am I supposed to answer them without him thinking I'm a certifiable basket case?"

Her diatribe was met with an unusual silence. Yet, the absence of a response only increased her anger. "I'm warning you. I'll not hesitate to sell this house at the end of my three years, if you keep causing trouble. Then, where will you be? The next owners might bring in paranormal investigators. They'll install cameras and microphones, and make a nuisance of themselves. Possibly even try to chase you away."

Still nothing. No door slamming, no tipping of pictures or dropping of candlesticks. Sitting cross-legged in the middle of her huge, lonely bed, she couldn't help but wonder what had shut down Lily's and Jake's show of restlessness.

No doubt the professor was ready to pack up his research and not come back on Monday.

Reaching out to turn off her bedside lamp, she sank into the plush mattress and released a long breath. The tingles that had invaded her body the minute the noises had started, slowly melted away. Apparently, storm-induced lovemaking wasn't the only thing to cause the sensations. The professor's expert kisses had set off a chain reaction as volatile as the lightning that had first sent Jake and Lily into action.

When Jilly arrived in the kitchen at eight the next morning, Nick was already there, standing in his usual spot, the inevitable cup of coffee cradled in his hands.

The memory of those same hands on her waist, against her back, caused her pulse to race. Obviously, she'd not slept away all of her frustration.

"Good morning, Nick."

His lips—his perfect lips—quirked up in a half-smile. "Just you, Jilly. You're the only one allowed to call me Nick."

"Great. I was getting really frustrated with Nicholas. It's such a mouthful."

"Speaking of frustration," he said softly. "I'm not sure what happened last night, not just out on the widow's walk, but afterward. I've never felt anything like that before."

"I'd imagine not," she agreed. "I doubt you've ever experienced sexual frustration."

His deep chuckle ratcheted up her awareness.

"Don't be so sure. I might have been a jock in college, but during the football season, I rarely had time to date. Between practice, games, and keeping up my four-point average, my adoring female fans were the last thing on my mind. Then, once the season ended, my standing at school flew out the window. I was nothing more than a history nerd."

"So, no serious girlfriends?"

He shook his head. "Nope. No on-again, off-again relationships. An occasional date or two, but most didn't last past the point when it became clear romance wasn't my focus."

"And where's your 'focus' now? Any time for more than an occasional date?" She couldn't believe she'd asked but, suddenly, his answer seemed far more important than she'd intended.

"I still have plenty to prove, to myself, to the university—especially if I want tenure. That doesn't mean I can't multitask. For the right relationship, of course."

She offered him a smile. Encouragement, should he be interested.

"Of course."

He turned away and faced the sink, breaking the intense connection between them.

"Since there were eggs and milk in your fridge, I assume you're a lacto-ovo rather than strictly vegetarian. On that hunch, I made a casserole. It'll be done in about ten minutes."

"A casserole? You do multi-task, Professor. Sounds great. Once we've eaten and cleaned up, we can get back to the research. I thought of a few things I hadn't mentioned before regarding the years between 1840 and 1900." She paused for a moment, then thought to add, "Just so you don't think there are even more spirits roaming the house, Vera McDougal, my housekeeper, is due here at ten. She'll be in and out of all the rooms on the first and second floor."

"Thanks, for the heads up. I'll keep that in mind."

Coffee refills in hand, they made their way to the library, and the next two stacks of journals and assorted papers.

Once they'd taken their seats, Nick asked, "How often do you have to put up with what happened last night?"

Jilly swallowed, uncertain of how much she wanted to share. "The humidity sets it off. The lack of an actual storm, I suppose."

"The legend," he prompted, "that they come together to make love during the violent nor'easters. I'm still not sure I believe it."

"Last night was just a temper tantrum. Frustration. I was surprised it stopped as quickly as it did. It can sometimes go on for hours."

"Actually, I might have been the one to stop it."

Her head snapped up, her gaze connecting with his. "What? How?"

"I appealed to Jake's humanity. I asked him to give a fellow man a break. Within minutes, the lights stopped flashing outside the window, the stomping and door slamming ceased."

"You actually spoke to the Captain?"

"Well, he didn't talk back, but I did ask for the noise to stop. And, believe me, the fact that it did was far more frightening than the actual commotion."

"As much as I hesitate to tell you this, last night was nothing compared to what happens when we actually get a storm."

He shared another of his devastatingly sexy grins, and asked, "Is it odd of me to say, I hope I'm here when one rolls in?"

"No, not really. After all, where would your research be without firsthand experience?"

He smiled again, his beautiful blue eyes lighting with

humor. His broad shoulders, fit body, and confident demeanor were definitely getting to her. Big time.

When Nick settled back in the chair behind the desk and drew a pile of papers toward him, Jilly breathed a sigh of relief.

Perhaps Professor Nicholas Martin didn't scare as easily as the other guests who'd come and gone over the years.

"So, where did we leave off?" he asked. Reaching out, he turned on the recorder.

"We were talking about the changes made by Lucy and Nate Bradford, and their lives outside of Fairwinds."

"He was a solicitor, wasn't he?"

"Yes, he had an office in Boston, so they traveled back and forth, children in tow."

"How many children did they have?"

"Four. Two sons, two daughters. The eldest child, a daughter named Alice, was a nurse during the Civil War and died during one of the battles."

"How horrible. So, who inherited Fairwinds?"

"William, the second son. Johnathan, the eldest, wanted to go west and signed over his rights at an early age. William married Eloise Thomas in 1875, and they had a daughter, Helene."

"She was the woman who married the bootlegger, wasn't she?"

"He wasn't a bootlegger when they married, obviously. He was a businessman. Not a very successful one at the time, living mostly off of her vast inheritance. He profited from transporting supplies around the country during World War I. Then, once prohibition took effect, he got into more unsavory businesses. After Helene died, he moved everything here to

Fairwinds, opening the tunnels for storage and ease of transport."

"Their daughter didn't approve?"

"Mallory hated what her father had become, and rebelled as often as she could. Malcolm kept her on a tight rein, which led to her making a game out of slipping the watch of her assigned bodyguards."

"Bodyguards?"

"He—Malcolm—had enemies. He insisted the bodyguards were there for her safety, but most believed it was because if anything happened to her, he'd lose his access to Fairwinds because of a clause in Helene's will."

"That's where your great-grandfather came in, correct?"

"He was an FBI agent who came to work for Malcolm under an assumed name. He was much better at corralling Mallory than any of the others. However, he was also kind and gentle with her. They fell in love, even before she knew the truth about who he was, and why he was there."

"Do you know why he had the report on the death of the man who murdered Helene classified, rather than making it public knowledge?"

"According to what's been written in the family journals, the details of the man's death came from his brother, the only witness to the fall from the cliffs. He claimed the ghost of Lady Lillian rose up in anger and caused his brother to fall over the edge."

"In other words, Simon was protecting Mallory from having to defend or deny the account of ghosts."

"Something like that, I suppose."

"Simon and Mallory turned Fairwinds into a rather renowned horse farm, didn't they?"

"Yes, they did. After unearthing the circumstances surrounding both Helene's and Rick Temple's deaths, Simon left the FBI and shortly afterward retired from Pinkertons to run the stable operation. Fairwinds Farms lasted from the mid-1920s up until the onset of World War II, with my Grandpa Steven taking over from my great-grandparents. However, the war brought many changes. Costs skyrocketed and breeding champion horses took a backseat to everything else. Then, after my father was born in 1958, Grandpa concentrated on his legal practice, and put my dad through medical school."

Nick closed the cover on the journal and pushed the last unread book to the side. Then, he turned off the recorder on his phone and gathered up his notebook and pen.

"That's enough for today. I've got plenty to get started on my report."

"And, I have your assurance, the recordings are only for your ears, right? Especially the part about the ghosts."

"Yes. I gave you my word, didn't I?" He paused, then added, "I should probably get packed and on the road."

"You're not staying for lunch?"

He gave a shake of his head, the motion knocking a loose strand of hair across his brow, and sending a quick jolt of awareness skittering across the surface of her skin.

"No, but thanks for the offer. I think I'll grab a burger for the road. Man can only live for so long on veggies. I'll be back early on Monday, as promised. If you're available for a verbal consultation, we'll go through this last journal then, maybe, go for that cavern dive we talked about."

"You'll stay Monday night?"

"Yes, to finish up my inventory. Then, I'll get back on the

road home by Tuesday afternoon. You'll be able to get back to work on your next sculpture."

"I still have work to do for my gallery showing, so that will definitely keep me occupied."

"The show is in Boston?"

"Yes. The Peele Gallery, downtown. Perhaps you can stop by and say 'hi'."

"I'll put it on my calendar."

Chapter 9

Nicholas gathered up his belongings and stuffed them into his duffle before packing his camera and tucking his cell into the side pocket of his briefcase.

When he went to the bedside table to retrieve his notebook, it wasn't there.

Strange. He could have sworn that was where he'd left it.

It must be on the desk in the library. No doubt he'd been distracted by Jillian, and his desire to pull her into his arms for a lengthy goodbye kiss.

Taking the stairs two at a time, he went in search of the elusive notebook.

Less than five minutes later, he was tapping lightly on the open door leading to Jillian's workshop, more appropriately named the grand ballroom. When he stepped over the threshold, he drew to a sudden halt.

She had her back to him, an oversized headset holding her curls at bay and, likely, she had no idea he was there. He inched closer, not wanting to startle her. Yet, wanting to get a closer look at what she was working on.

The mysterious project that had been totally covered the last time he'd been in the studio. Nearly six feet tall, the sculpture depicted a man—a pirate—and a woman wrapped in each other's embrace.

Was this how she envisioned Captain Jake and Lily?

He stood there, staring at the intricately carved piece, mesmerized by its beauty, and waited for her to realize she wasn't alone.

She spun around suddenly, her eyes widening, her gaze going from him to the sculpture and back again.

"What?"

The curt tone of her voice surprised him.

"I knocked," he said. When she didn't respond, he told her honestly, "It's magnificent."

She gave a quick shake of her head as if to clear it. "It's nowhere near done." Offering him a hesitant smile, she added, "Sorry I snapped at you. You surprised me."

"Have you seen my notebook? I could have sworn I'd taken it to the bedroom with me, but it wasn't there or on the desk in the library."

"I haven't seen it since you tucked it away when we finished talking. Do you want me to help you look for it?"

"No, that's okay. I've got the recordings. I can start with those. I probably just missed it among all the other items I stuffed into my bag. I'm sure it'll turn up at some point."

She nipped at her lower lip before asking, "You're ready to leave?"

He took a step closer to where she stood and lifted his hand to her cheek, using his thumb to brush away a smudge of clay. "I've only one thing left to do before I go."

"And what would that be?"

"I need to kiss you goodbye, of course."

She stepped willingly into his outstretched arms and lifted her head. "Of course."

The drive went much faster heading back to Boston than it had at the beginning of his research trip. Even with the stop for a burger, fries, and a soda, he managed to cut his travel time in half.

The two-and-a-half-hour drive gave him plenty of time to map out the paper he would write. The back of his SUV held a number of donations of artifacts willingly given by those who wanted to be included in the museum's display. He'd not received anything from Jillian, and he wasn't sure if he should ask.

There was something about Fairwinds that raised his protective instincts, whether it was the house itself, or the woman living in it. She'd certainly gotten past his usual defenses without any trouble.

Not that he intentionally shut women out in the past, he'd just never met anyone for whom he'd been willing to give up his sparse spare time. However, with Jilly, he could see himself commuting between Fairwinds and the university just to spend a few hours in her presence, in her arms, and—with any luck—in her bed.

It was half past four when he pulled into his garage and let himself into the house. He planned to spend a few hours putting together the beginning of his paper, the part devoted to the far less impressive homes. Tomorrow, he intended to concentrate all his efforts on Fairwinds.

***

It was nearly seven when Jilly put away her tools and cleaned the clay from her hands. She'd worked straight through the afternoon and early evening and was currently paying the price with an empty, and very unhappy, stomach.

As if on cue, a rumble rolled through her entire body, demanding her attention.

"Shh. I'll feed you in a few minutes."

A pile of brushes rolled from the table onto the floor, and

Jilly turned toward the sound. "That's enough out of you, Captain. I know you're the one who took Nick's notebook. You need to put it back where you found it."

Rather than clean up the brushes, she turned on her heel and left the room. Something to eat first, then a nice long soak in the big, clawfoot tub. Perhaps a night of pure relaxation would get her mind off Nick, and those few perfect kisses they'd shared just before he left.

If she couldn't get him out of her head, she was destined for another long, lonely night.

She'd just settled in at the kitchen table with her tofu veggie stir fry when her phone rang. Scrambling for the counter, she slid her finger across the lock screen and hit the blinking green button.

"Nick?"

"Who's Nick?"

"Oh... it's you." She drew a breath, hit the speaker button, and sat back down to finish her meal.

"Is that any way to greet the man you're dating?"

"Was dating," she corrected around a mouthful of tofu. "Stone, our on-again, off-again, is definitely 'off' and has been for at least four months."

"I took a step back to give you time to settle your father's affairs and put that wretched house up for rent so you could come back to Boston where you belong. With me."

"I can't rent it. My father's will stipulates that I live here for a minimum of three years."

"Why would your father make such a ridiculous demand in the first place?"

"I'm not sure, but he rarely did anything without a purpose, so I have to trust he had a plan of some sort."

"Sam Bellows was in for a private class the other day. He says you're coming to the city for a show at his gallery the weekend after next. I figured you might want a place to stay that wasn't a hotel."

"I'll be fine in a hotel, thank you."

"My bed comes with a warm body. Actually, a really hot body."

"I'm not interested in your hot body... such as it is."

"What does that mean?"

"I guess what I'm saying is that you're far more in love with your body than I am."

"That's cruel, Jilly-girl."

She sucked in a breath, and bit back on an outright scream. She hated being called Jilly-girl.

"I've got to go, Stone. I have a project to work on and a deadline."

"You never did tell me who 'Nick' was. Are you two-timing me?"

"For the last time, I can't possibly be two-timing you when we're not one-timing each other any longer."

"So, is this Nick fellow the warm body in your bed now?"

"That's none of your business."

"Go back to your clay, Jilly-girl. And, have fun rattling around that weird house of yours. No doubt, your new friend won't last long when the doors start slamming and books fly through the air."

A quick chuckle escaped her throat before she could rein it in. "I'm not worried. The Captain only throws things at the people he doesn't like."

***

Sunday morning dawned overcast and dreary. Nicholas

rolled over in the bed and wrapped his arms around the spare pillow, wishing it were Jillian he was reaching for instead.

The alarm sounded a few minutes later, drawing him from a light doze. Pushing himself to a seated position on the edge of the bed, he raked a hand through his hair and stretched his back.

He'd spent an extra hour the night before making sure he'd finished the details on the first five houses, so he could concentrate solely on Fairwinds for the entire day. Without his notebook, he would have to rely on the recordings on his phone to piece everything together.

Two cups of coffee later, he took a seat at his desk and hooked his phone up to his computer, engaging the expensive audio equipment he'd added last year to listen to—and edit—his underwater recordings.

The thought of hearing Jillian's smoky voice in ultra-sensitive stereo sent a charge of adrenaline surging through his body, settling most predictably between his legs.

They'd shared little more than a dozen kisses, yet all he could think about was making love to her... with her. He'd thought the feelings would lessen now that he was home, but they only seemed to be getting stronger.

Pulling up the first recording, he put on his headphones and pressed 'start'.

Static crackled across the line, and he adjusted the volume to filter out the background noise. Jilly's voice came through loud and clear, her love for her ancestral home evident in the way she spoke about her family and Fairwinds, as if it too were a living thing. She'd just gotten to the part where they discussed the rumors of Fairwinds' supposed ghosts when another sound broke in, a low hum, almost a growl.

Giving another slow push to the volume slide bars, a loud screeching sound caused him to yank the headphones off and toss them on top of the desk.

"What the hell?"

He closed the first recording before putting the headphones on again. Moving on to the second recording—their discussion of the family of Lady Lillian's sister, Abigail—he made a second set of notes. Thankfully, the recording came through loud and clear all the way through.

On the third recording, they were in the middle of discussing the death of Alice Bradford, when another low hum broke into the recording. He increased the filter adjustment and waited for Jillian's next words.

'She was a nurse during...' The distinct sound of a woman's sob interrupted Jillian's words.

Nick's heart hammered wildly. Was he actually picking up EVPs on these recordings? Or, was it only his phone's voice recorder that was causing the unusual background noises?

Rather than continue to play directly from his phone, he downloaded the individual recordings and ran them through the scrubber on his audio equipment to eliminate as much static as possible.

Settling in with another cup of coffee, he moved on to recording number four. They were talking about her great-grandma Mallory, and the humor he could hear in Jillian's voice drew his smile.

'She had a habit of escaping her father's tight rein. Once she attempted to leave by climbing down the ivy vines and trellis. About ten feet above the ground, she lost her hold and fell.'

'What happened?'

'Great grandpa caught her. According to the legend, that was when she—literally—'fell' in love with him.'

There was a pause in the recording, yet there was something there. Closing his eyes, he pulled up the memory of the breeze that had blown across the rooftop. He'd asked if she'd felt the breeze. Rewinding five seconds, he turned up the volume.

A woman's soft laugh. Yet, Jillian hadn't laughed despite the humor in her story.

"Okay," he mumbled to himself. "This is crazy. Unbelievable. Yet, here it is."

He thought back about their short time on the roof, the incredible widow's walk. The beautiful brass weathervane. Another memory intruded—Jilly's mention of Captain Wilder's monogram on the keel—J.J.W. and the name of his ship.

Where had he seen something similar before?

Pushing away from the desk, he climbed the stairs to the second story bedroom he'd converted into a storeroom to hold the items he pulled from the ocean on many of his personally funded dives.

He opened the heavy chest and laid back the bubble packaging. The first item he pulled out was the outer casing of a compass, most likely from the early nineteenth century. The next item, a pouch with a handful of silver coins dated 1822. Both were tagged with a date from last summer—his second private dive of the year. The next item was wrapped in both bubble wrap and a soft velvet cloth. The tag on the outside of the package was later in the summer, the location of the dive farther up the coast than the first.

His hands shaking, Nicholas carefully peeled away the wrapping before lifting the spyglass to the light. The outer lens was cracked but not broken. He turned the fragile piece in his hand. Holding the brass fitting closer to a nearby lamp, he wiped away the accumulated dirt with his thumb.

The initials J.J.W. and *The Phantom* were etched into the brass fitting.

"Son of a bitch."

He sat there on the floor of the storeroom for another hour, cradling Captain John Jacob Wilder's lost spyglass in his lap. Then, rewrapping it, he placed it in one of the heavy cardboard boxes he used to transport items to the university.

Given his fast-approaching deadline, he had no choice but to hunker down and finish the first portion of his presentation prior to returning to Fairwinds. To Jilly.

He was usually happy to get lost in his research. However, at the moment, all he wanted was to finish up as quickly as humanly possible.

Chapter 10

By the time Nick hit the road on Monday morning, the temperature had already climbed to a stifling ninety degrees. The humidity hovered around eighty-five percent. No doubt, Fairwinds would be on full noise alert.

Pulling into the gas station to fill up his tank, he grabbed a cup of iced coffee from the café next door and got back on the road. The sense of urgency he felt over getting to Jillian was troubling him.

He wasn't sure why, but he knew he had to get Fairwinds as soon as possible.

Pulling into the circle drive at half-past ten, he grabbed his duffle, briefcase, and camera and bolted for the door, lifting the brass knocker just as the door was wrenched open from the inside.

Jillian stood in the doorway, dressed in a little more than a skimpy pair of running shorts and tank top that clung to every curve she possessed. Sweat glistened on her bare skin and ran down her chest to dip into the valley between her breasts.

Her red hair had been pulled back in a ponytail, the few loose strands clinging to her flushed cheeks.

The sudden ache in his gut nearly drove him to his knees. The urge to carry her to the first flat surface he could find and make love to her, had him tightening his grip around the handles of his tote and camera bag.

"Hey, there," she said between puffs of air. "I saw you pulling into the drive as I came in through the back."

"I didn't realize you were a runner."

She huffed out a laugh and admitted, "I'm not usually. But between the heat and the humidity, Captain Jake is driving me crazy. I had to get out of the house."

"There's rain in the forecast for later today. No doubt we'll have to postpone our cavern dive."

"Rain only lowers the humidity a bit. Until we get a heavy storm from the northeast, they're both going to be intolerable. You might wish you'd stayed in Boston."

"Why don't you go grab a shower while I get things set up in the library? There's something I want you to hear, and something I want you to see." He paused, giving her a smile of encouragement. "Worst case scenario, we can weather their tirade together."

"I'll appreciate the reinforcement. Give me five… uh… ten minutes, and I'll be right back down."

As badly as he wanted to suggest he join her in the shower, he swallowed back the offer and gave her a broad smile.

"Take your time. I'll get organized."

***

Jillian stripped out of her sticky clothes and stepped beneath the cool water of the shower, letting the tension in her body wash away with the sweat.

Well, most of it anyway.

She'd been so tempted to invite Nick to follow her upstairs. Yet, she'd not had the nerve. Hopefully, she hadn't wasted her one opportunity to entice the professor.

Within twenty minutes she was showered, dressed, and had a pot of coffee brewing in the French press. Placing the pot, cups, and creamer on a tray, she made her way to the library.

Nick had the last journal and some loose papers spread out across the desk. He'd also brought additional equipment with him. On the corner of the desk was a cardboard box tied with twine.

"You look like you're ready to get back to work," she commented on her way through the door.

"I am, but first I want you to listen to this recording. I downloaded it off of my phone and onto my computer, then made a digital recording of it."

He started the recording.

"That's us, up on the widow's walk," she said, listening intently. "We were talking about Mallory's great escape."

Nick held a finger up to his lips, requesting her silence. The recording played on.

'Did you feel that?', he'd asked on the tape.

A faint noise sounded in the background, and he stopped the recorder.

"What was that?"

"Listen closely," he prompted. "I'm going to turn it up a bit and slow it down."

He replayed the short, five-second portion again.

"It sounds like a woman laughing."

When he nodded, she drew in a sharp breath.

"That's what I thought too. It wasn't you and it wasn't me—obviously. So, who else was on the widow's walk?"

"Lady Lillian."

"In the four recordings on my phone, I found anomalies in all but one. Strange EVPs in the background that were too faint to positively identify. This one was the loudest and, still, it's not something I could confirm with absolute certainty."

"Ever since I was a child, I've known their spirits were

here… in the house… on the grounds. I grew up on the stories, reading the same diaries you're now going through. Still, the skeptic in me held out for a more plausible explanation. At least until my twenty-first birthday."

He leaned across the desk and lifted her hand in his before asking, "What happened on your twenty-first?"

"I'd come home from school for the weekend. It was late March. My father admonished me for taking a huge risk by driving on the snowy roads. For some reason, I just felt like I had to come home. I had to be here for something important."

"I gather there was a storm. A true nor'easter."

"Yes, there was. My father was at the hospital making rounds when it began. He called me to say he was going to stay there for the night in case they were overrun with car accidents or other trauma and asked if I'd be okay." She pulled in a deep breath. "Of course, I told him 'yes'. After all, I was safe in my own home."

"Then what happened?"

"I was asleep in my bed when the storm began. The wind rattled the windows so fiercely that it woke me up. After that, all hell broke loose. The doors to the widow's walk blew open—as they always did—and, right on cue, Captain Jake came up from the tunnels, his heavy footfalls echoing through the house. I burrowed beneath the covers, because I knew what was coming."

"They were going to make love."

"The wilder the storm, the more intense their joining, or at least that's how it seems. It went on for hours… both the storm and the activity… until I finally fled my room and came downstairs to wait it out in the parlor. The power was already off. I rummaged around the kitchen and pantry drawers for a flashlight but couldn't find one. So, I lit candles and started a fire. Then, I curled up on one of the settees and tried to go to sleep."

"Did you? Fall asleep?"

"Eventually. Even ghostly lovers have to take a break from time to time. Or, so it seems. I awoke briefly just before dawn. The fire should have been out, or at least dying. Yet, there were fresh logs set. The candle stubs had been replaced with full tapers."

"Jake, I presume."

"I thought, at first, my father had come home and was responsible, but when I sat up with the intention of going to find him, a shadow passed around the room. When I glanced toward the fireplace, I saw…"

"Yes?"

"The Captain. He was standing there in breeches and a flowing shirt, the fireplace poker in his hand, as if he were about to give the embers another poke. I pinched myself to make sure I wasn't dreaming, then I blinked. When I opened my eyes, the poker was back in place, and he was gone."

"How long did the storm last?"

"The worst of it was already over, although the snow was still falling. The wind had died down. I made my way up to the third floor, curious as to whether or not they were still there, but the bedroom door was wide open, and the French doors to the widow's walk were closed. At some point during the night, their time together had ended."

Nick released her hand and slumped back in the chair.

"That's a fascinating story," he said finally. "Are you sure you weren't dreaming?"

She shot him a purposeful glare. "Positive. After all you've heard since you arrived, combined with what you heard on your audio recordings, are you seriously still doubting their existence?"

"To be honest, I'm not sure what to think. I subscribe to the old adage, 'seeing is believing', and until I see proof with my own eyes, I'm reserving judgement."

"Geesh, you are so stubborn." Lifting her gaze to the ceiling, she shouted, "Captain, could you come down here and hit this doubter upside the head with the notebook you stole from his room?"

Nick's deep chuckle lightened her mood. Somewhat.

"Yes, please," he added in, still laughing. "Bring back my notebook."

They shared another chuckle, their laughter dying down when their gazes met, his flaring with a brooding intensity she'd not seen before.

"What's in the box?" she asked, needing to defuse the intimate moment before she threw herself across the desk and begged him to take her then and there.

He cleared his throat, before explaining, "Something I think you'll find very interesting." He untied the string and lifted the lid. Folding back the bubble wrap, he reached in and withdrew an antique spyglass.

"It's beautifully preserved," she said, her voice catching. "What a wonderful discovery."

He laid it in her hand, and told her, "Look closer. At the brass fitting."

She turned the delicate instrument over in her hand, her eyes widening when she saw the etching. "*J.J.W.* and... *The Phantom.*" Raising her head, she made eye contact. Blinking back the threat of tears, she whispered, "This belonged to

Captain Wilder?"

Nick's deep voice softened, and he nodded slowly. "It would appear so."

Jillian ran the tips of her fingers across the smooth brass fitting, caressing the etched writing.

"Did you find this on one of your university-sponsored dives?"

"No, on one of my personal dives. That's why I still have it."

"It's amazing. A wonderful find for your collection."

"It doesn't belong to me. It's the Captain's and, by right of inheritance, it now belongs to you."

"I can't take this. It's priceless, and you found it. It should be yours."

"Believe me, I've struggled with my decision to return it to Fairwinds over the past day and a half, ever since I realized what I had. Yet, as much as it would enhance my project, in the end, I realized this is an important piece of Fairwinds' history, not my history." He reached out and closed his hand around hers, holding the gift tightly in their joined grasp. "I'll find other treasures."

Her heart skipped a beat, and her pulse raced, from both Nick's generosity and the warmth of their joined hands.

"I don't know what to say."

"Say, you'll accept my gift."

Jilly sank back in the chair, the treasured piece of Jake's history snug in her closed hand and waited while Nick gathered up his research and piled it neatly on the corner of the desk.

Once he'd finished, Jilly looked up from her close inspection of the spyglass, and confirmed, "Thank you, Nick. I will accept your gift, on behalf of both Fairwinds and the Captain."

"Is there somewhere you can put it for safekeeping?"

"We have a wall safe, but I don't know that we've ever used it." She paused, a thought coming to her in a rush. "I know just the place."

Standing, she cradled the spyglass in one hand, and then held out her other in his direction.

"Where are we going?"

"I'll show you but, first, we need to get a screwdriver and a step ladder."

Chapter 11

Nick wasn't sure where they were going, but he quickly realized he'd follow Jilly anywhere, as long as they were together.

Screwdriver and step ladder in hand, they climbed the staircase to the second floor, and then the narrower set of stairs to the third. When they reached the third-floor bedroom, Jilly pushed the door open and went inside, motioning for him to follow.

"We need to loosen the braces around the Captain and Lady Lillian's wedding portrait so we can take it down."

"Is that where the wall safe is located?"

She gave a shake of her head, her wild curls flying around her shoulders. "No, that's downstairs in the library. This is much more secure."

"Not if it can be accessed with a screwdriver, it isn't."

"You are now only the second person alive who knows about this, after me of course. And, like the tunnel entrances, I trust you'll keep it to yourself."

He drew his fingertip across the seam of his mouth. "My lips are sealed."

Once he'd removed the bottom two braces, he was able to wiggle the painting free of its top anchors and lower it to the floor. Behind the heavy portrait, there was a hole in the wall.

"Reach in and grab the wooden chest," Jilly instructed. "Bring it over to the bed."

This wasn't quite the way he'd pictured getting Jillian on a bed but—for the moment—it would have to do.

Laying down the slightly warped box, he sat on the edge of the mattress, Jillian directly across from him.

She opened the lid slowly while dust bunnies flew through the air. Grimacing, she admitted, "I haven't dusted in a while. Sorry." Taking out the first item, a small leather pouch, she poured the contents out onto the bed. "Eight pieces of gold. According to the stampings, from the early 1700s. Lady Lillian's wedding ring." Picking up the next item, she continued on. "The infamous key to the dungeon room."

"Are you sure that's what it's for?"

"Yes, Simon fit it into the lock, and it turned, but he never actually removed the lock or opened the door. The key was immediately put away for safekeeping."

"It's a mighty large box for such a small bounty."

"There were also journals and some dried-up ink and quills, but the journals were put with the other historical documents, and the quills and ink well donated to the local museum in Mystic Point." Leaning close, she whispered, "I think they were sorely disappointed in the donation. They were expecting something far more important, I'm sure."

They added the spyglass to the box and put the leather pouch in before returning the chest to its place of honor. Remounting the portrait, Nick fit the anchors back in place and added the screws.

When he looked back to where Jillian was waiting, she was standing beside the bed, straightening the quilt and brushing out the wrinkles.

"How about we make a fresh pot of coffee and get to work?" Her offer was made with a tentative smile, drawing his attention—as it always did—to her luscious mouth.

How about we go mess up the bed in the guest room? The wicked thought shot through him with lightning speed.

"Sounds good. I'll get back to organizing the last few documents," he said instead.

By five that afternoon, they'd reviewed the final fifty years of family history, and swapped some stories about the local area, including her colorful recount of Mystic Point's history as the go-to place for illegal drink during prohibition.

Jillian had gone to make their supper, promising him something more substantial than a vegetable dish and salad. He was about to put away the last of the early journals, when a loose paper fell free from beneath the spine of the oldest book.

He opened the weathered paper, being careful to not tear it.

There, in what he recognized as Captain Wilder's handwriting, was a crudely drawn map of the roof, the chimneys, and the side of the structure that faced the bay. Faintly printed on what appeared to be the outside cornerstone of the third-floor bedroom was Jake's official mark.

Pushing himself from behind the desk, he rushed to find Jillian.

She wasn't in the kitchen, or her studio, so he climbed the stairs to the second floor and called out her name. Still, nothing.

Dark clouds hovered over Fairwinds, the rain the weatherman had promised was rolling in off the bay.

Taking the stairs up to the third floor, he made his way to the bedroom. He needed to see where the map led, to see if there was something hidden in the blocks of the structure.

Nick let himself out through the double doors and onto the roof walk, circling the house to the far corner. Rain began falling, and lightning flashed off in the distance. Thunder rumbled so loudly it shook the ground.

He kept close to the building until he'd reached the spot shown on the hand-drawn map. Nothing appeared out of place; there were no obvious breaches in the solid foundation. No markings. Quite possibly, whatever had been there was removed and the spot sealed over in the intervening years.

Making his way back to the French doors, he turned the knob but it refused to budge. The next bolt of lightning crashed down just short of the cliffs. Rain fell in earnest, drenching clear through his shirt.

He was about to call out for Jillian, when she appeared on the opposite side of the thick glass. With a twist of her wrist, she unlocked the door and pushed it open.

"Get in," she demanded. "Quickly, before she gets here."

The moment he stepped across the threshold and into the room, the doors slammed shut behind him. He turned to look out over the roof and his heart stopped beating.

There, floating above the roof, was a white apparition, her gown flowing freely around a slim body, her dark hair flying behind her in the swirling wind.

The very foundation of the house began to shake—heavy footsteps echoed through the hallway.

They made a beeline for the bedroom door, but it shut in their faces.

"Come on. Hurry." Jillian held out her hand, drawing him back into the center of the room. "We've got to get out of here. Now." Pushing aside the corner of the heavy rug, she raised a trap door in the floor. "Down here."

"Down where? You're joking, right?"

"No, I'm not. Please, hurry."

She went in first, lowering herself to the second stair. He followed right behind and reached to close the hatch. He was within a foot of having it shut when the doors to the widow's walk blew open, a bright light shone into the room, and in the middle of it, Lady Lillian's ghost floated forward.

Nick desperately wanted to watch, but Jilly was tugging at his arm, silently imploring him to shut the hatch and follow her down the rickety staircase. The last thing he saw before the trap door shut was a glimpse of two mud-crusted black boots at the foot of the bed.

"So, this is where the staircase ends. Now what?"

Jilly gave another tug to his soaked shirt. "I know it's dark, but if we go slow—"

Above their heads, the noises began, a loud whirring sound, as if they were standing in the eye of a hurricane. Bright light seeped through the cracks in the trap door. He lowered himself down another step until he and Jilly were standing chest-to-chest; breath-to-breath.

"Dammit, Jilly, I'm sorry."

She pressed her fingertips to his lips. "It's okay, you didn't know, and the storm... the—"

He swallowed her words, taking her mouth in a crushing kiss. When she sighed, he slipped his tongue between her parted lips, turning up the heat full blast. Their ragged breathing echoed the frantic activity taking place less than five feet above their heads.

When she pushed her hands beneath his shirt and across his chest, Nick was certain he was going to explode. Reaching for the hem, he stripped the damp cloth over his head and tossed it to the bottom of the staircase.

"I've wanted to kiss you like this forever," he whispered against her mouth. "Among other things."

"Let's get out of this wretched stairwell and we can discuss the 'other things' when we're not breathing mouthfuls of cobwebs and dust."

"Yes, let's. It sounds as if it's getting pretty heated up there."

"They're just getting started," she said, laughing.

"Really?"

"When you only get to do it a few times a year, what do you expect?"

They made their way down the stairs, the iron risers shaking beneath their weight. Nick clung to her hand. When they reached the landing, Jilly stretched out her hand in search of the latch that would release the hidden door. "I've never done this in the dark before," she mumbled. "Yes! Found it."

A moment later, the panel in the wall slid open and she stepped forward, and gave his hand a tug. They stepped through the opening and into the rotunda.

"Saved by the hidden passage." He gave a last glance into the dark space before the panel closed. "I guess I'll come back later with a flashlight and look for my shirt."

Her giggle tickled his senses.

"Much later, I hope."

"Definitely," he agreed. Scooping her up in his arms, he slipped through the doors of the rotunda and made a dash for the staircase. "We can't let the Captain and Lady Lillian have all the fun."

Chapter 12

Jillian let out a gasp when Nick tossed her in the middle of the bed in his room. When he followed her down onto the mattress, it was all she could do to keep from tearing off her clothes before reaching for the last of his.

She spared a moment's thought about what was happening at the other end of the house, one floor up. Was Nick's obvious passion being driven by the same unknown force she always felt—was feeling now—when the Captain and his lady came together?

Or, was what they were feeling real?

"Here," he said, reaching for the front of her blouse. "Let me get those for you."

His fumbling would have been endearing, were she not so darned horny. She closed her hands around his to slow his frantic efforts to slip the tiny pearl buttons from their holes. "No need to rush. We've got all night."

Nick released a sigh, his warm breath washing across her cheek. "I'm usually much more adept at this," he said. "But my heart is pounding so hard, I'm having a hard time focusing on anything but getting you naked and making love to you."

"I like your focus," she admitted with a soft chuckle. "It's the same as mine. However, I think we'll both have more success if we slow down a bit."

He released his grip on the front of her shirt and smoothed his hand across her breast, cupping her in his palm. Closing his eyes, he breathed in and out in slow, measured increments, his gentle massage of breast relaxing her as well.

"Jilly, I've honestly never felt this way, this anxious." Opening his eyes to meet her gaze, he told her, "I know you probably think it's because of the Captain and Lady Lillian, but it's not. At least not completely. I've wanted to kiss you, touch you, make love to you since the first day I arrived here at Fairwinds."

"Wow! All I wanted was to see you naked."

Her comment drew his startled laugh. "Naked? Really?"

She cuddled into his embrace and laid her hand against his bare chest, the tips of her fingers teasing his nipples. His hand flexed against her breast, and he snagged the tight peak between his thumb and finger.

"I really didn't think you were the professor I was expecting. I'd hoped you were here to model for me. In the nude, of course."

"No, not me. I have no problem getting naked, but not so you can turn me into some clay statue."

Pushing herself up until she sat in the middle of the bed, she reached for the hem of her blouse and pulled it over her head. "The buttons are only decoration. This is faster." When she reached for the front closure of her bra, Nick was there to help.

Once the clasp was released, he pushed the satin and lace cups aside. A long, low whistle slid from between his tightly pursed lips. "Damn."

"Why, thank you. The twins are my best asset."

His gaze moved over her body, from the top of her head to where her toes peeked out from beneath the hem of her jeans. When he licked his lips, Jilly nearly melted on the spot.

"Now that my heart has stopped trying to jump out of my

chest, I say we get the rest of our clothes off and get serious."

Releasing the snap at the waistband of Nick's khaki slacks, she agreed. "Serious is good."

She made quick work of the zipper closure and urged him to lift his hips so she could slide the garment down his body, leaving him in a very tight-fitting pair of black briefs. Her hand trembling slightly, she reached out and wrapped her fingers around his arousal through the thin cotton material.

Between the two of them, they managed to divest Jilly of her jeans and the skimpy thong underneath, leaving her naked in the middle of the big bed.

Nick slid down her body to take her breast into his mouth, taunting the hard crest with the tip of his tongue, the scrape of his teeth, before kissing his way across her chest to show the opposite breast the same mind-boggling treatment.

When he slid his hand across the plane of her belly and cupped her womanly mound, her hips rose and her legs parted in willing invitation.

The first touch of his finger across her sex drew her muffled scream. When he breached the damp opening, she clutched the bedspread in her hands and raised her hips even higher.

He slid his hand forward and back, stroking her in perfect time with the pull of his mouth on her breast.

Jilly closed her eyes tight and reveled in his attention, her breathing labored, her heart hammering an uneven rhythm. "Nick, please. I need… I need…"

Her words caught on the first rush of her climax, her body convulsing around Nick's doubled caress.

She took no more than a few moments to recoup before she was on her knees and reaching for the top of Nick's briefs, peeling them down his legs, uncovering him completely to her appreciative gaze.

When she closed her hand around his bare flesh, he sucked in a breath. "Be careful. We don't want a premature explosion."

"No," she agreed, laughing softly. "We certainly don't. I've got plans for you, and they don't include anything premature."

He pulled her back down onto the bed and into his arms, then pressed a gentle kiss to her lips. "I know it might be a little late to ask, but are you protected? Or am I going to have to retrieve my pants from wherever they landed when you whipped them across the room?" When she opened her mouth to answer, he laid his fingers across her lips. "Do you hear that?"

"What?"

"Nothing, that's just it. The noise from upstairs has stopped."

"They're taking a break." Motioning toward the window, the rain still beating wildly against the frame, she told him, "They'll come together again. As long as it's storming, Lady Lillian won't have to leave."

He smoothed his hand across her hip. "They can listen to us for a while. They just can't watch. So, do I need to find my pants?"

"I'm on the pill," she told him. "However, if you wouldn't mind—"

Nick rolled out of the bed and went in search of his wallet. When he returned to the bed, she greeted him with a broad smile. His blue eyes flared with desire.

"We're all good now." Rolling her onto her back, he slid his thigh between hers and parted her legs.

"Well then, Professor, I say we give our upstairs neighbors a run for their money."

A very satisfying hour later, Jilly lay content in the circle of Nick's strong arms, her head pillowed on his shoulder, her leg resting atop his muscled thighs.

"Damn! That was..." she whispered against the side of his throat. "That was something else."

He held her hand, their fingers intertwined, and resting in the center of his chest. "Yes, we are pretty spectacular together."

"I don't think I've ever had that many orgasms in one session of lovemaking."

She could feel his smile when he pressed his lips to her forehead.

"What can I say? I'm thorough with everything I do." Giving a slight nod of his head toward the ceiling, he added, "Especially when our competition couldn't wait for us to finish before they began again. I gotta give it to the Captain, for a ghost in his three-hundreds, the dude's got game."

"You know, you never explained why you were up on the roof."

He nuzzled beneath the curtain of her hair, and pressed a kiss to the sensitive spot behind her ear. "I've been busy."

"Well, we're not... busy now. So, why were you out on the walk?"

"I found an old hand-drawn map hidden in the spine of one of the Captain's original ledgers. It was a sketch of the roof. Supposedly, there was a cornerstone with his monogram carved into it. I wanted to know if it was still there."

"It wasn't, was it?"

She felt the slow shake of his head against her shoulder.

"No, nothing. At least not now. Was there once something hidden in the outside structure?"

"According to what my father told me, sometime in the mid-1800s, there was a violent storm—the remnants of a hurricane, I believe—that swept through Skullery Bay. It damaged a portion of the roof. When they were making repairs, they found the broken cornerstone. That was where they discovered the dungeon key. They'd hoped to keep the monogrammed block of stone, but it was too badly damaged, so they replaced it with sturdier cement blocks."

"I know this is going to sound *out there*, but given how long that map was hidden in the journal spine, do you think the Captain meant for me to find it?"

"I'm honestly not sure. Jake and Lily made it their mission to chase away nearly every boy… every man… I've ever shown an interest in. Until you."

"They obviously care about you if they've spent all these years protecting… uh…screening the men in your life. I'm not sure whether to be honored, or frightened, at the thought of having their trust."

"I've often wondered… What do you think it's like for them? I mean, obviously, they have no real bodies."

Nick shrugged, the lift of his shoulders raising her head slightly. "I haven't got a clue. Hell, four days ago, I was adamant there was no such thing as ghosts. Otherworldly beings. Whatever we should call them. Now, I'm laying her with a beautiful, sexy woman in my arms, and eavesdropping on spirit sex. I may know history, but I don't know shit about what's happening up there."

"My grandma used to say they went to another place, an

alternate existence or universe, where—to them—they were still alive. I'd like to think they can have that, a brief time when they're still together."

"How about we try to catch an hour or two of sleep? Then, maybe we can have a second, or third, round of our own."

"Sounds heavenly. The sleep and another round of your very inventive love making."

He yawned and drew her tighter to his body. "What can I say? I'm an overachiever."

***

Nick awoke just before dawn. Jilly slept soundly at his side. He lifted his head far enough to glance out the window. Sometime during the last hour or so, the storm had ended.

There was no activity on the third floor and he wondered if Lady Lillian had been sent back to widow's walk, alone and at the mercy of another storm front. And, Captain Jake, destined to walk his beloved home alone; allowed only as far as the tunnels.

If Jilly had any doubt as to his desire without Jake and Lily's influence, she had no cause for worry. Just lying there, holding her, he wanted her again. And again.

They'd made love three times, and each joining had been better than the one before. He'd thought his life was perfect as is, but he'd been wrong. He did need more than just his job, his hobbies. He needed Jilly. She completed him.

However, she was bound to Fairwinds, whether she wanted to admit it or not. She'd talked about selling her family home once the three-year stipulation in her father's will was up. Yet he felt fairly confident she'd never follow through. As much as she grumbled about the size of the house, the noisy resident ghosts, and the distance to city comforts, Fairwinds was in her blood.

That put the possibility of an ongoing relationship between them in flux. He'd worked too hard to give up his chance to make a name for himself in his field; to hold a great position at a prestigious institution.

Not that he wouldn't drive from Boston to Mystic Point every weekend if she'd have him. Still, she deserved so much more. She deserved a full-time relationship, possibly marriage and a family. At the moment, he wasn't in a position to give her everything she deserved.

They had another day together before he had to go home. He was due to report to the department head on Wednesday morning to give an update on his progress and lay out at least part of his research in detail.

"Good morning." Her soft whisper tickled the side of his neck.

"Good morning to you, too." Drawing her close, he pressed a kiss to the top of her head. "The storm stopped an hour or so ago."

"Well, I guess that's the end of that then."

"For them, maybe."

"As enticing as that may be, right now I need a bathroom, and then some food. I'm starving."

"I never did get that special dinner you promised me last night."

"Well then, I suppose I should get up and make us a special breakfast."

Chapter 13

Jilly took her seat at the breakfast table and reached for a second slice of toast. Just the sight of Nick sitting across from her, his hair finger-combed into semi-obedience, his chest bare, and his unsnapped khakis hanging low on his hips, made her heart skip a beat.

"How's your breakfast?"

"Shrimp omelets," he said around a forkful of food. "I'm impressed. Although, I think I'm far more in need of more coffee at the moment."

"I'm making another pot. It'll be ready in a few minutes. As much as I love my French press, I really wish I'd bought a larger one."

"I live for my old-fashioned drip coffee pot. Eight cups at a time in a thermal pot. A caffeine addict's nirvana."

"What more do you have to do before you leave?"

"I want to double check the inventory of those maritime charts, I've one journal to date, and then I'd like a couple more pictures of the property." He raised his head and met her gaze, his blue eyes widening. "And, of course, I wouldn't mind making love with you one more time."

She shot him a broad smile. "I was hoping your thoughts were the same as mine."

"Jilly? About after I leave—"

She held up her hand. "I'm not expecting a grand gesture here. You've got a fantastic position at the university." Glancing around the room, she added, "I've got Fairwinds—at least for another two-and-a-half years."

Nick slid his hand across the table and grasped her fingers, drawing them to his lips for a kiss. "There's no reason we can't have both, if you're interested."

"A long-distance relationship? I'm not very good at those."

"I've never had one, so I honestly don't know what to expect. However, I do know, despite your grumbling, you'll never give up Fairwinds, or the Captain and Lady Lillian."

"When I first moved home, I was on the fence for sure. However, having you here, going over the family history definitely has me teetering on the side of staying put."

An understanding smile lit his handsome face. "And it didn't even take the full three years. Do you think, perhaps, that was why your father put the stipulation in his will to begin with—to give you the chance to appreciate your family home as an adult?"

"The man always had a master—if not somewhat devious—plan."

"Why don't you give it some thought... Us, I mean? You're welcome to stay with me when you come to Boston for your gallery showing. We can talk more about the possibilities while you're there."

"I'd like that. Very much. I can't promise a commitment, but spending the weekend with you sounds wonderful."

Jillian lay stretched out on the bed, her body still pulsating from another thorough round of love making.

The sound of running water was like a metronome in her head, the constant rhythm of the splash against the porcelain sink echoing her heartbeat.

"Are you going to lay around all day after I leave," Nick

called from the doorway of the bathroom.

"You wore me out, so I'm entitled to a nap."

"Wore you out? Woman, I was lucky I didn't pass out when you took hold of the reins."

Offering him what she hoped was a teasing smile, she asked, "Are you sure I can't tempt you to stay?"

"I'm already two hours later leaving than I'd planned. It's a two-to-three-hour drive… if the roads are clear. And, I still have to put my presentation together for the board."

Jilly pushed herself to the edge of the bed and sat up. Clutching a pillow to her chest, she stood and made her way slowly across the room. The look of sheer panic in Nick's eyes was worth her awkward attempt at a modern-day fan dance.

"Jilly," he warned, shaking his head from side-to-side. "I have to leave. Soon."

Stopping in front of him, she let the pillow slide to the floor. His gaze followed, raking the surface of her bare body with his heated stare.

"Soon is fine. At least it's not immediately."

An hour and a half later, Nick made his way down the stairs to where Jilly waited in the foyer.

"You do realize, I'll be working all night now. No doubt, my eyes will be bloodshot when I give my presentation to the committee."

"Yes, but it was worth it—at least for me."

He pursed his lips to hide an outright grin. "You're insatiable."

"If I'm not mistaken, Professor, the last time was your choice."

"What can I say? I couldn't resist the temptation."

She glanced down to where he clutched his duffle in one hand and his camera bag in the other. The memory of his hands, caressing her skin, teasing her most intimate places, caused her to draw a deep breath.

"You've got everything?"

"I need to grab my briefcase and the extra copies of the maritime charts. They'll be a wonderful addition to the display. Thank you for sharing them."

"You're welcome. I don't think we need two of each."

When they slipped into the library to grab the envelope containing the charts, Nick came to a sudden stop in front of the desk. There, in the middle of the blotter, sat his lost notebook.

"Well, I'll be. My notebook." Looking in her direction, he asked, "Where did you find it?"

"I didn't. *Whomever took it, must have had a change of heart and returned it.*"

"The Captain?"

"I think so. Given he brought it back, that's as good a stamp of approval as any he's given—especially to a male visitor. That and not chasing you out the door in the first place."

"Be sure to thank him for me."

"You could do it yourself, you know."

Giving a shake of his head, he told her, "No, that's okay. I'll leave the ghost-talking to you."

Once Nick's car pulled out of the driveway, Jillian closed the door and set the lock. "Thank you, Captain," she whispered. "For returning Nick's notebook. We both appreciate it."

Off in the distance, the door leading to the butler's pantry slammed shut. No doubt, Jake was on his way to the tunnels on his daily rounds to the gates and back.

Perhaps she'd spend some time working on her sculpture of the Captain and Lady Lillian. Or, maybe just curl up in the bed she and Nick had shared and wrap herself around his pillow and pretend he was still there.

Stop feeling sorry for yourself. He's offered you all you're both able to give at the moment. You'd be a fool not to take it.

Like she'd told Nick, long distance relationships weren't her strong suit. Actually, relationships of any kind were iffy at best. She could count on one hand the number of relationships she'd had that lasted longer than a month or two. On one finger, the only man who'd lasted longer than six months, and he'd turned out to be a dick.

You know, your ancestors commuted between here and Boston frequently, by carriage and on horseback, when it took two days instead of four hours. Quit making excuses, or you will end up an old spinster, even without the Captain and Lady Lillian's interference.

Damn. She hated it when her conscience was right.

Chapter 14

When the alarm sounded at six-thirty the next morning, it was all Nick could do to roll over and shut off the offensive noise.

Every muscle in his body ached—albeit in the best way possible. In three years of high school and five years of college football, he'd never been worked so hard. Jillian was a wicked taskmaster, and he was her willing servant.

He'd not made it to bed until nearly three. Sleep had come quickly, yet had been filled with dreams of Jilly. Her luscious body, her silken hair, the feel of her warm heat wrapped snugly around his cock.

Cursing the sudden change in his body, he pushed himself to his feet and headed for a cold shower. Due at the university by nine, he'd have to hustle if he wanted to grab coffee and a muffin at the nearby diner.

"Good morning, Dr. Martin."

Nick raised his gaze from the pile of materials on the floor at his feet and met the broad smile of Dr. Berkley's young assistant.

Nodding slightly, he responded. "Good morning, Miss Clary."

"Sabrina, please." Her bright red lips puckered around her drawn out name. "Dr. Berkley will be with you in a few minutes. If you'd like, you're welcome to sit here beside my desk."

"That's okay, I don't want to disturb your work. I'll wait over here by the window."

Dr. Berkley was the other associate professor assigned to the project. A man in his late forties, he'd been passed over for tenure twice, and had been quite vocal about playing second fiddle to 'that young upstart Dr. Martin'.

No doubt, the man's constant complaining was what kept him right where he was… at least four rungs down the hierarchy. Were it not for the fact the man was an expert in one of the more obscure disciplines of American History, no doubt he'd have been shown the door ages ago.

"Dr. Martin," Berkley greeted from the door to his cramped space. "The others will be here shortly. Do you want to review what you've got so far?"

Nick gathered his presentation and boxes of donated artifacts from the floor and followed the older man into his office. "There are two additional boxes of donations in the back of my car, most of them not up to university standards. I brought the more promising items in with me."

"Let's see," Berkley said, reaching for the manilla envelope on top of the pile. Carefully withdrawing the maritime charts from inside, the man sucked in a breath. "These are magnificent. Hand-drawn, the paper dates from the early to mid-1700s. Exquisite."

"I concur," Nick agreed. "I have reason to believe they were drawn by Captain John Jacob Wilder, a pirate who sailed the waters off Skullery Bay. Or, if not him, then by one of his trusted crew."

"Wilder? Isn't he the fellow who died at sea? If I remember correctly, according to the many stories surrounding Fairwinds, his ship sank during a violent storm."

Nick nodded. "He and his twin brother, Aiden, perished together."

"Fairwinds. That was it. The home could have been something, a showcase for New England architecture. Seems to me, though, it was plagued by poor management, unexplained deaths, and ridiculous tales of ghosts."

"The home certainly had its problems over the centuries. But, at the moment, it's beautifully restored. The current owner has painstakingly preserved the home's history."

Berkley shifted his attention to the first page of Nick's initial report. "You went to Hollyhock?"

"Yes, Miss Hancock was quite helpful."

Berkley chuckled, something Nick didn't realize was possible. "Does the old bat still have a dozen cats?"

"Six, at last count," Nick clarified.

Thumbing through the next few pages, Berkley recited the list of homes. "Graystone, Bullard, Smithfield, and… damn… you got into Willowtree?"

"Not without a fight. While the owner was willing, her very aged butler was less than welcoming. I thought he was going to beat me off with his cane."

Their colleagues arrived a few minutes later, and the group of five went through everything Nicholas had assembled, accepting and rejecting materials equally.

"Nice work, Dr. Martin," Terry Pritchett, the department head commented. "Of course, we'll still have to lay out the actual display and review the photos to decide which to feature."

Dr. Taylor, Pritchett's right-hand man asked, "Have you decided on a centerpiece for the collection?"

Nick drew a breath. Fairwinds was the obvious choice. Yet,

to put Jilly and her home out there as the focal point might bring unwanted attention to both the home, and its previous owners. "I'm waffling between Willowtree and Fairwinds."

Pritchett gave a shake of his head, and echoed Berkley's earlier comments. "Not Fairwinds. Too much questionable history surrounding that place. Harvard can't glorify a property that's had so many suspect deaths, so many supposed hauntings."

"Ordinarily, I'd agree. Sir. However, the majority of the materials and reports I've collected from Fairwinds far exceeds the donations from the other properties."

Despite his earlier misgivings, Berkley spoke up in Fairwinds' defense as well. "These maritime charts alone are worth more than all of Willowtree's journals and etchings."

Nick thought quickly of the tunnels, the legends, the stories behind Fairwinds history. Of how the pictures, and his notes, would enhance not just the project, but his career as well.

"The grounds at Fairwinds are magnificent. The house is the most well maintained of the six, the view from the cliffs stunning," he explained.

"What about the rumors of tunnels? A pirate's treasure trove?"

Nick pulled in a quick breath and held it, then he shook his head. "The tunnels, or what there may have been once, were closed off four or five generations back. There's nothing there to see, much less report on."

Giving the pocket of his sport coat a pat, he assured himself the four pictures he'd taken of the dungeon were safely tucked out of sight.

"Okay," Pritchett agreed. "We'll go with Fairwinds. Just

make sure we can substantiate every fact we put on display."

At half past six that evening, Nick punched Jilly's number into his cell and then laid the device down on his kitchen counter and engaged the speaker.

"Hello?"

"Hello, gorgeous. Miss me yet?"

There was a pause before she asked, "Who is this?"

Nick welcomed the relief her humor offered. "It's me... your sex slave."

"Oh, yeah. You." Laughing softly, she teased, "I'd nearly forgotten."

"Lucky you," he teased. "I can barely walk."

"Some big, tough football player you are. Wuss."

"I've got news to share," he said, pulling back from their playful banter. "They've chosen Fairwinds as the central focus for the museum's display."

"Really? Are you sure that's wise?"

"Don't worry, Jilly, I won't let any secrets slip. I've even deep-sixed the tunnel photos. As far as the committee is concerned, the tunnels have been closed off for a century, if not longer."

"Thank you."

"I'm also not going to report on the deaths, or the ghost stories. History only. Pictures of the house, the grounds, the view from the cliffs."

"That's wonderful. Have I seen all the pictures?"

"I've got one more file to open and review. I'll choose the best half dozen or so and email them for your approval."

"Are you still coming back on the weekend?"

Nick closed his eyes and sucked in a draft of air. "I can't.

Sorry. The university got permission for an exploratory dive ten miles off the coast just south of Boston. There's supposed to be both American and Canadian ships down there. We'll be teaming up with a crew from Halifax."

"When do you go?" she asked.

"Friday through Monday. We'll be billeting on the boat, so no travel back and forth."

"Do you know the other divers? Do you trust them to have your back?"

The soft quiver in her voice made his heart clench. "Are you worried about me, Jilly?"

"I suppose," she admitted. "Is that a bad thing?"

"No, sweetheart, not at all. It's nice to have someone concerned for my safety."

"Other than your mother?"

"Yeah, other than Madeline the Magnificent."

Jilly let loose a soft laugh. "That's what you call your mother?"

"No, that's what my mother calls herself."

"Really?"

"You'll understand when you meet her."

Meet her. Damn, that just slipped out, didn't it?

"Maybe, someday," she confirmed, her gentle tone letting him know she'd caught his slip up.

"You're still planning to stay here with me when you drive down next weekend, I hope."

"That depends on a couple of things."

Panic hit him square in the gut, and he asked, "What couple of things?"

"First of all, will you properly stock the fridge with fresh veggies?"

"Yes, I will. From the organic market down the street."

"Second, is your bed big enough for two?"

"Jilly, sweetheart, my bed is big enough for three, but I'm not sharing you with anyone."

"That's good to know. Is Thursday evening too early to show up? I need to set up my display first thing Friday morning for the opening."

"I expect to be back from the dive on Monday around six. You can show up any time after that. As a matter of fact, the sooner the better."

"It will have to be Thursday, Nick. I have to arrange for the pick-up and delivery of one or two more pieces before I can leave Fairwinds."

"The ghost lovers?"

"That's *not* what I'm calling them. Maybe I'll let you help me decide on a name when I get there."

"I look forward to putting our heads together. Among other more interesting parts."

They ended the call a few minutes later. He promised to call her again before he left for his weekend dive and, then again, when he returned.

He'd not been joking when he'd told her it was nice to have someone thinking about him, worrying about him. He'd never much thought about it before.

But, with Jilly, it felt right. Perfect, in fact.

Chapter 15

Jillian rushed from one end of the house to the other in a frantic search for everything she'd need for her show. You'd have thought—after all of the events she'd done over the past few years—she'd have the routine down pat.

However, Nick kept popping into her thoughts, breaking her concentration. The realization that by seven tonight, she'd be in his arms, sharing some of his perfect, heart-stopping kisses, was enough to derail her plans for the umpteenth time.

The parcel delivery service had shown up as promised at nine that morning, loaded two carefully wrapped sculptures into their heavy-duty van and promised delivery to the gallery by three that afternoon.

All that was left to do now was to fill her small suitcase.

She'd never packed and unpacked so many times in her life. Clothes were scattered everywhere. Three days of outfits for her show were easy enough to plan. It was the clothes she'd wear, or not wear, for Nick that was giving her fits.

Too sexy, not sexy enough.

Finally, in a state of frustration, she stuck her hand in her underwear drawer and grabbed a handful of thongs and matching demi-bras and tossed them on top of her makeup case, along with two rather skimpy nightgowns.

Not that she expected to wear those for very long. If at all.

About to set the house alarm and go out the door, she turned in the foyer and raised her gaze to the ceiling.

"You two behave yourselves. Jake, no tracking mud across

Vera's clean floors. Lily, no leaving smudges on the glass of the French doors when you know you can't get in. And, for heaven's sake, if a storm should blow through, don't make a mess of the bedroom." She drew a breath, then added, "I'm getting tired of picking up those damned candlesticks."

Off in the distance, a door slammed shut, and she grinned.

The moment she stepped onto the flagstone driveway, a breeze blew across her cheeks and lifted her loose-hanging hair to fall softly against her shoulders.

"Be safe, Fairwinds," she whispered softly. "I'll be back soon."

Stopping to gas up and grab a bottle of water just an hour short of Boston, Jilly turned on her GPS and entered Nick's address. Immediately, the map popped up, the coordinates landing smack dab in the middle of the Fenway Kenmore district of the city.

Great older neighborhood. Pricey, but worth it for its beauty and history.

At half-past six, she pulled her car to a halt in front of an enormous brownstone. The impressive structure drew her low-key whistle.

Damn! They must be paying professors really well nowadays.

By the time she'd retrieved her suitcase from the back of her mini-truck, Nick was there at her side. Taking her bag in one hand, he put his other arm around her shoulders and drew her to his side.

"You made it, and in good time too."

"Pretty much a straight line until you get into the city." Staring up at Nick's home, she commented, "Nice digs."

"Thank you. It was a graduation inheritance from my grandfather. His father built it in the late 1800s. I'd be happy to give you the tour." Turning her in his arms, he suggested instead, "Or, we could just stand here on the open street and neck."

"A tour would be nice—at least as far as your bedroom."

"Hmm... sounds like a great compromise."

He led them up the stairs to the narrow stoop, and through the heavy double doors adorned with a beautifully detailed stained-glass window. The foyer—or what little she saw of it before Nick scooped her up in arms—was also perfectly detailed turn-of-century architecture.

"I can walk, you know. Or, at least swoon at your side as you drag me off to your lair."

"I prefer the feel of your curves pressed to my angles, sweetheart. Besides, this way I get to be the swashbuckling hero and toss you in the middle of my bed to have my way with you."

Her smirk drew his laughter.

"You've obviously been hanging out with Captain John Jacob Wilder too much." Shooting him a mock glare, she warned. "Do *not* refer to me as your wench."

"I'd never think of it, M'Lady."

As much fun as their teasing banner had become, when Nick gave a firm shove to his bedroom door and swooped her across the threshold, Jilly was almost positive he'd earned the right to be a swashbuckling hero, if he wanted to be.

The huge, four-poster bed with intricately carved headboard and footboard resembled a ship. The surrounding bed curtains hung like sails from a mast. At the foot, an antique chest provided the perfect finishing touch to the room.

"Okay, I've changed my mind, you can call me your wench if you want to. This room is amazing."

"My grandfather was a history nut—which probably influenced my love for the subject. He also loved nautical décor. He had it everywhere. My mother hated the house and moved out as quickly as she could. I've updated most of the rooms, but I didn't have the heart to change this one."

"Thank goodness."

"So, shall I set you down gently? Or, will it be toss and ravish?"

"As excited as I am to be ravished by my very own pirate, I've spent the past three-and-a-half hours in a car, and what I'd really like is a shower."

He lowered her slowly down the length of his firm body, but didn't release her.

"That can definitely be arranged, as long as I'm allowed to scrub your back."

"And my front?"

His grin spread, rearranging an already handsome face into something sinful and heart-stopping.

"I'm especially good with fronts."

Boldly, she slipped her hand between them and pressed her open palm to the fly of his cut-off jeans. The hard shape of him caused a definite hitch in her breath. Raising her gaze to his, she licked her lips and told him, "Fronts happen to be my specialty, as well."

∗∗∗

Nick lay back in the bed, his heart still pounding, Jilly slowly kissing her way back up his body. She hadn't been kidding. She really knew her way around the front of a man's body. Every inch of it.

His lips dusting her forehead, he asked, "What time do you need to be at the gallery in the morning?"

"By ten at the latest. Sam usually has everything mapped out, but I like to oversee the unwrapping and placement of the last two pieces. Plus, I'm sharing the exhibit with a photographer who documents artists' work. He's got a few pictures of my earlier pieces I'm anxious to see."

"I can drop you off on my way to the university if you'd like. The graphics department has some banners for me to review. They'll hang in the hallways leading to the museum, so they need to be perfect."

"Thank you, but I'll need to take my own car. I've got brochures and other smaller items in the back." Toying with the hairs in the middle of his chest, she asked, "Will you be available for lunch? Back here at the house?"

"I can make myself available."

"So, in other words, you're easy."

He tightened his hold on her shoulders and drew her across his body, taking her mouth in a deep, wet kiss. When they finally came up for air, he told her. "Damn straight, my darling wench. Especially for you."

By eight the next morning, after a long night with little sleep, they were both up and rambling around his comfortable kitchen. While Nick filled his favored drip coffee pot, Jilly chopped veggies for their omelets and poured them glasses of juice.

He'd never had someone in his kitchen before—not like this anyway. Jilly was semi-dressed in one of his staid professor shirts—as she called them. However, the fact she'd only bothered closing two of the eight buttons, was playing havoc with his desire.

He'd not yet recovered from their early-morning tumble, and here he was as hard as a rock again, wanting to throw her atop the kitchen table and take her right there. No preamble, no teasing, just pure, raw sex.

"I can feel you leering at me, you know."

He couldn't hold back his laugh, and didn't bother trying. "And, does that bother you, Jillian?"

"Nope, not in the least. Other than the obvious. We don't have time."

He came up behind her and wrapped his arms around her middle, snaking his hands beneath the tease of a shirt until he could cup her bare breasts. "There's always lunchtime. Our nooner."

"More like our one-o'clocker, but who's keeping track?"

"I am, Jilly, I am."

If it were possible for an entire day to get totally fucked up, today was the day. The banners were all wrong. Wrong house, wrong text, wrong everything. And, if that wasn't bad enough, the brochures were filled with typos and inaccuracies.

Obviously, the flirtatious Miss Clary was not proficient in spell-check.

Settling in at his desk, Nick opened the files he'd insisted Miss Clary forward, and he began repairing the numerous errors.

At half-past twelve, he realized he couldn't put off the inevitable forever. Picking up his cell, he pressed Jilly's speed-dial icon. Thank goodness he'd given her a spare key to the house, so she'd be able to go home and change for tonight's opening cocktail party. Heaven only knew when he'd be able to get there himself.

    Hopefully, before it was over.

Chapter 16

"So, Jilly-girl, where is this mysterious Nick you were telling Sam about earlier?"

Jillian shot her ex-boyfriend a glare, then shared the same expression with Sam Bellows, the gallery owner.

"Obviously, Sam enjoys sharing private conversations, when he shouldn't." Making a quick, and hopefully discreet, glance around the packed gallery, she added, "I'm sure he'll be along soon. He got stuck at work with some snafu on his big project."

"He's a professor of history, right?" Sam asked. No doubt doing his best to make up for talking out of turn earlier, he added, "At Harvard, too. He must be a smart fellow."

Stone let loose a mocking laugh. "Smart maybe. Geek, for sure. No doubt a featherweight with thick glasses and a hunchback from carrying so many books."

"I'll have you know—"

The press of a warm hand against her bare back stopped her words in their tracks.

"Sorry I'm late, sweetheart."

Jilly breathed a sigh of relief and leaned into Nick's side. "Not a problem, darling." Smiling broadly, she turned to Sam and Stone to make the introductions.

"Sam Bellows, Stone Parker, this is Dr. Nicholas Martin. Nick, this is Sam, owner of this beautiful gallery, and… Stone. A friend. A *past* friend."

***

When Jilly's ex, Stone the yoga man, extended his hand, Nick reached out as well. The man's grasp was firm and tightening with each passing second.

Biting back on a smirk, Nick tightened his grip as well. There was no way he was going to back down from this ass.

Jilly and Sam exchanged glances, then looked down at his and Stone's joined hands. No doubt, Jilly was mortified by their macho display. Or, at least he thought she would be. Instead, she broke out laughing.

"Really? *Testosterone spill in aisle four.*"

Nick released a long breath, shot Jilly a grin, and gave Stone's hand one final squeeze before letting go.

For all his bravado, the man began flexing his fingers and shaking his hand in the air.

Jilly burst into another round of laughter. "Did I forget to mention? Nick was also a star football player for the Harvard Crimson."

***

Steering them to the far side of the gallery, Jilly stopped in front of her latest sculpture.

Nick let loose a low whistle and gave the finished piece and up and down appraisal. "*The Lovers*. I like it."

"I took your inspiration and just nixed the 'ghost' part."

He pulled her close to his side, and whispered, "I truly am sorry I'm so late."

"You got here at the perfect time."

"For the testosterone demonstration? He started it."

"And, by the look of his red fingers, you finished it." Shaking her head, she gave him a teasing smile. "Boys and their games."

"Speaking of games and my inflated testosterone, that's

one sexy dress you're wearing. Although it seems the designer ran out of material before they finished the back." His fingers brushed the curve of her ass.

The saucy wiggle of her hips sent the dress shimmering across her body. "Perhaps you should have kept your hand at my waist."

Leaning close, he pressed his lips to the side of her long, sleek throat. "Now, where's the fun in that?"

The gallery closed at ten, the guests filtering out slowly. By ten-thirty, the only people left were he and Jilly, Sam, and Randy, the photographer sharing the exhibit.

"Jillian shared a few of your photos of Fairwinds with me," Randy said, offering Nick another glass of champagne. "You've got quite an eye for detail and depth."

He waved off the drink before admitting, "It was one of the few skills I acquired from my father. As much as I enjoy photography as a hobby, I'd never try it full time."

"Was your father a professional photographer?" Jilly asked.

Nick nodded but didn't elaborate.

However, Randy wasn't as easily put off. "Martin? Right? Your father wouldn't happen to be *Paulie M*, would he?"

Jilly's gaze moved from him, to Randy, and back again. "Who's Paulie M?"

Sam released an exasperated sigh. "One of the most famous foreign correspondent photographers. He's been in the middle of nearly every conflict and peace keeping mission over the past thirty years. His photos have won numerous Pulitzers." Turning in Nick's direction, Sam guessed, "Four? Five?"

Before Nick could answer, Randy announced, "Six, at last count, if I'm not mistaken."

"Yeah, six," Nick confirmed. "Although, according to my uncle, he'll likely get another nomination for the pictures he took last month in Sudan." Wanting desperately to change the subject, Nick asked, "So, Sam, how did Jillian do tonight? Surely some of these high rollers did more than just drink your champagne and eat crab puffs."

"She sold four pieces outright. Of those that were up for sealed bids, all got at least three bids each. The only one *not* for sale was the one that got the most interest." Reaching into the pocket of his silk jacket, Sam withdrew a small envelope and twirled it between his fingers. "A private offer from one of our most wealthy patrons, in case you change your mind, Jillian."

Nick watched Jilly with interest.

"Don't even open it," she said. "*The Lovers* is not for sale, and I have no desire to know how much I've turned down."

Sam slipped the envelope back into his pocket. "I'll hang onto it in case you change your mind."

A shake of her head sent her curls flying. "I won't."

It was nearly midnight when they finally got home. Once his front door shut behind them, Nick pulled Jilly into his arms. "Now, about that curvy butt of yours." Sliding his hands beneath the material that hung low on her hips, he cupped her bottom in his palms and gave a gentle squeeze.

Much to his delight, she stepped forward, pressing herself to his chest, his arousal. "Why, Professor, are you trying to tempt me into misbehaving?"

"Yes. Is it working?"

"You bet. Now, how about carrying me off to your bed like a good pirate lover?"

***

Jilly rolled over the big bed and wrapped her arms around Nick's warm body. Even in sleep, his muscles bunched and jumped beneath her touch.

"You keep that up and we won't get out of here on time," he growled.

She slid her hand lower. "It's not me who's keeping things up."

"Morning arousal. Nothing… okay, maybe a little something… to do with you."

"How about you use the bathroom first and then make us coffee? I'll take a quick shower, and meet you in the kitchen to help with breakfast."

"No two-person shower?"

"Nope."

"Spoil sport," he teased.

"Will you be keeping me company all day?" Giving him a shove toward the edge of the bed, she teased, "You know—to keep me safe from yoga man?"

"I've got to check in with the graphics guys one more time, just to be sure they got everything done. But, for the most part, I'll be around today."

"It's a blessedly short day, ten to six. Then, tomorrow morning ten until one for the champagne brunch where we open the envelopes and announce the winning bids."

"You truly don't want to know what the private offer was for your masterpiece?"

"I'm pretty sure if I opened it, I'd get sick to my stomach thinking about how much I'm giving up."

"It's not like you're a starving artist." He shot her a sly smile. "I've seen the Fairwinds records, Jilly. I'm fairly certain, that's not everything. You could live the rest of your life without ever selling another sculpture."

"It's not the sale, Nick. It's the creation."

"I agree." Pushing himself from the edge of the bed, he turned toward the bathroom. "The love of discovery is why I dive. Whether I find something valuable, or something worthless, it's all in the finding."

Jilly walked into the kitchen twenty minutes later, dressed and ready for her day. Nick stood at the stove in a pair of jeans and a dark T-shirt. Just the sight of the denim stretched across his firm buttocks, took her breath away, and made her want to cop a feel.

"Casual, I see."

"No reason not to be. Don't worry, I'll dress up for tomorrow's big event."

"You've got another two weeks before the new semester starts, right?"

"Yes, but we're due back the Wednesday before, so more like ten days. Why do you ask? Are you thinking of inviting me for a visit?"

"You know I am."

"We could finally go cavern diving like we'd planned."

"Among other high energy activities."

He released a long sigh, his gaze narrowing when he raised his head. "I need to ask you something, Jilly."

"Of course. Anything."

"Is there more to this relationship than just sex? Don't get me wrong, the sex is great. But, if that's all it is, I'd kind of like a heads up."

"I'd like to think we're compatible in more ways than just the bedroom. I mean, we both love history—you more so than me. You have an eye for art, and don't seem to mind me playing in the mud and clay. Like I said, though, I'm not good with long distance relationships. I tend to get engrossed in my work and forget the other person is even there."

"That's likely because the other person doesn't remind you often enough." When she didn't respond, he added, "Why don't I finish up with the museum exhibit on Monday, then drive back to Fairwinds for the last week of my summer vacation? We can dive, walk the beach, and picnic on the grounds. Do our best to find some common interests outside the bedroom. If you think it's worth risking being in a relationship with me, then I'm willing to try. I'll even be the one to make the drive back and forth between here and Mystic Point—at least most of the time."

"You're willing to take a chance, even with all the baggage that comes with me and Fairwinds?"

"Even with… actually… your Fairwinds' baggage is one of the things I love about you."

"Love?" Shaking her head, she took a swig of her coffee and bolted for the door, Nick's veggie omelet completely forgotten. "I've got to go. I want to move the display around so it's fresh for today's visitors."

"Jilly… wait."

"I'll see you when you get to the gallery."

Chapter 17

Jillian tightened her grip on the steering wheel and blinked back her tears.

Why the hell did Nick have to say the 'L' word? He'd gone and messed everything up with a single comment.

That's all it was... an off-hand comment. It's not like he proposed marriage.

Parking in the lot behind the gallery, she pulled in a calming breath, exited the car, and let herself in through the rear door.

A little manual labor would do her good. Shove a few things, drag a few others. Anything to keep her mind off Nick's words and her less-than-stellar reaction.

It was after one o'clock when Nick finally arrived. He was carrying a tote from the local vegan restaurant, and he made a beeline for where she was standing.

"I assume you're hungry, given you skipped breakfast."

"Starving. Thank you."

"Why don't you sneak in the back and relax for a bit? I'll stand guard over your work, especially *The Lovers*."

"I could use a break." Standing on her tiptoes, she pressed a soft kiss to his cheek. "I'm sorry about running out on you this morning. You freaked me out a bit."

"That wasn't my intention. However, now is not the time, or place, to sort things out. We can do that later, at home."

"Yes, we can."

She felt better after seeing Nick again. Taking a seat

behind Sam's cluttered desk, she opened the carryout container and inhaled the wonderful scent of coconut salad dressing.

Perhaps she and Nick had more in common than she first thought. After all, no other man in her past had ever taken the time to make note of the contents of her fridge. Or noticed that she stocked up on coconut salad dressing. Not even the jerk who'd introduced her to vegetarianism.

They were on their way home when Nick asked, "Are you sure you didn't mind leaving your car at the gallery?"

"Are you kidding? I'm due for a new car anyway. There's nothing in it of any value, so if someone steals it, I'll be forced to replace it." She reached across the width of the car and laid her hand against his. "Besides, this way, I know you can't back out on tomorrow's brunch."

"I wouldn't do that. Truth be told, I'm anxious to see how well you did on those sealed bids." Giving her fingers a squeeze, he told her, "I've always wanted to say I know a famous—and rich—artist."

"Don't get all excited. They may be sealed bids, but they're not earth shattering."

"If you're anything like me, you'll spend most of it on supplies. I do the same thing with any money I make from my dives. I put it all back into the next one."

"Once Sam takes his cut, and I split the profits in half, supplies are about all I'll get."

"Half? Isn't your accounting separate from Randy's photography sales?"

"Yes, of course. However, half of my income is earmarked for something else."

"Really? Don't tell me, you're paying off an ex-lover I don't know about."

"No, nothing that salacious." She pulled in a breath and explained. "For the past century, or more, the resident owner of Fairwinds has been supporting a specific Mystic Point charity. It started right after World War I, with my great-great grandma, Helene Bradford McGuire."

"What kind of charity?"

"A veteran's home, *Hansen House*. Unfortunately, over the past century, they've had a steady influx of resident patients. They also house retirees who were once employees of the home. Helene, and her daughter, great-grandma Mallory, spent both money and time volunteering. Their donations were usually yearly. My father's donation was time—medical expertise. Because I'd moved away from home, I found it easier to send a check after a successful show."

Nick's rough cough, before he spoke, made her heart clench.

"You never cease to surprise me, Jilly. And always in a most profound and generous way. Whether it's your care of Fairwinds, your acceptance of your temperamental roommates, or a charity." He reached out and clasped her hand in his, giving her fingers a gentle squeeze.

Jilly pulled away from his hold, his words touching her far more than she expected, far more than she wanted—at least for the moment. "I'm in the mood for seafood," she blurted out. "New England crab cakes with a spicy remoulade."

"Naughty girl. The next thing you know, I'll be able to coax you to Molly's Diner for one of her greasy burgers."

"Don't hold your breath on that, Professor."

They reached Nick's house shortly after seven. Dinner had been fun, filled with light conversation and Nick's teasing about where she should put *The Lovers* when she got the piece back to Fairwinds.

"So, have you made your decision yet?"

Panic hit her. *Was he talking about them, a relationship?*

"My decision?"

"About the sculpture?" he said nonchalantly.

If he caught her sigh of relief, he didn't comment.

"I like your idea about putting it up in their room. However, I'm not sure I can get the delivery men to climb two flights of stairs."

"Not a problem, Jilly. I'll move it for you."

"It's heavy."

"You have a dolly, don't you? That's all I'll need." He paused and shot her a cocky grin. "Remember? Big, strong, football player."

"That's true. You have no trouble carting me around."

"Speaking of which…" He crooked his finger at her and beckoned her forward. "Come here, wench."

When she wrapped her arms around his neck and leaned into him, he doubled over, as if he were in pain.

"Oh my god, Nick. Are you okay?"

He chuckled and swept her up in his arms. "It must have been that second helping of crab cakes you ate."

"You're positively evil."

The wag of his eyebrows had her laughing.

"Not yet, sweetheart, but I can be."

Jilly was in the kitchen the next morning enjoying a cup of coffee, when Nick came in to join her. He was dressed in beige linen slacks, a peach dress shirt, and lighter peach tie. His sun-kissed brown hair hung loosely over his brow. Just the sight of him set a hummingbird loose in her middle.

"Holy cow, Nick, you clean up nice."

He gave her an up-and-down appraisal, a warm smile lighting his face. "You're not so bad yourself, Jilly. That sundress is very sexy."

She raised her head and met the twinkle in his gaze. "No glasses?"

"Contacts. I so rarely wear them I forget I even own the darned things."

"I have a great idea. Let's skip this whole shindig and stay home in bed. I'll even take your tie off with my teeth."

Nick grinned. "As tempting as that all sounds—especially the tie part—this is *your event*, after all. It wouldn't be wise for you to skip it. Besides, you did me a big favor by inviting me. The least I can do is make sure you get there."

"What big favor?"

"Madeline called while you were in the shower and invited me to brunch at the country club. I didn't have to tell a white lie to get out of it."

"What did you tell her? I don't want to come between you and your mom."

"I told her I was already going to brunch with a friend at the gallery. I think she was impressed that I was getting some culture along with my eggs Benedict. Besides, there's nothing you could do to come between me and my mother. She's already done that for herself."

"How so? If you don't mind my asking."

His shoulders lifted on a shrug. "She's domineering. Spoiled, stuck up, and always meddling in mine and my siblings' lives. It gets tiring after a while. Very tiring."

"Well then, I'm glad I could help out with your excuse, even if I'd rather stay here and take another cruise on the big pirate ship."

***

The gallery was buzzing with a full complement of customers. Some were there to see if their bid was successful, some were there strictly for the free eats, others were merely curious.

Jilly was the center of attention, and rightfully so. Nick chose to stay off to the side and keep tabs on the crowd. A few devoted fans had gotten too close for comfort, and he put himself between them and Jilly.

Once they'd given up, and moved away, he'd returned to his post along the wall. The door opened, the chime of the brass bell heralding yet another arrival.

"Shit."

Raising his head, he stared across the open space and met his mother's stark glare.

"There you are, Nicky." Once she'd reached his side, she glanced around the gallery, and then back at him. "When you said brunch at 'the gallery', I assumed you meant the Boston Fine Arts, or the Klein, not some privately owned shop."

"Nope, neither of those. The Peele. And it's a fine gallery, Mother. How did you find me anyway?"

"I made a few calls. It wasn't difficult to pin down who was hosting a brunch."

"Yes, of course. Your many connections."

"I saw Randy Finnerty when I came in. Please don't tell me you've befriended a photographer."

"Randy's a nice enough fellow but, no, my friend is

sculptor Jillian Barclay."

"This is her show?" Madeline asked, waving her hand around in the dismissive way he hated.

"Yes, it is," he confirmed a bit too harshly. "Come on, I'll introduce you."

They approached Jillian just as Sam was steering away another clinger.

"Jillian," he said, drawing her attention. "I'd like to introduce you to Madeline Martin. My mother. Madeline, this is Jillian Barclay, the featured sculptor."

Jilly stuck out her hand, and his mother grasped it gently.

"It's a pleasure to meet you, Mrs. Martin."

"How do you know my son?" Madeline asked, her dark gaze raking Jilly from head-to-toe. "He's never mentioned you before." Glancing from side-to-side to make sure they weren't overheard, she lowered her voice and confided, "I hope you're a friend with benefits because I was beginning to think my son had taken a vow of celibacy."

Nick could tell Jilly was fighting back the urge to burst out laughing. His reaction was the exact opposite, his mother's usual tactlessness rankling his nerves. At least a dozen premium swear words ran helter-skelter through his head.

When a server passed by with a tray of mini quiches, Jilly snatched one up and popped into her mouth—no doubt to avoid further conversation. The next waiter had a tray of mimosas and, not surprisingly, his mother lifted one into her hands and downed it in a few gulps.

"Are you staying for the opening of bids?" he asked. "Or, are the ladies waiting at the club?"

"I'm sure Ms. Barclay will do just fine without my presence. I just wanted to see what you were up to, given you rarely share." Swishing her hand to ward off the next tray of finger-foods, she explained, "I prefer my brunch sitting down."

"Thank you for stopping by," Jillian said. "Your son speaks of you often. It's nice to finally meet you."

Madeline gave an exaggerated roll of her heavily made-up eyes. "I've no doubt he talks about me. Whether what he says is repeatable or not, is up for debate."

He narrowed his gaze and aimed it squarely in his mother's direction. "I'll see you for Kendall's birthday dinner next month."

"You should bring your sculptor." Tugging on his jacket to draw him close, she told him, "Your sisters won't believe me when I tell them that you have a lady friend."

"We'll see." Nodding toward the door, he asked, "Shall I walk you to your car?"

"Not necessary, Nicky. I took advantage of the valet. I can certainly get myself to the kiosk on my own." Madeline took a few steps toward the door, but then turned back and met his gaze. "You shouldn't wear peach, Nicky. It washes you out."

Nick released a long, suffering sigh, but bit back on the first retort that came to mind.

The moment Madeline went through the front door, Jilly jabbed her elbow in his ribs. "So, that's Madeline the Magnificent, is it?"

"Sadly, yes. In all her stuck-up glory."

"Does your father call her 'Magnificent', as well?"

Her question drew his deep laugh. "Hardly. They've been divorced for nearly twenty years. I think his favorite name for her is 'Bitch of Beacon Hill'. Sometimes worse."

Chapter 18

Nick paced the length of the grand entry hall leading into the university's museum wing. *She was late.*

"Dr. Martin," Dr. Pritchett called from the doorway leading into the exhibit. "It's time to get started."

"Be right there."

Pritchett gave a deep chuckle. "I realize you're nervous. I could tell earlier today when you did the presentation for the visiting professors." He paused, then added, "You'll do fine. The board of regents, a handful of donors, and their invited guests, are far less intimidating than your peers."

The last of Pritchett's words were drowned out by the sound of shuffling footsteps coming in their direction. Nick raised his head, his smile spreading when he saw Jilly rushing toward him.

"Sorry I'm late, Nick," she said, her gaze begging his forgiveness. "Traffic was backed up coming into the city."

He pulled her into his arms, and pressed a kiss to the top of her head. "You're here now, that's all that matters."

Once Jilly had taken a seat, he walked up to the podium and stared out over the large crowd. The walls of the smaller entryway were lined with pictures from all six homes included in the project. The lesser artifacts sat out on tables around the room. A teaser of sorts, but nowhere near the finished exhibit.

"Good evening; welcome to *Discovering New England's Historical Homes*." Nodding to his left, "Dean Wilson, ladies and gentlemen of the board, honored guests."

Nick consulted his notes, then raised his head and locked gazes with Jilly. Launching into the shortened version of the speech he'd given earlier to a few dozen icons in historical studies, he relaxed back and let the words flow.

He'd made it through the first five homes with relative ease, before closing in on the last few minutes of his speech.

"The final home, and the centerpiece of our display, is Fairwinds, an estate dating back to the mid-1600s. Located on the outskirts of Mystic Point, Fairwinds overlooks beautiful Skullery Bay. Originally built by shipping magnate Theodore Langdon, the home passed from him to his son in 1710, when the younger Langdon married. In 1737 the home came into the possession of Captain John Jacob Wilder, a man considered to be one of the most feared pirates of the time, and his wife, Lillian Grace Langdon. Throughout the centuries, the home has been passed down from one generation to the next, never once leaving the possession of the extended Langdon/Wilder family."

***

Jilly stood off to the side and waited while Nick was shuffled from a member of the board, to a wealthy donor, and back to the small group of professors.

The invited guests milled around the cavernous exhibition room, moving from one portion of the display to the next, always ending on Fairwinds.

Nick had done exactly as he'd promised. He'd presented Fairwinds history with respect, in great detail, and kept references to the tunnels, the home's secrets, and the possibility of ghosts out of the presentation.

She couldn't remember a time in her life when she felt this proud. Yet, apprehensive at the same time. Nick's hard work was sure to enhance his career, make him even more in demand than he already was and, in turn, steal even more of the time they'd hoped to carve out for each other.

"Hey, beautiful," he said, closing the distance between them. The smooth tenor of his voice did its usual job on her emotions, her desires. "Are you pleased with the display?"

"It's magnificent, Dr. Martin," she said, a smile tugging at the corners of her mouth. "Truly wonderful."

"There's someone I'd like you to meet." Closing his warm hand around her elbow, he ushered her forward. "Dr. Tasha Cunningham," Nick said, drawing the attention of a statuesque woman standing among a small crowd of attendees. "This is Jillian Barclay, owner of Fairwinds."

The woman turned around; her smile aimed at Jilly. Tasha Cunningham was stunning, mid-forties perhaps, and obviously accomplished.

Was she one of Nick's faculty peers?

"Miss Barclay, it's so nice to meet you. Dr. Martin speaks highly of both your home, and you as well. He said you were very open and willing to share your lovely ancestral estate with him."

"The agreement to participate in the university's project was originally made with my father. However, once I met Dr. Martin and listened to his ideas, I was convinced he'd do Fairwinds justice." She made a show of waving her hand toward the display. "And he has. It's perfect."

The department head Nick had introduced her to earlier called him over. Giving both Jilly and Dr. Cunningham a quick nod, he said, "If you ladies will excuse me for a minute. I'm needed elsewhere."

"Take your time, Nicholas," Tasha said. "I'm sure Miss Barclay and I can find something to talk about. Perhaps she can tell me about all the ghost stories surrounding Fairwinds."

Jilly caught the look of panic in Nick's gaze, and she offered him a smile. "Yes, Professor, go attend to business. Dr. Cunningham and I will be fine here on our own." Once Nick walked away, Jilly asked, "Are you a professor here at Harvard, Dr. Cunningham?"

"No, I'm here on behalf of UCLA, Los Angeles. Despite my

PhD, I'm not a professor. I'm in charge of design and implementation of the university's many projects. We've been thinking of doing something similar on the historical homes along the California coast, and so I was sent here to take a look at Harvard's model."

"Nic... ah, Dr. Martin did a wonderful job of capturing the best of all six homes, not just Fairwinds."

"Yes, he did. My colleague, Dr. Perkins, and I were very impressed. So much so, we're hoping to coerce Nicholas into considering a move to UCLA to oversee the history aspects of our similar display. And afterward, become part of our teaching staff. We could certainly use a younger influence in the history department, especially one as astute as Dr. Martin."

"I know he's happy here," Jilly felt compelled to point out, a rush of panic filling her chest. "Teaching at Harvard is something he's always wanted. Or, so he told me."

"Here at Harvard, he's at least four or five years away from a full professorship, if not more. We have two positions coming up next year. We're hoping to make that a selling point when we deliver our formal offer."

"Formal offer?" Her alarm increased; her throat went dry.

Would Nick accept? Would he leave her before they'd even had a chance together?

"We teased him with the possibility earlier today. However, we wanted to see his presentation skills."

Jilly swallowed hard, and asked, "And, how'd he do?"

"Excellent," the woman confirmed. "As we expected."

Meeting the older woman's gaze, Jilly asked, "Why are you telling me all of this? Surely, it's Dr. Martin's decision, and has nothing to do with me."

"Really? The man lights up like a roman candle whenever you're within ten feet of him. You're going to tell me there's nothing between the two of you?"

"I don't think that's any of your business."

"It may not be," Tasha Cunningham conceded. "I'd hate to see Nicholas turn down such a great offer over a relationship, serious or not."

"It's obviously his decision. Of course, I'd never stand in his way or try to put any undue influence on him."

"Good. So, how about we discuss the ghosts of Fairwinds. What's the legend? That the famous pirate and his wife haunt the estate?"

"Stories, old wives' tales, and silly legends, Dr. Cunningham. Nothing more. Sorry."

When Nick opened the front door to his home later that evening, Jilly stepped across the threshold and turned in the foyer. Once Nick had followed her inside, she wrapped her arms around his neck and pressed her lips to his.

A quick groan escaped as she deepened the kiss, sliding her tongue into his mouth to seek out his undeniable heat. His passion.

Scooping her up into his arms, he made a beeline for the bedroom. Rather than toss her into the middle of the big pirate bed, he laid her down gently and followed her down onto the plush mattress.

"Damn, Jilly. I've been wanting to kiss you like that all night long." He slid his hand beneath the edge of her blouse and took possession of her breast. "All I could think about was touching you, stroking your soft skin, and burying myself deep inside your body."

"Well, then, why are we still dressed?" she said, her tone purposely light, teasing.

"I've no idea, my beautiful wench, but I'm perfectly happy to remedy the situation with the utmost haste."

***

Nick rolled over in the bed and slid his arm around a

sleeping Jilly, pulling her back against his body, fitting her soft bottom to his semi-aroused flesh. The urge to wake her up and make love to her again was foremost in his mind.

Yet, they needed sleep.

She'd been ravenous. Demanding. And he'd loved every minute of it. At the time.

Now, lying here, the beat of her heart tickling his hand where he held her breast, he had to wonder why she'd been so adamant in their lovemaking.

It was almost as if it were going to be their last time.

He sucked in a breath. *Was she breaking up with him*?

The past few weeks had been wonderful. Even the beginning of the school year hadn't slowed down their weekend plans. At first.

True, he'd had to back out on her last weekend when the university had gotten one last dive permit. And, they'd missed their weekend to cavern dive because of his sister's birthday dinner.

Jilly had fit in perfectly with his family. Even his mother was coming around and had kept her usual level of snark to a minimum.

He'd hoped he and Jilly could take their relationship up a notch; that she might consider coming to stay with him during the week and then they could go to Fairwinds on the weekends. A semi-living together arrangement.

Nick thought back about the evening event, the opening of the display. Had he made a mistake with the section on Fairwinds? She'd done nothing but compliment him. She'd clung to his side, graciously met each and every person he'd introduced her to. She'd even charmed Dr. Cunningham—

Dammit!

Had Tasha Cunningham mentioned the job offer? Was that why Jillian seemed to be practicing her goodbye?

He'd intended to broach the subject over breakfast. Not that he'd made a decision of any kind, but he'd at least intended to warn Jillian of the possibility.

Chapter 19

Jilly glanced out the library window to watch the first of the fall leaves hit the ground. The rose bushes had been pruned; the arbor now barren. A fitting metaphor for her life. It had been ages since she'd seen Nick, since they'd made love.

Restlessness drew her to her feet and out of the library. Climbing the stairs to the third floor, Jilly made the short walk to the bedroom, closed the door behind her, and took a seat in the middle of Jake and Lily's bed.

"I need to talk," she said, her gaze scanning the width and length of the room. "I don't know if either of you are paying attention, but I desperately need to straighten things out in my head. And, I figure since fall is closing in fast, and the storms will start soon, you'll both be too busy for me."

Out on the roof, the weathervane spun, the creaking sound sinking beneath the closed French doors.

"Those first few weeks after my gallery show were perfect. Nick was wonderful, attentive, we had fun together. And, well... the sex was great. Better than great." She pulled in a breath and continued. "I even enjoyed meeting his sisters and brother at Kendall's birthday party. And, Madeline, for all her snobbishness, is a stitch. But mostly, I loved being with Nick."

Across the room, the candlestick tipped over but didn't fall to the floor.

"Is that limp candlestick supposed to be a comment on the fact I've not seen him for three weeks now?" In Nick's defense, she explained, "He was able to schedule two more weekend dives before the weather shuts them down. His class load increased. Apparently since the success of the museum exhibit, he's been in high demand. His contract locks him in for a full year, but after that he'll likely have more than just UCLA to consider."

The double doors shook, but remained closed, as if Lily was reminding her of the fact that she and Jake were at the mercy of the weather, some things were out of their control. And, in contrast, Jilly had control over her life. *All she had to do was take it.*

"I know, in the beginning, I balked... spooked... when he let the 'love' word slip. But now, I'd give anything to hear him say it again. And more." Gathering the hem of her shirt in her hand, she ran the cotton fabric through her fingers. "I'm just so scared I'll screw things up. That, even if he does love me, he'll get tired of waiting for me to commit to something more permanent."

Footsteps sounded in the hallway outside the bedroom door and Jilly suspected the Captain had grown tired of her problems, and was heading back to the tunnels.

"I do love Nick. I know that now. More than I ever thought it possible to love another human being. Yet, I could never, ever stand in the way of his success. And, what if I'm more like my mother than I want to admit? What if I give settling down a real shot, and can't follow through?"

You'll never know until you try.

"I'm scared. I—"

The knob on the bedroom door turned slowly, causing Jilly's heart to beat a wild tattoo. The idea that Captain John Jacob Wilder was about to present himself—in full form—made her pulse race in time with her wildly beating heart.

"You know," a warm, deep voice said through the half-opened door, "all you have to do is admit you love me, and I'll be yours forever. Whether you want me or not."

The moment Nick stepped into the room, Jilly launched herself from the bed and into his open arms.

"You're here. Early, too."

"My Wednesday and Thursday classes were cancelled because of building renovations." Shrugging his broad shoulders, he told her, "There was no way I was staying home alone when I could come to Fairwinds and be with the woman I love."

"You do? Love me?"

"Yes, of course. Probably since the first day I met you. Or, at least the first time I overheard you talking to the Captain and his lady." When the candlestick fell the rest of the way from the mantle, Nick reached out quickly, grabbed it before it hit the floor, then let loose and hearty laugh. "Yeah, yeah, Captain. I'm pretty damned fond of you and Lady Lillian as well. Just don't expect me to confide all my deepest secrets to the two of you."

"They only listen occasionally anyway," Jilly said softly. "I wouldn't worry about them learning any dark secrets." Her heart hammered, yet she knew she had to ask, "What about UCLA? No doubt you'll have other offers to consider as well."

"I turned down UCLA's generous offer. I did agree to consult on their project, from a distance, but I'm perfectly happy on the east coast. Plus, it didn't hurt that Harvard has offered me a full professorship for the next school year."

"That's great... for you... I mean."

"For both of us. Assuming there is an 'us' in the equation."

She pulled in a breath and nodded. "An 'us' sounds great."

His crystal blue gaze locked on hers. His full lips quirked up a teasing smile.

"So, do you?" Nick asked.

"Do I what?"

"Want me? Love me?"

"Yes, and yes. Forever,"

Off in the distance, thunder rumbled. A streak of lightning shot across the horizon. Nick swept her off her feet and headed for the staircase leading down to the second floor.

"Time to give the ethereal lovers their privacy," he whispered. "And, perhaps, create a legend or two of our own."

The End

AUTHOR'S NOTE

"*I can shake off everything as I write; my sorrows disappear, my courage is reborn.*"
--Anne Frank

I truly believe this is why a lot of us write, why we endeavor to create something lasting, inspiring, entertaining. Or, it could just be because we're all introverts, and writing allows us to stay inside and drink coffee all day.

This anthology has been a blessing and a challenge. Yet, worth it in so many ways. As both Lisa and Kathryn have said, thanks go to all those who took the time to read this and be gentle in their critiques—even while telling us where we screwed up! Thanks to Beth and Theresa for their eagle eyes and kind words.

I hope you enjoyed all the books in this anthology. But… wait… you're not quite finished. We've saved the best for last!

~ Nancy

The Last Kiss

In Conclusion...

RITA Nominee & Best Selling Author
Lisa A. Olech
(With a Little Help from the Captain)

Grand Epilogue

Standing at the mouth of the caves, Jake caught the chilled smell of crisp ocean air. The wind was changing.

"Ah, the sea." Jake raised his face to the sharp scent of salt and miles of endless water. Closing his eyes, he was back at the wheel of *The Phantom*. Her decks gleaming in the sun. The men—his men—busy at their tasks. Their energy high as they headed off to new adventures. Tasting the spray on his lips, riding the gentle sway of the ship as she left Skullery Bay, tightening his grip on the pegs of the wheel as the sails first caught the fullness of the wind, and she came alive beneath him and began to fly across the waves.

Jake shivered as a gust chilled his skin. *Wait...* The wind *had* changed. He didn't need to check the weathervane atop Fairwinds to know. Once again, he could feel the cold. Smell the air. A surge ran through him as he spun on his heel and raced back through the twists and turns of the tunnels.

A storm was brewing! He'd watched the building of the clouds all day. Hoping against hope. Dammit, just the sight of gray skies brought an ache to his cock these days. How long had it been since the last time they'd been together? He'd lost track. Too long. It was always too long.

You'd have thought after more than two hundred and eighty years he'd have had his fill, but no. He'd never get enough of Lily. Never. Not in two hundred and eighty years, not in an eternity. Not two hundred and eighty eternities.

Call it a curse, call it a twist of fates, the fact that they could only reunite—physically touch—during a storm was both maddening and exhilarating. His step faltered briefly as he adjusted the position of his erection before continuing to race up the stairs. Boots pounded and echoed in the now empty house as he made his way to the third floor.

Lily, his Lily. Soon she'd be in his arms again.

Reaching their bedroom, he closed the door with a slam mere moments before the fire leapt to life, and he could once more feel its heat. Time returned and transformed the room to new. The growing winds caught hold of the French doors and wrenched them open, blowing wind, rain, and his beautiful Lily into the room.

Jake caught her as she flew into his open arms. Their mouths met in a frantic, hungry kiss. Relief crested and crashed over him. In all this time, he'd never given leave to the amazement of this. The pure miracle of what happened to them with each passing of a storm. Jake never made the assumption that this magic would continue to occur. That they would always be able to be together. He sent a silent prayer of thanks skyward.

"My, darling…," Lily murmured between kisses.

"You're mine again," he whispered, as he wound his arms around her and held her tight, ravished her mouth and clutched at her skirts, dragging her even closer.

"How much time do we have?" she panted, tugging at his shirt.

Jake rained kisses down her neck. She still smelled of roses. He pulled at the lacings of her beautiful pink gown. "I would think hours."

Lily worked to untie the sash wound about his waist. "That's what we thought last time. Don't you remember?"

"A summer storm." He walked them back toward the bed as they both continued to tear at each other's clothing.

"I loathe those. They are nothing but teasing. A taunt. Leaving us unsated, wanting more."

"I *always* want more of you." Jake slipped a hand into the open neckline of her shift, past the loosened top of her corset to cup the delicate roundness of her breast. So soft. "Always," he growled.

When he dipped his head to sip at her nipple, Lily sighed and clutched a fistful of his hair. "Did you say hours?"

He straightened and gave her a small smile before tossing her onto her back across the mattress. "This late in the season, it could be days."

Lily raised up on her elbows and smiled a sultry smile. Her hair wild and windblown, one perfect creamy breast exposed, her gown askew, her lips kissed pink, she looked beautiful. Ravished. The pressure in his breeches made him groan.

"Only days? Then you best be quick getting me out of my skirts."

Outside, lightning split the sky. The clouds darkened the afternoon into night. Rain slashed at the window panes, but they barely noticed in their haste to strip one another bare. No care was given toward delicate silk or fragile lacings. With a rough yank, Lily dislodged two buttons from the flap of his breeches. In frustration, he pulled a knife from his boot and made short work out of the tangle of ribbons holding her underskirts secure. Lily let out a startled gasp, but the ruining of the garment only served in heightening her fervor.

With each layer removed and tossed aside, their breathing increased. Between deep ravenous kisses, hands stroked and caressed. Soon skin against skin, heat against heat, soft against hard, they tumbled onto the bed.

Jake wasted no time positioning himself between her legs.

Lily swept one silky thigh up and over his hip to wrap around his waist. She opened for him. Giving herself to him.

His arms trembled with forced control as he tried to still the urge to simply drive into her and satisfy his own lust in a mindless rut. Looking down into her beautiful face, his breath fluttered the fall of hair upon her cheek.

Lily arched her back and pressed her moist sex against the stiffness of his cock. She whimpered, "Please, Jake. Don't tease me. Take me now!"

Lightning branched across the clouds and lit the room before the loud crack of thunder made Fairwinds shudder. In one powerful thrust, Jake buried himself deep within her. He roared with the pleasure of it before pulling back and plunging into her again, and again.

Beneath him, Lily gasped and writhed and soon matched the rhythm of his thrusts. She clawed at his back, his arms, as if she needed to be even closer to him, pulling him deeper and deeper still as they both raced toward their release.

The crescendo of the storm outside mirrored the building of their fervor. Sweat glistened on their steamy skin like the rain slicked rocks along the cliffs. The howling of the wind echoed in their moans and cries of pure pleasure. For a few glorious moments, they *were* the storm. Nature's raw power surged through them both. The intensity filled them and carried them into a hurricane of passion to lift them higher and higher until together, they became the stars.

Dropping into the chaos of the bedding, Jake fell panting onto his back. He pulled Lily to fit alongside. He tucked her against him so her curves matched and fit the contours of his own body. She draped a leg across his. The wet heat of her sex rested against his hip as she fought to catch her breath.

They continued to kiss and stroke one another. Sated and satisfied, they still craved the other's touch, needing to keep their intimate connection for as long as they could.

Lily moved to lay on top of him. Cupping his cheek, she kissed him with such tenderness it made his heart squeeze.

"I love you," she whispered against his lips.

"I love you, too. Not for a single moment have I stopped." Jake smoothed the hair away from her beautiful face. "Every time we're together I can't help but wonder. Do you suppose we are stuck somewhere between heaven and hell? Heaven when I can hold you in my arms and love you like this, and hell when that blasted door slams with you on the other side having to wait for the bloody wind to turn again?"

"It feels that way. I know it feels like heaven when you touch me." She ran a finger over his lip. "But what is our choice? How many times have we laid in each other's arms, listening to the rain lash against the windows and questioned this? How many times must we contemplate what is obviously our fate?"

"All these years, Lily, we haven't tried to test that fate. Aye, we've talked about it. A hundred times. Come close to walking out that door, walking out of Fairwinds, hand in hand, but we've never made it further than the threshold of this room. We could have spent all these years—"

Lily pushed away from him and sat up shaking her head, turning from him. "Where would we have gone, Jake? Where could we have spent all these years if not here at Fairwinds? Do you really want to know? Do you want to see what happens if we both try to walk through that door? What if we're torn from each other's grasp? What if I never see you again? I never want to take that chance."

Jake lifted himself to one elbow and stroked her back. He swirled a finger around the beautiful, ragged-edged claret heart that marked her hip. "But what if we stay together? Imagine if we're able to go on to—to…"

She looked back over her shoulder at him. "To where?"

"To a better life."

"Don't you mean to a better death?" Lily got out of bed and crossed the room to stand by the fire that crackled once more in the fireplace. The firelight kissed her skin golden. Turning, she poured them each a glass of brandy from the decanter that never emptied and brought them back to bed. "Are you so unhappy with how things have been?"

Jake set the brandy aside without drinking. He pulled her back into the sheets. "Not when I'm holding you in my arms. Tasting your lips. Taking my fill of your body, but dammit, Lily, I'm tired of being held captive to the whims of nature. I want to be with you always."

"I am with you." She kissed him.

"You know what I mean. I want to take your hand and stroll with you through the gardens. I want to sit across our dining room table from you and enjoy a sumptuous meal. Dance with you in the ballroom again. I want to take you on *The Phantom* and feel the roll of the decks beneath our feet. Watch the gentle wind fill her sails, as we aim her bow for the rising sun and never look back."

"I would love all those things as well, but I couldn't bear losing what we *do* have together." She wrapped an arm about his neck and swept her other hand over the muscled ridges of his abdomen and up to caress his chest. She pressed a kiss over his heart and whispered against his skin. "I never want to risk losing this. The intensity of our coming together." Lily kissed her way up his neck. "I can survive a thousand years knowing we'll still be able to bring each other to such heights of pleasure." She swept a hand lower and took his heat in her hand. "Our passion only grows with each passing year. It's blinding. Earth shattering. It fills this house and shakes it clear to the foundation. Our love is in the very stones of Fairwinds. Our shouts of delight echo through the halls."

His cock pulsed in her hand as she stroked him. "You do scream your pleasure so even deaf can hear," Jake teased.

She released him and looked at him with wide eyes. "Are you complaining that I'm too loud?"

"Your cries drown out the wind." Jake's gaze ran down the front of her body. His hand palmed and caressed her breast, teasing a tightened tip. Heat sparked between them again. He guided her hand back to his erection.

"Have you listened to yourself, Captain Wilder? When you find your release, you moan like a foghorn."

"Woman, you frighten the horses in the stables."

"You frighten grown men to flee from this house," she countered.

"Only those that don't find solace between the thighs of their own women." Jake swept his hands over the curve of her ass and down the back of her legs before lifting her to straddle him.

"We have been generous like that, haven't we? Sharing our...our enthusiasm." Lily slid the clef of her sex along his hardness.

Jake's fingers dug into the ripe fullness of her thighs. Her movements causing a low guttural moan to escape his throat. "Our lust."

Lily's movements quickened. "Burning desire," she

countered.

"Raw need." His words broke as Lily raised herself and sank slowly onto his cock. The sensation of her wet heat surrounding him made him groan. "Dear God, I wed an insatiable wench."

With slow agonizing swirls of her hips, she rode him. Jake kneaded her breasts and clutched at her waist, lifting his hips, urging her to move faster and end his sweet torment. The ends of her hair tickled his thighs as she arched and fused them together with a grinding press. Her body rose and dipped like the endless waves of the sea until her pleasure crested and crashed carrying him with her into the tempestuous depths.

Jake drew her down and crushed her in a tight embrace. The racing of her heart echoed against his. Perhaps if he held fast to her, when the storm ended, and the sky and seas found their calm again, if he refused to let her go…

No. He swallowed the sudden lump in his throat. How many times had he tried just that, only to have her vanish from his hold like smoke to take her place once more on the walk? Within his sight, yet out of reach, until the next time.

Jake pushed the thought from his mind. He wouldn't dwell on such things when they were finally in each other's arms. There were decades of pacing the halls of Fairwinds for such thoughts. Tonight—this storm was far from over.

A steady soaking rain continued to blow beyond their windows. The wind still wrestled through the tops of the trees. Lily slipped off him and snuggled into his side. The musky scent of their lovemaking surrounded them. She breathed a gentle sigh of contentment. "So, it's decided? We stay?"

Jake tightened his hold and kissed the top of her head. "Good God, yes. We stay."

"Good." She kissed his shoulder and nestled closer. "When do you suppose Jilly and Nick will return from their honeymoon?" Lily teased the hair on his chest with a fingertip.

"I don't know." Jake lifted a shoulder.

"Do you think they'll have children?"

"Hard to say."

"You like him, though. I mean, he did return your spyglass."

"She likes him. That's all that matters."

"Ha!" Lily raised up and gave him an incredulous look. "All that matters? You've judged every relationship that has ever crossed the threshold of Fairwinds, Captain Wilder. Don't you lay there and pretend otherwise." Lily tossed a hand. "Slamming doors and knocking things about. Stomping through the halls like a petulant child."

Jake stifled a smirk and raised an eyebrow. "But *I* never scared anyone off the cliffs, my dear."

Lily huffed. "Horrible men. Dangerous men. Evil. There was no love in any of their hearts." She rose and moved to the small table near the fire where, as always, a small meal stood waiting for them. Bread, cheese, fresh fruit. Where it came from, like the brandy, they never knew. It was part of the storm magic, somehow. Lily offered him a bit of cheese, but he shook his head. His only hunger was to taste her as the firelight flickered and caressed each inch of her.

Tearing off a piece of bread, she took a bite and sighed. "I do miss bread." She took another bite. "Do you know who I miss most? Cora. Dear soul."

"She always spoke so highly of you. It was lovely of you to help her cross over when her time came."

"And you leaving gold coins about for Nate to find your

treasure. It was right for them to have it." Lily sighed. "We've seen so many come and go. Fall in love under our roof. Build their lives and raise their families. Families from our families. Lucy and Nathanial, Simon and Mallory, now Jilly and Nick. It's been nice watching each couple fill Fairwinds with new love."

"But not without problems."

"Everything has always worked out for the best."

"Aye, with a little help from us."

"Sometimes with a lot of help," Lily agreed.

"Are we talking about the cliffs again?"

"No." Lily crawled back into bed and fed him a slice of apple. The sweet crisp flavor burst on his tongue. She ate a piece of the fruit herself before licking her fingertips. "Perhaps that is the reason we're still here. We're needed. They've all needed us in one way or another."

"All I need is you." He reached for her again and kissed her.

Lily lay beside him once more and curled into him. Soon her gentle breathing told him she slept. Yet another facet of the magic during these times together. Coming back into their full bodies, the simple acts of eating and sleeping, feeling each other's touch, and making love were all once again open to them.

Jake fought the pull, however. Too often the storm would blow out to sea only to have Lily taken from his arms while he slept. Not this time. He stroked her back and thought about their comings and goings. The joy and sorrow of it all. He breathed in the sweet scent of her hair and kissed the top of her head.

Like the ceaseless waves that continued to caress the

shore, he and Lily would return to each other here at Fairwinds for as long as the fates allowed. For their love was deeper than the ocean and stronger than death, and he wouldn't trade that for all the treasure in the world.

Sooner than either of them had hoped, their night together crept toward day, and a sliver of dawn's light could be seen beneath the storm's blanket of clouds. The winds began to calm.

Jake gave Lily a nudge, "Lily, wake up. The storm fades. I need to kiss you goodbye."

"No." She tucked her chin and snuggled closer. "It's too soon. You said days."

He untangled their limbs. "I wished, but I was wrong."

"I hate this," she moaned.

"I, as well," Looking out, Jake noted the lightning skies. "But we need to hurry." Getting out of bed, he gathered her to him.

"Hold me tight."

"I don't want to hurt you." He wrapped her in a strong embrace.

"Tighter."

"Stop talking and kiss me before it's too late."

A sob wrenched from Lily's throat at the desperate meeting of their lips. She clutched at his hair and pressed the full gloriously naked length of her body against his as they deepened their kisses.

"I love you, Lily. I'll love you forever." Jake ground out, cradling the back of her head as he tipped to meet her lips again.

All at once she slipped from his grasp like water through his fingers. The French doors slammed shut. The storm was over. Their glorious time together finished far too soon. The fire sat cold and dark in the hearth once more. Candles no longer burned. The only thing to bear witness to their night of passion was the rain-soaked boards of the floor. Jake pushed at the dark stain with the toe of this boot.

Outside on the widow's walk, Lily stood in the flowing white of her shift as the sun lifted out of the sea behind her and haloed her hair. She gazed at him with sad eyes and lifted a hand to the glass.

"I'll love you, too," she answered. "Forever…plus one day."

The Final End

Meet the Author

LISA A. OLECH—loves art, pirates and a cranky curmudgeon she affectionately calls the Wizard of O. Currently the author of eight Romance titles in both the contemporary and historical genres, she uses witty dialog with a side order of sexy to bring to life multi-faceted, adventurous, smoldering characters you'll not soon forget.

A 2018 RITA Award nominee for her book, Within A Captain's Soul, the final book in her Captains of the Scarlet Night series, Lisa's won a variety of writing contests and achieved the ranks of Amazon Best Seller with her debut book in 2014.

Living on the shores of On Golden Pond, Lisa shares a drafty, old Victorian house with a wizard and two schizophrenic cats she brought into the house in an attempt to fill her empty nest and keep her from talking to herself in a British accent. As an author, artist, Justice of the Peace, and aspiring beekeeper, Lisa finds true inspiration in the beauty and love that surround her. And, she takes full credit for three homes on her quiet New England street now proudly flying the Jolly Roger from their flagpoles.

Visit Lisa at: lisaolech.com

Meet the Author

KATHRYN HILLS—The rich history and many mysteries of New England are the perfect backdrop for many of Kathryn's books. Winding roads lined by old stone walls, forgotten cemeteries, grand homes with shadowy pasts…all sparks for her imagination. Whether it's a quaint seaside town or the vibrant city of Boston, it's easy for this "hauntingly romantic" author to envision the past mingling with the present. No surprise, some of Kathryn's favorite stories involve time travel. And ghosts! Sprinkle in some magic, and you're off on a great adventure.

When not writing, this best-selling author is researching, gardening, or cooking up something special in her chaotic kitchen. She shares her colonial home in the north woods with those she loves most – her wonderful husband and daughter, and three crazy dogs.

Visit Kathryn at: kathrynhills.com

Meet the Author

NANCY FRASER—*Jumping Across Romance Genres with Gleeful Abandon*—is an Amazon Top 100 and Award-Winning author who can't seem to decide which romance genre suits her best. So, she writes them all.

Nancy has published over forty books in full-length, novella, and short format. When not writing (which is almost never), Nancy dotes on her five wonderful grandchildren and looks forward to traveling and reading when time permits. Nancy lives in Atlantic Canada where she enjoys the relaxed pace and colorful people.

Visit Nancy at: nancyfraser.ca

Made in the USA
Middletown, DE
05 September 2021